Hester Browne's *New York Times* bestselling series is
"fun and frothy" (*Daily News*, NY) . . .
"entertaining, whip-smart" (*Chicago Sun-Times*)
. . . **"effortlessly witty and utterly winning"**
(*The Washington Post*) . . .
and **"delish"** (*Glamour*).

The Little Lady Agency
and the Prince

"Browne's less-than-perfect princess is still a delight. . . . It remains impossible to become disenchanted with . . . brassy, sassy Melissa Romney-Jones."

—*Kirkus Reviews*

"This reader was overcome with happiness after tearing open the package to reveal a most coveted item: a new novel by Hester Browne. . . . Might be the best yet. . . . Melissa Romney-Jones and her charmingly dysfunctional family and friends are back in full force. . . . Reading Browne's books is like watching a Doris Day romantic comedy. . . . From start to finish, this tale is a joy to read."

—*Library Journal*

"Browne's Little Lady Agency series . . . keeps entertaining time and again."

—*RT Book Reviews*

The Little Lady Agency and the Prince
is also available as an eBook

Little Lady, Big Apple

The Little Lady Agency

HESTER BROWNE

THE

Little Lady Agency

AND

THE PRINCE

POCKET BOOKS

New York London Toronto Sydney

Pocket Books
A Division of Simon & Schuster, Inc.
1230 Avenue of the Americas
New York, NY 10020

First Pocket Books trade paperback edition September 2008

For information about special discounts for bulk purchases,
please contact Simon & Schuster Special Sales at 1-800-456-6798
or business@simonandschuster.com.

Manufactured in the United States of America

10 9 8 7 6 5 4 3 2 1

Library of Congress Cataloging-in-Publication Data

ISBN-13: 978-1-4165-3906-3
ISBN-10:   1-4165-3906-9
ISBN-13: 978-1-4165-4006-9 (pbk)
ISBN-10:   1-4165-4006-7 (pbk)

THE

Little Lady Agency

AND

THE PRINCE

one

My name is Melissa Romney-Jones, but pretty soon, you'll be able to call me Melissa Romney-Jones-Riley! My fiancé, Jonathan, thinks it has quite a ring to it, although we've had one or two discussions about whether it should be Riley-Romney-Jones or Romney-Jones-Riley. Whichever, it certainly isn't any more ridiculous than my professional name, Honey Blennerhesket, which . . .

Actually, let's start at the beginning.

As Melissa, I am many things to many people: long-suffering daughter of notorious Member of Parliament Martin Romney-Jones; undereducated but perfectly mannered Old Girl of several fine boarding schools; and the delighted fiancée of the debonair, successful, and charming Jonathan Riley, a paragon who gives estate agents and American men a good name. I'm what parents like to call a "nice girl," i.e., cheerful, practical, sturdy in the leg and ample of bosom, and entirely without embarrassing tattoos. Not what you'd call a sex kitten, in other words.

But then there's my other life. Add a satin corset, and some serious red lipstick, and I'm Honey Blennerhesket, bootylicious trouble-shooter for London's hapless bachelors and chaps generally in need of a woman's multitasking mind. As far as they're concerned, there's no domestic problem Honey can't sort out, no etiquette dilemma she can't advise on, and no sticky social situation she can't winkle them out of faster than you can say "Gina Lollobrigida." It's weird, but I can't be bossy when I'm everyday Melissa, yet somehow when I'm walking in Honey's stilettos I turn into a whirlwind of retro-glamour and female dynamism. A supernanny for grown men, if you like.

I've tried to keep my two identities apart, but my two lives have a habit of running into each other. Even the name of the business—The Little Lady Agency—comes from the annoying manner in which my father, an unreconstructed male chauvinist pig, would refer to my mother, and indeed any woman, as The Little Lady. If men want to engage *this* little lady to run their lives the way my mother runs my father's, they pay very handsome hourly rates. But in return, I sort out their problems, advise them gently on the real reasons they're going wrong socially, and ideally, leave them not only spruced up but also in a better state to tackle things themselves.

I really do love my job. As my flatmate, Nelson, says, it's a form of social work. And he should know, being the third most well-meaning person in Britain, after Bono and Jamie Oliver.

In fact, it was by shamelessly playing on Nelson's mile-wide humanitarian streak that I'd managed to enlist his reluctant help in The Little Lady Agency's first job of the day.

"You understand that I'm doing this on the sole condition that I don't tell a *single* lie?" he stressed for the ninth time, as he flipped through the stack of glossy mags on my office coffee table.

Nelson was my oldest friend. He looked how you'd imagine an English cricket hero should—tall and strapping with a shock of blond hair. At thirty-three, he was a couple of years older than me, but really he should have been born around 1815, when he could have spent his time striding across some vast estate, tending kindly to his peasants, railing at the iniquities of the slave trade, and eating enormous gourmet meals.

Instead, he worked in fund-raising and administration for a charity and spent a lot of time sailing with his school friend Roger Trumpet, who, coincidentally, had the personal hygiene habits of a nineteenth-century serf.

"Absolutely," I reassured him. "I'll be doing all the talking. You just have to look patient. You're good at that."

"But what I don't understand is why Jethro Lorton-Hunter needs you in the first place," he said, furrowing his brow like a baffled Labrador. "If his girlfriend's so flaky that she can't bear to see him talking to another woman, why doesn't he just tell her to pack it in? Before he packs *her* in?"

For all his eligibility—and despite having lived with me for years—Nelson understood women about as well as I understood computer programming.

"Because it's not as simple as that."

"It never is," he sighed. "Explain."

Jethro Lorton-Hunter brought his own personal cloud of gloom into my office three days ago when he arrived for his consultation. Like most of my clients, he'd been sent on a friend's recommendation; apparently I'd "done wonders" for his mate George's party chitchat technique, to the point where George now had three girlfriends. Jethro's problem was his girlfriend, Daisy, who was an absolute sweetheart, apart from one thing: she went bug-eyed if she saw him talking to another woman.

"It's because of some stupid mix-up at a party," Jethro sighed, nervously shredding a tissue into flakes. "We were playing that game with the orange, you know, where you pass it along with your chin, and, well, you know how things roll down Tilly Chadwick's . . . *chest* . . . and then Daisy walked in—it was *totally* innocent, but you know how some people jump to conclusions and no matter what you say you can't convince them otherwise. Daisy's been like the secret police ever since. Convinced I'm eyeing up women *every time* we go out." He stuck his hands in his thick black hair. "She even accused me of flirting with a *traffic warden* this weekend! I mean, Daisy means the world to me, but nothing I say makes the slightest difference, and it's driving me nuts." He raised his big eyes to me. "What can I do?"

I heard that phrase at least four times a day. "Don't worry," I said, patting his knee. "There's a very quick way to fix this."

". . . so," I said to Nelson, "we're going to go have lunch with Jethro and Daisy, who thinks I'm—or rather Honey is—an old schoolmate of Jethro's. I'm going to give him the full Honey Blennerhesket charm offensive, and Jethro's going to make a big show of being utterly uninterested in me." I smiled encouragingly. "All you have to do is sit there and give her the impression that you're my boyfriend."

"But I'm not," Nelson pointed out. "If I was being your boyfriend I'd need to get my teeth fixed, a much more expensive suit, and a faint air of superiority."

Nelson wasn't all that keen on Jonathan. I put it down to jealousy, plain and simple, combined with the fact that they were, in many ways, quite similar. Their manic attention to detail, for one thing.

"You don't have to lie," I said, ignoring the dig. "Just . . . play along. Listen, I need to get changed, so could you put the coffee machine on? I could do with a quick cup before we leave."

"Fine," said Nelson. "I'll pretend you use my razor to shave your legs. Oh, hang on—*you do*."

I gave him a reproachful look, then slipped into the spare room, removed Melissa's comfy wide trousers, and began decanting myself into Honey's stockings. My office had once been a little one-bedroom flat, and in the old bedroom I kept my foxy Little Lady wardrobe of pencil skirts, neat tweed suits, and deep V-neck cardies. I had the sort of unmanageable figure that made high street shopping pure misery, even with my bestfriend, Gabi's, encouragement, but somehow, my ample bosom and even more ample hips filled Honey's fitted outfits like cream in an éclair, as if things constantly threatened to burst free, but in a good way.

I wriggled into a tight black pencil skirt. In the beginning, when I'd tried to keep my agency a secret, the clothes had been more of a disguise than anything else, but since the bombshell uniform had seemed to focus both the client's mind and mine on the job at hand, I'd continued to use it. There was no way our little plan for this afternoon would work, for instance, if I was just plain old Melissa. Believe me, I was perfectly resistible as Melissa.

"So what are you going to do to the poor man?" yelled Nelson.

"Oh, you know, the usual Honey stuff." To be honest, I never really planned *anything* as Honey: it just seemed to come out of its own accord. I buckled a waspie belt round my waist. At least having hips like a Russian doll meant your waist looked smaller by comparison. "I've told Jethro that he has to ignore me, whatever I do, go on about how happy he is with Daisy, and if necessary, ask me to stop flirting because he's *simply not interested*. Just don't let her slap me."

"Don't worry, I'm the office first aider," said Nelson. He did a gratifying double take as I sashayed into the main office and slid my feet into a pair of patent leather peep-toe sandals. "Good Lord. How does anyone get any work done with you dressed like that? How do you walk downstairs? How do you *breathe*?"

"I'm a woman of many talents." I winked, then paused as I caught a glimpse of my curvaceous reflection in the mirror. Something was missing. I was still too . . . Melissa.

"Do you think I should . . . ?" I made a halo motion around my head.

"Should what?" he said sternly, as if he didn't already know what I was talking about.

"Should I . . . put it on?"

We held each other's gaze.

He knew I was talking about The Wig.

I used to offer a rather ingenious service whereby I'd pretend to be a client's girlfriend—just to tide them over a tricky social hump, you understand. Weddings, meetings with nosy mothers, that sort of thing. To stop other people from recognizing me—I know an *embarrassing* number of people—I'd bought a blond wig because I hadn't wanted my freelance girlfriend work getting back to my family. But the weird thing was, tossing my fabulous blond mane around gave me an amazing thrill. I wasn't frumpy, reliable Mel anymore, I was a fearless, quick-thinking blond goddess.

It was how I'd met Jonathan, actually. He'd moved here from New York after a horrendous divorce, and he'd needed a smoke screen to keep himself from being matchmade to death by all the hostesses desperate for gorgeous thirty-something bachelors. So when he and I had gotten together for real, Jonathan had decided for obvious reasons that he hadn't wanted me wearing the wig for work anymore. I could see his point. I was never quite sure what would happen myself when I put the wig on. So I'd promised him it would stay in the box.

And it had, more or less.

I bit my lip now. The wig would be the cherry on the cake. Things always turned up a few notches when I wore the wig. And I needed to look like a real knockout to convince Daisy of Jethro's devotion. . . .

I turned on my heel and wiggled off to the spare room.

"Oh, Mel," groaned Nelson. "I'm not sure I can cope with the wig."

Heading straight to a filing cabinet that housed the personal details of enough London bachelors to fill a *Tatler* Eligibles list, I lifted the lid off a fabulous old red satin box.

Carefully, I opened it and withdrew a coil of gleaming blond hair. The golden strands shone as I smoothed and stroked the wig around my hand. My secret weapon.

Between you and me, I did miss it.

Jonathan was in Paris. He would never know. Nelson wouldn't tell. And Jethro would thank me later.

Deftly, I began pinning up my own thick brown hair.

We'd arranged to meet for lunch at Cecconi's in Burlington Gardens, and I spotted Jethro and Daisy through the big windows as we got out of the taxi. They were holding hands over the table, and Daisy looked the image of sweetness in a white sundress and strawberry blond Heidi braids.

"Is Jethro looking at me?" I asked Nelson as I paid the driver.

"Mel, of course he's looking at you. There are people in *offices* looking at you."

"Don't be silly," I said, blushing. "And call me Honey."

As we made our way into the restaurant, I saw that Nelson was right: people were looking at us. That was the wig—my very own exclamation mark. It suddenly dawned on me that though I'd run through the Honey persona with Jethro, I hadn't told Jethro I'd be arriving in a blond wig. That, presumably, was why he was looking so very shocked. I tried to look at him reassuringly but Honeyishly at the same time, and psyched myself up into Honey Mode.

"Jethro! How long's it been? You haven't changed at all!" I cried, opening my arms and advancing on him for a social kiss or two.

I sensed Nelson stiffen behind me, and at once a dark cloud passed across Daisy's pretty face, rather like when you try to take a bone away from a Jack Russell.

"H-h-honey," he stammered, his eyes running up and down me frantically. "Lovely to see you again. This is Daisy, my girlfriend. Daisy, this is Honey, an . . . an old friend."

"Hello!" I said, mwahing her pink cheek. "This is Nelson Barber— Nelson, Jethro Lorton-Hunter and Daisy—"

"Daisy Thomsett. We've been together eighteen months," she said at once, shooting daggers at me.

I made to sit down, and both Nelson and Jethro went to pull my chair out. I shook my head warningly at Jethro and glared at Daisy's half-empty glass.

"More water, Daisy?" he said instead, turning his attention back to her, as we'd practiced at his consultation.

"Yes, please, darling," she said, without taking her narrowed eyes off me.

I leaned my elbows on the table so my cleavage rose up in my red shirt like two fresh white loaves. "So, Jethro," I purred, "you're looking well."

"Yes," he said, staring at my cleavage. "That's domestic bliss. Daisy really looks after me. I've never been so happy."

I coughed, and he dragged his gaze upward. "Lucky Daisy," I cooed.

"Lucky in what way?" demanded Daisy.

"Lucky Daisy to have a boyfriend who's complimentary about her in public," said Nelson, opening his menu. "Something Honey here is always complaining about."

"Nelson!" I began, knowing he meant Jonathan, who wasn't what you'd call demonstrative in public, but he flashed me a quick smile and put his arm around me.

"Although she knows I adore her," he added, giving me a boyfriend-ish squeeze. A little too boyfriend-ish, maybe—one grip of his strong arm practically cuddled me onto his lap. Not that he seemed to mind. Nelson and I were Friends Who Hugged, but this was something else. This was stage three dating handsiness. I boggled my eyes at him from under my blond bangs.

"Who could resist that smolder?" he went on, beaming adoringly. "Certainly not me."

"Or me," added Jethro. "I mean, I *could* resist. Ha! I don't have eyes for anyone but Daisy!"

"Then stop looking down her top," snapped Daisy so emphatically that Nelson and I sprang apart—almost as if we really were going out.

This wasn't going quite as planned: for my cunning reverse psychology to work, Jethro's ignoring needed to match my flirting exactly, and . . . it wasn't. I must have thrown him off with the unexpected blondness. Daisy was looking crosser by the minute.

"Funny Jethro never mentioned you before," she said suspiciously. "I'd say you were the sort of old friend who'd stick in the mind."

"Oh, Jethro, I'm crushed!" I pretended to look hurt, then shrugged toward Daisy. "He's a one-woman man, obviously!"

With excellent timing, the waiter appeared before anyone could say anything else.

"Ready to order?" he asked, pen poised.

"Oh, I think we're ready," glowered Daisy. "More than ready."

I opted for spaghetti and ate it in a deliberately Sophia Loren manner, all slow twirling and lip-licking. Daisy stabbed her ravioli viciously, and I had to keep kicking Jethro under the table to stop his gawking at me and start talking up Daisy's many charms. If it hadn't been for Nelson's heroically taking charge of the conversation, I don't know what I'd have done.

"So, Honey," said Daisy as our plates were cleared, "does it take you ages in the morning to look so . . . glamorous?"

"I prefer the natural look, personally, Dais," said Jethro at once. "Some women don't need all that makeup and what-have-you."

"You think I don't make any effort?" she demanded.

He looked bewildered. "No. No, just that . . . Oh, God."

"Women!" said Nelson, as if he knew anything about it.

"It does take a while," I said, shooting Jethro a flirty glance. "All the hooks . . . and clips . . ."

Honestly, I couldn't help it. It was the wig.

Jethro swallowed hard. "Waste of time!" he croaked manfully.

"I don't think I could be bothered," snapped Daisy. "And I have a job to get to in the mornings. Unless it's part *of* your job?"

"It is," I affirmed.

"Oh, she's a different girl at home," Nelson assured her. "You wouldn't recognize her."

"Anyone got room for pudding?" asked Jethro, trying to change the subject. "The strawberry tart sounds nice."

"I'm not all that fond of tarts," seethed Daisy.

"I'll just have a black coffee, I think." I put my napkin on the table. "Would you excuse me?" I said, as Nelson and Jethro half rose from their seats.

"What a good idea!" said Daisy grimly. "I'll come with you."

She practically hustled me into the loos. Then, as soon as the door swung closed, she turned on me with a ferocity I hadn't seen since my sister Allegra had her car towed.

"What are you playing at?" she demanded. "Jethro is off-limits! Off-limits! Leave him alone, you hear me?"

"Darling," I said, leaning against a washbasin and affecting a sorrowful expression. "If only. Jethro is utterly devoted to you. He told me so when I—"

Daisy's eyes boggled. "When you what? Has he been meeting up with you behind my back? I knew it! Right, I'm going to have it out with him this minute."

Oops.

"God, no," I said quickly, grabbing her arm. "I mean, we spoke on the phone and . . ."

Nelson's constant warnings about not spinning a web of complicated lies reverberated in my head.

Keep it simple.

I put a hand to my throat and smiled bravely. "I must admit . . . Jeth is a *wonderful* man. A real keeper. He made it very, very clear to me that you're the only woman for him!"

Which was true.

"He said that?" she asked hopefully. "And he wasn't . . . drunk?"

"Oh, yes." I nodded, as her guard fell and revealed a sudden flash of something I recognized: vulnerability. Poor Daisy. She must have had a bounder in her past. I'd had enough bounders myself to spot the ugly scars of paranoia. "I wouldn't stand a chance. He's absolutely mad about you. Adores you. In fact, I wouldn't be surprised if he—"

Daisy's eyes lit up and she grabbed my hands. "Really? Ohmigod! You think he's about to *propose?*"

"Um! Who knows?" I gasped, but she was already barging back into the restaurant, doors swinging behind her.

"I think that went off all right," I said, as Nelson and I strolled arm in arm down Piccadilly afterward. I'd changed out of my crippling high heels into the more manageable pair I kept in my vast handbag, and shaken out my brown hair from underneath the wig. It was one of those rare early spring days in London when the trees are out, the sun is shining, and you feel as if you're breathing in summer instead of the usual grime.

What with that and a strong sense of a job well done, I was positively floating along.

"Indeed," Nelson agreed. "It was nice of the manager to give us that champagne. Not that they had much choice after Daisy announced her engagement, mind you. I heard her telling the waiter how like Jethro it was to have arranged lunch so near Bond Street, for Tiffany's."

"Well, what about you being such a great pretend boyfriend?" I gave his hip a nudge with mine. "If you're that good at pretending, I have no idea why you're still single."

He looked sideways at me. "I learned from the queen of pretend girlfriends. Look, this is my office—are you taking the rest of the day off?"

"Certainly not," I said. "I've got a wardrobe consultation, a broody mother, and an unknown family drama to fix this afternoon." I leaned up to kiss Nelson on his cheek. "Thanks for your help."

"My pleasure," said Nelson. "I'll see you back home."

The flat Nelson and I called home was a few streets away from my office, in a friendly but rather run-down residential area behind Victoria Coach Station. We had nearly the same postcode as Buckingham Palace, which impressed Jonathan's mother to no end, but it really wasn't that posh at all. Still, I thought, noticing the first flickers of pink blossoms on the cherry trees as I walked home that evening, I'd miss its shabby gentility when I moved to Paris.

My living arrangements at the moment were rather complicated, due to the fact that Jonathan had just taken a job running the up-market Parisian branch of Kyrle & Pope, a tony estate agency, while I still had to run the one and only branch of the very London-based Little Lady Agency. Consequently, I was working hard in SW1 from Monday to Thursday lunchtime, and living at Nelson's, then hopping on Eurostar to Paris and into the arms of Jonathan for the rest of the week.

Not seeing each other all the time did have its romantic advantages, if you know what I mean. Jonathan had been living there for nearly four months, and we still hadn't found time to go up the Eiffel Tower.

However, I couldn't go on living in two places, and Jonathan had been nudging me for a while about exactly *when* I was going to move to Paris. I did want to, honestly. It was just . . . quite a wrench.

When I got home, Nelson was going through the post and yelling at a radio phone-in show, as was his wont. I kicked off my shoes and put a bottle of wine on the table next to him.

"A little thank-you for this morning," I said. "Do you want to open it now? I've had a hellish afternoon trying to coach a client into telling his dragon of a mother he's living with his girlfriend and has been for the last five years. Not to mention the fact that his father's practically got him lined up to marry his cousin. God, sometimes I just don't know where to start."

Nelson looked up from a selection of bills. "It's a good thing these people don't know you and your own family arrangements, or else they'd find it hard to take your Nightmare Family Management very seriously."

I would have disagreed with him if it hadn't been true. The Romney-Joneses were, not to put too fine a point on it, a bunch of melodramatic, self-centered schemers. Jonathan thought they should all be in therapy, which of course we had been, for about a month in the early nineties, until my father had found out that the therapy bills cost as much as the mortgage.

"More to the point," Nelson went on, "I hope you're going to put some of those Nightmare Family Management skills into action this weekend."

"Oh, don't. At least I'm taking Jonathan home with me for backup," I sighed. "We need to start talking about the wedding, and Mummy's invited everyone for a family dinner—Allegra and Lars, Emery and William, Granny—"

"The whole lot. Blimey." He wandered over toward his room, pulling off his tie. "Maybe you should take the wig with you? Might help you put your foot down."

"I don't think Jonathan would go for that," I said heavily. "He has quite strong views on the wearing of the wig."

Nelson paused on the other side of the room. "Mel. I was joking."

"Any chance of a foot rub?" I asked hopefully. Nelson's foot rubs were legendary. He had very strong thumbs and could turn me to jelly in seconds. That and his cooking made him Flatmate of the Year, indefinitely. "I'm walking on knots here."

"Sorry, running late," he said, catching sight of the kitchen clock. "Maybe later?"

He vanished into his room, and while I was still making pleading noises, he reappeared, wrapped in a towel at his waist, and headed for the bathroom. "You'll have to get your own supper tonight. And can I borrow that fancy bath oil of yours? I've run out," he yelled over the sound of the boiler cranking into action.

My jaw dropped. One, Nelson was suggesting *I* make supper. Even when he'd been rushed into hospital overnight with blood poisoning, he'd left instructions about what I should heat up from his freezer of delights. Two, he wanted to use *bath oil*. Three, he was wandering around the flat *in a towel.*

The sight of Nelson's upper body, which he kept Englishly under wraps for as much of the year as possible, was a rare thing indeed. Even though we'd known each other forever, we'd agreed on dressing gowns as part of my moving in.

So it was quite startling to have his upper body so suddenly unveiled, and I couldn't help noticing his newly rounded biceps, flecked with a thick crop of freckles where his T-shirt sleeves stopped and his tan started. He'd spent a lot of the spring crewing some yacht with his mate Roger, and heaving all those mainsails around had clearly had an effect.

Before I could recover my dropped jaw, he slapped a hand over his stomach.

"What are you staring at?" he demanded, turning away from me so I couldn't see whatever it was he was so self-conscious about. "Haven't you ever seen an appendectomy scar before?"

Mel! I told myself, with a brisk mental shake. That was the trouble with having a boyfriend you only saw on the weekends. By midweek, I could almost fancy Gordon Brown.

"Bath's about to run over!" I caroled. "Use whatever you want! I'll make the tea!"

And I turned on my heel and scuttled to the kitchen.

Nelson never lingered in the bath, and after ten minutes, he plonked himself down at the kitchen table. He was now dressed in a pair of jeans and a blue shirt, and he toweled his damp hair as I pushed a mug of tea toward him.

"What's the big rush?" I asked, hoping he'd stay long enough to put dinner on.

Nelson stopped toweling and looked up. "*Dur*. I'm taking your friend Jossy Hopkirk out for dinner. We're going to a new organic pub in Islington. Come on, *you* set up this date."

"Oh, yes."

In an effort to kick-start Nelson's love life, which, to be honest, had been a little lackluster of late, I'd turned to my bulging address book and set about creating a program of blind dates for him, in the hope that he too might get to enjoy the delights of couplehood currently experienced by me and Jonathan. I had high hopes for Jossy. She had an advanced driving certificate and worked for a donkey charity. Competent parking and animal aid featured high on Nelson's Top Ten requirements in female company.

"Is that a new shirt?" I asked curiously. Nelson seemed to be making more effort than normal—a haircut, a fresh shirt, the trip up to North London. . . .

"Ah, you noticed!" he said. "Yes, it is."

"Good!" I said. "That's . . . good."

"You like it? It's the right color?"

"Yes. It's great."

I wasn't sure what this was about. Nelson normally spurned my help in clothes shopping. He was the one bachelor I wasn't allowed to fix up.

"Suppose I should really get you to give me a final checkup," he went on, as if he'd been reading my mind. "Sort out my wardrobe, and all that. Before you . . . go."

"Before I go where?"

"To Paris." He ran a hand through his hair. "Have you sorted out a date yet? For your big move?"

I blinked. "No. Not yet."

For the second time that evening we stared at each other in silence.

"I expect I'll be discussing that with Jonathan this weekend," I said, trying to sound excited.

I mean, *of course* I was looking forward to setting up home in Jonathan's gorgeous Parisian apartment, and it wasn't like we'd never be in London again, but leaving Nelson and the flat I'd lived in for so long was something I hadn't spent too much time dwelling on.

Nelson made a really obvious attempt to look jolly. "Yes, well, I need to know, so I can aim to get one of these blind dates of yours moved into the spare room," he said. "Place wouldn't be the same without tights over the radiators and nine different shampoos in the bathroom."

"And then there's my rent!" I said, in an equally lame jokey tone. "I know it's subsidizing your organic food addiction."

He pulled a face. "And what if she doesn't like *eating*?"

I felt a terrible pang in my chest at the idea of Nelson patiently putting up with some dreadful bimbo's messy kitchen habits and yappy friends talking over the archaeology programs he watched on the telly. We'd come to an understanding over the years.

"I'll miss you, you grumpy sod," I blurted out, grabbing his hand over the table.

"I'll miss you, you daft baggage," he said, squeezing my hand. The phone rang on the wall next to me. It was half six, the time Jonathan called me from work every day. His timekeeping, like everything else about him, was meticulous.

I squeezed Nelson's hand apologetically. "That'll be Jonathan. We'll talk later, OK?"

Nelson looked as if he was about to say something, but then he shoved his chair back. "Right. I should get a move on."

"You look v foxy, by the way," I added, reaching for the phone. "I hope Jossy's made as much effort!"

Nelson mumbled something I didn't catch, but I wasn't really listening. My skin was tingling with delicious anticipation as I picked up the receiver and reeled off our number.

"May I speak with Mrs. Melissa Romney-Riley-Jones?" inquired a smooth American voice.

I sighed with pleasure and leaned against the kitchen wall. "Not quite yet. In a month or two?"

"Not sure I can wait that long, Mrs. Romney-Riley-Jones," said Jonathan.

I didn't care what order the names were in, I would never ever get sick of hearing them strung together.

two

Jonathan Riley was the first man I'd ever dated who'd actually seemed finished.

That wasn't just because he had a great job, or his coppery hair was always perfectly groomed, or his suits were handmade. It wasn't even because he was, in my opinion, quite knee-wobblingly gorgeous, with his strong cheekbones and a devastating smile that crinkled up his gray eyes. Jonathan had a special kind of polish, the sort you see in those Golden Era studio portraits of Hollywood stars. Nelson could snort all he liked about stuffed shirts, but I'd never seen Jonathan lose his temper or be rude, and he'd quite literally swept me off my feet in our fairy-tale courtship of dinner dances and trips around London. I'd almost stopped believing that sort of romance was possible.

However, while it was easy to be poised and stylish in smart Parisian cafés in the company of a man who made me feel like Grace Kelly, there was something about the sight of Romney Hall's wrought-iron gates that brought out the quivering adolescent in me.

And that's where we were right now. The happy hours since I'd picked up Jonathan from St. Pancras International station had flown by all too quickly, and suddenly we were walking away from the safe haven of the car, and toward the ivy-covered dragon's den.

"Now, remember, darling," I said, squeezing Jonathan's hand to disguise my own nerves. "If you really can't bear another moment, wink at me, I'll pretend to faint and we'll just have to leave. I've done it before. People are always passing out at my parents' parties, for one reason or another. Leaving in a fury. Or a taxi."

Jonathan raised an eyebrow with an expression of adult amusement that calmed the butterflies cavorting inside my stomach, and replaced them with an altogether more pleasant fluttering sensation.

"It's only forty-eight hours," he said, putting his arm around my waist as we crunched across the gravel drive. "And I have met your family before, remember? It won't be a shock."

"They never fail to shock me, and I've known them for twenty-nine years," I replied dourly. My family was held together by a series of long-running disputes and grudges, and so far Jonathan had managed to remain impressively neutral in the face of shameless flattery and pitching. Although Daddy was an MP, the rest of them were just as bad.

"Well, OK, if they're vile to me this weekend, I'll take it as a sign that I'm part of the family," Jonathan replied. "It'll be a compliment!"

"Hmm," I said, checking the cars automatically. They were all there: Daddy's Jag, Mummy's battered Mercedes station wagon, Granny's little red sports car, some vast American SUV that I assumed belonged to my sister Emery and her husband, William, and a black BMW X5 with blacked-out windows and Swedish plates, which could only belong to my other sister, Allegra, unless Mummy had engaged a particularly Gothic caterer for this evening.

Allegra was married to a Swedish art dealer, Lars, and was meant to live in Stockholm. We still saw quite a lot of her, unfortunately.

I paused as we reached the huge oak front door, and I suddenly grabbed Jonathan's hands in my own gloved ones.

"I just wish they'd be normal," I wailed urgently. "I just . . . Don't let them put you off marrying me!"

"Oh, honey! Don't be ridiculous! *Nothing* could do that," said Jonathan. "Anyway, it's a celebration," he went on. "How rude do you think they'd have to be to stop me from marrying you?"

"Well . . ."

Jonathan cut off my fifteen examples by wrapping his arms around me and kissing me with considerable passion. Once I got over the shock of actually snogging against my front door—something I'd never *ever* done—I melted happily into him and would have carried on enjoying the delicious tingle of Jonathan's hands investigating beneath my new jacket when the front door opened and we staggered back in shock.

"Oh, *God*," drawled my older sister, Allegra, folding her arms across her chest so the trumpet sleeves of her latest black dress hung down witchily. "It's Romeo and Juliet."

Blushing, I scrambled to adjust my clothing. Jonathan merely shook out his jacket sleeves and stepped over the threshold into the hall.

"Allegra, lovely to see you," he said, kissing her on the cheek.

"Hmm," she replied noncommittally.

I steeled myself as I followed him in. It was never lovely to see Allegra. She had the dress sense of an operatic undertaker and the sort of social manner that would have made her right at home in the more cutthroat days of the Roman Empire.

"Bonjour, Allegra," I said, kissing her alabaster cheek. "Ça va?"

"Hello, Mel," she replied. "Don't tell me you got that shirt in Paris?"

"Yes," I said, beaming.

"*Really?*" She frowned in disbelief.

"Yes!" I protested. "From Samaritaine!"

"I don't know *what's* going on with French fashion these days," she said, stalking back to the drawing room.

"Ignore her," muttered Jonathan as I spluttered impotently. "You look adorable."

I thought we could creep into the drawing room without a big scene, since Daddy was standing with his back to the door, holding forth about something, but I'd forgotten about the eyes in the back of his head.

". . . now where you're going wrong, William, is listening to the other chap's opinion. Schoolboy error! Distracts you from your own . . . ah, *Melissa*, nice of you to drop in at last!"

My father spun around with his usual vulpine grin of welcome, and I took an involuntary step backward.

On a good day, Daddy wasn't a bad-looking man, if you went for the ghastly silver fox type of Englishman, but he seemed to have undergone a makeover of television star proportions. His gray hair was teased into youthful fullness, the bags under his eyes had vanished, and his skin had taken on a Caribbean glow not usually associated with the damp native climate of the Cotswolds.

As his welcoming smile widened into a veritable rictus, I noticed numbly that he'd also invested in a whole new set of teeth that made even Jonathan's gleaming American dental work look rather shabby.

I assumed that was why he was smiling so much. My father liked to wring full value out of everything.

"And you've brought Justin with you, I see," he went on, as I searched for the right thing to say.

"*Jonathan,*" my mother corrected him, shimmering forward, her long white hands extended. "As you very well know. Ignore him, darling, he's just trying to be foul. Although you never really have to try too hard, do you, Martin?" She clasped Jonathan's arms and beamed up into his face as if he was the only guest she was really bothered about. "*So* glad you could come!"

"Belinda, not even a strike on the Channel Tunnel could keep us away," he replied, kissing her on both cheeks. "I've been looking forward to it all week."

Mummy liked Jonathan. He knew how to be really charming and still sound like he meant it.

"Hello, darling," she said, turning to me and squinching up her face in an air kiss. She seemed to be lightly tanned too. I wondered if my father had done a two-for-one deal at the village salon. "Braveheart's been missing you," she added accusingly.

Mummy was something of a dog lover, and it seemed only logical that Jonathan and I should have parked his West Highland terrier with her until we both got settled in Paris. From what I'd seen of

Braveheart lately, he was even less keen to move to France than I was, living as he was in the lap of doggy luxury.

But before I could start apologizing, my father grabbed Jonathan by the shoulder—no mean feat, since Jonathan was at least four inches taller.

"Now then!" commanded Daddy. "I've been waiting to show you something!"

Jonathan looked at me with a faint flicker of trepidation.

"It's just the sword," I whispered. My father claimed to have "acquired" the sword that executed Anne Boleyn. He liked to show it to potential sons-in-law. The first time William visited as Emery's official fiancé, he actually took it down and started swinging it about, nearly decapitating Mrs. Lloyd, the housekeeper, which, I think, shocked my father into signing whatever ghastly prenup William's lawyers had drawn up.

"Come on!" barked my father. "Just time to have a quick trip up to the armory before dinner!"

I patted Jonathan on the arm. One of the billions of things I loved about Jonathan was that he refused to be intimidated by my father.

"Great!" said Jonathan, in a cheerleading voice. "Bring on the, er, armaments!"

My father—or, rather, the TV actor who seemed to be playing my father—clenched his jaw and led the way out of the drawing room.

"Lars? William?" I looked at my brothers-in-law hopefully. "You're not going to join them?"

Both shook their heads rather too quickly.

With Jonathan gone, I made the kissy-kissy hello rounds: first, Allegra's husband, Lars, who was also dressed in head-to-toe black. I steeled myself to kiss Lars. He always had worrying bits of food detritus in his thick black beard, and he smelled vaguely of glue. Every time I saw Lars and Allegra they seemed to be in the middle of some endless row, which they kept on the boil like a pan of everlasting stock.

"Hello, Lars," I said, aiming a kiss at a clean bit of beard. "You're looking very well."

"See?" he hissed cryptically at Allegra. "See? Even Melissa can tell!"

"Ignore him," said Allegra. "He's on some ludicrous Swedish herb diet that is making him extremely flatulent and yet is apparently doing him no end of good. I, on the other hand, am running out of Diptyque candles and have had to ban him from the gallery."

"Allegra!" snarled Lars.

"I see you've had your hair cut," she observed, ignoring him.

I patted my chic new chin-length bob proudly. I'd been hoping someone would notice. "Thank you," I said. "Jonathan thinks it makes me look rather Audrey Hepburn!"

Allegra peered more closely. "You have got big ears, haven't you? I'd never noticed before. Lars, look. Hasn't Melissa got big ears?"

"No!" snapped Lars. "They're more protruding than big!"

"Don't be ridiculous," snarled Allegra. "They're enormous. Like some kind of ceremonial *cup*!"

"No! It's the angle! The angle that makes them seem large! You have no eye, Allegra! No sense of proportion!"

I swung away before Lars could get his tape measure out. Honestly. My family were the bitter end.

I turned my attention instead to Emery, who was perched uncertainly on the arm of a chair while her husband, William, made short work of a plate of smoked salmon mini roulades.

Emery was three years younger than me, with long hair the color of milky tea that fell in shiny curtains around her face like one of those martyred women you see washing garments in rivers in pre-Raphaelite paintings. Compared with Allegra's exhausting torrent of opinion, Emery was a calming sea of soothing vagueness.

Which wasn't to say she was completely without Romney-Jones wiles—vague or not, Emery had managed to entrance a high-flying, sports-mad American lawyer, bagging herself a house in Chicago, a pied-à-terre in New York, and a six-year-old stepson called Valentine at the same time. Over the years, however, she'd cunningly established herself as someone who simply couldn't be asked to do anything, whereas Allegra simply refused whatever requests were made of her. The end result was that I got three times the sisterly responsibilities.

Tonight Emery was wearing a floaty silk kaftan in peacock colors over skinny jeans, and a matching expression of unspecific bewilderment. She looked lovely. Lucky Emery had inherited my mother's beanpole figure, which allowed her to carry off loose clothing. I needed underpinnings, and lots of them—the one time I'd let Emery badger me into a smock top, four people in a row had offered me a seat on the number 19 bus home.

"Hello, Emery," I said, leaning forward to kiss her. On closer inspection, Em wasn't looking as ethereal as usual. In fact, her cheekbones were looking almost rounded. *Good.* I thought, with a glimmer of schadenfreude. About time she caught up with the rest of us.

"Hello, Mel," she murmured. "Like your hair. Takes years off you."

I didn't mean to, but as she raised her cheek for a kiss, I got a good view down her wafty neckline, and believe me, she wasn't the "Pancake Em" of old. It was dumplings ahoy down there.

"Mind if I don't get up?" she went on, as I bit my lip on a number of observations. "Not feeling all that well tonight."

"Oh, no! Really?" I slid down next to her in the huge armchair. "What sort of not well?"

"Don't know. I haven't been feeling myself for a while, actually." She pushed her hair behind her ear and sighed. Her kaftan rose and fell, and I realized it wasn't just the cheekbones: there was quite a bit more of Emery beneath the folds all round. "Sort of . . . like when you stuff yourself at Christmas lunch? And none of it seems to be going anywhere?"

I took in her glowing cheeks and her swelling bosom—and the baby penny dropped. "Congratulations!" I whispered, nudging her affectionately.

Emery's eyes narrowed. "Shh. I mean, I don't know what you're talking about."

I rolled my eyes. "Oh, listen, I won't tell anyone. *Congratulations!* Were you planning to announce it over dinner? Gosh, how exciting!"

Emery shot me a furtive look, closely followed by a nervous one around the room. "Will you shut up? I'm not talking about it. Some one might tell Daddy. You know what he's like—as soon as he thinks an heir's in the offing, he'll have me under house arrest here. And at least in prison I wouldn't have to listen to him giving interviews."

"I won't let on," I promised happily. "When's it due?"

Her porcelain brow creased. "Um. Not exactly sure."

"What?"

"Oh, come on." Emery rolled her eyes as if I'd asked something absolutely unreasonable. "I don't know—four months? Three months? Sometime in the summer?"

"But, Emery . . . ," I began.

"Darlings, you should have said drinks were being served!" caroled a familiar voice.

"I swear that woman can hear the opening of a wine bottle at five hundred paces," murmured Emery, as I wriggled out of the chair to greet our grandmother.

Granny was the only member of the Romney-Jones clan who ever addressed me as if I was her first-choice conversation partner, and to be honest, family evenings were only bearable if she was there. Even I had to concede that there was a faint whiff of scandal about Granny, but at least in her case it was a glamorous 1950s nightclubs-and-mink-knickers kind of scandal, rather than the tax "confusion" that my father was prone to.

"Don't you look chic!" she exclaimed now, enveloping me in a waft of chiffon and Shalimar. "What have you done with that charming American chap of yours?"

"Oh, he's seeing the sword," I said, letting her tweak and rearrange my black shirt. A quick sideways check in the dusty gilt mirror above the fireplace confirmed I'd gone from semi-Sloane to La Dolce Vita. I had to admit that Granny had The Touch.

"I was waiting till you got here before I came down," she muttered into my ear. "Bloody unbearable, the lot of them. William's been stuffing food down his gullet like a competitive eater since the moment he arrived, and Lars and Allegra have already broken a door."

Before I could ask Granny how on earth that had happened, there was a feverish banging of the dinner gong, and everyone in the drawing room leaped about three inches out of their armchairs.

"Dinner is served," cackled my father, wielding an enormous gong beater.

The dinner gong was a monstrosity my father took great delight in dragging out whenever we had company. He liked to claim it was an ancestral relic from the Raj, but Granny let slip that he'd picked it up from a cinema that had been closing down in Chippenham in the 1970s.

"He really will have to tone down that tan before too much longer," observed Granny. "Or else questions will be asked about holidays and local party funds."

At the door, Jonathan was standing at Daddy's side, looking only slightly disconcerted by his trip to see the sword. He offered me his arm to lead me into dinner and didn't make any comment about the glacial temperature of the house away from the main fireplace, which was good of him.

"How did the small talk go?" I whispered.

"I told your father I had a hunting rifle," he whispered as we clattered down the freezing hall to the dining room. "And that my prep school had a cannon we fired on the Fourth of July. You reckon that's enough?"

"Should be plenty," I said, relieved.

"I'll leave the Uzi till next time," mused Jonathan. "Keep that one up my sleeve."

I looked up at him in surprise. I think he was joking. It was quite hard to tell with Jonathan sometimes.

We filed into the baronial dining hall, which was looking even more oppressive than usual, since, in honor of the occasion, Mummy had elected to dispense with electric light and had instead found some vast silver candelabras from somewhere. Poor Mrs. Lloyd, the housekeeper, must have been polishing herself into a new housemaid's elbow.

The major advantage of this lighting arrangement was that layers of dust and cobwebs were rendered invisible, while the glass eyes in the mounted stags' heads gleamed and the deep oak paneling took on a National Trust grandeur it certainly didn't have by day.

"How marvelous!" said Allegra, looking predictably at home in the gloom.

"I won't be able to see my food," whined Lars, taking his place opposite me.

"Isn't that the best way with British food?" asked William cheerfully.

"William," murmured Emery automatically.

She *was* looking peaky, I thought, worried. Maybe I should mention something to Mummy about it.

Emery caught me looking at her and clenched her eyebrows at me.

While my father was dealing with the wine, Granny subtly rearranged the seating plan to her own best advantage. Not only was she surrounded by three men attached to other people—opposite William, and with Jonathan and Lars on each side—but she'd also bagged the traditional plum position: the seat that wasn't in my father's line of sight.

It was a long table, which made the battered silver basket containing the bread rolls seem even farther away. In fact, an outside observer might have speculated that the place settings had been shifted downward so that we all seemed to be sitting a little nearer to my mother at one end, leaving my father snorting and raging at a relatively safe distance.

To my embarrassment, having gone through all this ludicrous showing off, my parents had taken it upon themselves to serve Heinz tomato soup to start, and what looked like frozen lasagna to follow, with the remaining tureens filled up with new potatoes and that awful diced-carrots-and-peas mixture so popular with schools and hospitals. The fact that they'd pressed Mrs. Lloyd into wearing a pinny over her black slacks and were silver-serving this bizarre selection to us only put the tin lid on things.

The wine, however, was flowing as lavishly as usual, mostly toward my father's end of the table.

"Melissa!" he roared now, his new teeth gleaming in the candlelight. "Stop hogging the potatoes!"

"But I've only had two!" I dropped the serving spoon as if it had been red-hot.

Jonathan, installed at my father's right hand, gave me a look. He was always telling me I should stand up to my family more. For Jonathan's benefit, I forced out a nervous laugh, as if Daddy had only been teasing, although I was fairly sure he hadn't been. "I mean, is that a hint that you'd like the dish passed up the table?"

"No," he snapped. "It's not. If I wanted the dish passed up, I'd tell you. Jonathan, what in the name of God are you doing to my leg, man?"

Allegra, on his left, glowered at her plate. "It's Jenkins, Daddy. He's under the table, probably hoping to polish off *this* dinner too, the scrounging mutt!"

She punctuated the last part of the sentence with an obvious subtable swipe toward the older of my mother's two basset hounds.

"I'm afraid that's why we're eating low-fat lasagna, everyone," explained Mummy, projecting her voice from the other end. "Jenkins was awfully naughty and gobbled up the lamb while it was cooling on the kitchen table." She refilled her wineglass from the bottle nearest her. "And the petit fours too, I'm afraid. *Bad* Jenkins," she added, beaming indulgently as he galloped out from under the table as fast as an elderly and overweight dog could manage, obviously on the wrong end of my father's shoe.

"How did he eat the cheese?" Allegra asked, eyeing Jenkins suspiciously. "I saw it in the fridge."

"Ah, well, that's Melissa's fault." Mummy wagged a finger at me.

"My fault?" I protested. Pretty much everything that went wrong chez Romney-Jones was my fault, but this was a new one.

"That naughty Braveheart of yours helped him open the fridge."

"What?" I shot an embarrassed look toward Jonathan. I was supposed to have trained all the willfulness out of Braveheart—Jonathan was forever telling his friends what a dog whisperer I was.

Jonathan wrinkled his brow innocently. "Is there no end to that dog's new tricks?"

"I know." Mummy beamed. "I saw him up on his paws, prising the door open with his little nose. Very clever!" Then she saw my father's furiously dilating nostrils and hastily added, "But terribly wicked.

Still, plenty of cheese in the cellar instead! Did you know your father's been made honorary head of the Cheese Council, Melissa?"

"No!" I said. "Well done, Daddy!"

"I had no idea," said Jonathan politely. "Congratulations."

"You're not on Daddy's famous Cheese Diet then, I take it," said Allegra with a sardonic lift of her eyebrows.

"No," I admitted. "But I hear sales of Stinking Bishop are up twenty percent! You grate it over everything," I explained to Jonathan. "Even puddings—amazing how the weight drops off."

"Uh-huh," said Jonathan neutrally.

Allegra and Lars took advantage of this flurry of conversation to shoot a few phlegmy volleys across the table at each other in Swedish, culminating in Allegra spitting, "And I haven't forgotten about the *tin opener*!" in English while stabbing several diced carrots menacingly with her fork.

There was an embarrassed pause, then Lars glared and hissed, "Allegra, no smiling! Be careful of your stitches!"

Allegra scowled, then winced, then did a half scowl with extra-narrowed eyes.

"If you have any more lifts and tucks, Allegra, I shall have to have your birth certificate altered," observed Daddy, with breathtaking hypocrisy. "Your surgeon's had more input into your appearance than your mother and I."

"If only it were that easy," she shot back.

"Allegra! Martin!" cried Mummy, with an embarrassed glance at Jonathan.

Looking across the table, I was struck by Emery, who was sipping at her water glass and wincing. She always looked vaguely pained, as if the sheer unfairness of life was bearing down heavily on her wispy shoulders, but tonight she was looking about as strained as I'd ever seen her.

"Emery," I murmured as Mrs. Lloyd floated in and out of the shadows, clearing away the plates. "Are you feeling all right? Is your lasagna OK?"

"Oh, um . . ." She glanced at her half-eaten lasagna as if she'd only just realized it was there. Emery normally ate like a horse, albeit in such a stealthy way that no one ever saw the food vanish from the plate.

"Time for a spot of pudding, I think, don't you?" Mummy said, and before we even had time to wonder what it was, Mrs. Lloyd had reappeared as if by magic at the door. She was holding a tray with my grandmother's "priceless" crystal trifle bowl on it.

Jonathan looked at me, clearly impressed. I'd have to tell him later about the doorbell under the table. The one my father had overused so much with the last housekeeper, on account of the way his leg jiggled up and down whenever he became enraged, that she'd ended up throwing an entire dish of roast partridge at him.

Mrs. Lloyd started to advance slowly toward the table. She seemed embarrassed.

I shot her a sympathetic look.

"So, what delight have you whisked up for us, Mrs. Lloyd?" asked Mummy, beaming.

Mrs. Lloyd showed her the contents of the bowl, and Mummy's smile froze a little. "Oh. This was all that was left after . . . ?"

Mrs. Lloyd nodded.

Mummy recovered herself, as was her great skill in life. "Emery, darling! We made your favorite especially!"

"What?" Emery said doubtfully. "Lime Jell-O? Seriously?"

"Seriously?" demanded my father. "You're serving me Jell-O for dinner?"

"And Reddi-wip?" asked William, his eyes lighting up.

"Lovely!" I cried before an argument could break out.

By the time the vast platters of cheese and biscuits began to circulate, I spotted my mother sending covert glances toward Daddy's end of the table. Not that he noticed. He was now holding forth to both Jonathan and William about where the British had gone wrong in the War of Independence, using the silver cruet set as tactical demonstration.

I caught Jonathan's eye, hoping he wasn't too close to the end of his tether, but he smiled back at me and let the faint shadow of a private wink cross his face.

I think my mother saw, because she started to smile and fiddle girlishly with her diamond earrings.

"Anyway," my father went on smoothly, banging his hands on the table and rising to his feet. "I'd like to say a few words at this juncture, if it's all the same to everyone else."

Emery, Allegra, and I all flinched. Allegra actually groaned aloud, which I thought was brave of her.

Daddy fired a quick glare in her direction, then beamed in an avuncular manner at Jonathan, William, and Lars. I wasn't taken in by that carefully honed "open body language." I'd seen him through eight local and six national elections.

"First of all," he oozed, with a generous spread of his hands, "may I say how wonderful it is, as the head of the family, to have not only my own wife and children, but my sons-in-law and my future son-in-law around me too."

"And me, darling," added Granny.

"And my mother-in-law," snapped Daddy. "And of course Mrs. Lloyd. And the dogs. Anyone else?"

"No, I think mentioning the dogs would be twee," said Granny. "Do go on."

"Thank you, Dilys," he said sarcastically.

Blimey, I thought. *Granny is in a feisty mood tonight.* Baiting my father was one of her little treats in life, but this evening she had a special twinkle in her eye.

I loved Granny, but in her own way she was as much a loose cannon as anyone else in the family. More so, perhaps, because she had her own money and an address book that my father would have given both his new crowns for.

"You all know how very happy your mother has made me over the years, so you can imagine how thrilled I was when Jonathan decided to make an honest woman out of our own little lady of the night."

I flinched. Even though Jonathan and I had met at work—like *loads of people* do every day—Daddy, of course, persisted in misunderstanding the innocent nature of my agency, and of the way my relationship with Jonathan had begun.

He swung around toward me, nearly, but not quite, sloshing his wine in the huge goblet. He was far too experienced to spill. "Jolly well done, Melissa. Thought I'd never see the day, but here we are. My three daughters, married off to successful men, all with beautiful homes in foreign cities. What more could a proud father ask for?"

Allegra, who'd frankly boggled at the "family man" bit, now choked outright on her water biscuit.

"Something the matter, Allegra?" he inquired solicitiously.

She shook her head as William slapped her a little too enthusiastically on the back.

I looked at Jonathan and smiled. I'd never heard my father be so sweet about us! Even if he was putting it on for the benefit of the assembled husbands, it warmed my heart to hear he was proud of us. God knows we'd heard enough to the contrary over the years.

"So, please," said Daddy, refilling his glass from his own private decanter. "A toast, to Melissa and Jonathan! A perfect example of why it's better to marry the cow instead of buying the milk!"

I glared at him. There was absolutely no need for that.

"Melissa and Jonathan!" echoed my grandmother. "May the milk never run dry!"

"Melissa and Jonathan!" mumbled everyone else.

I glanced across the table and was relieved to see Jonathan looking more amused than annoyed. He looked so sexy in the half light, the shadows only making his cheekbones seem sharper and his jaw more square and manly. I was hoping Mummy had put us in the four-poster room. Not only was it romantic, but it also had the only central heating pipe that actually worked.

"So have you set a date?" inquired Granny.

"Not quite yet," I admitted. "We're rather hoping to get the move sorted out first, and the guest list will take some organizing . . ."

"I have a lot of family and friends who'll be dying to fly over," explained Jonathan.

"Oh, I *adore* big weddings," sighed Granny, as Daddy made a faint strangled noise.

Allegra gave him a dirty look. "You haven't cashed in Melissa's wedding fund, have you, Daddy?"

"If I had my time again, I'd elope," he said, smiling ghoulishly. "Much less bother and you're already there on your honeymoon, aren't you?"

"He's cashed it in," said Allegra to no one in particular.

"Melissa will have a beautiful wedding, just like her sisters did," insisted Mummy, which didn't actually answer Allegra's question either. "When are you planning on moving to Paris, darling? We'll need to get started . . ."

"Not before the end of August," said Jonathan before I could reply. "Everyone's away until then, but I hope it won't be too long after that. A Christmas wedding, perhaps?"

He looked at me with a smile in his eyes, and my heart melted gorgeously. It was hard to get specific when my brain was constantly distracted.

"Wonderful. Now, on to other matters," said Daddy. "You may be aware—"

"We're not at one of your insufferable Olympics meetings now, darling," said my mother.

"It doesn't matter, Mummy," I put in, still toasty at the edges from the unexpected display of paternal love. "While we're all here, and so on?" I turned back to Daddy and smiled.

He beamed back, with sparkly teeth. "Thank you, Melissa. Now—your mother's little knitting hobby. You'll all no doubt be aware that your mother is enjoying her second exhibition in that god-awful gallery in Whitechapel," he went on. "What is it this time, Belinda? Nightmares in wool?"

"Nursery grotesques," said Allegra crossly. "And there's a waiting list."

While trying to give up smoking last year, my mother had started to knit hideously malformed woolly toys—six-legged cats, dogs with two heads, hybrid donkey-pigs, that sort of thing. Not on purpose, just because she'd been too stressed to follow a pattern. Somehow, and this is the bit I've never quite understood, Allegra had managed to turn them into the next big thing in New British Art, going from part-time useless gallery owner to hard-nosed art agent in one mohair swoop herself.

I know. *Weird.* Still . . . As Emery would say.

"Yes, well, there has been a *teeny* hitch there," my mother began nervously, but Allegra turned a fierce look on her, and she stopped. "Although nothing we can't fix," she added, not very convincingly.

"Jolly good," said my father, before I could ask what the hitch was. "Amazing what idiots will spend their money on. Anyway, it's up to you all to spread the word among your dim friends and drum up some trade for your mother. It's all going toward the roof, you know," he added, with a vicar-ish roll of the eyes toward the oak paneling. "Costs a fortune just to keep this place in Mr. Sheen."

"Is that your new wine merchant, Martin?" inquired Granny.

"No, Dilys," said my father, gritting his teeth with supreme control. "It's the name of a household cleaning product." He paused and bestowed a sad smile on us. "And I just wanted to say, while you're all together, how very important my family is to me . . ."

I beamed at my sisters, who were both regarding him with shameful cynicism. "See?" I mouthed at Emery.

But Daddy hadn't finished.

" . . . at this very important time for the main sales push for my Cheese Diet book," he went on seamlessly. "Very important for you all to help me show how everyone from tiny tots to *raddled old grannies* can benefit from the magic of Red Leicester. You'll be getting your personal appearance schedules in the post just as soon as little Katie at the publishers gets them finished." He winked. "I've managed to get hold of the list of bookshops whose sales count toward the *Sunday Times* bestseller lists, so I think I can rely on you all to stock up early on Christmas presents? Eh? Eh?"

I let my mouth drop open. So that was what the tan and the teeth and the family compliments were about!

The usual disappointment swept over me, causing me to blink rapidly. Just for once, it would be nice to come first, and hear how much I meant to him without . . .

"We're both very happy for you, darling," muttered my mother, spotting my distress and patting my hand. "And I for one am thrilled you've found a man who'll stand up to your father."

"What was that, Belinda?" inquired Daddy.

"Just saying what a welcome addition Jonathan is to the family."

"Absolutely. Great to have an estate agent on board. Now," he said, snapping his fingers at Mrs. Lloyd, "time for port and cigars, I reckon."

My mother pressed her napkin against her lips, then dropped it on the plate. "Come on, girls. Let's leave the men to their vile cigars and port, shall we?" She lowered her voice and added, "I'd like your opinions on a pair of shoes I bought the other day that your father doesn't know about."

"The truth, Mummy," said Allegra sternly.

Mummy paused and corrected herself, as recommended by her addiction counselor. "Well, more than one pair, yes."

"Total?"

"Three! Plus a bag!"

"Em, are you *sure* you're OK?" I asked, as Emery swayed unsteadily to her feet. "Won't you let me . . . ?"

"I'm fine, Melissa," she snapped with unusual vigor, but I was stopped from inquiring further by a light hand on my elbow and a waft of Shalimar up my nose.

"Can I have a word, Melissa?" murmured Granny in my ear. "On your own? Hang back and follow me to the drawing room in two minutes."

This sort of cloak-and-dagger routine didn't necessarily mean a great deal when it came to my grandmother. She could just as easily need an extra bridge player. There was a very thick streak of melodrama running through both sides of my family.

I excused myself on the grounds of needing the loo, and scurried upstairs to put our overnight bags in the four-poster room. Despite the spring weather, the house was like an icebox. If I was going to wear the gorgeous new Parisian silky pajamas I'd packed, the electric blanket would definitely need to go on now.

While I was hurrying back downstairs to deal with Granny, I heard an odd groan from the window seat on the landing.

I approached it with some caution, having had a bad experience with pulling back the curtains as a child: my parents had thrown some quite debauched parties in those days. In addition to the faint moaning, there was a pool of water trickling down the paneling and soaking into the carpet.

Gingerly, I pulled the curtain aside, to find Emery clutching her stomach and looking ashen.

"Oh, my God," she said, widening her eyes. "I've, like, *seriously* wet myself. It's so . . . embarrassing."

"Emery," I said, feeling the time had come to be frank. "Might you be a bit farther on than you thought with the baby?"

"Honestly, Mel, you know I don't keep a diary!" she snapped.

I gave her a searching look. Emery had spent most of her adolescence in a state of constant pregnancy scare, due to her inability to remember when her last period might have been. I distinctly recall visiting the doctor with her on one occasion, using *my* diary to jog her memory.

I didn't think we had time to embark on a similar debate now. I'd seen *ER*. Labor could progress very quickly, and Daddy would go berserk if Emery gave birth on the one good carpet in the house.

"Emery, we need to get your jeans off," I said firmly.

"Why? It took me half an hour to get them on." Her face suddenly contorted into a grimace of agony, and she grabbed her stomach. "Oh, God, that's like . . . argh."

I tried to unbutton the jeans, but I couldn't even get my finger behind the button. Emery seemed to have poured herself into them by sheer force of will.

"I'm going to have to cut you out," I announced, looking around for a suitable implement.

"You're not coming anywhere near me with scissors, Mel!" wailed Emery. "These are Earnest Sewn! They're limited edition!"

"Trust me, I'm a dressmaker," I said grimly.

"What's going on?"

I spun around. Granny was standing on the stairs.

"Anything I can do to help?" she inquired.

"Phone for an ambulance," I said. "It'll be quicker than arguing about who's sober enough to drive her to the hospital."

At this point, Emery let out a loudish moan—about as loud as Allegra would make on discovering her toast was burned—and somehow I managed to yank her jeans open, to reveal a surprisingly substantial, round bump.

Emery and I both stared at it in shock.

"OK," she admitted, "I might be a bit farther on." Then she gripped my hand so tight the bones cracked. "Don't let Daddy take over! Please!"

"Hello? Yes, hello. Good evening! I'd like an ambulance, if you'd be so kind," Granny was purring into the downstairs phone. "Well, right away, if you could do one. You see, my granddaughter appears to be having a baby . . . oh, thank you! Yes, I suppose I am terribly excited . . ."

"Granny!" I yelled. "Hurry *up*!"

A clattering of feet on the parquet and a gust of cigar smoke suggested that the men's port and cigar break was now over, just in time for the main show to begin.

"Good God!" bellowed Daddy's voice from the hall. "What the hell's going on up there?"

"Em?" William bounded up the oak staircase three stairs at a time.

"I'm feeling rather . . . ," murmured Emery, waving unspecifically at her kaftan.

"She's in labor," I explained. "We need lots of towels and some old blankets. William, help me get her into the drawing room. Lars, go and put the kettle on."

Lars blinked owlishly. "For hot water?"

"No," snapped Allegra, appearing behind him, "so the ambulance men can have a cup of tea when they get here. Hurry up, Lars!"

"Have you done this before?" demanded William, hoisting Emery into his arms as easily as if she'd been a gym bag.

"No, but Nelson did a first-aid course, and he was always practicing on me," I said. "Now come on, she needs to be somewhere more comfortable."

"The boot room," interjected Daddy quickly. "That sofa needs replacing in any case. Emery," he said, leaning over her and overenunciating right into her face, "hang on until you get there. Don't do anything on the main carpet."

"If you don't get a move on, I don't think there'll be much choice where the baby's born," I said.

Emery made a faint moan of horror.

"I'll get the brandy," said Daddy, as if this would solve everything.

As he strode off to his study, William set off down the hall, with Emery in his arms and Allegra following at a safe distance.

"Oh, the ambulance is on the way?" Granny said into the phone. "That's *wonderful*." Granny was winding up her conversation in the manner of someone discussing a weekend party invitation.

"Anything I can do?" asked Jonathan, leaning on the staircase.

"Get everyone a stiff drink and keep Daddy out of the way until it's all over—start him off on Scottish devolution or something," I said.

"Shall I send your mother in?"

I considered.

"Get her a couple of large gins first," I advised. "She's pretty squeamish."

"Will do," he said. He started to walk away, then turned back with a huge grin on his face. "You know, I love it when you cope like this, Melissa."

I smiled wryly. God knows I'd had enough practice over the years.

three

After helping to deliver my very first baby on Saturday night, then listening to the whole thing reenacted over the phone by my father for the benefit of the local press, with himself in the new lead role of Modest But Capable First Aider, I found the rest of the weekend to be naturally somewhat flat.

Or, looking at it more positively, nothing else happened.

Emery's baby turned out to be a boy, much to Daddy and William's delight. Daddy was actually more delighted than William, and went around saying he felt as if he finally had the heir he'd wanted for years, which made me, Emery, and Allegra feel *great*, as you might imagine, especially when he said it six times to six different journalists.

Even so, we were all bowled over by the tiny, pink shrimp of a baby curled up in the drawer from a Chippendale chest, lined with Mummy's spare pashminas and pillows.

But if his dark hair, balled-up fists, and cross expression didn't give away his Romney-Jones genes, his lungs certainly did. When he wasn't asleep, or plugged onto Emery, he screeched and screeched and screeched. Nothing would stop him. It was like being trapped in a house with the car alarms, the fire alarm, and the burglar alarm all going off at once. In fact at one point, my car alarm *did* go off, and we only noticed when Mrs. Lloyd came in and begged me to turn it off because the dogs were going crazy.

Emery, naturally, slept through most of it (or pretended to), and the district nurse ended up giving me the list of instructions and advice for new mums.

Not that anyone else seemed to be stepping forward to help. Lars and Allegra left after breakfast, arguing about who should drive back to their London house in Ham, and Granny bailed out soon after.

"I'm absolutely hopeless with babies, darling," she sighed regretfully, pulling on her kidskin gloves and adjusting her hat in the hall mirror as the deafening roar continued upstairs. "One was quite enough for me." She leaned up to kiss Jonathan's cheek. "So lovely to see you again, Jonathan dear. Take care of Melissa for me, won't you? Now, Melissa," she went on, with a meaningful twitch of the eyebrows, "would you give me a hand with my luggage?"

I'd almost forgotten about the "word" she'd wanted to have with me the night before, but when I'd loaded the monogrammed luggage into the tiny boot of her sports car, she took my hands and said, "Monday afternoon, tea at Claridge's. I have something I need your advice on," and winked.

"I'll need to check my diary," I began. "I'm rather frantic right now what with working a—"

"Splendid!" said Granny. "Love to Nelson!"

And she zoomed off, sending gravel and small birds flying in her wake.

Jonathan and I spent a pleasant hour tramping through the woods around the house with Braveheart and the rest of the dogs before I was summoned back to the house to "sort things out" for Emery. Maternity nursing isn't exactly a Little Lady Agency service, but I did what I could, made some phone calls and some lists. Emery, obviously, hadn't had a chance to lay in the normal supplies one needs when faced with a squalling infant, so I did my best to raise a cot, sterilizer, sheets, blankets, sleep suits, bottles, and burping cloths, while

William busied himself with the vital task of researching on the Internet the fastest possible buggy.

Meanwhile, Jonathan manfully chatted to my father, then at six o'clock, we escaped back to London, where Jonathan had booked us into the Dorchester's most honeymoon-y suite for the night since new tenants had just moved into his exorbitant flat.

"It has a spa," he said. "I thought you'd need to unwind." He dumped my overnight bag on the gigantic bed and massaged his temples as if to rub out the ringing in his ears. "What I really want is one of those hot oil body massages."

"Ooh, me too," I said, kicking off my shoes. "Should I ring reception and book them?"

Jonathan gave me his most smoldering look. "Who says we have to go down to the spa for that? Come here."

I must admit, Jonathan's idea of room service was pretty blissful.

In the morning, I drove him to the Eurostar terminal at St. Pancras, where we had an emotional good-bye (he ignored two calls on his mobile to demonstrate his extreme reluctance to leave me), and then I headed back to the Little Lady office in Pimlico to start the week.

As I crawled through the slow traffic, already missing Jonathan's wry smile and his subtle aroma of Creed and maturity, I picked at a croissant and tried to think of three positive things about the day ahead.

It was my trademark cheering-up device: find three things to be positive about, and even the most dismal situation doesn't seem quite so bleak.

One, I had plenty of work at the agency to fill in the hours until I joined Jonathan in Paris on Thursday evening. Condensing my usual busy week into three and a half days meant I really had to focus my attention on exactly who I was dealing with. Worryingly, once or twice, my mind had still been picking at the previous client's problem while I'd been sorting out the next—which had given poor Rory Douglas a shock, for one, when he'd come to me for advice on getting rid of a lingering houseguest and I'd absentmindedly started advising him on a more flattering haircut.

London drizzle began to obscure my view of the road ahead. I flicked on the wipers and focused on my positive things.

Two, I was seeing Granny for tea at Claridge's this afternoon, and that was always fun.

So long as whatever she wants you to do won't turn out to be something awful, nagged a little voice in my head. I pushed it to one side.

Three—and this really cheered me up—Nelson had his wine course on Monday nights, and that usually meant half a bottle of whatever they'd been tasting, plus Nelson in a "relaxed" mood. He routinely claimed that he wasn't even remotely drunk after these things ("We don't actually *drink* it, Melissa," he'd slurred the first night, "we 'preciate it . . ."), but on more than one occasion, I'd spotted him trying to boil the food processor, thinking it was the kettle.

Just to prove that I was right to think positive, when I pulled up outside the agency, there was half a parking space right in front of my door, and I popped the Little Lady Agency Smart car right into it.

The Little Lady Agency was on the second floor of a big Victorian white-faced terraced house, above an upmarket beauty salon so discreet it didn't even have a sign on the door. I wasn't entirely sure I knew what it was called, officially—it wasn't the sort of establishment I could possibly afford to frequent myself. Most of its clientele were dropped off by drivers wearing dark glasses.

I waved to Serena the Botox technician and removed my high heels to attack the stairs at a trot, as was my morning exercise habit. Three flights of stairs had certainly improved the state of my thighs over the past two years. Gasping very slightly as I reached the top steps, I reached into my capacious day bag for the keys and was delighted to see a vast bouquet of pink and red roses propped up against the post table.

I picked up the card. "Counting the hours," I read, unlocking the door and pushing it open with my hip, and my heart fluttered up into my throat as the fragrance filled my nose.

Jonathan had an unerringly silver screen touch when it came to romantic gestures. He must have arranged it before he'd left Paris, and I knew he was absolutely rushed off his feet bending the new French office to his considerable will.

I buried my nose in the arrangement again. At least three times a week, I had to rush-deliver flowers just like these to get someone out of a missed anniversary scrape. Jonathan didn't even wait until he had making up to do.

No, I thought, getting a crystal vase out of the cupboard, I really was a lucky girl.

My morning transformation from Melissa to Honey Blennerhesket always took at least fifteen minutes, and it was one of my favorite parts of the day, when I stopped being Melissa and started thinking, as well as looking, like someone entirely different.

I hummed happily as I got changed in the spare room, allowing myself a moment to note just how much longer my short little legs looked in black stockings. Then I slipped on the tight skirt, buttoned up the shirt, spritzed myself with perfume, and applied a glossy layer of scarlet lipstick.

Ready to go! I thought, smacking my lips in the mirror.

I rattled through the post, sorted out my schedule for the week, and went through the messages from the weekend. My two morning clients went smoothly—a wardrobe consultation and a preliminary chat about a party I'd agreed to help plan—and at two o'clock, I went off to Claridge's to see Granny.

She was ensconced in a deep easy chair in the corner of Claridge's lavishly appointed lounge, flicking through a copy of *OK!* magazine. Not for the first time, I fervently hoped that I'd inherited Granny's anti-aging genes. Sitting there in her slinky Chanel suit, her silver bob swinging around her cheekbones, Granny didn't look a day over fifty-five, despite the fact that her real age was somewhere between seventy-three and seventy-seven, according to which of her passports you looked at.

Nelson claimed I had her way with men, though I didn't see it myself. There's a difference between working *with* men and plain working them, and even if I was pretty good at the former, I knew from family lore that Granny was an expert at the latter.

When she spotted me, a broad smile crinkled up her bright blue eyes, and immediately she slapped the magazine closed and sprang to her feet.

"Melissa! Darling!" she said, spreading her arms wide and hugging me. "How lovely to see you! I've ordered the full tea, if you don't mind. Do you?" She held me at arm's length as I started to demur. "Oh, no! Don't say you're on one of those ridiculous diets? Haven't I told you a million times, men like a little something to get hold of?" she went on, as I settled myself and my huge bag into an armchair.

"Well, they've plenty to get hold of with me," I said. Not as glumly as normal, though, because if there's one thing having a boyfriend does for a girl, it boosts her confidence no end.

"Quite! I mean, what's the point of a corset if you've got nothing to winch into it?" retorted Granny as the tea tray arrived and the young waiter poured us both hot cups of Earl Grey. "Oh, I could do with this!" she said, seizing her cup and taking a sip. "I've been run off my feet."

Granny shook her head at the offer of lemon slices, and her hair shone glossily. However "run off her feet" she was, she'd obviously managed to fit in her Monday morning hair appointment.

"Have you heard the latest from home?" she inquired.

I shook my head.

"Well, William's put his back out shooting something, poor Emery's stuck there till the baby's old enough to fly, and so your father has sprung into action." She hovered a long finger over the cake stand, wavering between an éclair and the pristine pink fondant fancy I'd been eyeing up myself. Then she picked both and put them on her plate. "He's quite the doting grandfather. Anyway, he's dug up that desiccated old nanny of yours from retirement."

"Nanny Ag?" I exclaimed delightedly. "How lovely! Is she still working?"

I adored Nanny Ag. Her real name was Agatha Dunstable, and we'd been meant to call her Dunstable, but we hadn't. Allegra had called her Nag. Emery had been far too scared of her to address her by name in the nine years she'd been with us.

I *loved* her, though. When I was a child, Emery had gotten most of the attention because she'd been an angelic baby, and what little had been left had gone to Allegra, three years older, and her amazing, dinner-stopping tantrums. Allegra had refused to breathe until she'd gotten her own way, which had made for some dramatic soup moments. Nanny Ag, however, had come to us via a very troublesome family of Scottish lairds, so there hadn't been much she hadn't seen and heard, then trampled down with quite disproportionate ferocity for her size.

Even now, she always seemed to know what we were up to, and I still sent her Christmas and birthday cards and, in return, got short, spidery postcards detailing the weather in Grange-over-Sands, and a Blue Peter annual every Christmas. "She must be about a hundred and twenty by now, surely?" I added, wonderingly.

"Nannies start at seventy and don't age. She's arriving at the end of the week," said Granny. "Either your father has a short memory, or he's very keen to keep Emery at home for some nefarious reason." She raised her eyebrow. "I wonder what that could be?"

"That he's keen to spend some time with his grandchild and help poor Emery out?" I responded stoutly. "You don't have to look for nefarious reasons all the time. Anyway, what's this mysterious favor *you* want me to do?"

She had the grace to look abashed, but before she could speak, her phone rang.

I gave her a look. "Granny," I said in shock, "didn't you turn your mobile off when I arrived?"

My grandmother was even more of a stickler for manners than I was. Mainly so she could have more rules to break, but even so, I had been the only seven-year-old at prep school with her own evening gloves.

"Oh, dear, do forgive me," she said, checking the number. Her cat's eyes flicked up at me, then down at the phone, then a faint pinky blush spread over her cheeks.

Blimey. Granny never blushed.

She hastily rose to her feet. "Would you excuse me a second? I know it's terrible, darling, but I really have to take this call, so I'll just pop out . . ." She was edging her way through the chairs, but I could see that her eyes were twinkling with excitement.

An admirer, no doubt.

"Fine!" I said, seizing my chance to grab the other mini chocolate choux bun.

She was gone for a good five minutes, so while I had the chance I leaned over and picked up her copy of *OK!*

Nelson loathed all celebrity magazines and banned them from the house on the grounds that people like that should be firmly ignored, not encouraged, but secretly I loved flicking through the party pages, in case I spotted anyone I knew. Not that I moved in those kinds of perma-tanned, PR circles myself, but there was usually someone in there that I'd either been to school with, or Allegra had, or Emery had—we'd gone to about fifteen schools between us, what with Allegra's expulsions and Daddy's scandals—and pre-Lars, Allegra had had an international lineup of moody rich boyfriends. Actually, before I'd met Jonathan, I'd had some fairly colorful boyfriends too, but whereas Allegra's castoffs had tended to be rich theater producers or hedge fund managers, mine had been the sort of slip-on-shoe-wearing idlers who'd described themselves as "artists" because they'd once painted their bedrooms black.

Fool that I'd been in those days.

I peeled back the pages happily and poured myself another cup of tea while I breathed in the heady chemical aroma of pure *OK!* There'd been a crop of truly ghastly parties in London recently—I'd heard on the grapevine that an old school friend, Tiggy Waterford, had been dunked headfirst into a chocolate fountain by some dreadful oik at a Russian oil billionaire's birthday bash in Chelsea, who'd then compounded his outrageous behavior by offering to lick her clean. I think that's what she said, anyway.

Was that the same party? I peered closer at the page. That certainly looked like Tiggy. She was wearing some marshmallowy confection of a dress, and she'd put on a bit of weight since our pony-grooming days, so I could see how a particularly dim posh bloke might think it hilarious to use her as a dip . . .

"OK, *OK!*? I don't think Jonathan would approve!" exclaimed a voice right in my ear, and I jumped so hard I nearly spilled my tea. "Or Nelson," Granny went on, wagging a reproving finger with some glee.

I put the magazine down. "They don't *run* my life. I am allowed to read what I like."

Granny curled herself into the chair, tucking one leg underneath her. She tilted her head as if to disagree, then beamed at me. "Well, quite. I know what a splendid, independent businesswoman you are, and actually I want to talk to you about a little business plan I have." She paused significantly. "A *secret* one."

"By that, do you mean you don't want Daddy to know?" I sighed. "Because that's pretty much understood by—"

"No, no! I mean I don't want anyone to know! I need to rely on that famous discretion of yours." Granny pressed her red lips together and folded her hands so all three of her diamond eternity rings sparkled up into her face. "It's a matter of *international diplomatic importance.*"

Despite myself, I was intrigued. "Go on."

"You must promise not to breathe a word to anyone."

"I won't."

"And you must promise not to say anything until I've finished telling you the whole story?"

"I won't."

"Even if you want to stop me?"

"I won't! Just tell me!"

"Well," said Granny conspiratorially. "Do you remember my old, old friend Prince Alexander von Helsing-Alexandros? Of Hollenberg?"

"Not specifically," I said carefully.

My grandmother, I should explain here, had been what some people would call "a bit of a goer" in her younger days. Indeed, my father called her a lot worse. I prefer to think of her as having been rather ahead of her time. What everyone agreed on, though, was that in her day, Granny had been a real scorcher. Her wardrobe of couture cocktail dresses and saucy little fur capes, which I sometimes borrowed for more glamorous Honey occasions, spoke for itself.

Granny liked to throw a veil over the exact details of her past, even within her closest family, but as I understood it, she'd had a brief but apparently stellar career as a nightclub singer in the fifties, after which she'd lived in Mayfair for some years as the companion of a mysterious aristocrat, before marrying my grandfather, Lord Wasdalemere. Mummy had been their only child, and Wasdalemere had died when I was about four, after a particularly fabulous party thrown by Granny to celebrate one of his peonies winning Best in Class at the Chelsea Flower Show. He'd died, she assured me, a very happy man.

Call me an old romantic, but it really warmed my heart to know that Granny had been there at his side, right at the end.

Luckily for Granny, she'd been left pretty well off, and with her own income too (I assume from her hit record, *Cool Kitty Cat*). While she hadn't married again, I don't think she was lonely, put it like that. It didn't surprise me in the least that she had various princes in her past.

"Oh, you *do* remember Alexander!" exclaimed Granny. "He gave me that car—you know, the one I gave to you to learn to drive in."

"No, I don't think I . . . Oh, God," I said, as the jigsaw pieces fell into place and various events began to rise with white-hot clarity in my mind. I must have been the only girl in England who'd learned to drive in a Porsche 911, but my lessons with Granny had come to an abrupt halt when I'd driven it into a parked Range Rover while she'd been telling me how to three-point turn in the car park of the Hurlingham Club. "He was that man we went out to the Savoy with, so you could tell him—"

Granny nodded. "Wasn't he lovely about it? He's a darling man."

"So you want me to do some job for him?" I asked. "But I'm sure *you're* more than capable of—"

She shook her head. "No, no. Not him. His grandson, Nicolas."

"His grandson?" I made some mental calculations. "Should I know him too?"

"Hmm," said Granny, suddenly looking less frisky. "That's the point. You might do. He's not exactly discreet when it comes to maintaining an appropriate public profile. Poor Alexander has told him, and told him, but Nicky won't listen."

My heart began to sink. I could see what was coming as clearly as if it had had floodlights, warning sirens, and one of those moose-scooping things you see on the front of American trains.

"In fact," Granny went on, reaching for the copy of *OK!*, "he's in here." She flicked through it until she reached the back pages. "Look, he was at a ghastly nouveau party and attacked a poor stout girl with a chocolate fountain."

"That was my friend Tiggy," I said faintly.

Granny looked up. "Was it? Oh dear. Well, that's the sort of shenanigans Nicky gets up to. Trashing hotels, exposing himself at charity balls, that type of overgrown schoolboy nonsense. The boy's nearly thirty! He runs with a dreadful crowd of Euro-trash, he's bringing shame and scandal on his entire family, and he hasn't had a suitable girlfriend in his life."

"Isn't that the point of being rich?"

"Of course not. Besides, there's a bit more to it than that."

I was surprised to realize that Granny was genuinely uptight. The magazine was quivering in her tense grip, and her usually creaseless brow wrinkled with distress.

Alexander must be a very good old friend indeed, I thought. Granny was terribly loyal—one thing I was pleased to say I *had* inherited.

"Which is?" I asked.

Granny sighed. "Well, I should really let Alexander explain it properly, but in a nutshell, his family used to govern a little principality, on the Balkan coast. Very pretty, but tiny. Anyway, they were kicked out in the thirties, but *now* the government is willing to have them back, so long as they restore the castle with their own money and present some kind of Disney-fied royal family they can stick on the front of their holiday brochures."

"Wow!" I started to say, but Granny hadn't finished.

"*However,*" she went on, "they obviously can't do that while the idiot grandson and heir is turning up at parties dressed as a Palestinian suicide bomber."

Her voice had risen to a high quiver, and she took a sip of tea to calm down. "I'm sorry," she said. "But Alex is such a gentleman, and I'm furious about the way Nicky is turning his name into some kind of byword for drunken tomfoolery."

"And you think I can do something about it . . . how?" I asked gently. "I'd love to help, but I'm afraid I'm not very effective against that sort of professional cad type. I mean, Orlando von Borsch ran rings round me for years, remember? And he was just a stuffed olive heir, not a prince."

"Well, princes aren't what they used to be." Granny sighed deeply and passed me the magazine. "And I don't think he's a cad," she said. "I think he's just a very silly boy who's been allowed to play the fool for too long. It's not just women who get away with murder because they're pretty, you know."

I looked more closely at the pictures, and, despite myself, my heart skipped. Crikey. Prince Nicolas looked more like a rock star than a prince. Quite a saucy rock star too. One with several Ferraris in his garage and an ex-wife in every major marina.

"That's him?" I asked, pointing just to check.

She nodded.

"Wow. Well, I see what you mean." Nicolas was exactly the sort of man who used to make me forget myself entirely. Brown-eyed, ski-tanned, and with swimmer's shoulders and narrow hips, he was twinkling away at the camera with his arms round two equally tanned leggy lovelies, exuding the exact amount of charm to sweep a girl off her slingbacks but stop just short of smarm. His red silk shirt was open a button too far, revealing a flash of dark chest hair, but instead of looking sleazy, he merely looked as if he'd been having too good a time to notice. Ditto his artfully disheveled thick brown hair, which probably took longer to style than mine did. His only flaw was that the leggy lovelies were just a smidge taller than him in their Louboutin stilettos.

If his grandfather had looked like that when he was younger, no wonder Granny still had a soft spot for him.

I closed the magazine with some relief. There really wasn't anything I could do here: Nicky wouldn't give a girl like me the time of day.

"Granny, you know I'd do anything to make you happy," I said, "but surely a stern talking-to from *you* would have more effect." I paused, as Granny began to prepare her innocent face. "Oh, no. No. You've already said I will, haven't you? Oh, Granny!"

"Oh, Melissa!" she replied winningly. "Just a meeting?"

"To say what?" I protested.

"That no nice girl will look him in the eye if he carries on tipping people into chocolate fountains!"

I fixed her with a square look. "Granny, he's not in the market for a nice girl. Anyway," I went on, "Jonathan would go nuts. After that business in New York with Godric Ponsonby, I promised I'd scale back on the hands-on male stuff, as far as I could. Concentrate more on the lifestyle side of things."

"But that's your favorite part of your job!" exclaimed Granny, putting down her teacup in dismay. "Fixing up men!"

Granny had hit on a nerve. I loved polishing up awkward specimens into gleaming catches, just by applying some common sense and decent trousers, but I loved Jonathan too, and he'd made it clear that he wasn't so keen. It seemed only fair to compromise, especially since he'd moved halfway round the world so we could both start fresh in Paris. But I hated the idea of choosing between him and my agency.

A small voice reminded me that so far my best plan for combining Jonathan, Paris, and the agency involved the first and last Eurostar trains each day. Still, I thought, shoving the thought to one side, now's not the time to decide on a "best plan."

"Jonathan and I made a deal. He agreed to cut down on the overtime, and I agreed not to take on clients who really need a therapist, not a social or lifestyle makeover. He's right—it's very time-consuming," I said, raising my voice above her tuts.

But even as I said it, my eye returned of its own accord to the gleaming vision of Prince Nicky and his open-necked shirt. He had the sort of come-to-bed-you-sexy-lady eyes that didn't just follow you round the room from the magazine; they winked at you. No wonder his female companions looked like stunned deer.

"Melissa," said Granny seriously. "Do you do everything Jonathan tells you to? And I thought *I* was old-fashioned."

I squirmed a little, trying to fight back my own curiosity. Oh, what harm would it do to meet him? I was engaged to the most gorgeous man in the EU. If I did have tea with this fool, he'd no doubt show his true colors before the sandwiches were replenished. Granny would probably end up throwing the contents of the milk jug over him and the matter would be dropped faster than a hot scone.

With impeccable timing, Granny unleashed her most irresistible smile, the one that had allowed her to take advantage of London society for fifty years. "Darling," she said. "You're a chip off the old block. Don't tell me you wouldn't like to have tea with a prince."

When I paused, struggling with the terrible, familiar sensation that I was being played like a cheap fiddle, she added, "Two princes, come to that."

And with that, I'm afraid to say, I was sunk.

four

I drove back to the office, my head buzzing with contradictory thoughts, and even though I'd only been out for an hour and a half, the answering machine was stuffed with calls. Top of the pile was one Lady Dilys Blennerhesket.

"Hello, darling, so lovely to see you just now. Just to let you know I've spoken to Alexander and he'd be absolutely delighted to take us both out for dinner tomorrow night, if you're around. Obviously, by that I mean do cancel whatever you have on, won't you?" she added, at the exact same moment that I started to bridle about having prior engagements. "I think it's royal etiquette. He's going to make Nicolas come along, since he's in London at the moment, and you can see what you're up against. I mean," she added, "you can see what he's like. Seven for cocktails at the Blue Bar, then dinner at Petrus. That OK? Lovely! Speak to you later!"

I checked the time of the message again. Exactly two minutes after I'd left her at Claridge's. Hmm. Either she'd made a very quick call to Alexander, or the whole thing had been set up in advance.

"Hello, Honey, it's Angus Deering. I need to learn how to make a shelf, very quickly. Stupidly told this new girl I'd done lots of carpentry at school, now she wants me to assemble the whole IKEA range in her flat. Call me back? Cheers."

I scribbled a note. I'd found a terribly good handyman, who frequently gave crash courses to my less spacially aware bachelors. He also fixed their attempts while the guilty party was out at work, if necessary.

"Um, hello, I need to speak to Honey about the nail-biting cure for my son?"

I flipped open the engagement diary and jotted the details down on a Post-it note. My patented Hard as Nails nail treatment was one of my most popular services, but it was quite time-consuming, involving, as it did, fourteen randomly spaced calls a day to the nail-biter. I was thinking of farming it out to Allegra, who positively enjoyed shouting at people.

I deleted the messages and was going through the post again when the phone rang.

"Mel?" said a familiar voice above the clatter of a busy office. "Can you do me a favor?"

Gabi was my best friend, and she worked at the estate agency whose Paris branch Jonathan managed. She had an ear for gossip, an eye for a bargain, and a nose for sticking into other people's business. She was also funny, generous, and loyal: the very best mate I'd ever had, even if her dark petiteness made me look like the Jolly Green Giant next to her.

"Listen, are you around this evening? I need you to cast your expert eye over my wedding plans!"

Gabi almost sang the phrase "my wedding plans!" From the initial ideas I'd heard about the wedding, it was going to be the sort of occasion where entire roads were closed off and helicopters were involved. Even though the Big Day was sixteen long months away, Gabi had already visited every major venue in North London. I'd stayed out of it as long as I could, but clearly that political immunity was now about to end.

"I've had to sack that wedding planner I was telling you about," she added. "She said that doves were very last year. I mean, hello? Has she *been* to any weddings recently? *Everyone* has doves!" She paused. "I'm thinking about pigeons, you know, to put like a London spin on it. Do you reckon you can clean pigeons?"

I reached for the biscuit barrel. Although I had a massive diamond engagement ring, Jonathan and I still hadn't set a date for our own wedding. Just thinking about trying to organize it at the same time as Gabi's gave me hot flushes, and in any case, Jonathan wanted to "get things straight" in Paris first. What with moving and work and Jonathan's insane diary, his vague "Christmas" suggestion was as near as we'd got.

It wasn't a bad idea since we'd probably have the reception at home. And if the heating went off, the guests would already be dressed for inclement weather.

"Do you want to come over to ours for some supper?" I suggested. If Nelson was within earshot, it might just keep Gabi within the bounds of reality. "I should be finished here about six, and Nelson'll be back from his wine class by eight-ish."

"As long as Nelson's cooking," said Gabi cheerfully. "Actually, I need to ask him about getting some goats for the ceremony." I heard her clicking again. "Nelson . . . goats . . . ," she mumbled.

"Riiiiight," I said, then spotted a note in my own diary. "Oh, actually, Gabi, I should warn you—Roger's coming round for a trial-run manicure."

Gabi made an affectionate gagging sound. Even people who loved Nelson's friend Roger were not oblivious to his hygiene shortcomings. There was a good reason that a cider heir with a private income and a full head of hair would still be single. Not that that was the whole problem.

It's difficult to describe Roger Trumpet to anyone who hasn't met him, but put it like this: if Nelson was a golden retriever, and Jonathan was a very well-bred Irish setter, then Roger was like the oldest and gloomiest of my mother's basset hounds. Adorable on birthday cards, less so at parties, where he'd been known to clear the room in under twenty minutes, just by drinking a bottle of wine in a particularly baleful manner. He also usually smelled like he'd recently rolled in something untoward.

I was terribly fond of him, though, as was Nelson. Roger was, after all, the raw material on which I'd honed every homme-improving skill I had. Not, sadly, that I'd wrought much long-term effect.

"I hope he's paying you," said Gabi disapprovingly. "You want to watch out, people taking advantage of you left, right, and center."

Honestly. Virtually everyone I knew liked to haul themselves up to the moral high ground before asking for favors themselves.

"Absolutely, yes, Mrs. Lumley, we'll have those keys round to you by courier this afternoon!" said Gabi abruptly, which, I assumed, meant that her boss, Hughie, had rolled in from his long lunch, so we left the conversation there and I went back to the post.

The one intriguing handwritten envelope amongst the bills turned out to be from my office landlord, Peter, a very sweet retired violin teacher who lived in Stow-on-the-Wold. He "didn't see why he should spend his remaining years at the mercy of central heating," he wrote, and so the time had come to sell up and buy the little house in Sicily that he'd escaped to in his head during the thirty years of listening to children scraping away at "Frère Jacques."

Oh, how nice! I thought automatically, then realized with a start that this might mean it wasn't just Peter packing his bags for pastures new.

I reached for a second chocolate biscuit.

Peter wrote that he hoped the sale of the flat he'd bought in Pimlico for five thousand pounds all those years ago might now be able to fund that dream, but rather than turf me out on my ear, he wanted to give me first chance to buy it. If I was interested, I should get in touch with the estate agents who'd brokered the original letting agreement when he'd moved out a few years ago, but that I should do so within a month, before he opened it up to everyone else.

That estate agent had been Dean & Daniels, where I'd worked until it had been acquired and merged into Kyrle & Pope. You'd think that would put me at an advantage, what with my fiancé being the biggest fromage in their European operation, but having worked with estate agents myself, I knew that wasn't necessarily the case. And the asking price would be jaw dropping. Peter had been renting it to me at a very generous price for the past year or so, and even if a new owner let me stay, it'd be at about three times the amount I was paying now.

I put the letter down thoughtfully. It would be a really good idea to buy the office, not least because it would mean I'd be bringing something to my marriage to Jonathan. He had so much money, and property all over the place, whereas I only had my business, and though he was always going on about how much he admired my entrepreneurial skills, I knew he'd be amazed if I could pull off a little property deal of my own.

Plus, if there was one thing Mummy had always taught me, it was that a girl needs a flight fund—a little something up her sleeve in case of emergency. Not that I saw any emergencies in the future with Jonathan.

I pulled out my calculator and started doing some sums.

At six, I packed off my last client, a simple consultation about furnishing a bachelor flat so that it wouldn't remain a bachelor flat for too long. Once Simon was safely loping down Elizabeth Street with a shopping list for Heal's, I slipped thankfully out of my pencil skirt and back into my own comfy trousers, and drove home through the London drizzle, parking neatly in the half space next to Nelson's scooter.

Nelson was still out at his wine class, but he hadn't risked my tackling supper. Instead, he'd left a note on the kitchen table instructing me—rather bossily—about which freezer dish to put in the oven and for how long, and which bottle of wine I should open and when.

Nelson really would make someone a splendid wife, I thought, scraping unsalted butter onto the shepherd's pie topping, as directed in the accompanying diagram. While Roger's tramplike gloom explained his single state, Nelson was a whole other kettle of fish. It seemed absolutely incomprehensible to me that such an attractive, capable, baggage-free man should still be single at his age.

I reminded myself to ask subtly how the blind date had gone on Friday. Jossy was only the fourth in what I intended to be a long line of potentials. If Nelson was going to be fussy, he'd picked the right address book.

Jonathan might be home now, I reckoned, kicking off my shoes and arranging myself on the comfy sofa. I pictured where he might be in the apartment as the French ringing tone blared in my ear.

The apartment, on the fourth floor of an atmospheric old building in the trendy Marais district, was exactly what I dreamed a Paris apartment would be, from the long windows with the flower-boxed balcony looking out over the narrow street below, to the clanking elevator with the concertina doors, and the discreet buzzer system downstairs. Being Jonathan, he'd insisted on all mod cons as well as period ambience, so it had Wi-Fi and integrated stereo and all sorts of other high-tech gadgets slightly at odds with the original cast-iron fireplace and wooden floors.

There was a click, as my call was transferred from his home phone to his office phone, then another ringing tone, then a clipped woman's voice said, "Allo?"

My heart sank. It was Solange, Jonathan's new French PA. He'd always had frightfully competent robo-secretaries, but Solange was all that, *and* immaculately dressed. She was one of those skinny, manicured Frenchwomen who look effortlessly chic. I'd only met her in person once, but my attempts to charm her, as one ex-PA to another, had fallen *sur* stony *terre.*

"Allo, Solange!" I said, screwing up my forehead in concentration. "Ç'est Melissa! Um, Jonathan—est-il là? Um, s'il vous plaît?"

"Yes, he is here," she said in perfect English. "Had you forgotten about his committee meeting this evening?"

"Ah, oui, sorry," I said. It had slipped my mind. Jonathan was always getting onto committees. "Is he in it now?" I added, having run out of French.

"Yes."

"Oh."

Short cross-Channel silence.

"Oh, well," I said brightly. "Perhaps you could tell him I called? I'll ring again later. When he's home."

"Very well," said Solange.

"Um, do you have . . . any idea when that would be?"

"Around half past eight." There was a definite note of reluctance in Solange's voice. She really was the most discreet secretary in the world, I marveled. Maybe I should encourage my father to poach her for his own office. Heaven knew he needed someone super discreet.

"Well, thanks so much!" I said, trying to sound friendly. "Hope you're not stuck in the office for too much longer!"

"Good night, Melissa," iced Solange. "Thank you for calling." And she hung up.

I stared at the phone for a long moment, then went into the kitchen in search of some comforting Pringles to tide me over until the shepherd's pie was ready.

About an hour or so later, during which time I'd reread my Eating Guide to Paris and made a list of places Jonathan could take me to over the weekend, I heard the sound of raised voices and feet on the stairs.

Well, one raised voice, to be exact. Gabi's.

". . . was thinking about having a horse and carriage, because that's really eco-friendly and romantic, isn't it, but when I mentioned it to Aaron, he said his little brother would want to drive the carriage, but there's no way I'm letting Sol anywhere near a carriage because he's got nine points on his license already, and you can't even trust him with a shopping trolley, so do you know if those things come with their own drivers? I don't mind budgeting for that, but I'd want them to be in the same colors as the rest of the wedding party, and . . ."

The front door burst open, and Nelson came in, looking dazed, followed by Gabi, bearing two pink shopping bags and an armful of magazines.

". . . I'm thinking something unusual like *sand* because everyone goes for apricot or burgundy—Hi, Mel!—but if you're going to be an usher, you'd have to wear sand and it would wash you out with your coloring, don't you think? What do you reckon, Mel? Can you see Nelson in sand?"

"Can't I just wear my morning suit?" asked Nelson weakly, heading straight for the bottle of wine on the table.

Gabi rolled her eyes at me. "Like, yeah! If you want to be really, really predictable. What about shitake? That's in my reserve color scheme."

"We're going to have morning suits," I said tactfully. "When Jonathan and I get married. It makes it all much easier for you—they do suit everyone."

"No offense, Mel," said Gabi, pausing to unload her magazines next to me, "but you and Jonathan are going to have a very different wedding from myself and Aaron."

"It may even end up being in a different *century* at this rate," observed Nelson.

I glared at him, and he raised his eyebrows innocently. "I'm just saying. Can I get anyone a drink? I see you've already started, Melissa."

"I had to," I said. "It's been quite an odd day."

"Ooh, yes, please," said Gabi, settling herself on the other end of the sofa and tossing me *Vogue Brides*.

I held out my empty glass and opened up the magazine. *Vogue Brides* had the best "price on request" dresses. I could just see Jonathan, tall and distinguished in his morning suit, me in a simple bell-shaped gown, light streaming onto our upturned faces through the stained-glass windows of some smart London church. . . .

"Now, this is a Bordeaux," explained Nelson as he poured. "You can tell that because of the shape of the bottle? Can you see? It's got shoulders. Not a slopey shape. That's Burgundy."

"Fascinating. Fill her up," said Gabi.

"You should be looking out for black currant and leather," Nelson went on. "A classic Cabernet Sauvignon. What are you getting, Mel?"

"Um, a sort of grape-y taste?" I said, to humor him.

"I wish *Hello* did a wedding magazine," mused Gabi. "*OK! Bride*. How perfect would that be? I mean, not so much for the actual weddings, but so you could let your family and friends see how bad it looks when they don't dress up enough and have to stand next to people who *have* made an effort. . . ."

"Aniseed balls!" exclaimed Nelson. "That's incredible! I'm getting aniseed balls!"

"I'm sorry to hear that," sniggered Gabi. "Maybe you should cut down on the drinking?"

"Ho ho," replied Nelson.

"What?" I furrowed my brow. I never got Gabi's jokes.

"Never mind," said Nelson.

I put the magazine down. "Gabi, have you heard of someone called Prince Nicolas of Hollenberg?"

"Prince Nicky? I have, yes," she said.

"You're doing royalty now?" said Nelson, giving up on the wine lesson. "Has he got a crest you can put above your coffee machine?"

I ignored him. "How do you know him?" I asked Gabi curiously.

"Oh, Aaron took me to Nobu for my birthday, and he was there with his mates. He's got a very naughty smile." She shook herself. "Anyway, yes. He's one of those 'Ooh, look at *me*, I'm awful!' types."

"Righto," I said. "He sounds like a bit of a handful."

Gabi winked. "That too, from what I've heard."

I stared at her blankly. "Sorry?"

"She means he's a big fish. In a small pool," said Nelson, with a straight face.

"What?" I demanded, looking hotly from Nelson to Gabi.

"Oh, never mind," she snorted, and reached for another magazine. "What do you think about 'London through the Ages' as a wedding theme?"

But Nelson refused to change the subject so easily. "Mel," he groaned. "Tell me you're not planning on taking on a playboy prince as a client."

"Well . . ." I gave them both a short précis of what Granny had told me, at which point Nelson's groans turned into definite barks of disapproval.

"Don't!" he kept saying. "Seriously! Don't! Seriously! Don't!"

Gabi, however, was providing a more balanced counterpoint. "That's so cool!" she crowed. "You have to do it! Just think of the gossip! And the clothes!"

"But these people are complete *cretins*," roared Nelson. "She'll go mad within seconds!"

"Mel can handle herself," retorted Gabi.

"I'm not disputing that," said Nelson with a quick glance at me. "I'm just saying, is it safe to let a woman with absolutely no awareness of innuendo and a terminal case of rose-tinted spectacles loose with a . . . a . . . woman-eating man-boy like this Nicky?"

"I'll soon have him in hand," I said. "And he's hardly going to *eat* me, Nelson."

Gabi dissolved into hysterics and Nelson's mouth twitched, diminishing the effect of his Stern Big Brother glare. This happened a lot. I pretended not to notice.

"Anyway," I went on, "I need to do it. Peter's selling my office. Gabi, it's on with Kyrle & Pope—can you find out how much it's going to be? He says I can have first refusal, which is really very sweet of him, but I've only got a month to get my offer in, and I'll need the money from this job to make the deposit."

"You're going to buy the office?" asked Nelson. "Even though you're meant to be moving to Paris with Remington Steele?"

"Yeah," said Gabi. "Doesn't he want you out there at his beck and call permanently once you're Mrs. Riley-Romney-Jones?"

The pair of them looking at me was quite disconcerting.

"Well, I don't know if I could afford it yet," I protested, "but aren't you always going on about London property being an investment?" I looked at Nelson as a thought suddenly occurred to me. "Unless that was just hinting that you wanted me to move out?" I added, with a little pang. Maybe he'd *meant* it about finding someone new to move in.

"Don't be ridiculous," said Nelson. "Do you want me to explain mortgages to you again?"

"Even though she's engaged to an estate agent?" asked Gabi.

"Please," I said. "I want it to be a surprise for Jonathan."

"No problem." Nelson frowned. "Gabi? What's the matter? Can you smell gas?"

Gas leaks were a favorite paranoia of Nelson's. That and passive carbon monoxide poisoning caused by faulty gas fires. He watched a lot of House of Horrors-type workmen-exposé programs.

"No, it's not gas." Gabi's face was screwed up in a mask of concentration. "It's . . . are you wearing new aftershave, Nelson?"

"No!" he snorted. "I don't wear aftershave! Just—"

"—soap and water is perfectly good for any normal bloke," I finished for him. "We know. You've said it before."

"Then what is that smell?" she demanded. "Melissa, can you smell it?"

I inhaled deeply. Beneath the residual salty smell of Nelson's sailing kit and my scented candles, there was a definite musky, citrus smell coming from somewhere. It reminded me of the fifth form discos at St. Cathal's, where the local boys' school would be bussed in, in their own micro-climate of Lynx cologne and hormones. But it couldn't be that. "Oh, yeah . . . Um, I don't know. Nelson?"

The three of us sat there, sniffing hard and frowning.

Then there was a knock at the door.

"You get it," said Nelson, levering himself up. "I'll check the pie."

I went over to the front door, and when I opened it, I reeled backward as an intensive gust of the same scent hit me, in the manner of someone opening a hatch on the *Titanic* and getting a faceful of the Atlantic.

"Hiya, Mel," grunted Roger Trumpet, shuffling past me into the flat. "Oh, hi, Gabi."

You might imagine my mingled shock and delight at the thought that Roger had finally embraced aftershave. I also noticed, stunned, that a thorough shave had revealed a previously unnoticed cleft on his chin.

He looked . . . almost handsome.

"Roger!" Gabi exclaimed with a slight cough. "Jesus! What are you wearing?"

"Jeans?" replied Roger, puzzled. "Why? Are they wrong?"

"No, they're lovely!" I said, taking in the new white shirt too, and oh my God, were they *boots?* "Lovely! But I think she means . . ."

"Oh." Roger gave a shy smile. I'd rarely seen him smile, and the effect was quite charming. "You mean my new fragrance?"

"Fragrance?" gasped Gabi. "Is that what you're calling it?"

"Roger, you look great!" I exclaimed, not wanting to sound too amazed for fear of offending him. Roger was easily offended.

"What's going on?" demanded Gabi, who was less diplomatic. "Have you got a girlfriend?"

"Actually, I have met a lady, yes, since you ask," said Roger.

Nelson, Gabi, and I nearly dropped everything we were holding. Nelson recovered first. "Well done, Rog," he said. "Do we know her?"

"I doubt it," said Roger, mooching toward the sofa, where he carefully removed his new boots and flung himself down in more familiar fashion. Through my surprise, I noted that he was wearing socks without a single hole in them. For the first time in the fifteen years I'd known him.

"Why?" asked Gabi. "Don't tell me you've bought yourself a Thai bride."

"Gabi!" I protested.

"It's not unknown," she said.

"Her name's Zara and she's a model-waitress," he said. "I met her . . . quite recently." Roger's mouth clamped tightly, I noticed, on the further details.

"You're dating a model-waitress," repeated Gabi. She looked at me. "Mel, are you about to turn into a giant crab? Because this is a very surreal dream, right?"

"Shut up," said Roger, but I noticed the trace of a soppy smile beneath his affronted expression. "I knew you lot would make fun of me, that's why I haven't told you till now."

"How long's this been going on for?" I asked, delighted. "You dark horse!"

"Oh, a few weeks," shrugged Roger. "Can you do my nails, Mel? Zara says they're too long and scratchy."

Gabi looked horrified, and she held out her glass. "Nelson, can I have a refill, please? And tell us how your date with Flossy or whatever she's called went."

"Jossy," I said.

"Seriously?" Gabi said. "Your school register must have sounded like something out of Beatrix Potter."

"It went very well," said Nelson. "She's a very interesting woman, although I'm not sure all the food on the menu was totally organic, which I mentioned to the manager and—"

"Are you seeing her again?" interjected Gabi. We both gazed up at him with expectant expressions.

He smiled nervously. "Um, I'm not sure. I don't think so."

"Oh, Nelson!" I swatted him. "You've got such ridiculously high standards."

"I don't think so," he replied. "I just know what I like."

"Let me tell you now," I said, "perfect women don't exist."

Roger sighed in a revoltingly self-satisfied manner. "Don't be so sure."

"See?" said Nelson, winking at me. "Living proof that it's worth saving yourself for the best."

"Bet that's not what Zara's saying," grumbled Gabi, who then topped up our glasses.

five

The following evening, I arrived at the Berkeley Hotel, where the Blue Bar was, a good few minutes early, to give myself time for a last-minute outfit rethink, should I turn out to be under- or over-dressed. It hadn't been easy, working out what note to strike for dinner with two princes and my grandmother. I think Nelson had been teasing when he'd suggested white gloves and a bunny girl tail.

In the end, I'd opted for a plain black wrap dress with a vintage paste brooch anchoring my cleavage at a modest height. Well, as modest as a cleavage like mine ever is. I love wrap dresses, but I can never relax properly unless I know the hatches are safely battened, since my curves, I'm sorry to say, take some containing. I'd had to haul on my least attractive Pants of Steel to make sure there were no untoward bulges. But with my tortoiseshell glasses and my hair pinned back with a clip, I reckoned I cut quite a stern but chic figure, and the beauty of this outfit was that I could sauce it up in a twinkle of the eye, simply by putting my contacts in and lowering the brooch about two centimeters.

Not that I intended to sauce it up, you understand—there's something *wrong* about attempting anything like that in front of your own grandmother—but just because I was meeting this dreadful Nicolas as

Melissa, rather than armor-plated Honey, didn't mean I couldn't make a decent impression.

The Blue Bar is one of those fashionable places where everyone's head swivels when you come in, in case you're Someone, then swivels back when they've established you're Not. The small room was packed, and I couldn't spot Granny anywhere. Cigar smoke and hedge fund discussion hung heavy in the air as I inched my way through the hair extensions and Prada bags, checking discreetly to see if Prince Alexander was already here. There were at least four possibles in my immediate line of sight—far too tanned, groomed, and well dressed to be English.

A skinny woman with furiously plucked eyebrows gave my Diane von Furstenberg knock-off dress a very obvious once-over, and I felt the first flickers of What am I doing here? start to attack my stomach. *No*, I reminded myself firmly, *you've got just as much right to be here as she has. Her dress might be more Bond Street than yours, but you're having dinner with two princes.*

Even though I was suddenly very conscious of my VPL (visible panty line), I stared right back, focusing my eyes a foot to the left of her head, and smiled at the light fixture. Unnerved, after a second or two, she turned round to see who I was looking at, and, feeling a bit better, I got an elbowhold on the crowded bar and leaned as far forward as I could to order a drink.

Almost immediately the barman seemed to gravitate toward me. It was the weirdest thing: I just had to wish really hard to get served while leaning forward, and somehow I did. Nelson and Gabi always made me order for them when we went to the pub.

"A bottle of sparkling mineral water, please," I said, for something to sip while I waited. The chap to my right moved away, and I slipped onto the bar stool.

"Would you do me a favor and help me finish this bottle of champagne?" drawled the middle-aged man pressed up against my left arm.

I tried not to scan his face too obviously for signs of possible princeness. Last time Alexander and I had met, ten years ago, he'd been terribly reasonable about Granny's car, and I'd been over-whelmed with mortification and whiplash. He probably wouldn't rec-ognize me either, since I'd lost the braces and the strange haircut that Allegra had inflicted on me that summer.

"Er, thank you," I stalled. The tie looked expensive enough, for a start. "How kind of you. I'm Melissa."

"Hello, Melissa." As if by magic, a champagne flute arrived, and he filled it and pushed it over to me.

I didn't like to say Are you Alexander? straight out. He was already smiling in a manner that suggested we knew each other pretty well.

"So . . . ," I said, searching desperately for something to say that wouldn't incriminate me one way or another. "Are you staying here?"

Was that a shadow of a wink? "Perhaps. It depends on the company."

Argh. What did that mean? Was it a business trip he was on? I didn't think princes worked for anyone.

"Are you?" he went on.

"No," I faltered. "I, er, live just down the road."

"How convenient." He smiled in a very intimate fashion, and I could feel myself being pushed nearer him by the crush of customers queueing behind. I resisted as best I could, but there was a very per-sistent banker shoving his way to the bar behind me.

"I'm sorry, I didn't catch your name . . . ?" I began, but my voice was swallowed up by the barman shaking a cocktail very loudly in front of me.

"Have you been in the rooftop pool?" the man went on, as I began to panic. "The roof goes right back and you can swim beneath the stars—it's quite an experience."

"Oh," I said, with a little laugh. "Silly me! I forgot my swimsuit!"

"No need for that, necessarily . . ."

And that definitely was a wink.

Just as my mouth was opening and shutting in speechless surprise, I noticed the heads turning back and forth at the door, and I realized Granny had walked in—with a tall, elegant man who could only be Prince Alexander.

A strong gust of Givenchy Gentleman mixed with cigars hoved in from my left. It was hoving in very close. "What a pretty brooch. Does it come off?"

Aghast, I slapped my hand over my cleavage and leaned as far away as I could without falling off my stool, as Granny and Alexander glided across the bar like a pair of swans.

She was looking gracious in the sort of understated shift only the seriously stylish or very tall could carry off, with a set of diamonds that definitely weren't paste. He was looking impeccable in a navy suit that set off his gray hair and dark eyes. Together, they radiated a warm glow of confidence that made everyone else in the room look desperately overdressed. I noticed too that he had one hand just resting on the small of Granny's back to guide her into the room—a tiny, old-fashioned gesture that was simultaneously protective and proud.

I knew it well, since Jonathan did it to me.

When Granny saw me, she lifted a hand in greeting while Alexander turned to murmur something to the waiter who'd materialized out of nowhere.

"Excuse me." I apologized to the champagne man. "My date has arrived."

He boggled at me.

"Thanks for the champagne," I added, sliding off the stool as fast as I could. "Terribly sweet of you."

Across the room, a party of Russians was being unceremoniously turfed out of their prime spot so Granny could arrange herself on an easy chair, which she did with an air of delight, as if the table had been free all the time. She beckoned me over and I inched my way through the crowds, feeling quite nervous and unsophisticated again.

"Darling!" said Granny, half rising to give me a kiss. "You look absolutely gorgeous! I bet you can hardly recognize little Melissa, can you, Alex? Hasn't she grown up into a beautiful woman?"

Alexander turned to me, and, to the fluttering of my heart, made a very tiny bow of his head. Then he took my hand and raised it to his lips.

To be honest, huge cliché or not, I could have swooned right then and there, even if he hadn't looked like Clark Gable. Which he did.

My father might have been a Premier League Silver Fox, but Alexander was World Cup standard with the sort of old-school manners that flirted with self-parody but only in such a way as to make him even more attractive. His white hair was thick, swept back off his high forehead, and his brown eyes hinted at how dark and pirate-y he must have been in his youth. Yes, he had some wrinkles, but they were wrinkles of distinguishment. Wrinkles that laughed at Botox or face-lifts. Wrinkles that said, yes, I have wrinkles, but look at my handmade shoes! Alexander was clearly one of those rare men, like Paul Newman, who just kept becoming more attractive the older he got.

Not that I could see Alexander bothering with salad dressing. Caviar spoons, maybe.

"Of course I remember Melissa," he said, as a kindly twinkle came into his hooded eyes. "You've always had your grandmother's lovely smile. And now I see she has her grandmother's wonderful style too." The twinkle turned into a little private-joke sort of intimacy. "I hope there have been no more . . . driving incidents?"

"Gosh, no," I said, gasping a little. "I'm perfectly safe behind the wheel these days. Terribly reliable. You know, I'm still so sorry about—"

"Oh, these things happen," he said, as if one wrote off sports cars every day of the week. "There's nothing wrong with a lady who drives with a bit of élan, Melissa," he added gallantly. "It's rather exciting." He looked over my head and caught Granny's eye. "Your grandmother, for instance, was a *terror* behind the wheel."

"Not just behind the *wheel,* either," Granny murmured with an innocent look.

"Her navigation isn't up to much," I agreed. "She can only do directions via shops and people's houses."

"Quite," said Alexander. "These days, I find it much easier to let my driver worry about that sort of thing." He nodded at Granny, who gave him a twinkly smile. "Much nicer to sit in the back and admire the view."

"Oh, she's an awful backseat driver, though!" I said. "She's always . . ."

Was Alexander suppressing a snort?

"Melissa is by far my most charming grandchild," Granny inter-jected, "and has the sort of innocence that quite restores my faith in humanity. Anyway, cheers!" She lifted her glass. "To old friends!"

I raised my flute and looked around the room to see if the fourth member of our party was anywhere in sight. Granny and Alexander were already chinking their glasses and muttering some Greek-cheers-type phrase at each other.

"Um, cheers, but shouldn't we wait for Nicolas?" I suggested politely.

Alexander shrugged his shoulders and shook his head as if it rather went without saying. "He will be late. And I wanted to enjoy the pleasure of a quiet drink with you two ladies before the circus arrived. Can you blame me for wanting a few minutes of you to myself? We have so much to catch up on."

I giggled and looked over at Granny. She was smiling like the cat who'd got the cream, the cow, *and* the farmhand.

We spent the next hour or so having the sort of elegant, grown-up con-versation I used to daydream about when I was at school: Alexander asked intelligent questions about my experiences of Paris, where his family spent half their time, and what I thought of London compared to New York, and he gave every indication of actually listening to my replies, while our glasses were topped up invisibly and fresh nibbles appeared. We skirted a little around the topic of my agency, sticking mainly to the makeover side of things, and it seemed that Granny had filled him in—how much, though, I couldn't quite work out.

"You know, if I eat any more of these I'll ruin my appetite for din-ner," I said ruefully, scooping up another small handful of honey-roasted cashews.

"I like a lady with an appetite," said Alexander, causing Granny to smile Sphinx-ishly. Suddenly, a waiter appeared at his side and mur-mured something in his ear. Alexander frowned and murmured some-thing back, and the man disappeared.

Granny checked her tiny gold watch. "Alex, darling, I know you're being polite, but I simply don't think we can wait any longer for Nicolas." She gave him a private look. "In fact, I don't think we should. He needs to learn that you simply *can't* keep people waiting."

I popped a cashew in my mouth and was surprised to see a grim expression spread over Alexander's handsome face.

Oh, no. Had there been some drama already?

"He's already here, Dilys," he said through clenched teeth. "He's been here for a good thirty minutes."

"Really?" I almost laughed with relief. "Don't tell me—he's sitting round the corner? Oh, gosh, I've done that myself, so many times . . ."

"He's in the pool." Alexander clenched even harder.

"Oh, *no!*" said Granny. "How tiresome of him! He *knew* we had a dinner reservation . . ."

"In the rooftop pool?" I repeated. "Is he a keen swimmer?"

As if in answer to my question, a young man with the most outrageously room-stopping aura I'd ever seen appeared with a man I took to be the manager. I wouldn't say the manager was manhandling him, but there did seem to be a certain tension between the two. Maybe because Nicolas was wearing a fluffy white bathrobe.

Whatever it was, everyone's jaw dropped.

"Evening, all," said Prince Nicolas of Hollenberg, with a wink in my direction. "Nice tits."

I clapped a hand to my cleavage, not wanting to meet the flirtatious gaze he was directing up and down between my face and my chest. Even my neck was blushing.

"Nicolas!" hissed Alexander, his voice turning all clipped, like Captain von Trapp in *The Sound of Music.* The man was a total film star. "Can you explain yourself?"

Nicolas paused, then pressed his lips together as if in thought. He dripped onto the floor. I must admit that I was staring at his tanned feet because I didn't dare look any further up—whether for fear of encouraging him, or for fear of being hypnotized like a rabbit by his huge brown eyes, I didn't like to say.

Then he ran his hand through his wet hair and shook his head. "Not really. Fancied a dip. Hopped in. With a couple of friends." He sounded a little drunk already.

"We do not allow swimming in outdoor clothes," said the manager, with an impressive note of apology in his voice. "So we were forced to remove the prince from the pool."

"I am lost for words," said Alexander. "I am *aghast.*"

"I know!" said Nicolas. "I took my bloody *shoes* off."

Alexander shot Nicolas a look that would have reduced even Allegra to tears, but it seemed to have little or no effect.

"I take it you won't be joining us for dinner?" inquired Granny icily.

Nicolas shrugged. "No, that should be OK. I'm having some more clothes sent round on a bike."

"I'm delighted to hear that," said Granny, sounding anything but.

"What were you thinking?" demanded Alexander. He made a tiny gesture with his head toward me and looked even more furious. "I can't believe you could be so boorish as to keep our guests waiting—"

Nicolas rolled his eyes. "Oh, come on. Rooftop swimming pool— has to be done."

"It does not 'have to be done,'" snapped Alexander. "Why would it have to be done?"

"It's a *phrase.*"

Nicolas turned to me as if to say, *Huh! Old people! What do they know?* but I gave him the freeze. If he thought I was the kind of girl who was happy to be dipped in a chocolate fountain or tossed fully clothed in a swimming pool, he was very wrong indeed.

Besides, from what I could see, he was a good ten years too old to be excited about that sort of thing.

"Does she speak?" he inquired of his grandfather, nodding at me. "Or is she just here for decoration?"

Up to that point, I'd been somewhat tongue-tied, not because Nicolas was technically royal, but because he was astonishingly attractive. It pained me to admit it of a man so deeply in love with himself, but Nicolas had a real head-turning magnetism. Even in a bathrobe, with his black hair wet and slicked back, and five o'clock shadow tracing along his jaw, he looked as if he was en route to some A-list "come in your bathrobe" party.

However, equally obviously, he was also an arrogant, sexist, spoiled idiot, and for me, that overrode everything else, just like bad breath could ruin a fabulous outfit.

Even as I thought that, a little voice in my head was telling me not to be such a prig and to look at his fabulous swimmer's shoulders.

"Yes, she does speak," I said quickly, before Granny or Alexander could speak for me.

"And what does she say?" he drawled.

"She says, 'You're dripping onto my handbag.' "

He stared at me, and I stared back. If he'd been nice, I'd have been intimidated by his jet-set attitude, but being this uncouth didn't make him any different from the scores of surly blokes I dealt with on a day-to-day basis. Nelson and Jonathan had raised my expectations, as far as manners went. Even Roger might smell weird, but he was never *rude*.

Anyway, poor Alexander was now clearly mortified, as well as angry. And it was a new Lulu Guinness evening bag that I'd brought out especially for the occasion.

"I do have that effect on girls," he drawled, raking his hair back. It was so thick that no scalp was visible as his fingers ran through it.

"And what's that?" I said.

He winked at me. "Damp patches."

Granny took a sharp, disapproving breath.

I gave her a puzzled *What?* look.

"I know how to deal with drips," I said politely, moving my bag away from him. "They're quite easy to brush off."

"Book a room, wait there for your clothes, and join us as soon as you can once you're decent," said Alexander in a low, dangerous tone.

"Oh, yah, I booked a room already," Nicolas said, and turned his chocolate brown eyes toward me again. "Room 202. Two-oh-two." The long lashes brushed his cheek as he winked slowly. "Shall I write it down on a napkin?"

"If you think you need help remembering it," I said politely.

"Go!" thundered Alexander so forcefully that several heads turned and didn't turn back again.

There was a tense pause, then Nicolas shrugged, helped himself to my glass of champagne, and swaggered off.

I watched him go, unable to take my eyes off his bathrobe. He didn't shuffle, or slouch, as most of my English clients did. He sauntered.

What an idiot, I reminded myself.

Granny, Alexander, and I repaired to the luxurious dining room of Petrus next door, where Alexander wasted no time in ordering some wine for the three of us.

"I'm so sorry," he said, once our glasses were filled and the menus handed out. "He knew exactly what time we were meeting."

"I have no doubt," murmured Granny.

I glanced at her under the guise of studying the starters. She seemed more annoyed about Nicky's behavior than she ever had been about Allegra's carryings-on. And Allegra had been expelled from six different schools, married a man who'd already been technically married to someone else, and nearly arrested for international fraud.

"Never mind," I said, trying to sound blasé. "It was lovely to have some time to chat on our own."

Alexander inclined his head graciously. "You're too sweet, Melissa. I can only apologize on his behalf."

Granny tutted to herself. "Well, while we're still on our own, as you can see, Alexander really needs some outside help," she said. "And, as I've told him, I don't know anyone who could do a better job of knocking some sense into Nicky than you." She took a large sip of wine. "Any sense at all would be a good start."

"Dilys," began Alexander, with a swift look over the table at me, "you know, perhaps it's a little unfair to Melissa to—"

Granny held up a hand. "Not at all. Melissa's dealt with much more awful types than Nicky, haven't you, darling? That dreadful actor boy in New York, for instance—tell Alexander about him."

"Well," I began, turning pink, "Godric wasn't so awful—he was just a fish out of water, and I helped him to—"

"He was an embarrassment," interrupted Granny. "Have you heard of him, Alex, darling? Ric Spencer? English actor, was in that film with the big plane crash? Anyway, he was upsetting people, sulking in interviews, no idea how to behave whatsoever. And Melissa stepped in and smoothed off his edges, and now he's meant to be the next Hugh Grant, isn't he? Did you tell me he's in the running for James Bond?"

I blushed. "Yes, well, that was meant to be confidential . . ."

Alexander sighed deeply and spread his snowy white napkin on his lap. "Dilys, I don't doubt Melissa's . . . capabilities for a second. I just wonder if it's fair to land her with such a Herculean task." He smiled sadly at me.

"Just what exactly is this Herculean task?" I asked. "If you would explain exactly what it is, I'll be able to tell you whether I'm up to it or not."

Alexander and Granny looked at each other.

"He's your grandson, Alex," said Granny encouragingly. "Better explain before he gets back, don't you think?"

Alexander hesitated, then looked me square in the eye.

I tried not to melt.

"My father was the last reigning prince-governor of a small province on the Montenegran coast," he said. "It wasn't large, but we had a beautiful, ancient castle, and a wonderful forest where we kept truffle hounds . . . anyway, there was a revolution in the nineteen thirties, long before your time, of course—"

"And ours, darling," Granny reminded him.

Alexander allowed himself a little smile. "And ours. In any case, we were forced to abandon our family home in a great hurry and move to France, but I have dreamed of returning ever since. And now, I am so pleased to say, there's a chance that we can."

"Oh, how lovely!" I exclaimed. "Just like a film!"

"Ah." He raised a finger. "There are conditions. The country is not rich, and we must maintain the castle ourselves, which is not a problem. It would be an honor to do so. And we must allow people to look around some of it, and allow the BBC to film some drama there once a year, or somesuch. My lawyers are looking into that. But the main difficulty is that the government is very traditional. They want a family, a respectable family that they can show off to tourists." He shrugged his shoulders in a gorgeously European manner.

"Ah," I said, beginning to understand.

"My daughter, Oriane, is not . . ." He turned to Granny. "What is the best way to put this, Dilys?"

"Oriane reminds me very much of your mother," said Granny, looking at me meaningfully. "I think they have the same taste in *spas*. And *detox centers*. And kinesiologists."

"She is not the same after the last divorce," agreed Alexander.

"And Nicky's father?"

"We do not speak of him," he said gravely.

"Racing driver," murmured Granny under her breath.

"It has been made very clear to me that unless Nicky shows he can calm his behavior, take on some responsibility, the deal cannot go ahead. And my family will lose this last chance. I must confess, yes, I would like to see him settled down, and thinking of a family, instead of just his own pleasure. But not with someone who'll make the situation"—he paused—*"worse."* Alexander looked up at me, concerned. "I'm afraid he won't meet the right girl the way he is now. Would *you* want to marry him, Melissa?"

"Well . . . ," I stammered, not sure what the polite response was.

"No, you wouldn't." Alexander shook his head. "And that makes all of us so unhappy. Ours isn't an *illustrious* family, but it's an old one, and our name has never, ever, been dragged through the tacky papers this way. We do not want Nicolas to end up with a trapeze artist, in and out of the divorce courts, children everywhere. . . ."

"But, if he wants to . . . ," I began.

"Nicolas does exactly what he wants," said Granny tartly. "That's the point. Which is fine when you're a merchant banker from Epsom. But he wants all the fun of being a prince and none of the responsibility that goes with it."

Alexander raised his majestic, sad eyes to mine. "What I would like to engage you to do, Melissa, is simply show him the right way to behave. For a few months."

"Improve his profile," added Granny. "Be seen with him at a few art galleries and museums, instead of the usual round of bars and nightclubs." Her brow furrowed. "What's it called? That one Prince Harry goes to."

"Boujis," I said automatically. But a dread thought was dawning on me. *Be seen with Nicky?* What *exactly* had Granny told him about my agency? "You don't want me to pretend to be his girlfriend, do you?" I looked at Alexander. "Perhaps I didn't mention it, but Jonathan is my fiancé. We were engaged at Christmas. He would . . ." I stopped myself from saying *go nuclear if I did this again* and corrected it to ". . . be very reluctant to agree to my doing this."

Alexander opened his mouth, but Granny cut in. "Think of it more as image consulting," she said. "Like a PR expert."

Just as I was searching for the right way of pointing out that rebranding Prince Nicolas was more than most experienced PRs would take on, Alexander suddenly threw his napkin on the plate, got to his feet, and excused himself.

Nicolas had appeared at the door, dressed in a tight shirt with three buttons undone, a pair of dark jeans held up with a belt that screamed *This buckle is made from gold by Gucci!* and loafers.

I didn't need to inspect his feet to guess that he wouldn't have bothered with socks.

Granny and I watched as Alexander opened his arms wide and escorted his grandson out of the dining room with all the appearance of warm family feeling. I knew enough about displays of warm family feeling to suspect it was anything but.

"Probably going to lend him a tie," I suggested, to break the silence.

Granny put out a bejeweled hand and grasped mine over the table. I braced myself for some serious persuasion. No one in my entire family could ask for anything normally. More worryingly from my point of view, none of them could take no for an answer either.

"Please, darling," she said in a low, impassioned voice. "You're the only person Alex can turn to! I have heard him *dream* about that castle for forty-five years!"

"Ladle on the emotional blackmail, why don't you?" I said faintly.

"Think of it as a challenge then!" She arched her eyebrow. "And what about the knock-on effect it'll have for the rest of your business?"

"But Jonathan would never agree to let me do something like this again," I insisted. "Not after Godric. He hates the idea of me getting emotionally entangled in other men's problems—and this is obviously a big family issue!"

"Well, isn't Jonathan in Paris these days?"

"There are newspapers in Paris," I reminded her.

She made a dismissive gesture and played what was obviously her trump card. "Anyway, we haven't even discussed terms yet. I know Alex is prepared to be *very* generous."

"That doesn't make the slightest difference," I said stoutly.

Well, actually, it did, I told myself. If I was going to buy my office, it made *all* the difference.

But I wasn't sure I could do what Granny and Alex wanted me to do. Until I'd met Nicolas, I hadn't realized how far out of my depth I'd be; now that I had, I was pretty sure I'd have to say no. A sudden wave of disappointment hit me as the rosy mental image of me triumphantly showing Jonathan the deed to the flat vanished before my eyes.

"Oh, well then." Granny picked up a menu and began to study it. "What a shame. Never mind."

We examined the entrées in strained silence.

Nelson had gone through my accounts and explained that though my cash flow was enough to pay the mortgage, I needed to find at least twenty-five grand for the deposit.

How much would Alexander be offering as a down payment? I wondered. What if I tried? Gave it my best shot for a month?

I bit my lip.

"Alexander is such a darling," mused Granny, as if apropos of nothing. "He was all for giving you a separate clothing allowance too, since you'd have to dress up for events and so on, and he doesn't want to put you to personal expense." She looked up. "Isn't that thoughtful?"

I narrowed my eyes. "Don't bother going down that road. You know I make most of my own clothes."

She smiled beatifically. "You've got so many talents, darling."

We went back to studying our menus.

"And then there's the car," added Granny without lifting her gaze from the menu. "You'd have had to have a car and a driver. Wouldn't that be fun? No having to go mad finding a parking meter outside the shops!"

"I like my Smart," I replied, refusing to rise to the bait. "I never have to worry about parking spaces."

There was another long pause while glasses chinked and cutlery tinkled around us.

"Did I ever tell you Alexander has the most gorgeous old yacht?" Granny said conversationally. "He'd love to invite both of us out to the Med for a sail. . . . What do you think about the quails' eggs here? Nice, or not?"

"Granny, it makes no difference!" I said, finally snapping. "I know men like Nicky—they don't listen to girls like me. They can't even *see* girls who aren't thin, blond, and half dressed. You know I'd love to help, but, honestly, I can't!"

Her head bounced up, but I could see a triumphant sparkle in her Tiffany blue eyes. "Of course you can!" she exclaimed reproachfully. "I'm helping a dear old friend in a very trying time. I'm sure you'd do exactly the same." She paused. "If it was an old, dear friend of yours."

"Hmm," I said, trying to maintain my own stern expression. I knew what she was getting at. At least she hadn't stooped to mentioning Nelson by name, as Daddy would almost certainly have done. And she had a point: if Nelson's grandson turned out to be a notorious letdown, making Nelson miserable in the process, I'd be itching to sort him out by whatever means possible too.

Granny's radar must have picked up my weakening, because she went in for the kill. "You've always underestimated yourself, darling," she said. "And do I need to say that you would have my undying gratitude for ever and ever, amen? I mean," she added, as if it had just occured to her, "I did help you out when you needed that money to start up the business in the first place, didn't I?"

Oh, God. Granny really knew how to twang my heartstrings. And she was right about the loan: if she hadn't lent me the cash to start up the agency, there wouldn't have been an agency at all.

I turned my attention back to the menu and let her stew while I chewed it over.

At the end of three minutes I said, distantly, "I'll have to ask Jonathan."

"Thank you, darling," said Granny. "Oh, look! Here come the men!"

I looked up and saw Alexander and Nicolas making their way through the restaurant. Each sent smiles of recognition in different directions, but the smiles were very tight.

Whatever Alexander had said to Nicolas outside, it must have had some effect, because for the remainder of the meal, he was absolutely charming. After a little awkwardness, we worked out a few acquaintances we had in common, as well as some Parisian bars we'd both visited, and when I reminded him about poor Tiggy, the human fondue dipper, only a moment's concentration showed in his eyes before he laughed and promised to send her some flowers to apologize.

"That's a good habit to get into," said Alexander approvingly.

I got the impression that if he sent flowers to all the girls he dipped, there wouldn't be a gerbera to be had in Central London, but I didn't say anything. After coffee, Alexander and Granny left to go on to some other party "an old Greek friend" was throwing in Grosvenor Square.

I saw Alexander turn back anxiously as they were almost out the door, and the relief on his face when he saw me and Nicolas still chatting politely touched my heart. He'd seemed so moved when he'd talked about his old castle over dinner—the secret passages, the turrets, the magnificent gardens—that I'd found myself wanting to do anything to help him go back.

Maybe I *could* do something for Nicky, I mused. Maybe his arrogance was all show, like that of some other insecure men I knew who . . .

"Yeah, I'm still here. Yeah, he's gone. Taken Camilla with him and left me with the chunky granddaughter."

My attention snapped back to the table. Nicky was on his mobile, talking in a rich trans-Atlantic drawl that didn't quite tally with the polite English accent I'd just heard him use over dinner, and when he saw me glaring at him, a lazy smile crossed his face.

I glared at his phone.

"Yeah, one sec . . . What?" he demanded.

"Weren't we talking a moment ago?" I asked. "If it's an urgent call, I don't mind you going outside. But it's very rude to call while I'm here—it makes me feel awkward."

"I'll ring you back, darling," he said, without taking his eyes off me, then he snapped his phone shut. "Right," he said, straightening his coffee cup and spoon so it was neat, then folding his arms patronizingly. Now he sounded very Kings Road again. "Let's get a few things clear. I don't want some goody-two-shoes nanny following me round. And I don't imagine you want to be forced to have a good time and get drunk and go to interesting parties much either, do you?"

I started to bridle, but he held up a hand and carried on.

"However, my grandfather, in his desperation to get his moldy old castle back, has made it pretty plain that failure to comply with the plan he and your grandmother have hatched between them will result in a . . . how can I put it?" He put a finger on his chin, and I longed to slap it away. "A certain financial embarrassment for me?"

"He'll stop your allowance," I interpreted.

"Exactly."

"Well, that won't be a problem, will it?" I said, now too annoyed to hold back. "Because you'll have your salary to fall back on . . . Oh," I added, with maximum sarcasm, "don't tell me you don't have a job?"

Nicolas scowled. "I'm not the one pretending to be someone's girlfriend."

"I'm not the one pretending to be a teenage sex pest," I said, not letting my shock show. "Tell me, what *is* it you do for a living?

Because if you're a *prince* by profession, surely it would make sense to get the castle that goes with it. A prince without a castle is . . . what?"

"Still a prince," he insisted sulkily.

"Still a prince," I repeated. "But more of a . . . *prince in name only.* The artist *formerly known as Prince,* say, rather than Prince William."

We glared at each other until Nicky suddenly smiled. It was a fake smile, but it was so sunny and gorgeous that for a moment I was utterly thrown.

"Whatever," he said, checking his phone for messages. "We can play it a couple of ways. I can make your life so miserable that you'll give up within a fortnight."

"That would never happen," I said stoutly. "I have professional standards."

"Whatever. Sure you don't want to try?" Nicolas flicked a dark eyebrow at me. "Could be fun?"

"I'd hate to stand between *my* grandmother and the home she loved," I said meaningfully. "For the sake of a few months' good behavior."

"Oh, Melissa," he said, putting his hands flat on the table and leaning forward. "Can you *really* be as wholesome as you seem?"

"Appearances can be deceptive," I snapped. Then added, after a pause, "I mean, I'm sure, deep down, you're a perfectly . . ." I ran out of words and looked up to meet his eyes with the most innocent expression I could summon up.

"A perfectly . . . ?" prompted Nicky, gazing up at me from his thick eyelashes.

I swallowed and refused to meet his eyes. This was obviously how he gazed women into bed. It was a sticky moment.

"A perfectly decent man. No matter how keen you are to pretend otherwise. And your plan B was?"

He sighed, as if disappointed I hadn't said more. "Plan B was to go along with it. But you must know that I'm doing it for the sake of my allowance. And I don't want you pretending to be my girlfriend. There are too many girls out there who already think they are. I don't have time to put them all straight." He smirked.

"Nicolas, I have no intention of doing that," I said. "My fiancé would never allow it, for one thing. And for another . . ."

I stopped myself just in time.

"Do go on," said Nicolas.

Again our gazes met over the table, and I felt a dim and distant lust memory stirring. If my ex, Orlando, had been taller, smoother, richer, and altogether more golden god-ish, he might have gotten within smarming distance of Prince Nicolas of Hollenberg.

"You're really not my type," I lied.

He put a hand to his forehead. "I'm crushed," he said dramatically.

"Good." I tried to bury my nose in my water glass, but I couldn't keep a smile from sneaking onto my lips. Maybe he had a tiny sense of humor.

Nicolas caught me smiling and grinned back. When he wasn't trying so hard, he could be quite cute, in a boyish way. Or maybe he just thought he had me safely under his spell.

"You do realize, don't you, that you're on a wild-goose chase?" he said.

"In what way?"

"Grandfather thinks you're going to turn me into a throwback prince, teach me some proper behavior."

"Yes. And?"

Nicky leaned across the table and murmured confidentially. "Melissa, I spend more time hanging out with princes than you do, and I can assure you that this is how princes behave. Boujis. Klosters. Believe me. I am absolutely hitting the mark."

I leaned forward too, close enough for him to think I was about to kiss him. I wasn't, of course. "But modern princes don't get fairy-tale castles, Nicky. They go on *Celebrity Love Island* and make fools of themselves. So if you want the castle and the cash, you'd better start listening to this expert on throwback manners. OK?"

"Mmm," he said, apparently distracted by the brooch pinning my dress together. "Is this real?" He poked at it.

"No, it's paste," I said, leaning back to put myself out of harm's way.

"I wasn't talking about the brooch. Anyway." He winked and swilled back the rest of his wine. "Got a party waiting for me. Can I get you a lift anywhere?"

"No, thanks," I said.

"Be like that." He leaned over and kissed me on both cheeks, resting a hand on my waist as he did so. "Ooh. Big pants under here? Appearances, eh?" Then he gave me a cheeky wink and was gone while I was still grappling for the right thing to say.

If I'm being honest, I was a bit dizzy.

It was only when I stood up to leave and I felt a sudden draft around the thighs, and discovered the eyes of the whole restaurant on me and those very same wildly unflattering big pants, that I realized Nicky had not only unfastened the safety brooch at my cleavage but, he'd also undone my wrap dress with a practiced, undetectable hand.

Right, I thought grimly, pulling my dress together as best I could. Clearly the Melissa approach wasn't enough. From now on, Nicolas would be dealing with Honey.

six

When I climbed the stairs to our flat, alternately seething about Nicky's appalling attitude and cringing at my pant humiliation, I found Nelson still up, going over some figures on the kitchen table. He was surrounded by paper and cold cups of coffee, one hand pushed into his thick blond hair, the other hand twirling a pen round his fingers like a mini baton.

I didn't feel too sorry for him. Untangling complicated accounts was pretty much Nelson's favorite thing, after writing angry letters to the *Guardian* about the growing misuse of apostrophes in signage, and reminding me to pay the Congestion Charge. Despite this, he was also handy with a screwdriver and could do magic foot massages, so I forgave him his amateur sainthood. He didn't take himself that seriously.

Nelson's ability to do hard sums, combined with his inherent soft-touchness, meant that he was always being taken advantage of by hopeless causes. At the moment, for instance, he was helping out with a sailing charity based round the corner in Victoria. The idea was to take inner-city kids with "issues," put them to sea in an old tea clipper, and make them splice the main brace and keelhaul and that sort of thing until they discovered self-worth and gave up shoplifting. Nelson had spent the previous summer captaining the ship like a

seafaring Bono, and now the ladies-who-lunch running it had made
him a board member, partly so they could have their figures straightened out for free, and partly, I reckon, so they could admire Nelson's
lovely English ruggedness and fantasize about him hoisting sails and
hitching sheets, or whatever he did in his spare time with Not-Very-
Jolly Roger.

"If this is a hint about the rent, I'll give you a check tomorrow," I
said, and put the kettle on to make a pot of tea.

"It's not," he said absently, jabbing at his calculator. "Monday will
do. I don't suppose you want to go to a charity ball, do you? And
know roughly three hundred and thirty-nine other people who
might?"

"Of course I'll go!" I said at once. "How much are the tickets?"

"A hundred and fifty quid each? I know, I know," he added, as I
spluttered something about budgeting. "But Araminta's commis-
sioned a three-ton ice sculpture of HMS *Victory* and says it's impossible to compromise on the catering since it's Faye's goddaughter's
company . . ." Nelson sucked in his breath through his teeth, then
looked up at me with a wry grin. "How was your prince?"

"Which one?" I pulled a pretend starry-eyed face. "Oh, don't groan
like that. Who knows when I'll get to say that again in my life?"

"The one you're meant to be turning into Prince Charming."

"Nicolas? Oh, he was even slimier than I expected," I said, looking to
see if the biscuit barrel had magically replenished itself. Happily, it had.

"Ah. Where does he fit on the Orlando von Borsch scale?"

I nibbled a homemade shortbread biscuit. "He's way off that scale.
Way off. He makes Orlando look like Roger Trumpet. I mean," I corrected myself in light of recent transformations, "the *old* Roger."

"That bad, eh?"

"Worse than you could imagine," I said. "But the grandfather's a
complete sweetie. He even noticed my new shoes. The ones *you* said
made me look like Minnie Mouse. And he has the most gorgeous old-
fashioned way of talking to you—I mean, I can quite see the older
man charm thing now. . . ."

Nelson fixed me with his Paddington Bear Hard Stare. "You're not seriously going to take this on, are you?"

I hesitated over a second biscuit. "I don't know. I'd like to be able to help Granny out. And I can see how it could be quite interesting in some respects, because frankly, someone needs to tell Prince Nicky you just can't talk to women like that these days, and then there's the whole castle business . . ."

He widened his eyes as if I'd temporarily taken leave of my senses.

"Oh, listen, it doesn't matter whether I would or wouldn't, since Jonathan will never agree to it," I said, pouring hot water into the teapot, with some relief that this thorny decision was effectively out of my hands. "So at least I can give Granny a cast-iron reason that she can hardly argue about."

"Are you sure you want to go down that road?" Nelson went back to his maths with apparent unconcern, but the even way he said it immediately alerted me to a hidden spike of sensibleness.

"And what do you mean by that?"

He looked up. "Just that it's not like you to let other people make decisions for you. Especially not control freaks like Mr. Riley."

"Jonathan and I are going to get married," I reminded him. "And he's not a control freak. It's a decision for *us*." I stuffed another biscuit in my mouth and checked my watch. "Is it too late to ring him, do you think? I need to ask what the weather's like so I know what to pack. We're doing the Tuileries and some light shopping this weekend, and I need to take his secretary out for coffee on Friday."

"Ah, sorry," said Nelson, picking a Post-it note off the floor. "I meant to say—Remington called while you were out and said . . ." He scrutinized his writing. "The weather's lousy, there's a party neither of you will want to go to, and he knows you're probably dying to see your new nephew, so he doesn't mind spending the weekend at your parents. He'll meet you at Waterloo at five tomorrow and then something about a five-star hotel I didn't write down."

"Ha ha," I said, pouring him a mug of tea. "Very amusing. What did he really say?"

"That's what he really said. Is he on some kind of medication?"

"He's really making an effort with my family," I informed Nelson. "He spent nearly an hour with my father last weekend. I even heard Daddy laughing at one point. Jonathan's a *lovely* man," I said, pleased to shove Nicolas's smug suntanned face out of my head and replace it with Jonathan's all-American good looks.

Nelson squinted up at me. "Or a very clever one."

"Both," I said happily. "He's getting married to me."

Even after a full working week, an hour's delay in the Tunnel, and a horrible on-board meal, Jonathan still looked immaculate as he got off the Eurostar on Friday evening. His cashmere overcoat hung perfectly over his left arm, his jaw was very lightly stubbled; even the doors slid open for him, rather than stick, as they had done every time I'd tried to make the same graceful arrival at the Gare du Nord, leaving me stabbing at the buttons while ignoring the sea of tetchy French businessmen behind me.

I also loved the way his face lit up when he saw me on the platform, as it did now. Jonathan's natural resting expression was rather stern, which had been a bit off-putting at first. It was only as I'd gotten to know him better that I'd realized it hid quite a shy man beneath. And now I saw the frown swept away by a broad smile that made his gray eyes shine with delight. OK, the current logistical demands on our relationship weren't ideal, but it did mean that we were forever doing awfully romantic things like meeting each other off trains and counting off hours till our next kiss.

"Hey!" he said, putting his BlackBerry away and scooping me into his arms for a tight hug.

We didn't do kissing on railway platforms. Neither of us was into big public displays, and besides, I was quite happy to keep Jonathan's romantic abilities to myself, thank you very much.

"I have a lovely French evening planned for you," I told him as we made our way to the car park. "To make up for being here and not in Paris. We're going to go for a drink at the French House in Soho, then I've booked a table for dinner at L'Escargot."

"Parfait, chèrie," said Jonathan, then rattled off a load of French I didn't understand, but it sounded fabulous.

I must confess, I spent the first part of the evening just staring happily at Jonathan, holding his hand and listening to his accounts of the new properties he'd taken on in Paris. I loved hearing him talk. He had an incredibly sexy accent, and he'd been doing extra refresher French lessons, so his French was impressively good too. There's really nothing sexier than listening to a man speak a foreign language, don't you think?

"So, what have you been up to?" asked Jonathan, as the waiter took our pudding plates away. He stretched his hand over the table and entwined my fingers in his. "I'm sorry I've missed your calls. Solange puts my messages from you on different color Post-it notes—there are always too many blue ones I haven't been able to take."

"I'm on the blue Post-its?" I said, just to check.

He nodded.

"Oh, well, in a way it's nicer to be able to tell you my news in person," I replied. My brain was already racing, searching for the right way to broach the whole Prince Nicky topic. It was rather a big idea to present, and I needed to get the whole thing described and dismissed quickly, before it triggered Jonathan's gentle nagging about my taking on dreadful clients, and how much better my time and expertise could be spent.

"Absolutely," agreed Jonathan. "I'm all ears."

"Well," I began, "Granny's asked a favor of me . . ."

"Has she?" said Jonathan cheerfully, signaling for coffee. "She's a national treasure, your grandmother. My mother keeps asking me how she should address her at the wedding. Whether she should curtsey or not. Can you drop her a line and let her know?" He winked. "I think she'd like it if everyone else had to curtsey except her. Can you fix that? She loves all that English aristo stuff."

"Yes, well . . . Oh, thank you." I made room on the table for my espresso. "It's funny you should say that. . . ."

I explained Alexander's proposition very quickly, without taking breaths. When I'd finished, I sat back, waiting for Jonathan to say no.

I knew he'd say no in a very nice way, which was fine. I could repeat it verbatim to Granny.

"I see," said Jonathan thoughtfully. "That's quite some favor."

"Absolutely," I said, unwrapping my chocolate coffee bean. "I told her it wouldn't really fit in with the plans we're making and—"

"I don't see why not," he said.

"—that it wasn't at all appropriate for an engaged woman to be cavorting around with a man like that." I looked up. "What did you say?"

"I said, I don't see why you shouldn't do it," said Jonathan.

At this point, my jaw might have dropped open. Or Jonathan might have just put his finger under my chin and closed my mouth as an affectionate gesture.

"Why not?" he repeated. "I bet the fee would make it worth your while."

"Well, yes," I stammered. "But I thought you said—"

"It's a one-off, right?" said Jonathan. His face softened. "You have to admit, it's kind of romantic—restoring a royal family to their palace. Imagine knowing you'd made that happen. Maybe this friend of your granny's can get you made a dame or something."

"Yes," I said doubtfully. Jonathan had a weird American view of European royalty that I didn't think would last for long if he actually met Nicolas. "But it's not like he's a *real* prince. . . ."

Jonathan looked confused. "I don't follow. A prince is a prince, surely?"

"Well, yes and no." I struggled to think of the best way to put it. "There's a sort of sliding scale of how seriously royals are taken in England, depending on how much they do, and whether they're a prince of somewhere that actually recognizes their, um, *princeness*. For instance, Prince William's got a job in the army and stacks of royal duties like opening schools and visiting hospitals, plus he behaves himself. Nicky's rich, but he has no throne, no job, and he's really only a prince in the sense that it gets him to the front of queues in nightclubs. That impresses some people, but not me."

"Right," said Jonathan. "So where does this guy's family fit in the sliding scale?"

I took a deep breath. To be honest, I wasn't all that strong on the pecking order of defunct monarchies. "Well, if Britain, Spain, Sweden, Denmark, and the Netherlands are Premier League, then the Hollenbergs are somewhere around the bottom of the fourth division," I admitted. "I don't think they even had an army. I mean, *yes,* they're distantly related to all the right people, but there used to be *hundreds* of little monarchies in Europe, just to give Queen Victoria's billions of children something to do. But since Communism and World War Two and the EU and everything, there are stacks of redundant princes knocking around Chelsea, and most of them couldn't even point out on a map where they used to rule. Unless it's got a nice beach."

"And this guy's one of those?"

"I suppose so. But his grandfather's terribly serious about his duties, and if I help Alexander get the castle back, Nicky *will* have something to do—he'll have a role in promoting the principality, using the castle to get tourists in and film crews. Having something to do might be the making of him."

Jonathan gave me a knowing look. "Sounds like you're already itching to make him over."

"Well, I don't know if it's that easy," I said doubtfully. "I'm not entirely sure Nicky *wants* something to do."

He picked up a sugar cube. "Listen, go for it. It'll be the favor to end all favors for your family, for one thing. You sign the deal, fill your address book with tony contacts, then move to Paris with me. You say the family lives in Paris half the time, right? Well, he's bound to have some good connections there. You can put the money into a new business for the two of us, and we can start over together." The smile intensified, and he leaned across the table slightly. "As life partners *and* business partners."

My brain was still engaged with the Nicky problem, and I wasn't expecting this abrupt change of direction. "What do you mean, exactly?"

Jonathan beamed, like a child unveiling his special project. "You're always saying how I can't tell you that you work too hard when you're running your own business, right? And that Kyrle & Pope doesn't pay me enough for the hours I work for them? Well, I've been giving the matter some thought while I've been in Paris, and I reckon now's the time for us to set up on our own."

"You mean . . . start up a business together?" To be honest, I felt rather wrong-footed. Had we actually finished discussing Nicky? Or was Jonathan just moving on to what *he* wanted to discuss?

"You got it!" said Jonathan with a little snap and point of his fingers—a nervous tic I thought I'd just about beaten. "You know how much I love that amazing touch you have with houses. I mean, you were in the new apartment for what? A weekend? And you've made it look like a home already. Now, what if you were to do that as part of a service for new home buyers? I find the properties, you help them move in. And all those smart details you're so good at—finding the right staff, or working out where the schools are, the nice patisseries— people want to know that sort of thing."

"But I don't know Paris," I reminded him. "Not like I know London. Jonathan, just to go back to Nicky for a—"

"You'd get to know it quickly," he breezed on. "It's smaller than London. And we'd be targeting ex-pats, Americans, English families—they want someone they can trust. Someone who speaks their language. Someone who really reminds them of home, you know?"

"My French is *très mauvaise,*" I protested. "And, honestly, I don't know if—"

"Solange will find you a tutor," said Jonathan. "In fact, she might even coach you herself. She's offered to give me extra conversation lessons after work." He looked approving. "Really, she's the most organized woman I've ever met—aside from you."

"Mmm," I said. I wasn't as organized as Jonathan thought. I just made lots of lists. Still, it was flattering that he thought I was. "But, darling, let's not get too far ahead here. Are you absolutely sure you wouldn't mind my taking this job on? I'd have to spend a fair bit of time with Nicolas. I might even get photographed with him, you know. I mean," I added delicately, "you know how bothered you were when everyone thought I was Godric's girlfriend in New York."

"Bothered" was putting it mildly. I'd never seen supercool, super-grown-up Jonathan get so agitated as when I was shepherding Godric around, even though I'd known Ric the film star since he was Godric the gloomy adolescent.

Jonathan paused for a moment, then dropped a sugar cube into his coffee and stirred it briskly. "That was different."

"In what way?"

"We weren't engaged then. I don't *think* you're going to run off with this Nicolas, even if he is a prince." He looked up, his gray eyes very serious. There was a brief flash of vulnerability in them that I found utterly heart-melting. "I mean . . . are you?"

"Of course not!" I spluttered. "I mean, yes, I'm sure *some* women would find him attractive but—"

I was about to say I found him repellent, but Nelson's "Ding!" lie detector went off in my head.

Instead, I amended it to, "It's going to be very hard work making him look like a gentleman, put it like that. It might not be as simple as shouting at him and making him stop texting other people over dinner. And what with Granny knowing Alexander . . ." I spread my hands. "I'm already kind of involved. But I won't do it if you think it'll cause a second's upset between you and me."

Jonathan arched an eyebrow, and I wondered if I'd misread him. "Maybe I also want to prove to myself that I can let you go a little, and know you'll come back."

"Jonathan!" I exclaimed. "Stop it!"

"OK, OK. One thing, though," he added. "Wear the wig."

"The wig?" Now this was the U-turn to end all U-turns.

"Yes," he said seriously. "So I know that the woman with this guy is Honey, not my Melissa. It means you're doing a job, not getting dragged in for real. Then, when the job's done, and you've picked up your fee, we'll throw the wig into the Channel. Is that a deal?"

I hesitated and met his steady, searching gaze, trying to ignore the goose bumps that still prickled deliciously on my arms when Jonathan looked at me like that. My Melissa.

Did he just say "throw the wig into the Channel?" demanded the little voice in my head. *What exactly did that mean?* I wasn't sure I wanted to kill off Honey like that. At all.

Here was what I'd always wanted, I told myself. A real soul mate—someone who loved me, and more than that, someone who respected my independence, my business sense.

But throwing the wig into the Channel? When it could just go back in a drawer?

"You mean, close my agency?" I asked, to clarify.

"Well, yes." Jonathan looked miffed. "Be real, Mel. You're not going to be able to run it from Paris, when you're living there permanently, are you?"

I must have looked shell-shocked, because he added, "I'm not asking you to give up *working,* I'm just asking you to work in Paris, with me. Together. Isn't that what we both want? It's what I want. I thought you would too."

Jonathan gave me a hurt-puppy-dog look that was so far removed from his usual amused detachment that I felt a great rush of remorse sweep away my doubts. He'd be giving up his career to start this new project too, after all. Wasn't that proof of his belief in me? We'd both be taking the risk.

I could still buy the office. That would be like a little wedding present—our own London love nest.

"Of course it is," I said, reaching over the table to take his hands in mine. "Of course it's what I want."

In the morning, after breakfast in bed in our Mayfair hotel room, we set off for the country. I must admit that even though I'm not one of those teeny-weeny-bootie-obsessed women, I had popped into babyGap and Petit Bateau during the week to pick up a few little clothes for the as-yet-unnamed Baby McDonald, and was quite looking forward to seeing the little chap.

In fact, as we scooted down the country lanes, sunroof open, the Supremes blasting forth and Jonathan's hand on my knee, I really did feel an unusual sensation spreading through me: for just about the first time ever, I was looking forward to going home.

Obviously, that lasted until we pulled up outside Romney Hall.

I could hear Emery's baby crying even as we were walking across the drive to the front door. It was a ferocious wail, so insistent that it was hard to credit that it could have emerged from a child of Emery, and it sent shivers down my spine.

Jonathan put his arm around my shoulders and squeezed me.

"Feeling broody, huh?"

"No," I said. "Just scared that I have no idea how to get him to stop making that noise. Emery clearly can't."

"I'm sure he'll be as quiet as a mouse the moment you get your hands on him," Jonathan reassured me. "He's a guy, isn't he? I haven't seen you fail yet. . . ." He tightened his grip and leaned in to plant a sneaky kiss on the curve of my neck. "And strictly between you and me, when I saw you with that baby in your arms last weekend, well . . ." And he nuzzled his nose into the small of my neck. "It makes *me* quite broody."

The chilly shivers turned into rather pleasant ones, and I wouldn't have minded exploring the idea of a broody Jonathan a little further if an upper window hadn't been flung open and my mother's head hadn't emerged from the choking ivy surrounding the casement.

"Darling!" she shrieked. "Thank God you're here! You have to come up here at once! Allegra's locked me in!"

Jonathan and I sprang apart.

"What?" I demanded. "Then who's looking after the baby?"

"Aren't you meant to ask *why* Allegra's locked her in?" demanded Jonathan as we broke into a trot toward the house.

"First things first," I gasped, pulling open the front door.

As I did so, the level of wailing intensified, matched by the sound of Mummy hammering on the door upstairs and the furious ringing of a handbell.

My head swiveled as I wondered in which order I should tackle the chaos, but since it all seemed to be coming from upstairs, I decided to head up there and see which presented itself as the most urgent.

I was greeted at the top of the stairs by the bewildering sight of Allegra holding Mummy's study door shut, while alternately shouting and blowing cigarette smoke through the keyhole.

"Come on, Mummy," Allegra was bellowing grimly. "Get knitting! I need a cat and a couple of unicorns from you. This is an emergency! And give the cat two heads! Or do something bizarre with its ears!"

"Allegra!" I yelled. "Who's looking after the baby?"

"Melissa?" Mummy's voice floated plaintively through the solid oak door. "Tell her to let me out. The poor mite's going to do himself a mischief! Someone needs to see to him!"

"Why not Emery?" Jonathan murmured, but the answer to that was too obvious for the rest of us to respond to.

Instead, Allegra looked shifty. "Annoying, isn't it?" she called through the door. "Mmm. Is it making your blood pressure rise? Are you feeling the need to knit?"

"Let her *out!*" I roared.

"Is someone going to deal with that god-awful racket?" bellowed a fresh voice from downstairs. "It's worse than when we had the builders in, and I have an interview to conduct with *Waitrose Food Monthly* in an hour!"

I spun round.

Daddy had emerged at the top of the stairs to join in the fun. His own study was at the other end of the house, far, far away from every-one else, to the mutual convenience of all concerned.

He seemed to notice Allegra for the first time. "What the hell are you doing, Allegra?" he demanded. "I thought you were in Ham fighting with that monolithic soap dodger of yours."

"I popped over to collect Mummy's new animals for the gallery," she said without relinquishing her grip on the brass handle. "But Ivanka says they're too neat. Too normal. Not like the cack-handed monstrosities Mummy was producing six months ago, when the gallery was packed solid with collectors." She rattled the handle at this point for emphasis. "When she was *stressed,* and giving up *smoking,* and generally more *tense*. She's *useless* now that she's all Zen about life."

"So you're *trying* to stress her out?" I gasped.

"Art is a cruel mistress," replied Allegra, narrowing her eyes. "And I'm on twenty percent commission."

"Shouldn't someone see to the baby?" suggested Jonathan politely. "The poor little guy does sound kind of upset."

The handbell started ringing again, while the crying ramped up a notch from teeth-grinding to ear-splitting.

"Jonathan, would you go downstairs and put the kettle on for a cup of tea?" I said, taking control, since everyone else was looking dazed by the noise. The sheer force of it was paralyzing. "Allegra, let Mummy out. Now!"

Sulkily, Allegra let go of the door, and Mummy emerged, looking flustered.

"Thank you, darling," she said, passing a hand across her brow and eyeing Allegra's Marlboro Light longingly. "Do you have any aspirin, Melissa?"

"In my bag," I said automatically. "Allegra, should you be smoking, with a baby in the house?"

"If anything drives me back to the fags, it's going to be this baby," murmured Mummy, making a grab for Allegra's cigarette while Allegra was glaring murderously at me. She dragged deeply on it, while an expression of sheer bliss wreathed her face.

"Oh, for pity's sake!" snorted Daddy, and he marched past everyone toward the sound of the howling. "Do I have to do everything myself?"

I stared at my mother and sister, who were now squabbling like teenagers over the cigarette. I couldn't think of anything useful to say, so instead, I followed Daddy down the hallway toward Emery's room.

"What?" I heard him bark as he pushed the door open. The ringing of the handbell ceased, a window opened, and after a second or two, I heard the dull sound of a handbell falling into the shrubbery.

Emery was lying in her old bed, propped up on a variety of My Little Pony and Strawberry Shortcake pillows. Her hair cascaded around her, and the remains of several boxes of chocolates were visible. The nuts, I knew from experience, would be all that was left.

"Oh, good," she said when she saw me. "You're here. I think the baby's crying again," she added, as if we couldn't tell from the rattling windows.

"We noticed," said Daddy through gritted teeth.

"I suppose he needs changing or something. When's Nanny Ag coming?" Emery asked, foraging for a strawberry creme.

"Not soon enough," snarled Daddy.

Emery smiled beatifically. "Sorry? I didn't catch that."

"I said, 'Not bloody soon enough!'"

"Absolutely!" nodded Emery.

I looked at her. How on earth could she sit there so calmly through this screeching? Poor little Baby Mac was turning bright red with effort.

Giving up on Emery, Daddy turned back to me. "Well? Aren't you going to do something?"

"Me?" I protested. "Shouldn't the mother be . . . ?"

"Fancy a choc, Melissa?" asked Emery, proffering the box. "You can have anything you like. Oh, sorry—so long as it's a nut cluster—"

"For the love of Mike," Daddy snapped, and to my and Emery's total amazement, he lifted the baby out of his crib, trailing Aertex blankets and all.

To our further amazement, the baby stopped crying instantly, as if Daddy had yanked out his batteries.

Daddy and the baby stared at each other, nose to nose. Both noses were quite red. You could see the family resemblance. If I hadn't been so surprised, I'd have been touched.

"Oh, fabulous," said Emery, pulling at her ears and removing a pair of William's clay-pigeon-shooting earplugs. "How did you do that?"

"No idea." Daddy attempted to hand the baby to Emery, but the instant Emery touched him, the screeching began again. Horrified, she tried to pass him to me, but he screeched even louder, until I was forced to press him back into Daddy's arms, like a particularly fierce pass-the-parcel.

Then the baby stopped crying instantly.

"Oh, he likes you," Emery and I cooed in unison.

A strange expression crossed my father's face. Sort of horror, mixed with pride, mixed with delight at the fresh avenues opening up to him. In a film it would probably have been accompanied by warm, sentimental string music, or possibly stabby strings of unholy alliance.

"Of course he does," said Daddy. "He's the first male Romney-Jones to be born in this house for well over half a century."

"MacDonald," murmured Emery.

"Still a Romney-Jones to all intents and purposes." Daddy raised the tiny baby up to eye level and made a squinty-eyed face at him. The baby blinked rapidly.

Just before the baby could prove his Romney-Jones credentials by spitting in Daddy's eye, there was a gentle knock at the door, and Jonathan appeared with Mrs. Lloyd, who was bearing a tea tray.

"I tried," he said to me. "But Mrs. Lloyd insisted I'd screw it up. The pot warming, and so on. Would you like a cup of tea, Emery?"

"Lovely . . . ," she said, rearranging her curtain of hair quickly over one shoulder. Everyone seemed to preen themselves whenever Jonathan hoved into view.

"Ah, just the man," said Daddy, his eyes glittering anew. "Fancy something a bit stronger in my study?"

"Well, I . . . ," Jonathan began, casting quick looks at me and Emery.

"No point talking to either of them," said Daddy. "And I've got something to run by you that might, ah . . ." He went to pass the baby back to Emery, but he opened his little mouth in a warning manner and Daddy took him back.

"He'll start crying if he's hungry," said Emery with an absent-minded wave. "Or if his nappy's niffy. Or something." She smiled at my worried face. "You have to go with the flow with newborns, Mel."

I resisted the temptation to tell her that, in that case, she would be Cotswolds Mother of the Year in no time.

"Why don't you pop him in here?" I suggested instead, picking up the carry cot thing that William had dragged me into Peter Jones to help him buy. It could be fitted to a range of different all-terrain vehicles. "Then he might go to sleep."

Aware that all eyes were on him, Daddy self-consciously decanted the baby into the cot. It lay there, gazing up adoringly at him.

"You're looking very well, Emery," said Jonathan, taking advantage of the silence. "William not around?"

"Oh, he's gone off for a run, or a shoot or something. I gave him the keys to the gun cupboard—that's OK, isn't it? He said something about shooting something for dinner." Emery stopped rooting through the chocs long enough to look up at me. "I told him to take the dogs too. See, Melissa? You're not the only one who can multitask." She rearranged her pillows. "Would you mind awfully if I had a nap? I'm absolutely shattered."

"I can see," I said, pushing away the awful possibilities of William, a gun, Braveheart, local wildlife, and sundry other dogs. "I'll leave your tea here, then. Next to your magazines. And your iPod. And your mobile phone."

"Thanks so much," said Emery as she slipped on her eyemask.

Daddy spirited Jonathan off to his study before I could think of a reason to save him, and I can't say I was that keen to go and rescue him, to be honest.

Mummy and Allegra weren't in the kitchen, but the faint trace of cigarette smoke drifting in through the door out to the herb garden gave me a good idea where they might be. I was just helping myself to a cup of instant coffee and a couple of French Fancies when a tiny hand appeared out of nowhere and whisked the box away from me.

"Not before your lunch!" boomed a Voice from the Past. "And only then if I see a clean plate!"

"Nanny Ag!" I cried, turning around in delight.

Filling the space in front of me, although she was barely five feet tall, was Nanny Ag, the all-seeing, all-knowing Welsh moral oracle of my childhood. Even while she was glaring at me and the French Fancies, I could see her taking in the cobwebs, Mrs. Lloyd's defrosting lunch, the pile of *Telegraph*s waiting to go to the recycling bin, and the dogs' bowls, all very near the stove.

Standing behind her, peeling off a pair of leather driving gloves and wearing a stiff expression, was my grandmother.

"I see I've arrived in the nick of time," sniffed Nanny Ag. "Do your parents still *employ* a housekeeper, Melissa?"

"We'd have arrived even sooner if you'd let me go over forty miles an hour," murmured Granny. "Darling, would you get me a Scotch? I believe your mother keeps an emergency bottle of Glenfiddich just behind the Weetabix, if you look."

Nanny Ag looked askance, and I hesitated. Then I was saved by a sudden roar from Baby Mac, and, like a bloodhound responding to the scent (or more accurately, like a corgi getting a whiff of bare ankle), Nanny Ag was off, her sensible shoes stomping down the uneven parquet.

"I haven't finished with you, Melissa!" she yelled over her shoulder. "What do we say? Little pickers?"

"Wear big knickers," Granny and I finished automatically.

Well, I think Granny said "silk knickers," but she knew what she was supposed to say.

I looked out of the kitchen window and saw Mummy hovering on the path, listening. The moment she heard Nanny Ag's battle cry, a terrified look crossed her face and she scuttled back to the safety of the herb garden.

The crying stopped abruptly, and a faint echo of Welsh folk song began in its place. Daddy's study door also banged shut.

Granny nipped into the pantry, grabbed the bottle, and was about to pour a large Scotch into one of Mummy's nineteen WI market mugs, but she stopped and screwed the cap back on.

"On second thought," she said, looking up at me, "let's keep the option of a quick getaway open."

I held out my mug of coffee. "I'm not going anywhere. And if I am, Jonathan can drive."

Granny sloshed in a generous measure. "So?" she said. "Can I take some good news back to Alexander tonight?"

"You're seeing him again?" I asked curiously. "Twice in one week?"

"He hasn't been able to get over to London much recently, and he's making the most of it," she said airily, and raised her eyebrow. "Although now his wife's gone to the great *bag* shop in the sky, that may change. . . . Well?"

"I would love to help Alexander get his castle," I said. "And if that means working with Nicolas, then yes, I will . . . take it on."

Granny clapped her hands. "Oh, Melissa! I knew I could rely on you!"

"But there have to be rules," I said firmly. "I won't run around after him, like everyone else does. I have to wear my wig and be Honey so no one thinks *I'm* dating him. And I won't neglect my own business. I'm going to work out a series of appointments, and if he doesn't stick to them, I'm not chasing around the nightclubs of London looking for him. And I can only do it until I move to Paris with Jonathan, in September."

She tried to look serious, but the delight in her face was touchingly clear. "Alexander will be thrilled. He's happy to leave it entirely up to you."

"What Nicolas needs is to learn that there are some women who won't roll over at the first bat of his eyelashes," I said, indignation rising just thinking about how he'd undone my dress in Petrus. "And since I'm totally impervious to that sort of sleazy charm, I might just be the girl for the job. You can tell Alexander that I'm a safe pair of hands."

Granny winked. "Unlike poor Nicky."

I nodded, thinking how worried Alexander must be at the thought of Nicky as his next-in-line. "Quite. I wouldn't let him run a bath, let alone a country."

She paused, and sighed, as if I'd missed something, then offered me the verboten cakes. "Never mind, darling. French Fancy?"

seven

Being at home with Jonathan kept me awake at night. Not only because it was sweet revenge on my miserable adolescence to have fully licit romps at last in the four-poster bed, instead of just reading Jilly Cooper novels and pretending, but because I frequently lay there afterward, my brain ticking over all the possible things that might go wrong.

Like, what had my father been talking to Jonathan about for so long? Had he been making embarrassing allegations about people Jonathan might know? And would Jonathan, the soul of discretion, tell me? Then more general things: Would the central heating fail at the same time as a freak rainstorm exposed the leaky roof? Had Mummy remembered to take her chicken fillet bra enhancers out of the bathroom? Was Allegra still sleepwalking?

I listened to the steady in–out of Jonathan's breathing and stared at the strange tableau painted on the canopy of the four-poster. At one time it had probably been erotic, but time had flaked off certain key details, leaving a nightmarish jumble of arms, legs, and prudish blanks. My mind shifted once again back to the problem of Nicky, now a real problem, since I'd overheard Granny on the phone telling Alexander it was "all go" and then laughing girlishly.

I needed to make a list, I thought, slipping soundlessly out of bed and hunting for my slippers. If I had something to tick off, it would make it easier to get through, and at least there would be something I could type up and send to Alexander; Granny had hinted discreetly that there would be a retainer check to begin with, followed by a monthly sum. If I was going to make my mortgage work, I'd need at least three months' money.

Holding my breath, I allowed myself a moment or two to admire his lovely chiseled profile. Some people's faces slumped into gormlessness in sleep. Not Jonathan. He still looked gorgeous. Then I sneaked down to the kitchen, avoiding the three creaking steps.

Once fortified with some fruitcake and a glass of milk, I got my big "to-do" notebook out of my handbag. Using a back copy of *Tatler*, and a posh Kyrle & Pope Social Calendar, I started to list the events I could usefully take Nicolas to, but this time in a sober, image-enhancing state, as opposed to a lecherous, bad-headline-grabbing one.

So nightclubs, dubious fancy-dress parties, and balls for teenagers were out.

Polo matches, charity dinners, art galleries, and cultural events were very much in.

He might have a point about being a modern prince, but if the government of Hollenberg wanted an olde-worlde gentleman to go with their olde-worlde castle, then that's what they were going to get. There was nothing fusty about manners and dressing well, treating people courteously and having productive interests. After all, my life had improved immeasurably since I'd embraced boned lingerie and retro chic. I just needed to dig out the young Prince Rainier in Prince Nicolas. He already had Honey's bombshell qualities, but he could do with some old-fashioned poise.

I sat back and examined my color-coded diary. It was so packed with appointments and notes to myself that it looked like a particularly complex tartan.

I absolutely wasn't going to spend more than ten hours a week with this cretin, international diplomacy or not, and I had to draw a line somewhere—the point at which I moved to Paris for good. There was just so much to do. My stomach lurched at the combined thoughts of moving, packing, selling, and learning French, all in a matter of months, but I stuffed some more fruitcake into my mouth, grabbed a highlighter pen, and started scribbling until the twinge went away.

I started blocking out engagements. Ideally, I wanted to make them events where *I* had the connection so I could retain some semblance of control—over him, and over any coverage in the press. I could take him to Mummy's first night at the art gallery, for instance, and then there was an old school friend Kitty, now in PR, who was organizing a charity Sports Day. Nelson was bound to know someone at Cowes Week; Granny had seats at Wimbledon, where Nicky could be seen to admire the ladies' final without actively admiring the ladies. Add in the contacts I had on various society gossip columns. . . .

I twitched my mouth, wondering if that would be enough to convince Alexander's contacts that Nicky was a reformed character. He was smart enough to know the role he had to play, and if he channeled half the energy he currently spent on acting the playboy into something worthwhile, he could probably run the next-door principality too. Some proper clothes would help. I made a note to take him off to a new but very traditional tailor I'd found on Savile Row for some English suits. What else?

As Alexander had admitted, Nicky's reputation was a serious business problem. He needed someone to take over full-time when my contract expired. A solid, old-fashioned girl from a good family who'd put her foot down. Nicky didn't need an image makeover just for the papers; he needed one for prospective girlfriends.

While I was prepared to cut a few corners for the celebrity press, I couldn't inflict an unreconstructed Nicky on some unsuspecting nice girl. No, if I was going to do this, I had to make a real effort to tackle his transformation from the inside out.

WAYS TO MAKE N A REAL PRINCE, I wrote at the top of a new page.

1. Must be able to have dinner with a girl without trying to pick her up.
2. Develop interesting hobby or skill that demonstrates hidden sensitivity.
3. Must put people at ease, not make them want to punch him.
4. Should not spend more on grooming than his date.
5. Must know when to turn off mobile phone.
6. Find something worthwhile to do with his life.
7. Must stop dipping women in fountains and learn some respect for them.

The words finally stopped tumbling out, and I chewed my pen as I reviewed the list. That wasn't bad going after just the one meeting. I got the feeling it was a list that might well expand, but it was enough to be going forward with for the time being. It certainly focused my mind nicely for the weeks ahead.

Feeling much better about everything, I finished off my fruitcake. The cake tins in our house were always full. Not because my mother was a domestic goddess, but because she couldn't drive past the farm shop without buying at least four or five sponges. And since she was supporting the rural economy, it was a nearly blameless addiction. Well, apart from the pounds I put on whenever I went home and hit the lemon drizzle cake.

I was about to wash up the plate and sneak back to bed when I heard a distant wail and decided to stay downstairs until it stopped. A few moments later, the kitchen door opened and a ghostly figure in white silk slid in.

"Don't look at me, Melissa," commanded my mother. "I don't have my face on."

I looked up. Her hands were spread over her face, leaving only her eyes visible. They were the same pale blue as Granny's.

"That baby's got lungs like Allegra," she went on, opening the fridge while keeping half her face covered. "I completely understand now why my own dear mamma got herself and Daddy booked on a cruise every time I went into hospital with one of you."

"Mummy," I said. "What's the story with Granny and Prince Alexander?"

"What do you mean?" she asked shiftily, lowering her hands. I hadn't seen my mother without makeup for years. She looked like a slightly older, un-colored-in version of herself. With freckles.

"Do they go way back? He seems awfully fond of her."

"They had a romance when your grandmother was singing in a nightclub in London after the war," she said. "Don't look at my crow's-feet, Melissa. He was very keen on her, but his snobby old witch of a mother wouldn't let him marry someone who, you know . . ." She pursed her lips, creating a fascinating maze of lines.

"Couldn't help him get the castle back?" I suggested.

"Ye-e-e-es," said Mummy. "Something like that. Anyway, Alexander was one of Granny's friends in London for years. He used to throw lovely parties where everyone had to come as a film star, just so she could dress up as Rita Hayworth." She frowned. "That was quite embarrassing when Rita Hayworth came too. No one would believe it was her."

"Did they actually have a love affair, then?" I went on, trying to work out dates in my head. "Before Granny met Granddad? Was it a Love That Could Never Be?"

"Oh, yes. But there were lots of men who were in love with Granny, darling. Even when she was married to your grandfather. Alexander married some Hungarian trout, but he carried a torch for Granny for years. I think she always fancied the idea of being a princess."

"She was certainly no lady, despite her title."

Mummy squeaked with horror and covered her face. I looked up to see Daddy in his Harrods pajamas, clutching a silent, pink-faced baby, its eyes darting around as it tried to take in its surroundings.

"I had to," he said quickly. "How else was I going to get any sleep? Stop staring at the baby, Melissa, and make me some toast."

"My God," said Mummy. "There really is a first time for every-thing."

Naturally, it gave me great pleasure to kill several birds with one stone by making Nelson's sailing charity dinner the new improved Nicky's first outing. Not only would it take a whole table off Nelson's hands, making the charity ladies happy, but Gabi and Nelson might also help me keep Nicky in line, should he decide to abandon our agreement to go along with things for the designated time and act up.

Obviously, the first person I asked was Jonathan. He looked so di-vine in black tie, and his quickstep would make Nelson eat his words about the sexual orientation of men who could dance.

"I'd love to come, sweetheart," he said ruefully on Sunday evening as we drove back to London so he could catch the Eurostar, "but I've got a breakfast meeting with a potential new client first thing Thurs-day, and I want to be fresh."

"You couldn't get an early train back?" I suggested hopefully. "Please, Jonathan? It'd be like old times—me in my wig, at a dinner, in a swanky London hotel?" I dropped my voice. "I could get out that old black corset you haven't seen for a while . . ."

"Unfair! Stop making me feel so nostalgic. I can't, Melissa. And be-sides, if I was there you might not give the prince the full Honey treatment, don't you think? Get Nelson to take pictures. Or will I be seeing them in the paper?"

"Maybe," I said, rather sadly, before kissing him good-bye.

When I got back to the flat I casually asked Nelson, "So, have you got a date for the big night?"

Nelson stared at me like I was stupid. "Yes. You."

I flapped my hand. "Don't be silly. You can't take me, I'll be taking *Nicky.*"

"Oh." Nelson attacked his mash with some vigor. "Well, no, then. Maybe it's better that I don't have one—I don't know how much time I'll be able to spare. Wouldn't want to be rude and abandon my date, you know."

Nelson's not having anyone lined up fit in perfectly with my blind date campaign. He looked very dashing in black tie and would be illuminated from within by his twin passions of organizing and sailing.

"What? And lose a ticket sale? Why don't you let me find you one? What about Jossy?"

"Not Jossy," said Nelson, a bit too quickly.

I supposed that rather answered any lingering questions I had about him seeing her again.

Nelson and I locked eyes. I smiled encouragingly.

He cracked first.

"Oh, God, if you must," he sighed. "Pass me the gravy."

"I must," I insisted. "Don't you understand how in demand normal unmarried men of your age are? Even ones with your irritating amateur policing habits."

"When you put it like that . . . ," said Nelson. "And if someone with your dreadful parking skills can get a bloke, I don't see why I should spend my evenings all alone, forced to watch whatever I want on television, eating Pringles un-nagged, and using as much hot water as I like in my bath."

"I'll get onto it," I said. "It's my duty."

"If you say so. But, please, Mel—no low-carb nutcases," he said, pointing his fork. "No one whose dad pays her rent and definitely no one who's given their car a pet name."

"I'll do my best," I promised, as the social Rolodex in my brain started whirring.

I phoned Nicky on Monday morning to tell him about the dinner. After three attempts I finally got hold of him, at half past two in the afternoon. I finally tricked him into answering my call by withholding my own phone number.

"I cannot help you, I'm afraid," he shouted by way of greeting, in a thick Greek accent I knew wasn't his real one. "You'll have to speak to my representatives in London!"

"Nicolas, it's Melissa," I said stiffly. "I hope I'm not disturbing you?"

I only asked that because I could distinctly hear some kind of Barry

White-ish music in the background and the sound of running water. Or splashing of some kind. I wasn't very comfortable about conducting a business discussion with a client in the bath.

At once he reverted to his usual Knightsbridge drawl. "No, darling, you're not. I'm just having breakfast, actually—"

At half past two?

"—with an old friend."

At this point, a voice worryingly close to the telephone said, "Sod off, Nicky! I'm not *old*!"

"Hang on, Melissa," said Nicky, then everything went a bit muffled, as if the phone was being pressed against excessive chest hair. "How old *are* you, Charlotte?"

"*Scarlet*. I'm nineteen."

Then there was the sound of splashing. It sounded a bit like someone getting out of a bath in a huff.

I blushed at the unwanted mental images.

"And who's *Melissa*?" this old friend of Nicky's shrieked, her voice getting farther away.

More splashing.

My blushes turned to acute embarrassment, but they were tinged with creeping annoyance.

"Is this a bad time?" I inquired icily.

"No, no, everything's under control. . . . What was it you wanted? . . . Don't throw that! Scarlet, don't be a silly girl. . . . Don't throw the Krug in the bath! She's my PR executive! Do you want me to spank you?"

Splashing and giggling.

I bit my lip, mortified to feel like a voyeur in my own office on the one hand, and absolutely livid with Nicky that *he was making me* feel like that on the other. And to make things even more awkward, I didn't feel I knew him well enough to yell.

"We're going to a charity dinner in aid of sailing for inner-city kids," I said very quickly. "Dinner, a raffle, a charity auction, a few short speeches, maybe some dancing. Wednesday night. I've got a table of ten, and some of my friends are coming, so if you'd like to invite two of *your* friends to make up the table, that would be fine. I'll email you the details, but keep that night free, please?"

I didn't tell him I'd billed the entire table to Alexander. I reckoned that counted toward Nicky's charitable donation.

"And this is going to benefit me how?" he inquired. "Because you're not really selling it to me as a top night out, I have to tell you."

I bit my tongue on a caustic reply. "You're going to be seen making a generous donation to a worthy cause, there'll be plenty of photographers there who'll see you talking nicely to the charity organizers, all of whom are very well connected. You can say something about how your grandfather's yacht taught you all sorts of useful life lessons, and if you really can't bear it, you can leave by eleven o'clock."

"Pretty girls?"

"Lots," I said, crossing my fingers at the fib.

Nicky yawned. "Well, if it ticks a box for the old fella and gets this whole bullshit a step nearer finished, then I suppose I'd better turn up."

"Do that," I said.

A terrible splashing, combined with a sudden gasp from Nicky, suggested that my allotted time had come to an end.

"Oh, my God, you *bad* girl!" he groaned lasciviously, and I hung up before he could explain that he wasn't talking to me.

It took two cups of coffee and several biscuits before I completely regained my composure.

When I told Gabi I'd gotten her and Aaron a couple of tickets to have dinner at the same table as a prince, she went into a wardrobe overdrive that put Nelson's meticulous preparations in the shade.

"What are you wearing?" she demanded in her third phone call of Monday morning.

"I haven't decided yet," I admitted, shoving the phone under my ear so I could carry on typing my email.

"Yeah, right."

"Honestly. I haven't." I didn't add that when I'd tried on my fall-back black tie dress over the weekend, I'd found it rather more close-fitting than normal, on account of the croissants and that weird ten pounds of Happy Flab you always get when you move in with the love of your life.

"I read somewhere that you have to wear gloves."

"That might not be a bad idea," I said, ignoring the rumbling in my stomach. Solange had helpfully emailed me the "emergency diet" all the girls in the office used on such occasions. It seemed to involve a lot of *eau*. "I can't vouch for where Nicolas has been. Or how clean his hands are."

Gabi made a funny noise. "You're not helping, Mel! Short or long?"

"Gabi, it's a *dinner*. There will be lots of sailing types there, including Roger and Nelson, and Nicolas will probably skedaddle thirty seconds after the coffee's been served," I said. "Anyway, I'm not making a *huge* effort, because I don't want him thinking I'm tarting myself up on his account."

"Well, I will be," she said. "Aaron or not."

And then there was the matter of Nelson's date.

I had a million single girlfriends, but alas, Nelson's selection criteria were more mysterious and exacting than MI5's: it wasn't just a case of setting him up with the prettiest ones. Before the Jossy date, I'd arranged for him to go for dinner with the most gorgeous girl I'd known at secretarial college—Harriet had had legs so long that she'd had to sit at the end of the row, and every time she'd crossed them in class, you could have heard a communal hiss of sisterly resentment. Even so, Nelson had politely driven her home by half ten, and when pressed as to why the date had ended so soon would only say, "She thought the America's Cup was a pub in South Kensington."

However, I'd given the matter some thought and had found him what I reckoned would be the perfect match. Leonie Hargreaves was a friend of mine from the second of my three schools. When I'd known her, she hadn't been particularly pretty or brilliant, but she'd had a knack of calming down troublesome ponies by blowing into their ears, and I reckoned Nelson would appreciate that sort of thing. She was also very sensible about money and had been treasurer of virtually every society going—again, something I felt Nelson would appreciate more than a spectacular cleavage.

Though I hadn't seen her in years, we'd had a brief email chat after Christmas—work, family, catching up on other St. Cathalians' news, that sort of thing—and I'd ascertained at the time that she'd been single for a while, and was on the lookout for a new chap. Fortunately for everyone, she was free on Wednesday night, which I took to be a Sign. She also informed me that she'd just passed some very complicated tax exam, which I took to be an even better one.

Nicolas deigned to inform me by text message that his own invited guests would be "Chunder and Piglet"—or, as I was to put on the envelope, Selwyn Carter-Keighley, Esq., and the Honourable Imogen Leys.

"I made some calls and checked them out on the Internet at work," I confessed to Jonathan during our nightly phone call. "Selwyn seems to spend all his time being arrested for streaking at sports events, and Imogen is the heiress to some sort of ointment fortune. I think she and Nicky are an item. I have no idea what we're going to talk about. I might have to make a list of ideas and hide it in my handbag."

"You're taking Gabi," said Jonathan reassuringly. "There won't be any shortage of conversation."

I wound the phone cord around my fingers. I was sitting in the dark, the better to hear Jonathan's voice in my ear. He had a very sexy voice. I missed hearing him whisper in my ear when we were curled up in bed together.

"What are you wearing?" he asked.

Ooh. I'd read about this in a glossy mag recently: How Saucy Phone Calls Can Spice Up a Long-Distance Relationship.

"My black silk pajamas," I said breathily. "The ones you gave me for Valentine's Day. And I've just washed my hair, so it's all fresh and clean, the way you like it—"

"No," said Jonathan. "What are you wearing to the dinner?"

"Oh, um, I haven't decided," I stammered.

That was my main fear with Jonathan: saying the wrong thing at the wrong time. He was difficult enough to read when I could see him, let alone when all I had to go on was his tone.

"Although obviously I'm keen to hear about your pajamas too," he added, about two seconds too late.

I sighed. "Gabi and I are going shopping tomorrow, so I'll probably get something then."

"Nothing too spectacular," he said in what I *thought* was a jokey warning tone. "I don't want this guy getting the wrong idea and putting the moves on you. Dropping you in a fountain or something."

"Neither do I!" I said. "Anyway, it's for Nelson's charity. I promise you it's less than likely to get out of hand in any way, shape, or form."

"You're a friend in need to Nelson," said Jonathan drily. "And your granny. And this Nicky. But soon it'll just be you and me, right?"

"Right," I said.

"Now," said Jonathan in a much less brisk tone, "tell me about those pajamas. . . ."

eight

On Wednesday night, I rushed home from a tricky wardrobe consultation (Freddie Markham: allergic to all known fabrics, apart from Spandex and Kevlar) to get changed myself before Alexander's driver arrived at seven o'clock to collect me.

Nelson had already left. He loved the hysterical hours before a big event. If he could have run the dinner with a series of whistles and commands, he would have done so. Araminta was probably lining up right now to have her clipboards inspected, I mused, as I squeezed myself into my outfit for the evening: a crimson satin cocktail dress with a full skirt and a laced back that held me in to the point where more than two drinks was a complete no-no.

The exertion of doing up the lacing made me pant, but the effect it had was worth it—the resulting cushion of milky white cleavage was one that Marie Antoinette would have been proud of. I slipped on the matching red stilettos and affixed the pearl earrings Jonathan had given me for Christmas, then paused before the final part of the outfit:

My blond Honey wig.

The first time I'd pinned up my hair and slipped it on I'd felt so glamorous, and special, and free of all the hang-ups and family-inspired paranoias I'd dragged around for years. Falling for Jonathan, and knowing he'd fallen for the boring Melissa under the wig, had removed *some* of those hang-ups, but secretly, I still preferred the way I looked when I was spotlit by that halo of blondness.

Plus, the wig wasn't just about the hair. It was about letting out something else—a borrowed sass that I needed as self-defense from someone like Nicky. I hesitated for a brief second, then carried on. If you're going to fight fire with fire, you might as well make sure you have a big old flamethrower.

I slipped the wig onto my head and tugged it into place, deliberately not looking until it was sitting in exactly the right spot.

Then, holding my breath, I let my eyes lift to see my reflection in the mirror.

Wow.

My eyes sparkled, my skin took on a pale golden glow, and a long, slow smile spread across my face as my whole body seemed to elongate then settle back into a confident curve, filling out the dress.

Usually, I didn't spend much time looking at myself, preferring to ignore all the lumps and bumps as best I could, but as I applied my makeup, my face seemed to come to life. Darker eyeliner, flicked at the sides, brought out the gold flecks in my brown eyes. Deep red lipstick, the same scarlet as my dress, made me notice how full my lower lip was.

Standing back to see the whole effect, I was so pleased that I smiled at myself. What with work, and moving, and generally getting used to living with Jonathan, it had been ages since I'd looked this nice.

It was the wig that gave me this sparkle. And Jonathan seriously wanted to throw it in the Channel? Why? Did he want to pretend our Honey history had never happened?

But before I could dwell on that awkward thought, the front door buzzed. With one final preen, I grabbed my coat and bag and ran down the stairs, and when I opened the door, a gray-haired man in full green and gold livery was standing there, peaked cap and everything.

"Miss Romney-Jones?" he asked, holding out his hand to take my coat.

We descended the stairs rather awkwardly—I got the feeling he wasn't used to collecting people from first-floor flat conversions—and he directed me to a rather lovely old Bentley, which he'd parked in the middle of the road, blocking the way imperiously until I was ready.

"Are we going straight to the dinner?" I asked.

"I'm afraid we have to collect Prince Nicolas from his apartment first, miss," said the driver.

"Oh, good!" At least I'd know he would be turning up, in that case. "I hope he's ready!" I joked.

There was a discreet silence from the front seat.

Once we'd gotten under way and I'd broken the ice a bit with some compliments about his terrific sense of direction, he became much less formal and revealed that his name was Ray, that he'd worked for Alexander for thirty-seven years ("man and boy"), and that his least favorite task was collecting "that lad" from various nightclubs.

"Some nights I wait until four," he grumbled, "then he comes out, covered in God knows what, pardon my French, miss, usually with a dolly bird or two . . ." He stopped suddenly, and I could see in the mirror that he was looking stricken.

I don't know what it was, but people often told me the most personal things, even without my having to probe.

"Oh, Ray! Don't worry," I said hastily. "I'm not Nicolas's date, not that way! I'm just . . . accompanying him. My grandmother is an old family friend. Dilys Blennerhesket?"

A broad smile swept away the tension lines. "Yes, well, I'd have known that anyway from the family resemblance, miss!"

"Really?" I beamed. "Thank you!"

"You're her dead spit! Oh, now, she's a *proper* lady. One of the old school, if you'll permit me to say so. And"—he winked—"I'm not the only one with a high opinion of her."

"I adore her," I agreed. "She's the most charming person I know."

Ray looked like he was about to say something else, then changed his mind as his face gloomed up again. "Now, if Prince Nicolas could find a lady like your grandmother, I'm sure Prince Alexander would sleep easier at night."

"Mmm," I agreed as noncontroversially as I could. "How near are we to his flat? Perhaps I should call to make sure he's ready."

Nicky ignored three calls, but as we were pulling up outside a house in Eaton Square, he finally condescended to answer.

"If he tells you he's not in, ignore him, miss," muttered Ray. "My colleague Jim dropped him off from the airport an hour ago. Overnight bag, dolly bird and all."

"Nicolas, it's Melissa," I said. "We're outside your house. Are you ready?"

"Oh, no!" he gasped. "I completely forgot! Melissa, you won't believe this, but I'm actually in Hydra on a boat with some—"

"I know you're at home," I said firmly. "I can see you."

That last bit was a trick I'd learned from work. Amazingly, it never failed, even on men significantly brighter than Nicolas.

There was a sharp intake of breath on the other end of the phone. "But . . . I'm naked!" he said. "How much can you see?"

I decided to let that go. "We're outside," I went on, "so if you could put your dinner jacket on and come down here in five minutes . . . ?"

"Or?"

I tucked a strand of blond hair behind my ear. It felt quite odd, having hair that tickled my shoulders again. "Don't make me call your grandfather."

He hung up.

A mere seven minutes later, the other rear door of the Bentley opened, and Nicky slid in, his hair still damp from the shower. He was wearing a beautiful dinner jacket, with his white shirt not yet buttoned up, and he smelled of Mediterranean figs.

"Jesus!" he said, rearing back theatrically when he saw me. "Why, Miss Jones, when you take off your glasses . . . you're beautiful!"

"Thank you," I said. It was hard not to turn a little pink under such intense scrutiny, and such deep brown eyes, but I was trying very hard to be cool. Honey, I knew, would be cool about this sort of attention.

"Do you always wear wigs for dates?" he asked, looking me up and down with his unsettlingly direct gaze. He stopped assessing and winked. "Is it, like, your little kinky *thing*?"

"Of course not. It's better if no one knows who I am."

"Well, I certainly wouldn't recognize you. What did you do with Mary Poppins?"

"She's still here," I said, shifting over slightly to avoid his widespread knees. I noticed he was wearing Gucci loafers with his dinner suit. "Underneath."

Nicky gave me his most Sloane-seducing gaze. "Are you going to let me look underneath and check?"

"No," I said, as Ray set off toward The Hilton.

We drove round Sloane Square, and Nicolas used the centrifugal force as an excuse to spread his legs farther apart.

I shifted nearer the window.

He started to stretch his arm along the seat back and I twisted myself to lean against the door, out of reach. The bones in my dress dug into my ribs, but I forced a smile onto my face. He might be skilled at making passes in taxis, but I was equally well schooled in avoiding them. I hoped this was where lesson one started: teaching him that not every girl put out under duress.

"You'll rip your trousers if you're not careful," I observed.

He arched an eyebrow at me in response, and when I refused to rise to it, he said, "So, if you're in disguise this evening, what am I meant to call you?"

I hesitated.

"I mean," he went on, "people are going to want to know who I'm with. They do that," he added helpfully. "There'll be someone there to take names."

"I know," I said icily. Honestly, did he think I hadn't been to a gazillion charity dinners thrown by my own mother alone? "Don't call me Melissa. Call me . . ."

It was the logical thing to do. But it was also asking for trouble.

"Call me Honey," I said. "Honey Blennerhesket."

I must confess that it was rather fabulous to arrive at a hotel and have a liveried driver leap out, run round, and open the door for me.

Nicky flounced straight inside, but I stopped to say thank you to Ray.

"Any trouble, give me a call," he said, slipping me his card.

As I hurried through the foyer, anxious not to leave Nicky alone for too long, I couldn't help glancing into the mirrors and reflective surfaces as I passed, and each time I was quite startled by the confident blonde glancing flirtatiously back.

There were reasons Jonathan had banned the wig.

I reached the cordoned-off area where people were drinking blue cocktails, and scanned the crowd. Gabi and Aaron were standing right next to a massive anchor-shaped vodka luge, to which Gabi kept pointing excitedly and from which Aaron kept topping up his glass. Of the three outfits she'd bought at Selfridges, Gabi had opted for the very small gold halterneck dress and matching Gina sandals, and she'd forced Aaron into his black tie.

Aaron Jacobs was a futures trader in the City. He worked fifteen-hour days, earned more money than he had time to spend, and adored Gabi, in much the same way that a crocodile loves the little bird who perches on his snout and picks bits out of his teeth. Aaron had never seen me in my wig and so didn't recognize me when I leaned over and planted a kiss on his cheek.

"Gabi, seriously, I have no idea . . . ," he started, turning white underneath his tan.

"It's Mel, you plank," she said, swatting him with her teeny evening bag. "Ooh, you look nice," she added, turning to me. "Is that from your Prince-managing dress allowance?"

"No, it's my own, this time. Any signs of Nicolas?" I asked, checking the crowd. "We came together but he legged it inside and I can't see him."

"No, but your friend Leonie's already here," said Gabi. "Nelson did that whole 'Ah, hello, you must be Leonie' routine, and the pair of them went off to check that the raffle salesgirls understood exactly what they were doing with the credit card machines."

So they were bonding already over financial details. "Excellent!" I said. "And Roger? You know he's bringing this mysterious new girlfriend of his?"

Gabi shook her head. "No sign. I can't wait to meet Zara. What do you reckon? Short and so posh she's her own half-cousin? Or fat and grateful?"

"She's a model," I reminded her.

"So Roger says," Gabi snorted. "How many models does he know? She could be a hand model for all he knows."

"How about tall and gorgeous?" suggested Aaron.

Gabi and I both snorted with sarcastic amusement.

"No, baby," said Gabi. "*Blind* and gorgeous, maybe."

Aaron said nothing but carried on staring over our shoulders with such intensity that we were compelled to turn around.

Moving slowly through the crowd, which parted like the Red Sea to let them through, came Roger, miraculously shaved and coiffed but still sporting his father's moth-eaten old dinner jacket. On his arm, and getting all the attention, was a tawny blond gazelle-woman in a dress even smaller than Gabi's. And since she was close to six feet, compared with Gabi's five foot one, there was a lot more of her to cover.

"Noooo," breathed Gabi.

"Yessss," breathed Aaron, and got another swat for his trouble.

"Roger!" I said, since he was now in earshot. "Don't you look marvelous! And you must be Zara!" I extended my hand toward her. "What a beautiful dress!"

Her huge eyes went panicky, then she smiled hopefully at me and said, "Please!" Then she shook my hand, hard.

"Zara's Uzbekistani," said Roger. "She doesn't speak much English, I'm afraid."

"She doesn't need to," said Aaron. "I mean, I bet she, er, makes herself understood well enough."

"Aaron," snapped Gabi.

"Zara, this is my friend *Melissa*," Roger said, pointing to me and speaking very slowly. "And *Gabi*, and *Aaron*." He reached into his dinner jacket, took out a tiny dictionary, and proceeded to hack up phlegm in her direction, which elicited a shy nod.

"Challo," said Zara carefully. When she smiled, she looked like a baby giraffe, with her long lashes and her ludicrously long arms and legs.

"Hello!" we all cried, too enthusiastically.

"And I'm Prince Nicolas of Hollenberg," came a voice from behind my shoulder. *"Hello."*

"Chall-*o*," replied Zara, her eyes glazing slightly.

The word *prince* seemed to have leaped over the language barrier easily enough.

Nicky's arrival seemed to send an electric current through everyone. I could see Gabi positively quivering with excitement, and after a second or two of hot glances passing between Nicky and Zara, she couldn't hold herself back any longer. "Hello, Your Highness," Gabi said, sticking out her hand for him to shake. "I'm Gabi. Melissa's friend."

Without missing a beat, Nicky took her fingers, pressed them to his lips, and said, "Lovely to meet you, Gabi."

At this point Gabi nearly passed out with joy, and even I had to admit I was impressed. Only Roger looked a bit sick.

"She's told me all about you," Gabi replied, nodding toward me.

"I'm sure it didn't take too long," he drawled back, in a way that suggested he hoped very much everyone had been talking about him, for hours at least.

"No!" squeaked Gabi. Honestly, her voice had gone up a whole octave. I gave her a *Stop it!* look. Nicky wasn't *that* famous. How was I going to bring him down a peg or two if every woman he met acted like he was the most thrilling thing they'd seen since the first day of the Harvey Nicks sale?

Roger was casting despairing looks toward Zara, trying to catch her eye, but she was as starstruck by Nicky as Gabi was. I gave Roger a gentle nudge, but he only turned to me with a glum expression.

"Come on, Rog," I hissed. "Say something to her!"

"Like what?" he hissed back, as Nicky admired Zara's necklace rather too closely.

"Like . . . 'Shall we go through to dinner, *darling*?'"

I noticed that Nicolas hadn't got round to tidying up his outfit since his disheveled arrival in the car. His shirt was still open at the neck, with the tie undone, and he was standing so the gaudy orange lining inside his dinner jacket showed. His tan was honey bronze against the whiteness of the dress shirt, and a fine gold chain glittered like a gossamer thread in the dark hairs. Even as I was noting how tacky that was, a different part of my brain couldn't help melting at the exact same tackiness. He was the magazine illustration of "playboy prince," and suddenly at home in his social arena, he seemed more seductive than ever.

As he winked at Zara and Gabi's forehead creased in combined disapproval and lust, I battened down the rising tide of nerves that seemed to have bubbled up in me. If Roger wasn't going to step in and tackle this shameless routine, I would.

First thing, Mel, don't let him see you're nervous, I told myself.

"Would you like some help with your bow tie?" I asked politely. "It's customary to start the evening with them done up."

"Are you angling to do it for me?" he replied with a lazy wink. "You don't have to make excuses to get up close and personal, you know, *Honey,* Just say the word."

"Not at all," I replied, tingling slightly at the suggestive way he'd said Honey. "I thought perhaps you might be more used to the ready-tied type."

Without letting his eyes move from mine, Nicolas grabbed the ends of the bow tie and knotted it into a perfect bow in a few swift movements.

"I've done it a lot," he explained patronizingly. "Over the years."

I wished I wasn't impressed by that awful sort of showing-off, but I couldn't help it: I was.

Not that I intended to let him see. "I see you've introduced yourself to the girls in our party, but have you met Roger Trumpet?" I asked coolly. "Zara's *boyfriend.* And this is Aaron Jacobs, Gabi's *fiancé.*"

"I'm sure we're all going to get on like a house on fire," he said, looking exclusively at Zara.

"She's Uzbekistani," explained Roger. "So talk slowly."

Nicolas threw his hands in the air. "Why didn't you say?" he cried, and rattled off a lot of what I took to be Uzbek. I didn't get to see Zara's reaction, apart from some tinkly laughter, because by then

Nicolas had swept her off into the dining room, one hand moving dangerously close to her tiny model-like bottom.

Roger, Gabi, Aaron, and I were left staring at each other.

"Go on, Roger!" I urged. "After him!"

"What's the point?" he moaned, slumping against a pillar as if he'd just been mugged. "Do you know how long it took me to learn 'You look nice' in Uzbek? Might as well just go home now."

"Roger, you're a . . ." I racked my brains for something encouraging but, at the same time, true. "You're a decent chap, and he's a lounge lizard!"

"And *what* a lounge lizard," breathed Gabi longingly.

I glared at her, then at Roger.

"Oh, for heaven's sake!" I spluttered, and went after Nicky and Zara myself. Using my best wiggling-through-a-crowded-restaurant skills to ensure I reached the table first and prevented Nicky from rearranging the seating plan, I plonked myself firmly down on his left, saving my other side for Gabi. The others followed behind like ducklings.

"You're very keen," Nicky said to me with a raised eyebrow as Roger helped Zara rather emphatically to a bread roll.

"Just keen to keep an eye on you," I said, reaching for the water jug.

"That's what I thought," he replied. "Do play a little harder to get."

"No, that's not what . . ." I started, then stopped. If there was one thing I'd learned from my Honey experiences, it was that flustered reactions only encouraged men like Nicolas.

I smiled blandly at him instead, and he made a big show of checking his watch.

"I'm loving the décor," said Gabi, looking around. "Aaron, what do you reckon about these chairs for our wedding reception?"

It was easy to see where Nelson's financial nightmares had sprung from: ships could have been built more cheaply. There were vast blue and white floral arrangements everywhere, twinkling fairy lights wrapped round every vertical point, not to mention the giant ice sculpture of HMS *Victory* at the far end.

I felt Gabi's elbow in my ribs, and when I turned around she was making her "blimey!" face.

"What?" I said, following her excited nodding, and realized she was nodding toward Nelson, who was approaching our table deep in lecture with a girl I assumed was Leonie Hargreaves.

"What have you *done* to him?" she hissed, impressed.

I started to say, "Nothing," but then, looking at him again, rather lost my train of thought. I'd known for years that Nelson looked his best in formal wear—black tie, white tie, ceremonial tartans—but tonight he was a dead ringer for Daniel Craig, with his broad shoulders and freshly washed blond hair tamed. He looked so handsome even *I* had to admit to a little flutter in the chest.

"He is your best advert yet," said Gabi.

"Well, I can't really take credit . . . ," I murmured.

"I would," said Gabi. "I mean, *I would.*"

"Shh!" I said. "He'll hear you."

Fortunately, Leonie was exactly as I'd remembered—brown hair, nice figure, Laura Ashley dress. To be honest, I was quite relieved: having pitched her to Nelson as a perfectly charming, normal woman, I'd half expected her to have undergone some drastic transformation into a sex kitten.

She hadn't. And from the way she was regaling Nelson with tales of double-entry bookkeeping exams, it was clear she hadn't changed her hobbies much either.

I quickly made another round of introductions, and at once I could sense a shiver of something untoward between Nicky and Nelson. My heart sank. It was bad enough listening to Nelson's chuntering about "real" princes versus made-up playboy ones without having Nicky disliking Nelson as well.

It probably didn't help that the second before I introduced them, Nicky leaned over to Zara and quite obviously stared down her dress, garbling something in a language I couldn't make out, apart from the phrase "tit tape," followed by a dirty wink.

"What did you just say?" demanded Nelson.

"I was asking Zara how she's keeping her dress up," replied Nicky smoothly.

"Surely that's for her to know and *Roger* to find out?" said Nelson, with a meaningful look. "And if you ask me—"

"Well, let's hope whatever it is holds firm, or we'll *all* be finding out!" I said merrily. "Nicolas," I went on, to drag his attention away from Zara, "are your friends still coming?"

"Oh, God, no point waiting for Pig," said Nicky, pouring himself a large glass of wine. "She's always late for stuff. And last time I spoke to Chunder he was in Moreton-in-Marsh, so he might be late too."

"When was that?" I asked.

"About an hour ago? But don't worry, he's got a very fast car, and only six points on his license at the moment. Chill out," he added, seeing my wide eyes.

"Is this them?" asked Gabi as two figures barged through the tables.

I knew exactly what Nicky's friends would sound like, even before they were close enough for us to hear the braying. He had a round, red face, a straining cummerbund, and a ski tan that had left pale sunglasses marks around his eyes; she was pale orange, skinny, and was swishing long blond hair extensions that probably weighed half as much as she did. They both sported matching expressions that blended boredom and irritation, and I knew, with a sinking heart, that even Nelson was going to struggle conversationally tonight.

"Yup," said Nicky, standing up and waving. "Over here, Pig!" he yelled, smirking as everyone turned round to look at him.

"I think they've spotted us, Nicolas," I said. "And everyone's spotted you too, so you can sit down."

He sat down.

Roger, Nelson, and Aaron rose to their feet as Nicky's friends approached, not that Imogen made any acknowledgment of their gesture.

"God," she sighed. "I hope this isn't going to take too long—I'm bored already and I've only handed my coat in."

I shot a glance at Nicky, to prompt him to introduce us. He raised his eyebrows back.

"Go on," I hissed, suddenly realizing he'd probably already forgotten everyone's names.

Gabi and Zara were looking expectant.

I pressed my lips tightly together. I'd told him everyone's names, twice. People were always going to remember his name, on account of the prince thing; that made it even more important that he learn to remember theirs.

To my surprise, Nicky read my look and cleared his throat. "Um, Pig, Chunder, this is Honey, um . . ."

"Aaah," I hummed helpfully, as he looked blankly at Aaron.

" . . . Adam?"

I glared at him, and he quickly amended it to, "Abel . . . no, Aaron. Aaron."

"Gaaaaah," I prompted.

"Gabi," said Nicky, shooting me a look. "How could I forget Gabi."

"Are you OK, Melissa?" asked Nelson, and I nodded.

"Gabi, Zara, and, er, Richard? . . ."

"Roger," I said brightly. I noticed he didn't seem to have the same trouble with the girls' names.

"Roger, and Leonie?"

Nicky stopped very obviously as he turned to Nelson. "I'm sorry, I've completely forgotten your name."

"Nelson," snapped Nelson. "If you forget again, there's a large visual clue on the stage."

"You're a florist?"

"No," said Nelson, turning purple. "HMS *Victory*."

"Sorry," drawled Nicky, "not a big follower of English history. Anyway, Selwyn Carter-Keighley, Imogen Leys. I always forget, are you an honourable, Piglet?"

"Or just a common piglet?" inquired Gabi.

"Don't call me Piglet," said Imogen icily. "It's a pet name." She gave me an even icier look. "A special name *Nicks* has for me."

Gabi shot me a *Like that, eh?* look.

"Lovely!" I said. "Thanks for that, Nicky. Shall we get some more wine?"

"Yes," said Nicky, Nelson, Gabi, and Roger as one.

Somewhere between the starter of prawns "Mary Rose" and the main course of sea bass "Jutland," Nicky excused himself to go to the loo. After fifteen minutes he still hadn't returned and my mind was filling with all sorts of lurid waitress-bothering.

"Oh no!" I said, putting my napkin on the table. "I've totally forgotten to get raffle tickets! Will you excuse me if I pop out and get some, in case I miss the draw?"

"Do you know where to go?" asked Nelson.

"Um, no," I said, already scanning the room for dazed or panicked female staff.

"Then come with me and bring your purse," he said, pushing back his chair. "Everyone else got some? Leonie?"

"I have one," she said. "For the sake of the charity—I don't usually do lotteries. They're a terrible investment."

"Gabi?"

Gabi nodded. "Certainly have."

From the look on Aaron's face, I suspected she'd paid with a credit card.

Nelson and I ran into Nicky *and* the raffle right outside the dining room. He was standing by a six-foot anchor of white carnations, his arm extended around a buxom teenager so as best to circulate any armpit hormones, putting the charm on her. The dazzled girl's eyelashes were fluttering so hard she could only have seen Nicky in stop-go animation.

". . . and it's moored in Monte Carlo at the moment," he was saying. "Do you know Monaco, darling?"

"No," she breathed. "But I'd love to go."

Nicky's smile broadened. "It's just the place for topping up that lovely all-over tan you've got there. I can just see you on deck, soaking up the sun . . . now, tell me, have you got an all-over tan, or if I peek will I see strap lines?"

I pulled Nelson behind a pillar so they wouldn't see us. "Oh, God, he's so predictable," I murmured. "Who's that?"

"That's Araminta's daughter, Sophie," he whispered back. "She's in charge of the raffle. I'm not sure it was the best idea—I told her to write the phone number on the back of the tickets, but she's been putting her own on."

I leaned back out and caught Nicky's eye in the fleeting moment that he wasn't twinkling at the bedazzled Sophie. I could hardly go and drag him off her, in a public place, but he had to pack it in before . . . well, before anything.

"No flirting!" I mouthed crossly.

Sophie dipped her head to check something in her raffle ticket bag, and Nicky pulled a "confused" face and cupped one hand to his ear.

"Stop flirting!" I hissed, making appropriate hand gestures.

Nicky shrugged and pretended he couldn't hear me.

I ducked back behind the pillar. "I *knew* this would happen," I muttered, half to Nelson and half to myself. "He's not going to take the blindest bit of notice of me."

"You can't appeal to his decent side?" suggested Nelson.

I pulled a face. "The only side I can appeal to is the one that cares about having his allowance cut off."

"If Sophie's dad catches him looking at her like that it'll be more than his allowance that gets cut off," said Nelson. Then he tipped his head to one side conspiratorially. "Mind, you are wearing the wig. . . ."

"Meaning?"

Nicky was now making good on his tan-examination threats. Sophie's spaghetti straps were already under serious strain from her ample frontage, and it would only take one playful tweak for a "girls overboard" situation.

"Meaning," said Nelson, nodding meaningfully, "are you here as Melissa . . . or Honey?"

Right on cue, I heard Nicky say, "Oh no! I am sorry!" as he held up one inadequate, and now semidetached, strip of satin and Sophie clapped one hand to her exposed shoulder with a nervous giggle.

"Honey," I said, even as my spine started straightening up in my boned bodice and a familiar confidence began to spread through me, as if someone had been pulling a string from my toes to my head.

"I don't think Honey would put up with behavior like that," Nelson went on remorselessly. "I bet Honey would just shimmy over there and . . ."

But I was already shimmying, despite all the alarm bells ringing in my head.

I also tried to ignore the little flicker of excitement running up the backs of my legs like stocking seams.

"So that's where you've got to!" I cooed, bowling up at Nicky's right hand. "We missed you!"

A flash of annoyance crossed his face, but he soon disguised it with his usual ironic expression. "Pleased to hear it."

"Aren't you going to introduce me?" I asked, then before Nicky could respond, I extended a hand. "Hello, I'm Honey."

"My flatmate," said Nelson, appearing behind me. "And Prince Nicolas's *date* for the evening."

Nicolas shot him a dirty look at that, but Nelson just gave him his best vicar-ish smile.

"Honey, this is Sophie Belvedere," he went on. "She's in charge of raffle tickets."

"Head of in-house lottery sales," gasped Sophie, with a quick sidelong glance in Nicky's direction. "Prince Nicolas was just telling me about his grandfather's yacht," she added breathlessly. "It sounds fabulous."

"Indeed," said Nicky. "I was just asking Sophie here if she'd like to join me on a weekend cruise later in the year."

Sophie's eyelashes went into overdrive.

"Now, hang on, Nicky!" I said with a little laugh. "That wasn't quite the plan!"

"Wasn't it?" he replied, his little laugh more steely than mine.

"No!" I smiled. "The plan was, *Sophie,* that Prince Nicolas's grandfather, Prince Alexander, would offer a long weekend on the yacht as one of the top raffle prizes! He's a terribly keen sailor himself, as is Prince Nicolas . . ."

I looked at him for confirmation at this point. His jaw was hanging open slightly, but his mind was clearly working at its maximum velocity.

"Hang on . . . ," he began, but I rushed in before he could.

"I know it's awfully last minute, but Sail Away is definitely a charity both princes are delighted to be *associated with,*" I said, getting close enough to Nicky to nudge him. "And what could be nicer than offering someone the opportunity of sharing their own boat?"

I nudged Nicky again. He had the nerve to nudge me back.

"Tremendous fun, sailing," he said. "Comes in handy—learning how to tie things up, and so on—"

"Nicky would host the weekend, of course," I went on smoothly, "and I'm sure the winner would have a wonderful dinner somewhere as part of the prize—"

"I had no idea you were a sailor," said Nelson, in a tone that suggested that he still didn't. "Do you spend much time at sea? What sort of yacht is it you sail?"

Nicky looked condescending. "One with crew quarters? It's not the sort of yacht one actually sails oneself, you know."

"Ha ha ha!" I cut in, before cattiness could set in. "Anyway, sorry to spring this on you, Sophie, but Nicolas is terribly spontaneous. Why don't you pop back in and make an announcement? Let people get their checkbooks out before the main draw!"

"*Thanks,*" said Nicky sarcastically when Sophie bounded out of earshot.

"No," said Nelson, shaking his hand in a hearty English fashion. "Thank *you*. I can't wait to hear all about this boat of yours. Is it what we salty sea dogs call 'a gin palace'? That's a technical term, by the way."

"Stop it, Nelson!" I hissed.

As quickly as the rush of Honey adrenaline had swept through me, I could feel that dizzying confidence seeping away, and suddenly I was just standing in the corridor, with one irate socialite and a rather smug flatmate. I still had no idea where it came from, but when it did, it was like having a whole other woman thinking in my brain. Which made it all the more freaky when it was just me again.

I could see that Nelson was spoiling to give Nicky a short test on the history of sailing, so I packed him off after Sophie to get the raffle tickets while I steered Nicky back into the dining room.

"Listen, it's great publicity," I said, trying not to notice how well cut his dinner jacket was and how well his shoulders were filling it. "All the magazines are here—I've seen at least two photographers and someone my sister knew at school who works on *Harpers.* You'll be photographed with the organizers, you'll be helping inner-city kids, you'll be looking spontaneous and generous. . . . It's perfect."

Nicky stopped and frowned. "Is it too unreasonable to ask that you check with me before you do things like that?"

"And lose the spontaneity?" I gazed at him innocently. "Anyway, your grandfather said I could do whatever I needed to, if it made you look good."

"And what if some gorgeous married woman wins the prize? What am I supposed to do then?"

"Play deck quoits with her husband."

"You can play deck quoits," said Nicky, holding the door open for me.

"Me?"

"You'll have to come too."

"But . . ."

He paused in the doorway, his arm over my head. "But of course. Aren't you meant to be my on-call PR?"

I took a deep breath and inhaled a lungful of Nicky's strong cologne. I suddenly saw why Sophie had looked so intoxicated.

"That's why you came running over when you saw me talking to her, right?" he added smugly. "I mean, it wasn't because you just didn't like me talking to another girl?"

I dragged my attention back to my mental list of improving rules and drew up my spine so I was looking straight into his lazy brown eyes. "Yes," I said, forcing myself not to drop my gaze or blush at the arrogant way he was smirking at me. "It was because I wanted to remind you that when you take a lady out for the evening, she should be the only woman in the room as far as you're concerned."

"Even if she's my on-call PR?"

"Particularly if she's your on-call PR."

"Well, you've managed that," he said, not dropping his gaze either. "Consider my eyes strictly glued to you for the rest of the evening."

Secretly, the outrageously suggestive look that accompanied this made me go all hot and cold, and I made him walk in front of me, so I could compose myself.

Back at the table, Roger had taken advantage of Nicky's absence to engage Zara in conversation, and the pair of them were smiling and nodding away happily. Roger, especially, looked dazed to the point of slipping under the table.

"Ah," I said, sliding into the seat next to Gabi. "Look at Zara and Roger! I think they're holding hands under the tablecloth!"

"Holding *hands*?" Gabi snorted. "You think?"

"Yes," I insisted as she dug me in the ribs. "What else would they be doing? I think it's romantic!"

"Yeah, yeah," said Gabi. "You carry on thinking that then."

Chunder, or Selwyn, or whatever I was meant to call him, seemed to be in the middle of a *hilarious* mobile phone call, while Imogen's laserlike stare, which had followed me and Nicky back from the door, seemed to etch *He's mine* into my head.

Leonie began telling a glazed Gabi how much money she could be saving by moving her credit cards every six months and investing the money in short-term stocks. Aaron seemed more interested than Gabi, and was leaning over the table, the better to pick up Leonie's advice.

"So, how many cards do you have?" I heard Leonie ask.

Gabi squirmed. "Um, just five."

Aaron looked suspicious, as well he might have. I knew for a fact that she had at least eight.

"Store cards, or credit cards?" she persisted.

"Anyway, Leonie, now she's back, tell us—what was Melissa like at school, then?" asked Gabi, desperate to change the subject.

Imogen leaned forward to get Nicky's attention, so the front of her dress gaped, revealing an expanse of flat, golden chest. She had those visible bones between her neck and her cleavage, like Paris Hilton. I didn't think my body contained those bones. I'd certainly never seen them.

"Darling," she said. "Where are we going afterward?"

Nicky shot a look at me. "I might just go home," he said nonchalantly.

Imogen's face registered shock. "Home? What? Why?"

"Where's that then?" bellowed Chunder, snapping his phone shut. "New bar?"

"No, home," said Nicky. "Where I live."

"You are *so* not going home," snapped Imogen.

Gabi, Aaron, Nelson, Leonie, and Roger tried not to stare at the mini-domestic unfolding in front of them. Zara merely smiled, oblivious.

Nicky didn't bother to reply. He just raised an eyebrow, in the manner of a young Roger Moore. I couldn't work out whether I should get him to stop doing that.

"You told me that the whole point of wasting an evening here was that we could go on somewhere else afterward," hissed Imogen. She was trying to hiss in an undertone, but there wasn't really much point when we were all sitting so close together. "There's no way I'd have worn my Missoni—you promised me we'd only have to spend an hour or two with the do-gooders, then go somewhere *interesting.* . . ."

She looked around the table. We were all trying to convey utter disinterest, but I could see Gabi's lip twitching. Gabi didn't take being talked down to by posh people. There were Kyrle & Pope customers all over SW1 still trying to work out where the odd smell in their bathroom was coming from who could vouch for that.

"What?" Imogen demanded rudely.

"Were you in *EastEnders?*" asked Gabi innocently. "Only I'm sure I've seen your face before."

Imogen snorted furiously. "Of course not!"

"No, now you mention it, I'm just thinking of the *dress,*" said Gabi. "I've seen that *dress* on someone from *EastEnders.* That's it."

Imogen was about to retaliate when the puddings started to arrive and distracted everyone. They were brandy-snap baskets in the shape of sailing boats, with spun sugar sails and cargos of strawberries and cream, afloat on a sea of red sauce.

"Look carefully at those," Nelson instructed us. "Admire them. You have literally no idea how much they cost per unit. And neither does Araminta."

"They're too nice to eat," I said, watching in horror as Roger crushed his in half and scooped most of it into his mouth. Then he remembered Zara and played delicately with the rest.

"Raspberries and cream would have been more than ample," sniffed Leonie. "It's not as if most of the anorexics here are actually going to eat them."

"Absolutely," agreed Nelson, tactfully ignoring the second part as Gabi and I dug into our puddings. "You can't beat good English raspberries in season, and thick double cream . . ."

"Nelson is fantastic in the kitchen," I added, as Nelson was highly unlikely to blow his own trumpet. "Completely organic."

"There you go, Pig," said Nicky. "Not as boring as he looks."

Nelson gave him a funny look.

"I love a man who can cook, don't you, Leonie?" I went on. "There's something so sweet about eating a meal someone's gone to the bother of cooking for you."

"And why eat out when you can stay in and have the same food for a fraction of the price?" she agreed enthusiastically.

"Because someone else washes up?" suggested Gabi. "And you get to leave your flat? And dress up?"

"Lots of reasons," I said hurriedly. "But staying in's good too. Especially on a school night!"

A light went on behind Imogen's eyes, and she leaned across the table. "Don't tell me you're going home with her!" she hissed, cutting her eyes at me.

"Duh!" said Nicky offensively.

"She's going home with *me*," said Nelson, at which Nicky, Imogen, and Leonie all looked startled.

Then various clankings and bangings on the PA system suggested that the raffle was about to be drawn.

"Tickets out!" said Nelson heartily. "Here you go, Mel, these are yours," he added, handing me two. He passed a small wedge of tickets to Nicky. "Very generous of you, um, thanks."

I noticed he hadn't called Nicky by his name. None of us had, apart from me. It was quite awkward. Not only was Nicky royal but he also clearly moved in much more gilded circles than anyone Nelson and I knew, and between us, we knew some of the crustiest, tweediest English people alive.

"Good evening, everybody, my name is Araminta Belvedere," boomed a woman's voice over the clattering. As she spoke, a second wave of glass chinking and shushing threatened to drown her out. "Before we get on to the fun part of the evening, I'd like to spend a moment or two talking about the Sail Away charity itself. . . ."

Gabi, Leonie, and I adopted our listening-carefully-and-seriously faces. But Chunder took out his mobile phone again and started to dial. Imogen leaned over the table toward Nicky.

"Nicks," she said, without bothering to drop her voice. "There's a new bar opening behind Davies Street and . . . what?"

She stopped arching her eyebrow playfully when she caught me staring at her.

"I can't hear Araminta," I whispered sweetly. "Could you hold on a moment until she's finished?"

"I'm at some dinner!" roared Chunder. "No! Half an hour! Yup!"

"Sh!" shushed Nelson.

Imogen narrowed her eyes. "God, we're not at school! Who *are* you, anyway?" She looked at Nicky in appeal. "Seriously, Nicks . . . ?"

Nicolas opened his mouth to defend Imogen, and I quickly added, "Ooh, Nicky! Araminta's bound to mention you and how generous you've been any minute!"

Immediately, Nicolas focused his entire attention on the speech, and Imogen scowled, thwarted.

Araminta ran through the first batch of prizes—a case of champagne, a sailing jacket, a day's use of an Aston Martin, a really quite super toaster that I had my eye on for my wedding list, his 'n' hers haircuts at the salon Mummy went to in Belgravia.

"And as I announced earlier, the star prize"—Araminta giggled girlishly—"is a weekend's cruising with sailing enthusiast Prince Nicolas von Helsing-Alexandros of Hollenberg on the family yacht, *Kitty Cat!*"

A general "Ooh" went round the room. Nicolas rose a little in his seat to acknowledge the ooh, brushing off the ripple of applause with a modest wave.

"*Cruising* enthusiast, maybe," sniped Nelson.

"Shut up, Nelly," said Nicolas, out of the corner of his mouth.

"And we'll agree to paparazzi them for *Hello!* magazine—double-page spread!" called a voice from the other side of the room, creating another ripple of laughter and applause.

"And the winning ticket number is . . . blue, seven nine seven!"

We all scanned our numbers. Gabi seemed to be looking on her lap, as well as at the three strips on the table.

"It's me!" exclaimed Leonie, waving her single ticket.

"You're kidding me," said Gabi in disgust, throwing a second batch of tickets onto the table.

"Oh, you jammy thing!" I said to Leonie. "Did you really just have the one ticket?"

"Yes. I'm just quite lucky like that," said Leonie. "Do you know when this is likely to be? I'm not sure I can get time off work—I'm saving a couple of days' holiday to get my new mortgage sorted out."

"Don't talk to me about mortgages," I groaned, at the same time as Nelson said, "Ah, maybe you can give Mel some recommendations."

I glared at him as Leonie's eyes illuminated with thrifty zeal, but before she could launch into her mortgage advice, Sophie appeared, her strap pinned safely down with a large brooch. She leaned over Nicky's shoulder, blushing from her forehead all the way down the cleavage of her dress. "Hello, um, Your Highness, would you mind coming up to the front to present the winner with her prize? We'd like to do some photographs, if it's OK with you?"

"He'd love to," I said firmly, getting up from my seat.

"You're coming too?" asked Nicky. "Oh, yes. I suppose you have to. Make sure I don't look at anyone else."

"Why do you have to go?" demanded Imogen. "If anyone goes, it should be me."

"Why's that, Piglet?" asked Nicky.

"Because I'm your . . . oh, piss off," she snapped.

"Don't worry, Imogen," I said, smiling as nicely as I could, "I'm just going to make sure they get his best side," and I ushered Nelson, Leonie, and Nicky through the tables.

The massed cameras flashed while Nicky presented Leonie with a little wooden sailing boat in Sail Away colors, surrounded by delighted organizers, and I must admit, I did feel a warm glow of achievement.

I'd cleared the first hurdle. Nicky hadn't acted up too much—obviously he wanted this over as soon as I did—and I'd handled it pretty well. Five more months of this, and they'd be begging him to take over from Prince William.

As I was thinking this, I felt someone pinch my bum.

Since it was unlikely to be Nelson, I shifted my stiletto heel backwards and trod on the offending foot.

"Mmm," said Nicky, which was actually worse than a yelp would have been.

nine

Nelson was up bright and early the next morning when I stumbled into the kitchen in search of a cup of tea. Judging from the chirpy but flat way he was singing as he made breakfast, the joys of counting the raffle money and bagging up the cash had given him a refreshing night's sleep. The sun was practically glinting off his halo as he wielded his special omelette pan. The suave Daniel Craig of last night had been replaced by the more standard-issue St. Nelson.

"You look exhausted," he said. "What you need is a good breakfast to put some color back in your cheeks. How many eggs?"

"Just one," I said, helping myself to tea from the pot. "Saving myself for dinner in Paris with Jonathan. We're going to a very nice restaurant."

"Aha!" said Nelson, doing his fancy one-handed egg-cracking. "That ought to take away the taste of last night."

"And what do you mean by that?" I said. "I'm not hungover, you know."

"I know you're not. I was referring to the mental strain of shepherding that human virus all evening."

"You and Nicky didn't hit it off then?" I asked innocently.

"You're lucky I didn't actually hit *him*," he replied. "Though given time I'm sure it can be arranged."

"Nelson!" I protested, putting some bread in the toaster. "And I thought you'd like him, what with his sailing and everything."

"Hardly!" Nelson's good mood seemed to evaporate. "The showing off! It set my teeth on edge. 'Our Milan flat this' and 'When we were skiing' that. . . . It's just so . . . so . . ." He shook his head. Nelson came from the sort of old English family where revealing what you got for Christmas was deemed ostentatious. "And, I have to say, Melissa," he went on, looking at me like a cross dog, "I was watching the way that oily shortarse was looking at you all evening and I came very near to saying something. He's just . . . Ugh." Again he trailed off and stabbed at some bacon with his spatula.

"He's just *what*?"

"You know what I mean."

"No, I don't." Nelson could be like this—most protective of me. It was very sweet, but he did have the sort of standards of gallantry even King Arthur would have found hard to live up to.

"I didn't like the way he was treating you," he said, his nose wrinkling in revulsion. "Too much *casual touching*. And did you see the way he was sliming all over Zara?"

"Yes," I said. "I told Roger he needed to put his foot down."

"And too much bloody back chat. Especially with you. Doesn't he realize you're doing *him* a massive favor?"

"Oh now, come on, that's repartee," I said, grabbing the toast as it popped up. "I quite like *that*. It reminds me of how Jonathan and I used to flirt when we first met. I rather enjoyed it, I must admit—it only seems to happen when I'm all wigged up. The magic of Honey, and all that."

Nelson turned around in his stripy apron, his face a mask of horror. "Oh, no, Melissa. No."

"No, what?"

"Don't tell me you fancy this creep?"

"Ha! Of course not!" I buttered the toast.

"Ding!" said Nelson sarcastically.

"I'm serious. It's just . . . work."

"Jonathan was work at first," he intoned. "And look where that ended up."

"Quite," I said, taking a buttery bite. "With an engagement ring. I'm hardly going to fall for someone like Nicky when I'm about to marry a proper man, like Jonathan. So, no, I don't fancy Nicky, but if I'm going to be spending time with him, I need to be able to find him amusing in some respects. If that's all right with you?"

"It's fine with me," said Nelson huffily, going back to his pan. "I just worry about you."

I put down my toast and went over to hug him from behind. "I know. And I appreciate that."

Nelson abandoned his huff long enough to lean back in acknowledgment of my hug, but then he remembered something else. "You have checked this whole yacht business out with the *real* owner, haven't you?" he asked. "I mean, it's one thing you promising my power drill to Gabi for fixing her wardrobe rail, but promising a charity a ninety-foot oceangoing yacht's something else."

I narrowed my eyes. "How do you know it's a ninety-foot oceangoing yacht?"

"I googled the *Kitty Cat*. She's . . . rather special," he said, his mouth twisting up at the strain of admitting it. "Proper 1920s motor yacht, really stylish. Not that someone like P. Nicky would appreciate it. They're just floating caravans for rich people."

"Don't be all jealous," I said, reaching for more toast. "Alexander said I could do anything I liked, so long as Nicky started to look halfway decent."

"If I owned something like that I wouldn't want that greasy toerag anywhere near it," said Nelson. "God knows what you'd find down the sides of the bunks."

Deftly, he divided the contents of the pan between two plates and brought them to the table. I poured him a cup of tea, and we tucked in.

"And *another* other thing," Nelson went on, wagging his fork. "I've been looking into his family—how come there are hundreds of so-called princes, and never any actual kings? Too idle to step up to responsibility, if you ask me."

"Nelson," I warned. "Stop it. You're starting to sound like Daddy."

He recoiled at that. It was about the worst thing I could say to him. We'd known each other so long that he knew exactly what I thought about men like my father.

"I just don't want to see you getting taken advantage of," he said, his face softening. "You always insist on seeing the best in everyone, but sometimes you need someone there to point out the worst too."

"Oh, come on. He hasn't been that bad yet," I said, conveniently deleting the wrap dress/swimming pool incident. "Give him a chance. It's not in his interest to give me a hard time."

"Call his grandfather," said Nelson. "Just so everything's out in the open."

"I'll speak to him this afternoon," I promised. "Before I leave for Paris."

"Ah, Paris," said Nelson, with a half smile. "Don't forget my Poilâne bread, will you?"

"I won't," I promised.

Packing the remainder of my week into Half-Day Thursday was no mean feat, and checking the time and counting off the minutes until I'd be sipping my G&T en route to the reassuring arms of Jonathan made the time go quicker and slower at the same time.

Finally, I dispatched Corin Burgess after his intensive ironing class and sat down to dial the number Prince Alexander had given me for everyday inquiries. He'd actually given me two; the other was for dire emergencies. It would, he assured me, get through to him directly, or be diverted straight to their lawyer. I got the feeling that it was an arrangement that had been used before.

The phone began to ring at the other end. I slipped my heels back on, sat up straight in my leather office chair, and took deep breaths while I ran through what I was going to say. Obviously, I couldn't say that I'd offered the prize as a way of stopping Nicky from putting the moves on the organizer's daughter. And it would be gilding the lily to suggest that it had been Nicky's own idea.

I glanced at the Swiss cuckoo clock above my bookshelves. Quarter to one. The Eurostar left at ten past three, and got in at seven minutes to seven, after which Jonathan usually whisked me straight off to dinner somewhere. . . .

"Hello?" said a silky coffee commercial voice.

I felt my pulse quicken with nerves, then told myself sternly to calm down. Alexander was just one of Granny's old friends.

"Hello, it's Melissa Romney-Jones here. Do you have a moment to talk?"

"Melissa, my dear! Of course!" he said. Alexander really had that knack of making you feel like you were the only person in the world he wanted to talk to. "What can I do for you?"

I explained about the charity dinner, omitting Nicky's hitting-on-Sophie and the bum-pinching, but throwing in the leaving-early-to-go-home and the smiling-nicely-for-the-cameras.

". . . and so we thought it would be a nice gesture to offer a weekend's sailing and sunbathing as a star prize," I finished up. "It went down so well with the organizers—they rang this morning to say it's going into at least two gossip columns this evening, and I made sure Nicky said something nice about the happy holidays he'd had learning to sail on the family yacht." I paused, as the reality of what I'd done belatedly sank in. I'd taken a bit of a liberty. "Um, I hope you don't mind."

"And was this your idea, or Nicolas's?"

I swallowed. Better to be honest. "Mine, I'm afraid."

"Melissa!" said Alexander with a delicious, dark laugh. "It's a delightful idea! I applaud your quick thinking."

"Oh, good, I'm so glad," I gabbled. "The dates of the charity cruise would be absolutely up to you . . ."

"I hope you'll be joining the lucky winners?"

"Well, yes," I said. "It was actually my flatmate and his date who won."

The dark laugh rippled down the phone again. "Even smarter!"

"No, actually, that was just a coincidence—"

"Whatever you say. I am putty in the hands of quick-witted women. If Nicolas had any sense he would be too."

I blushed.

"Now, maybe you can help me," Alexander went on. "I wanted to surprise your grandmother with a little present, for her jewelry case—does she have a favorite jeweler, do you know?"

Running through Granny's favorite jewelers kept me on the phone for another twenty minutes.

Despite my good intentions, it was nearly two-thirty before I was ready to leave. I was doing my final check round the office for the one thing I always forgot, when my mobile rang.

It was Jonathan.

"So, are you set?" he said quizzically. Jonathan was never, ever late for anything. He kept his watch set ten minutes ahead.

"I'm standing on the pavement waiting for a cab," I fibbed, leaning out of the window for authentic background noise.

"Good, well, I'm just calling to check you're bringing something smart to wear tonight," he went on. "I've booked dinner at Georges, you know, that place on top of the Pompidou Center?"

"Lovely!" I looked down at the dove gray work suit I'd been planning to change out of in favor of a pretty rose-print skirt and chic black blouse. "What do you mean by smart, though? Smarter than I normally wear?"

Jonathan seemed to be in traffic or something because I didn't hear the whole of his reply. I just caught the bit about going straight there off the train, and then "pretty important" and "can't wait."

"I can't wait either, darling," I said happily.

Then, of course, the cuckoo clock had to go and chime the hour.

"What's that?" demanded Jonathan suspiciously. "You're not still in the office, are you?"

"No!" I fibbed. "I'm just walking down, um, Ebury Street, and there's a cuckoo! Ooh! Taxi! See you soon!"

I debated for a frantic few moments, then slipped into my fail-safe black dress, the one Granny had twisted my arm and my Visa card to buy, and stuffed gold flats and red heels in my bag to cover all "smart" bases.

I still got excited by the Eurostar—the chug through London's suburbs, then whooshing into the tunnel, then the very French flat fields leading up to Paris's graffiti-tagged outskirts.

When I got into the Gare du Nord, Jonathan was there to meet me on the platform, and I'd barely got my gold flats on when he started babbling happily about the exciting developments on the new job front, as well as the current one.

It was all go on all sides, apparently.

"I've been talking to some contacts here about building a client base, and the more I look into it, the more potential this project has," he said as we walked toward the taxi line. "I thought it would be a good idea to get some wheels in motion, perhaps dry-run a few moves just to see what needs work, and research and so on. . . ."

I gazed out the taxi window, listening to the rise and fall of his voice as we sped through the ratty area around the station toward the center of town. The taxis in Paris smelled different from the London and New York ones somehow, but I couldn't put my finger on exactly how. I really hadn't spent very much time here at all. It was odd to think that in a few months, it wouldn't just be my home, I'd be expected to make it home for other people.

"You look great, by the way. Very chic. Have you made a new list for exploring this weekend?" asked Jonathan, breaking into my thoughts. "I know we never get through half of your must-sees." He nudged me. "Can I trade you two cute little patisseries for a decent wine bar? We can make up for the ones we missed finding while we were in the country with your family."

I snuggled closer to him. "You know, I have other things I need to make up for besides discovering little shops."

"Really?" said Jonathan. "You're not going to learn about Paris if we just stay in all day . . . and I need you to be my expert!"

I sat up, to check if he was being serious or dry. I decided, disappointed, that he was being serious.

"Anyway, we're nearly here," he said, checking in his briefcase for something. He said something quickly to the driver, who pulled up sharply to let us get out.

I realized we were right next to the Pompidou Center—the huge industrial-looking building with its insides outside. Some students were lurking about, possibly demonstrating about something, and tourists were pointing at things I felt I should know about. But Jonathan was striding ahead, and I had to walk fast to keep up.

"I really appreciate you being so understanding about this, Melissa," he said as the doormen let us into the lift to go up to the top-floor restaurant. "I know it's a bit of an imposition, but it could be a real opportunity, and there'll be plenty of other nights out for us. I'll make it up to you tomorrow."

"Um . . . ," I began. Had I missed something here? "What are you talking about?"

Jonathan saw me looking rather blank and stopped walking. "I told you on the phone this afternoon. The couple we're meeting for dinner? To discuss relocation plans?"

"Oh," I said. "No, I didn't catch that."

Jonathan looked annoyed for one second, as I'd seen him do at work when human error derailed his planning machine. "I did explain. It's a contact I've made—could be the first bit of business for you and me, for our agency. Dom's in Paris for business meetings tomorrow, and Farrah's here with him for some shopping, and we managed to find a window for an informal discussion. Just a chat." He put his arm around me, subtly hugging me and moving me along at the same time. "I knew if they met you, met *us,* it would make a far better impression than just me talking on the phone. You're my secret weapon! Half an hour with you and they'll want to move out tomorrow, so long as you're in charge."

"Oh, I don't think so," I said. But even though I could see his point, a stroppy part of me couldn't just let our romantic evening go, not just like that. "The thing is, Jonathan, I was really looking forward to it just being us tonight. I've really missed you! Can't it wait until the morning? I'm not feeling very prepared."

"Sweetie, it was the only time Dom could do," he said. "He's a busy guy. I'm sure they'll need to go somewhere else afterward, so if you want we can take our dessert somewhere different? Get ice cream and walk along the river, maybe. Hey, how about that? Our evening can start over then."

He squeezed me again, and I felt a churlish desire to stamp my foot, even though I knew how childish that was.

"It's for you *and* me," Jonathan reminded me. "Our business. That's what you want, isn't it?"

"Yes," I said, conscious that we *had* spent lots of unplanned time with my family recently. He hadn't made a big deal about that. Fair's fair, I told myself, but I wished I'd learned some French menu vocab on the train.

The severely clad hostess led us toward a table where two people were already seated. I tried not to let my head swing from side to side at the spectacular décor so as not to seem touristique, but it was stunning: long red roses in the middle of each table, stainless-steel floors, and huge white leather chairs. And the view over Paris was so amazing that I could hardly drag my eyes from it to watch where I was going. Obviously, the clientele was ignoring it.

I looked round at Jonathan, to make a last-minute plea to keep it short so we could be together on our own, but he was already making "Hiiiii!" gestures to the couple at the table.

I battened down my disappointment until later and put on my professional pleased-to-meet-you face.

"Melissa, may I introduce Dom and Farrah Scott," Jonathan said. "Farrah, Dom, my fiancée and business partner, Melissa Romney-Jones."

"Hello!" I said, shaking hands and sitting down. "You'll have to excuse me. I've literally just stepped off the train."

"Oh, I hate the Eurostar," said Farrah. She pushed back a thick wodge of toffee-colored hair from her face so I would get the benefit of her French manicured nails. She was, as Gabi would have said, "expensively put together": highlighted, buffed, tanned. Immediately, I felt as underdone as a damp crepe.

"We flew in," explained Dom. "It's pretty quick from Manchester. Where we operate from. I mean, people always calculate time to Paris from London, but I always say, Come on! There *are* other business centers in the UK!" He gestured to the waiter to hurry up with the wine lists.

I hadn't been in Paris long, but one thing I had learned was that it was impossible to speed up a French waiter.

"Dom and Farrah are relocating here from Cheshire," explained Jonathan. "Dom works in venture capital, and Farrah is a PR executive."

"How interesting!" I said. "Who do you work for?"

"For myself," she replied. "I have my own company. FSPR. Farrah Scott Personal Redefinition."

"I'd always go to a woman for PR," said Jonathan. "You're just so much better than guys at really knowing how to play things. Melissa has her own management agency in London, but of course when we launch she'll be coming on board with me to offer that sort of service alongside mine."

"Yeah?" said Farrah, raising her eyebrows at me. "Like concierging?"

"Um, well, something like that," I said. It was very hard to explain The Little Lady Agency without sounding like a hooker, no matter how many times I'd been through it. "I act as a sort of freelance . . ." I nearly said *girlfriend,* but stopped myself, just in time. ". . . a freelance advisor for single men who need a bit of help keeping everything running smoothly. You know, all the things girlfriends do for free!"

Farrah didn't give me the amused eye roll of recognition I normally got. Instead, she stared at me as if she didn't know if I was joking or not. Even as I watched, I saw a certain contempt set into her expression.

I swallowed. Dom was already grinning at Jonathan, but I knew I'd hit the wrong note with Farrah. It did sound a bit antifeminist, when you put it like that. "I mean, there's a lot in that old saying that if men had to pay their wives they'd never be able to afford the overtime," I stammered, trying to recover my composure. "Which is where I come in, to sort out their wardrobes and streamline their diaries and arrange decent parties and—"

"We don't need our wardrobes arranged," she said. "I have a stylist in Altrincham. So does Dom."

"Melissa's being modest—she's more a life coach than a concierge,"

Jonathan stepped in. "And her focus in our partnership will be facilitating your move so you can hit the ground running, and not have to worry about where to send the dry cleaning, that kind of thing."

"Yes," I said, looking over at him. It wasn't exactly what I did, but . . . "I like to find out where the nicest markets are, and which boulangerie has the best croissants, and where you can walk your dog. You know, the sort of things you might not have time to find out otherwise. Things that really make you feel you're settling in."

"That sounds sweet, but we don't get a lot of time for relaxation," explained Dom. "I think we'll be flying back to the UK at weekends, if at all possible."

"But you can arrange grocery delivery and dry cleaning and a personal trainer—things like that, yeah?" asked Farrah. "Because I'm just not going to have the time, and it would be good to know that was being taken care of. Bills, taxes, water rates, yeah?"

Jonathan was looking at me expectantly, and I heard myself say, "Well . . . yes, I suppose so!"

Groceries? Dry cleaning? Was I going to be some kind of upmarket chalet girl?

"Whatever you need, I'm sure Melissa can find the answer," said Jonathan smoothly. "She's an expert in making people's lives easier."

I smiled. I was starting to get a bad feeling about this.

The pouty waiter appeared, and I ordered the delicious-sounding duck. Farrah ordered the salade niçoise but without the dressing, the anchovies, the potatoes, any additional salt, and half the tomatoes.

It was going to be a long meal, I could tell already.

We chatted about Paris for just over an hour—or rather, Dom and Jonathan did—and eventually Jonathan had the bill brought over, after Dom had failed to catch the waiter's eye for fifteen minutes.

Jonathan, I noted, paid, so subtly that it was hard to spot when he'd actually done it.

"Thanks for a really rewarding discussion," he said, shaking hands as we left. "That's given us a lot of points to focus on."

"Us too," said Dom. "You've got a great idea there—the technical and the homely at the same time. Like it a lot."

"Anything you need to know," said Jonathan, "you've got my number. You too, Farrah."

She paused in the arranging of her scarf. "Well, actually, I'll need to find a trainer."

Jonathan looked at me. "Over to you, Melissa!"

"A trainer?" I repeated. Was she a part-time high jumper or something?

"A personal trainer?" Farrah raised her eyebrows. "I don't care how much it costs, but whoever Kylie Minogue sees would be good."

"Um . . ." I felt floundery. Personal trainers? That was something I knew *less* than nothing about.

"That's the kind of insider knowledge that Melissa's so good at getting," said Jonathan confidently.

My heart sank. "Um, yes!" I said, in response to a gentle nudge from Jonathan. "Absolutely!"

"Listen, guys, we'll be in touch," he said, and we all shook hands again and went off into the Paris evening. Dom and Farrah toward some trendy new bar that I pretended to have heard of, and Jonathan and I toward a coffee somewhere considerably less trendy, I hoped.

True to his word, we headed toward the river, where Jonathan bought me an ice cream, and we walked along the Left Bank, listening to the jostle and gabble of buskers and street sellers, soaking in the fresh spring atmosphere.

I'd have been more soakable if my mind hadn't been racing, trying to work out how on earth I could find out what the trendy members' clubs were in Paris.

"That went well, don't you think?" said Jonathan. Now we weren't in a business situation, he'd reverted to the familiar off-duty Jonathan I knew and much preferred. By off-duty, I mean he'd taken his cuff links out and rolled up his sleeves a little, revealing fine strands of pale gold hair.

"All thanks to you, though," he added. "Dom thought you were great. It's a smart move, you know, letting them feel that no detail is too small. Bills, clubs, cleaners . . . builds confidence in the whole package."

"So are you actually organizing Dom and Farrah's move right now?" I asked.

"In a manner of speaking."

"Oh." I licked my ice cream. "Does that mean you've handed in your notice at Kyrle & Pope?"

He paused. "Not yet. Not exactly. You want another glace?"

I peered at him out of the corner of my eye. It really wasn't like Jonathan to be so evasive.

"No," I said. "I'm OK with this one. So when are they moving?"

"It depends. I'm looking at a couple of properties for them, but they're looking at September now too."

"And when are you going to resign?" I stopped walking and looked at him. "What's the timetable? Because obviously I need to resign from my clients too."

I ignored the little flip in my stomach as the words left my mouth. I kept saying these things bravely as if it would make it seem more real to me, but if I were being honest, it was harder than I thought. I kept telling myself that Jonathan was making sacrifices too, but when grown men yelped at you over the phone because the Little Lady Agency Christmas present service wouldn't be available . . .

Jonathan smiled and shrugged. "I hadn't fixed a date beyond September, but we can if you want. Say . . . September thirtieth. How about that?"

"Don't you have to give Kyrle & Pope more notice?" I asked curiously. "It'll take them ages to find someone who can take over from you."

"I'm . . . hmm, playing that one by ear, shall we say," he said, slipping his arm around me in a distracting manner. "Anyway, that's quite enough business. Here we are, walking along the Seine—how much more romance could you want?"

"None," I assured him, as I leaned happily into his side and pushed my misgivings as far away as I could.

ten

My knowledge of Paris was based largely on films—*An American in Paris, Paris When It Sizzles, The Day of the Jackal* (Nelson's favorite)—and to an extent, my weekends with Jonathan didn't disappoint.

His apartment, for a start, was in an old-fashioned building in the Marais, hidden from the street by one of the anonymous gates I found so fascinating. Jonathan had picked up the "in" areas immediately, and he took great pains to demonstrate how close we were to the Place des Vosges, a huge seventeenth-century square where aristocrats had once paraded and where chic young mothers in Puffa jackets now wheeled their Puffa-jacketed offspring.

I was much more excited about wandering through the boutiques and narrow alleyways of the Marais and beyond. I made lists of places and things I wanted to find for my own interest, as well as for the benefit of future clients—the glowing brass and glass cafés on the Left Bank where every customer looked like a philosopher or a writer, the higgledy-piggledy flea markets at Porte de Vanves, and the stalls of old books in the Latin Quarter. There were so many gorgeous details to drink in about Paris. Even the Metro was stylish, with its Art Nouveau flourishes and decorated station walls, unlike the spare Underground signs (and the frankly incomprehensible New York subway, all numbers and no names). I wanted to eat tarte au citron and drink noisettes at polished counters and wear cropped cigarette pants, and buy a scooter and swan around in my own Truffaut film.

In real life, though, I couldn't find a pair of cigarette pants that didn't make me look like a bowling pin, and Jonathan refused to get a scooter. The romance of my arrivals seemed to have worn off because he also insisted on spending most of our time together trekking around residential areas. Everywhere I looked there was another dramatic set of wrought-iron carriage gates with a mysterious courtyard just beyond, or another boutique with one perfect red leather bag in the window. Jonathan indulged me for maybe an hour, then insisted we get back to business. I tried to tell him that it was my business to know where to get the perfect bag, but he laughed and dragged me away to the next "up-and-coming area."

But on balance, if I could just get over my innate English fear of feeling stupid when I tried to speak French (and taking it personally when the French speaker sniggered at me), I didn't see why Jonathan and I couldn't make a little corner of Paris's bustling village our own.

When I came back on the Eurostar on Monday, I brought some delicious 1950s glass teacups I'd found for the office in a flea market, and some fresh Poilâne bread for Nelson. I also brought back the delicious Parisian May weather.

My mood was further improved when I called in at the newsstand on the corner to get the new week's magazines, and discovered, on picking up the new *OK!* and *Hello!* that Nicky's appearance at the Sail Away dinner had made the back pages, albeit tucked away in a corner.

"Someone you know, love?" inquired the newsstand guy, as I squeaked with delight at the phrase "Prince Nicolas of Hollenberg revealed his boyhood enthusiasm for the delights of the ocean wave, while generously donating a cruise on the family yacht as the star prize in the raffle."

"Yes," I said, beaming. "Me!"

I showed him the page: it was just a tiny picture, but you could clearly see me standing next to Nicky, with Nelson and Leonie in the background. We all looked glassy-eyed and shiny of forehead, but Nicky looked perfect, staring into the camera with a practiced smile.

"Ooh, dear," said the newsstand guy, looking at the magazine, then looking at me. "It's true what they say about the camera piling on the pounds, eh?"

"It's the way I'm standing," I said stiffly, then realized he thought I was Leonie, the only dark-haired girl in the picture.

"Who's that blond bird?" he went on in more approving tones. "What a cracker! Eh? Eh?"

"Quite," I said, and hastily swept up the magazines, grabbed the new *Tatler* and a packet of chocolate digestives, paid, and left.

Once I got in and changed into my work clothes, I checked the messages, then settled down with a coffee to peruse the magazines properly. One of the perks of my office was that my accountant (Nelson) encouraged me to spend lavishly on glossy mags to write off against tax as "research." Obviously, I then had to devote time to reading them too, also for "research."

There was a little shot of Roger and Zara too, probably because, apart from Nicky, she was the only one of us who looked sufficiently glamorous to belong there. Her cheekbones stood out a mile. So did Roger's horrible hand-me-down dinner jacket, although I had to admit his new clean-shaven look was making him seem almost eligible. Chunder and Piglet were also featured under their real, betitled names, positively snoring with ennui, alongside some cricketers and a couple of friends of my mother's.

As I was turning the page to see if I recognized one of the chinless men lurking in the background, the office phone rang.

"Hello?" I said, hoping it would be Jonathan.

It wasn't.

"The Little Lady Agency?" I said again. "Good afternoon!"

There was a long pause at the other end.

"Hello?" I said, again. This wasn't unusual. Clients called me in states of high agitation. Sometimes they were hiding from their not-quite-ex-girlfriends, or trapped by the tie in their washing machines, or paralyzed with indecision in the household appliance section of John Lewis.

"I Iello?" I said one more time.

"Melissa?" said a surprised voice.

I put the pen down. "Hello, Emery," I said heavily.

Emery's phone manner was enraging. She always managed to sound surprised when someone answered, and she quite often appeared to have forgotten who she'd rung up to begin with.

"I can't speak for long," she said, in a more focused way than normal. "I'm in the garden and I've got a leak issue."

"A leek issue?" Emery wasn't what you'd call a keen gardener.

"No, a *leak* issue, I mean, with my . . . you know. Anyway, Mel, you've got to come home."

This was the way things used to be in the Old Days. Before I'd started my agency and gotten some self-respect and a backbone, I'd forever been plagued by imperious Romney-Jones demands to "pop home" to run up some curtains or placate a furious cleaner. But gone were the days when my family could summon me like a dog.

I didn't mind *listening* to Emery from afar, though. "What's happened now?"

"Daddy's acting up about what to call the baby, and he and Nanny Ag are at daggers drawn over the nursery, and Mummy's knitting weird baby jackets instead of Allegra's animals. I found her yesterday using Braveheart as a model."

"Em, come on, that's just normal," I said. "Can't you get Nanny Ag on your side? She likes you."

Emery's patented sigh gusted down the line.

Still, I wasn't falling for that.

"Well, what about William?" I asked. "Isn't he home to back you up?"

"He's had to fly back to Chicago for work. Anyway, he and Daddy fell out about . . . oh, I don't know, he shot something he shouldn't have."

Poor William. Reduced to stalking the estate in search of fresh food. I felt my resolve waver in a rush of sympathy, but I stiffened. It was a slippery slope down to organizing the whole darn shooting match, and what with Nicky and swotting up on tailors and manicurists in Paris for Jonathan, I just didn't have time.

"Look, Em, you're a mother now," I said. "You've got every right to put your foot down about things. Just tell them! Try shouting."

"I tried shouting. . . ." Emery's voice wobbled, and I knew her limpid blue eyes would be welling with tears. "It was too weird. I was nearly sick. I knew it would be like this. Just come back for the evening? Please, Mel? We're meant to be talking about the christening, and Daddy's stressing us all out about the guest list already."

I looked at the diary. Now that I wasn't going to have to break it to Sebastian Ogilvy that red jeans hadn't been in fashion since the late eighties, I could leave the office at 3 p.m. And I supposed Gabi could come over and talk about her catering plans over lunch, rather than after work . . .

"You could pretend you were coming home to see Braveheart," said Emery, a little too quickly for the one Romney-Jones supposed to be too ethereal for machinations. "I can say I rang you because he was off his food, or something? Please? You could set off really early in the morning and be back at work by ten. And," she added as the coup de grace, "I *need* you, Melissa. I need my sister here. I mean, Allegra keeps popping up to yell at Mummy, but she's not the same as you. She scares the hell out of poor Baby."

There was a pause while I imagined Allegra flitting malevolently around the nursery like something out of "Snow White."

"Please?" she added, her voice wobbling.

"Oh, God," I said, caving in like a sand castle. "Fine. Just make sure Mrs. Lloyd makes something nice for supper, because I'm not driving all that way to argue over a bowl of mulligatawny soup."

"Fab!" said Emery, sounding better at once, before she rang off.

Hating myself for being such a pushover, I made another pot of coffee and helped myself to the box of magnificently rich French chocolates I kept in the top drawer of my desk, to be doled out as daily rewards. It was a diet trick personally recommended by Solange. ("Just have a little of the best, Melissa." Disapproving stare at my stomach. "That is the trrrouble with the English. You stuff yourself with rrrrubbish.") I could see where she was coming from, but due to the stressful nature of my work, I'd already scoffed nearly the whole top layer.

Picking up the phone again, I rang Nelson at work, to let him know I wouldn't be in for dinner.

"But I've got some nice Welsh lamb chops!" he said, sounding disappointed. "I was going to cook them tonight. Can't you just ring home, have them put you on speakerphone, and tell them off from the comfort of your own kitchen?"

"No," I said glumly. "They'd all just shout at once. Anyway, I thought if I went now and offered some advice, it would save time later."

"The only thing that would save time with your family would be to put them on television and let the public vote them into space, week by week," said Nelson.

"You don't know the half of it," I said, thinking with dread of the horrors in store at the christening. Daddy was bound to invite every relative he wanted to show off to. It could run into hundreds. "Anyway, I'll be back tomorrow morning, so rather than waste it, can't you—"

"It won't go to waste," he said airily. "Leonie's coming round."

"Leonie?" I felt an odd twinge in my stomach that might have been jealousy. Nelson cooking romantic dinners-for-two instead of our cozy sofa suppers? "You didn't say she was coming for *dinner.*"

"Didn't think I had to," said Nelson.

"Oh. Of course not," I said. "Um. I didn't realize you two had reached the dinner-at-home stage."

"I thought it might be nice to get to know Leonie a little better, before we have to go off sailing for a weekend," said Nelson patiently. "For someone who was doing a good impression of Cupid last week, you don't sound very pleased."

"Oh, I am. If there's going to be lots, why not invite Roger too?" I said quickly.

"I might," said Nelson, sounding a bit odd. He paused. "There isn't a *reason* you don't want me to invite Leonie, is there? You're not . . . jealous, are you?"

"No! No!" I exclaimed. "No! I just thought she was a bit . . . dull. That's all. But anyway, it's absolutely up to you who you have for dinner. I'll be back tomorrow, so save me any leftovers!" I said a bit too cheerfully, and rang off.

When Gabi came round for her lunchtime chat about canapés, she was more robust in her opinion.

"Leoneezer Scrooge is coming for dinner?" she exclaimed. "Oh, God help Nelson. They'll spend all evening comparing credit card rates, then haggle with the minicab about how much her fare home will be."

"You didn't take her advice about putting a little away each week for your pension then?"

"No," said Gabi, opening her copy of *Brides*. "And you can tell Nelson to tell *Leoneezer* that I won't be taking her advice about going to the Isle of Man for my honeymoon instead of Barbados either. It isn't 'just as romantic.' I'm not going anywhere Aaron can watch Sky Sports."

"Hmm." On paper, Leonie was just the girl for Nelson: financially responsible, good job, attractive, not prone to Sloaney shrieking or watching reality TV. Everything I'd wish for him. So why couldn't I feel happier about it?

Gabi looked up when I didn't respond. "Don't worry, Mel," she said. "She'll start telling Nelson to cut back on his organic olive oil and that expensive deli habit he has, and he'll give her the flick soon enough."

"I'm not *worried*," I said. "I . . . just want him to date more people till he finds, you know, just the right girl."

"The right girl. You're waiting for him to *find the right girl*?"

"Of course I am," I said. "He deserves someone really fantastic."

Gabi's eyes widened. "Yeah, right, Melissa," she said mysteriously, and went back to making notes on mini Yorkshire puddings.

I drove home to find a strange silence filling the house. I don't think I had ever come home to silence, other than the time Mummy had had a sushi evening and everyone had had to be kept in at the cottage hospital overnight.

"Hello?" I called, letting myself in.

My voice echoed in the empty hall as I looked through the post lying on the table. Normally everyone leaped on the post the moment it hit the mat, but today's was still lying there. Mummy's subscription copy of *Harpers*, some letters from the bank, circulars . . .

I recognized the distinctive blue notepaper Jonathan's solicitors used, and I picked up the letter. It was addressed to M. Romney-Jones.

How odd, I thought. I wonder why they've sent it here, and not to our new address in Paris? Maybe it was some tax arrangement.

"Melissa!"

I spun round to find my father standing right behind me. Strapped to his chest in a suede papoose was Emery's baby, opening and shutting his shiny round eyes in sync with my father's rapid blinking. He seemed to be growing very quickly and had already developed adorable little bracelets of fat around his wrists and knees. The cute effect, however, was almost completely counterbalanced by the sheer incongruity of his being attached to a middle-aged schemer in a tweed jacket.

The fact that they shared identical squashed red noses was plain spooky. It was like Daddy had found a miniature of himself.

"Daddy!" I said. "Hello!"

I spotted Emery peering over the banister at the top of the stairs. When she saw Daddy, a thwarted look crossed her face and she vanished.

"Where is everyone?" I asked. "I thought—"

"Is that letter addressed to you?" asked Daddy, wagging his finger.

I looked down at it. "Well," I said, "it's from Jonathan's accountant, and it's addressed to M. Romney-Jones, so I assume it—"

"Esq.," said Daddy, snatching it off me and tucking it into the papoose behind the baby. "M. Romney-Jones, Esq. And they should have put MP. Come this way," he went on before I could ask what on earth Jonathan's accountants were doing writing to him. "I expect you'll need a cup of tea after your long drive. You look worn out."

I ignored the insult and let myself be shepherded toward the drawing room. This display of pleasantness could only mean Daddy wanted a favor, and that meant I needed my wits about me.

"I thought I'd come over to check if Braveheart's shots were up to date," I explained. "I'm not staying—"

"You can stay as long as you like," said Daddy, making himself comfortable in his armchair. The baby's fat little legs stuck out cutely, but any desire to nuzzle them vanished as Daddy leaned forward and said, "Now, there's something I need to discuss with you."

I swallowed and thought of the letter. Had Jonathan got his solicitors to arrange a prenup? That would make sense, even if it wasn't terribly romantic.

"You'll be aware that my book is about to go into its major second phase of promotion," he said, as if it had been selected for the Booker Prize. "And I need the family to rally round with the publicity plans."

"Ah, yes," I said quickly. "I got the schedule, and I'm afraid that I'm going to be in Paris for the dates you suggested—"

"I don't want *you*, Melissa," Daddy interrupted. "I was after that prince you're dating. If he could come along to the baby's christening, it would help publicity no end. Emery and I are thinking of asking him to be a godfather."

"I'm not *dating* him," I protested. "You can't just *borrow* him for publicity, Daddy. Besides, I don't think Nicky is really the sort of person I'd trust anywhere near a baby."

I couldn't see Nicky as a responsible godfather. A Godfather, maybe—in his own imagination.

Daddy peered at me and the baby leaned forward with him, its little forehead puckering. "I don't expect him to do it for nothing," he said. "What sort of, ah, encouragement do you think he'd need?"

I boggled. "Encouragement?"

"Sweeteners, Melissa," said Daddy crossly. "Cash. Honestly, sometimes I do wonder where you sprang from."

Before I could reply, the door burst open and Mummy stormed in, with Allegra in hot pursuit. Mummy paused for a second when she saw me, flashed a quick smile in my direction as she usually did for the press in moments of political embarrassment, then went back into rage mode.

"If he's trying to get you on his side, then ignore him!" she snapped, pointing an accusing finger at Daddy. "It's Emery's decision, not his!"

She sat down on the chair opposite his and glared at him so hard I thought his hair would burst into flames. Allegra flung herself on the sofa. I noticed that she was carrying a ball of knitting wool and a pair of needles.

"Cast on for you, Mummy?" she inquired.

"Yes," snapped Mummy. "It'll stop me injuring your father with the needles."

"Do keep it down, Belinda," said Daddy in injured tones. "Think of his little ears." And he put his hands tenderly over the baby's head.

"Where's Emery?" I asked.

"I'm not sure, darling." Mummy grabbed the needles off Allegra and started knitting angrily, her fingers almost knotting in the wool. A self-satisfied smile spread across Allegra's face. "She went for a lie-down after lunch, and we haven't seen her since."

"And Nanny Ag?"

"Annexing the nursery," said Allegra. "And, given half a chance, annexing Emery, then the kitchen, then the rest of us, the power-crazed old trout."

"I see." I clapped my hands on my knees. "So . . ."

The clock ticked as everyone glared at each other.

I tried to think of something easy and nonconfrontational to talk about.

"I can't keep calling him Baby McDonald," I said cheerfully. "Has Emery decided on when he's going to be christened?"

Like a mighty river bursting through a dam, it all kicked off, punctuated by the startled yapping of Braveheart and Jenkins, who had been sleeping behind the curtain on the forbidden window seat.

". . . really not up to you, Martin! If Emery wants a New Age ceremony it's her decision . . ."

". . . ludicrous, irresponsible, just what I expected . . ."

". . . nothing wrong with Tiger as a name, for a *dog* . . ."

". . . Martin is a perfectly good name . . ."

". . . yeah, maybe for an *old man* . . ."

". . . bloody mutts under control then we wouldn't need to Febreze the tapestries . . ."

". . . William's feelings?"

A short sharp clapping of hands brought everyone to an abrupt halt, dogs included. Standing at the door, with her hands on her hips, was Nanny Ag. Standing next to her, her head hanging like a guilty schoolgirl, was Emery. Even the fact that she'd already managed to squeeze her boyish hips back into her precious Earnest Sewn jeans didn't seem to be cheering her up. She looked as if she'd spent the past three days in a tumble dryer.

"It's time for Baby's feed, Mummy!" announced Nanny Ag, marching toward us with her arms outstretched. "So I'm going to have to take him off you, Granddad."

"I'm really not too keen on this Granddad and Grandma business," said Mummy, wincing. "Can't he just call him Martin?"

"No," said Nanny Ag. She had to raise her voice over the furious wailing now emanating from the baby, who had also turned himself cherry red in protest at being plucked from the bosom of his grandfather.

Daddy smiled smugly.

"Here you go, Mummy!" said Nanny Ag, depositing the squirming, screeching infant in Emery's unwilling arms. "Now then," she said, addressing us, "Mummy will see you in the dining room for her own supper in half an hour, before getting a nice early night." She turned her fierce gaze on the dogs, whistled once, and, to my astonishment, both trailed toward the door, tails between their legs. Jenkins looked so contrite that his ears dragged along the floor.

Gosh, I thought. *No wonder Emery phoned me.* It was just surprising she hadn't asked for a file in a cake as well.

Looking on the bright side, supper was a marked improvement on recent fare. A security chain had been installed on the fridge, and until Braveheart learned how to crack combination locks, Mrs. Lloyd's groceries were safe.

Granny arrived just as we were about to sit, making me wonder if Emery had called her in as reinforcements too. And then Emery herself appeared at the same time as the salmon terrine and toast corners. She looked stunned.

"Fresh from the milking parlor!" observed Allegra. "Our very own little Buttercup."

"Do shut up, Allegra," said Emery, wafting toward her seat. "Better a milk cow than a drugs mule."

I looked up in surprise, as did Allegra. Motherhood seemed to be taking some of the vague off Emery.

"Well, darlings, now we're all here, maybe this is a good time to discuss the christening, I mean . . . naming ceremony." Mummy sent a nervous glance my way.

"I don't see what's to discuss," said Emery calmly, helping herself to some toast.

"You can't have my first grandson named in some hippie woodland frolic!" roared Daddy. "I won't have it!"

"No one's asking you to *frolic*," she said. "Just wear a garland."

"A garland!" said Granny. "How chic!"

"What about names, first?" I asked hastily.

"Martin," said Daddy at once. "Family name."

"No, it isn't, darling," said Mummy, "it's *your* name. Anthony has the family name, since he's the oldest."

Daddy was the youngest of four sons. His eldest brother, Anthony, had gotten the nominal titles, Uncle Gilbert had gotten the brains, Uncle Tybalt had moved to Australia to farm, and through some family skulduggery so complex even Daddy hadn't seen through it at the time, Daddy had been landed with the house no one had wanted on account of its leaky roof, uncertain foundations, and threadbare furniture. This had powered his all-consuming ambition to become an MP and somehow avenge himself on the lot of them.

"Anthony is an effeminate name," huffed Daddy. "Fit for hairdressers and tennis coaches."

"I have a list," said Emery to me. "And so does William. He emailed me his third version this morning. What do you think?"

She passed me a piece of paper and I read aloud. "Tanguy, Parsifal, Basil, Gascoigne, Ptolemy and . . . Jasper."

I looked up.

Mummy, Daddy, Granny, and Allegra were looking green. Emery carried on eating her terrine.

"Right," I said. "I take it those are your choices? OK. William has picked Austin, Alonzo, Drake, Becker, Lyle, and Jimmy."

"Now, Drake I like," said Daddy, jabbing his butter knife in my direction. "Add Churchill, Winston, Bannister, Redgrave, Isambard, Kingdom *and* Brunel . . ."

"What are *you* leaning toward, Emery?" I asked.

"I like Parsifal," she said. "After Granddad Blennerhesket. Percy, for short."

"That's nice," said Mummy. "Isn't it, Mummy? Remembering Daddy like that."

"Um, yes," said Granny, "but it's not a very 'little boy' name, is it? Percy."

"I rather think he looks a bit like Daddy," said Mummy fondly. "Don't you, Martin?"

"Oh, absolutely. The red face?" suggested my own father. "The red nose? The fixation with eating and sleeping?"

"Do you have any more suggestions?" asked Granny pointedly.

"I don't mind Austin," said Emery.

"After the good old British motor manufacturer?" beamed Daddy.

"No," said Emery. "After the American city where William and I had a nice minibreak. I'd be happy with Parsifal Austin."

"Really?" I asked. "You're sure?" It just wasn't like Emery to be so definite.

A more familiar consternation muddled her expression. "Well . . . I quite like Ulysses too."

"No, darling," said Mummy. "He'd have to be awfully handsome to carry that off. You have to choose a proper name."

"If you'd only thought of that when you were choosing a name for me," said Emery crossly, "I might not have spent fifteen years of my life being called *Board.*"

We all tried to muffle giggles. Poor Emery, not being the sharpest tool in the box, had assumed Board was some reference to her flat chest and had stuffed her bras furiously until someone had explained the joke to her. By then she'd been seventeen and had started to be called Socks instead.

"Well," said Mummy with a pointed look down the table, "if your father had been sober enough to make himself clear to the vicar, you would have been called Emily Jane, as I specifically requested."

"And if your mother hadn't been so out of it at the christening, she might have noticed the silly arse of a vicar getting it wrong," he retorted.

"I had thirty-one stitches!" she snapped. "And you had a crate of Dom Perignon!"

This was news to me. I'd just assumed Daddy had assumed Emery would be a boy, then had refused to budge on his weird name choice.

"What?" demanded Emery, flicking her gaze between the two of them. "You mean I wasn't even *meant* to be called Emery?"

"Not really," said Daddy, helping himself to the last bit of toast. "Still, hasn't done you any lasting damage. Anyway, why not call the little chap Percy—I'll be reminded of Wasdalemere's dreadful poetry, and that ridiculous table tennis he used to make us all play after dinner. God, I can just hear him now . . . 'Your serve, Dilly?'"

Granny threw her napkin on the table. "He is not going to be called Parsifal, and that's an end to it!"

I was surprised to see just how upset she seemed. Since Granddad had died, she'd had quite a merry widowhood, but maybe this was stirring up sad memories for her.

"I know!" I said, as a genius idea struck me. "If you want to call him in memory of someone we all loved, I can think of the perfect name!"

Four faces turned to me, baffled.

"Emery! Your first pet!" All our dogs were buried in their own special graveyard in the woods, with proper headstones and everything. Mummy planted dog rose bushes on each one.

"Bodger?" Emery wrinkled her nose. "I can't call him Bodger, Mel. Nice idea, but that would be weird."

"Bodger was a cat, darling, he doesn't count," said Mummy as she turned to me, her eyes sparkling with tears and love. "She means Cuthbert!"

"Cuthbert!" we cried with a wash of affection, even Daddy. Bertie had been our first basset hound. When he'd died, we'd all worn black for a week and buried him with his basket, blanket, and half a pound of mature cheddar.

"Wonderful idea!" cried Granny. "Bertie McDonald! I'm in love with him already!"

"I'll let William choose the rest," decided Emery graciously.

The next morning, I had to get up at some unholy hour to get back to London before the rush hour started, long, long before anyone else managed to drag themselves from their pit.

But to my surprise, as I crept downstairs to make myself a quick cup of coffee to brace me for the M25 ahead, I caught a flash of black and white movement in the kitchen, and for a moment, I almost believed Mummy's ludicrous stories of the violated cavalier maid her psychic advisor insisted lurked around the servants' quarters.

On closer inspection, however, I realized it was nothing of the sort: it was Nanny Ag.

"You're up early," I whispered, putting on the kettle.

"Routine!" she bellowed with scant regard for the others sleeping. "Mummy needs to be woken to express milk at six forty-five, then Baby has his first feed at seven!"

"Six forty-five?" I said incredulously. "But Emery's knackered!"

Nanny Ag gave me a reproving look. "We don't like words like that. The queen would say 'fatigued.'"

I swallowed and tried to batten down the rising feeling that Nanny Ag, far from being the beacon of reliability I'd remembered, was actually something of a bossy-boots. "Can't she wait until half seven?" I tried with a persuasive smile. "She's really awfully tired. And the baby seems to be sleeping pretty well."

"Mummy and Baby need their routine. They both need waking for a feed. They'll thank me for it later," she said, putting a couple of dry crackers on a plate.

"That's not for Emery, surely?" I asked, peering at the crackers. "Doesn't she need something a bit more . . . nutritious? Look, I can whip up a bit of French toast if you like. I learned to do it when I was a chalet girl, and I'm actually . . ."

Nanny Ag turned to me and gave me the Glare of Disapproval, not to be confused with the Glare of Disappointment, and, worst of all, the Glare of Dismay. "Melissa. Nanny knows best. No one's at home to Mrs. Meddler. What this house is crying out for is some order!" And she picked up her tray of dry crackers and sterilizing equipment and made for the stairs.

A terrible picture of poor Emery being wrenched from her warm bed flashed through my mind—not to say the idea of Bertie being woken after only just dropping off. He wasn't going to like that.

I don't quite know where it came from, but in a flash I was at the door, blocking her way. "Nanny Ag," I said sweetly but firmly. "You will kill everyone in this house if you try to introduce order all at once. They can't go cold turkey like that. Why not leave it until half seven?"

We glared at each other for a second or two.

Slowly, Nanny Ag put the tray down on the kitchen table. "You never used to be so headstrong, Melissa," she said, with a note of wounded disappointment.

"No," I agreed, and picked up my car keys from the table.

eleven

What with constant baby-related calls from home, French refresher CDs, and my appointments around London with Nicky, I'd barely have noticed fresh spring turning into warm summer if it hadn't been for the cherry tree outside the office blooming and then fading with the heat. Well, that and the slow but sure blooming of Nicky into a much less oily person altogether.

As the weeks went by, I'd set about implementing my list of improvements, starting with getting him fitted for a proper suit at Huntsman and persuading him to play some tennis at Queens Club instead of just propping up the bar. After a couple of polite face-offs, he finally seemed to be bending to my will—or else imagining life without his allowance. Which is to say, he now answered my calls on the second attempt. I called that progress of sorts.

From the incessant texts he sent me, Jonathan also seemed to be making progress with plans for our new business, though he was still rather cagey about when he was leaving Kyrle & Pope. But then I was being equally cagey about how I planned to wind down the agency. Gabi suggested saying nothing to my clients until the last moment, then pretending I'd been abducted by aliens rather than upsetting them, but Nelson wouldn't hear of it, so reluctantly, I drew a line through my appointments diary after September 30, and made myself stick to it. I kept telling myself that it wasn't so much the end of a book as the start of a new chapter—in French, with a coauthor—and I tried really hard to get myself excited about my perfect excuse to learn about French shopping.

One Wednesday morning, Jonathan rang my mobile as I walked down the tree-lined street to the office. Despite the bright sunlight, I was still half asleep, but from his caffeine-buzzed tone he'd obviously been at his desk for ages.

"Hi, sweetie," he said, then before I could reply, breezed on, "you member Farrah Scott? Dom's wife?"

"Oh, yes!" I said, rubbing my eyes. "Was the trainer OK?"

By pulling every string I could think of, and calling in a favor from someone I knew in the Foreign Office (don't ask), I'd managed to find Farrah a very fashionable trainer, who did hardcore British Military Fitness, but around the smarter streets and parks of Paris.

"Fabulous. Can't wait to start when she gets here. In fact, Farrah called me yesterday because she wants you to check out the right club to join in Paris. Somewhere she can hold client meetings."

"A members club?" I asked, now fully awake. I'd been dreading a request like this. I knew most London places pretty well, but that was after years and years of meeting different people who went to them. But I had no idea at all about Parisian clubs—and not knowing many people who knew Paris that well meant it would take me ages to learn which were which, and who you could expect to bump into in the loos.

And as for getting Farrah onto the membership list . . .

"Um, I'm not really sure I can—" I began, but Jonathan cut me off.

"I told her that was exactly the sort of thing you were so good at," he said confidently. "You can look into that for me, can't you? Ack, I've got a call coming in—listen, we'll talk later, OK?"

"OK," I said since there wasn't really much else I could say.

Feeling rather ambushed, I climbed the stairs to the office and let myself in. There was only one message on the answering machine, and I played it as I took off my jacket. "It's in the paper today, Melissa," squeaked Poppy Lowther, a friend's younger sister who'd done a favor for me.

I'd no sooner finished listening to the message when the phone rang. But before I could even get my normal Little Lady office greeting out, I was cut short by a ferocious snarl.

"What the *hell* are you doing getting me banned from Greens?"

"Nicky!" I said reproachfully. "Is that the way to greet a lady?"

Nicky replied with something that definitely wasn't the way to speak to a lady, especially before ten o'clock.

"If you're going to talk to me like that, I'm going to have to hang up on you," I said with some regret. Regret for myself mainly, because though I wouldn't dream of letting on to Nicky, the office had taken on a more glamorous hue just from his call. "Don't make me do that. I've only ever had to twice."

"You will not hang up on me," growled Nicky. "Tell me what you're playing at—or have you just gone mad? I tried to get into Greens last night for a drink, and the silly mare at the door wouldn't let me in."

"Oh, that."

"Yes, *that*." He spoiled the effect of his growling by coughing with the effort. It was, after all, very early for him. "Do you realize I just about keep that place afloat? There are not one but two champagne cocktails named after me."

"Well, I haven't seen the papers yet myself, but if you look in this morning's *Daily Mail*," I said serenely, "you will see a story in the gossip column, all about how Prince Nicolas of Hollenberg has been banned from the notorious society—"

"The *Daily Mail*?" demanded Nicky. "Hang on, there's a copy here."

I heard scrabbling. "Where are you?" I asked.

"Up," he said. "And that's all you need to know." I strained my ears and picked up the flicking of pages, and from the clinking in the background, I guessed he was in a coffee shop somewhere. Or still in a bar. "Is there a photo?" he added, unable to control his vanity.

"Yes," I said. "I supplied one."

There was a howl of horror as Nicky found the page in question. "Jesus and Mary! You're kidding! I look like—"

"You look like a jolly nice chap," I said. I'd sent them a photograph I'd snapped during one of his fittings at Huntsman for his new suit the previous week. Stripped of his open-necked-shirt-and-Gucci-shades combo, Nicky had actually looked rather sweet in a normal white shirt.

"I look like a total dork!" he roared. "And . . . oh, my God! 'Besotted fans of playboy Prince Nicolas of Hollenberg will have to seek him out elsewhere now he's banned from his usual haunt, Chelsea private members club, Greens. Society doorgirl Poppy Lowther revealed that doe-eyed Nicky has been banned for good behavior.' Good behavior? What the hell is that about?"

"Well, if you read on, Poppy will explain," I said.

" 'Once known for his wild antics and drunken exploits, recently the eligible young aristo seems to have turned over a new leaf. From what I've heard,' says clipboard princess Poppy, 'Nicky's days of Nazi uniforms and pole-dancing with Olympic show-jumpers are over. He used to party all night then stay for our famous Brunch-of-the-Dog, but now he's into his early nights. I've even heard he's started detoxing! And we can't have that sort of behavior here—we've got a reputation to maintain!' " There was a pause, then Nicky continued, in a more suspicious tone, " 'Rumors are circulating that this new leaf might have something to do with Nicky's new flame—a mystery blonde who's replaced ointment heiress Imogen "Piglet" Leys as his regular party popper.' "

It was my turn to be outraged. "What?"

"Oh, don't play the innocent," said Nicky. "You told them to put that in, didn't you?"

"I most certainly did not," I protested. Blood drained from my face, then rushed back into it.

Party popper? I'd been to *one* dinner with him! Well, and a couple of parties. And a quick frogmarch round an art gallery, then a coffee afterward that had sort of turned into lunch at the Ivy. Oh, and a cocktail reception at the Irish embassy.

" 'Sources close to the prince are hinting that this curvy honey has got London's most eligible bachelor abandoning strip clubs and police cells for golf clubs and wedding bells.' Curvy *honey*? Don't tell me you didn't plant that!"

"But I didn't! I mean, generally yes," I said, flustered, turning pink, "I admit I got Poppy Lowther to say that—she's the younger sister of one of my old clients, and I did drop the story to a friend of mine who works with Richard Kay at the *Mail*, but I definitely didn't—"

"Thank God there's no name," said Nicky. "Yours, I mean."

"Well, quite," I said.

"You should be relieved," he went on. "You don't want to see Piglet when she's mad. I've seen her throw people."

"*People*?"

"Don't laugh. She gets you round the knees and hoists, like you're a caber. Some Scottish Army bloke taught her. Broke Cully Hatton's collarbone at Cowes last year."

"Oh," I said, making a mental note to stay outside grappling distance of Imogen Leys in future. "Oh, dear. Well, I'm sure if she knew the whole story—"

There was a faint snort at the end of the line.

"What?" I demanded, suddenly conscious that Nicky actually seemed to be prolonging the call. My senses abruptly went into panic mode as I counted down the seconds until I said the wrong thing. "I suppose you're imagining Imogen chucking me now, are you?"

"No," chuckled Nicky, rather sweetly. "I'm imagining you chucking Imogen. I'd say you were about a match for each other. I've got to hand it to you, Melissa—banned for good behavior? God Almighty. You're so going to ruin my social life before this is over. Any other clubs I should know about?"

"Not so far."

"You realize, thanks to you, I'm going to need a whole new set of friends at this rate? The ones I've got think I've gone mental. Ha!"

As his tone turned more conversational, I started to relax and tried to picture what he'd be doing on the other end: laughing, rolling his eyes at the same time, scratching at his ear as I'd noticed he sometimes did when he was amused at something.

My skin tingled, and I reminded myself that Nicky flirted with everyone. Not just me.

"Well, just keep remembering how much this means to your grandfather." I twisted the phone cord around my fingers. "I mean, would it kill you to stay at home with a DVD instead of falling out of a nightclub?"

"Depends on the DVD," he said saucily. "Unless . . . Melissa!" he gasped in fake delight. "Are you offering to stay in *with* me? Is it a date?"

"No," I said. "I am not offering. Daylight hours and well-lit evening engagements only."

Nicky sighed. "I'll have to stick to clubs you don't know about then," he said darkly.

A thought suddenly occurred to me. "Nicky," I said, "I don't suppose you're a member of any clubs in Paris, are you?"

"I might be," he replied. "It depends if you're going to get me banned from them."

"No, no, not at all," I said hurriedly. "I, er, I just need to find some details for a client. Someone's moving to Paris and needs to know where the right places to go are. I said I'd look into it for them."

"Seems like an odd way to do it. Shouldn't they ask round themselves? See if they like it, like the people?"

"Well, yes, that would be the way I'd go about it," I agreed. "But they're moving fairly soon, and to be perfectly honest with you, I don't know the city very well yet."

"Ah, but I do," he said. "Had some top nights out there. Who's the client? Man? Woman?"

"Man and woman," I said, my heart thumping. "Fashionable, young married couple. Very, um, modern."

"Hmm. OK," he went on, to my surprise. "Leave it with me."

"Would you? I'd be so grateful!" I said, visions of Jonathan's impressed face swimming in front of me.

Nicky let out a long breath, which sounded inappropriately

intimate, gusting luxuriously as it did straight into my ear. "Good. I like to have favors owing with beautiful women."

Ooh, I thought with a little thrill: "*beautiful women.*"

"Are you flirting with me, Nicolas?" I asked sternly.

"I'm trying," he said. "It's quite early, you know."

Too late, I saw the bear pit of owed favors open up in front of me, but I rallied myself before Nicky's radar could pick up any distress signals.

"I'm glad you're up and about," I said, "because that means you haven't forgotten about the polo match we're going to this afternoon."

"How can I forget any of the appointments I have with you?" he drawled playfully. "Even if I could, you've written them in my diary."

Now that *was* flirting. I felt the blood rush to my face, and I had to pull myself together before it showed in my voice. "Ray's picking you up at one o'clock at your flat. Smart casual, please. And shave. Prince William will be playing."

"Just checking—you haven't put me down to play too, have you, Melissa?" he inquired. "I mean, polo isn't another of my hidden passions, like sailing?"

"No," I said. "But supporting elephant charities is."

"Elephants! How nice. Would you like me to bring anything for the raffle?" he bantered on ironically. "A car, maybe? An elephant? Or should I prepare to surrender my Rolex at short notice?"

I smiled despite my best intentions. "Just yourself will be quite satisfactory."

"I always aim to satisfy," he drawled, and I could virtually see his dark eyes twinkling as he peered over the top of his Gucci shades.

I had several sneaky reasons for escorting Nicky to the charity polo match at Cowdray. First of all, Alexander had sent me the tickets with a charming note about this being one of the events of the Season he enjoyed most, but since he was unable to attend, he'd consider it a huge personal favor if Nicolas and I could represent him there. More to the point—as Alexander and I both knew and didn't need to say— it was yet another occasion where there'd be photographers and columnists from the usual glossy magazines who could write about him being polite and sober, and the more evidence there was of that in the press, the better.

Thirdly, Prince William was playing. And I wanted Nicky to experience the novelty of not being the most important person there.

Did that sound mean? It wasn't meant to. I just wanted Nicky to see that he didn't need to be the center of attention all the time. That his title wasn't the only interesting thing about him.

I was slowly putting together my own explanation for why Nicky was such a dreadful attention seeker, and, more to the point, what I could do about it. I'd realized very early on in my Little Ladying that with most clients there was always something under the surface that needed fixing, sometimes not even related to the ostensible problem. Nicky was no exception.

I'd gathered from a chat with Granny that he'd been brought up by nannies at home with Alexander and his grandmother, Celestine. Nicky's mother, Oriane, had spent "her better years" schlepping around Europe with rock stars, and she had been recovering from it ever since. As far as Granny knew, Oriane now lived in the south of France, where she made bead necklaces that sold for ludicrous amounts in Ibizan boutiques, while poor Jean-Marc the racing driver had just vanished, apparently, in 1982. Whether it had been of his own accord, even Granny didn't know.

Obviously, all this, even without one being an evicted semi-royal, would give anyone a complex. Granny assured me Nicky was seeing "at least" two therapists. But in the short term, how could I put a lid on the resultant fooling around?

It was Nelson, ironically, who'd given me an unwitting clue when he'd been grumbling to Roger over the phone about "the Nicker-snapper." Roger had taken agin Nicky about as badly as Nelson had, although with rather more cause, if you asked me, given Nicky's shameless flirting with the object of Roger's affection. To listen to the pair of them, you'd honestly have thought you'd been in an old biddies' tearoom somewhere.

"I know," Nelson had been saying. "He thinks everyone's looking at him, even when they're not! And it's not even like he's a real prince!"

I'd glared at him across the room and made *pack it in* motions. This whole "real prince" thing was getting rather old.

Nelson had roundly ignored me. "If you ask me, he has to have people staring at him, or else he'll realize he's just a common, cheesy freeloader. If people stop looking, he'll stop existing!"

Long pause, while Roger had obviously let rip at the other end.

"I don't think Zara really thought that, Rog."

Another long pause, accompanied by much forehead-furrowing.

"Don't worry, Roger." He'd turned round at this point and said, talking down the phone but staring straight at me, "No, I have no idea what sensible women see in men like that, either." Then his eyes had rolled, and he'd sighed heavily. "Roger, no, I don't think he's in denial about being gay, mate. Sorry."

At that point I'd gotten up and left the room before he could see I'd been Googling for photographs of Nicky in his swimming trunks.

I went through the rest of my morning's appointments in a rather distracted mood. My mind kept shuttling back to the newspaper and whether Alexander—or anyone—would think I was up to something, getting myself mentioned alongside Nicky. A couple of times I nearly put down my pen and went out to get a *Mail*, but each time the phone rang and a fresh new crisis emerged, until finally, at quarter to one, Ray, Nicky's driver, called for me, and I had to leave for the polo match.

"Looking very lovely today, miss, if you don't mind my saying so," said Ray as he opened the door of the Bentley for me.

"I don't mind at all!" I said, slipping onto the soft leather of the backseat. Under heavy persuasion from Granny, I'd finally taken myself and the credit card Alexander had given me to Selfridges and let the personal shopper pick out a simple blue and white polka-dot wrap dress, which was a much more expensive version of three other dresses I already owned.

Somehow, though, with the Honey wig, it looked substantially less simple.

"Late night, last night," Ray informed me as we waited outside Nicky's flat.

"Really?" I sighed. "Oh, dear. Where?"

"Round at his friend Selwyn's in Notting Hill."

"Not out on the town?" I said hopefully.

"No," said Ray, sounding surprised. "And, if you ask me—"

Sadly, Ray's opinion was lost, as Nicky chose this moment to slide into the car next to me, and the atmosphere changed as if someone had turned on the lights.

"Hello, Supernanny," he said, leaning over to kiss my cheek.

I pretended not to be bothered, but a sudden wave of butterflies flew up from the pit of my stomach, fluttering high up in my chest, making my skin tingle and my heart beat faster. The temperature in the air-conditioned car seemed to go up a few degrees, and I felt hot under my thin cashmere cardie.

He was wearing a white shirt, jeans, and a dark jacket, transformed into glossy mag style by an air of careless confidence, and his thick, dark hair was rumpled, as if he'd just gotten up. It was probably a look he'd spent all morning working on, I reminded myself.

"There you go," he said, passing me a bit of paper, "your list of Paris clubs. And I thought you might like to see this," he added as we set off, and chucked a copy of the *Daily Mail* at me.

"Thanks! I really appreciate that, Nicky." I slipped the list of clubs in my jacket pocket and flicked through the paper to the offending page, trying not to seem bothered.

There it was: the small photo I'd taken of Nicky in the bottom left of the page, next to a cutout of a beaming Poppy Lowther in skintight jeans. I scanned through the lines: "Prince Nicolas . . . eligible young aristo . . . curvy honey . . . ointment heiress . . ."

I felt my face burn.

He took the paper off me, rolled it up, and rapped me playfully on the arm. "It's going to take me years to rebuild my reputation after you've finished with me."

"Yes," I said, trying to keep my expression nonchalant, "but at least you'll *have* a reputation."

"Of sorts." He settled back in his seat and carried on reading. "Anyway. Well done. The old man will be chuffed. What's your star sign?" he added, shaking out the paper.

"I thought only girls were interested in that sort of thing," I said warily.

"Which is precisely why I am. Come on, what's your star sign?" He twinkled his brown eyes at me, and something inside me melted. Not on purpose. Like when you accidentally leave ice cream out.

I heard myself say, "Pisces," and only just stopped myself from adding, *February twenty-ninth.*

"Pisces . . . Pisces . . . 'A significant other disapproves of your current plans—stick by your guns. Your instincts are always right.' Hmm." He looked over the paper. "Does that mean that stick-in-the-mud flatmate of yours? Nelly?"

"No!" I said quickly. "And don't call him Nelly."

Nicky gave me a sly look. "I bet he calls me worse."

"Not at all," I lied. P. Nicky had just been the start. The Fake Prince of Bel Air, Slick Nick, Nicker-snapper, were just some of the more repeatable variations bandied about between Roger and Nelly.

Nelson.

"Ah, my mistake!" Nicky pointed his finger at me and looked pleased with himself. "It's the *fiancé* who's disapproving."

"You make *fiancé* sound like some kind of illness," I observed.

"Nothing wrong with engagements," said Nicky airily. "I've had three of them myself."

"And?"

He peered over the paper. "I got treatment for them. Cleared up in no time. Hmm. What's the fiancé's sign?"

"Capricorn," I replied automatically, and immediately wished I hadn't.

"Oh, dear," said Nicky. "Cash, cars, and credit cards, eh?"

"What?"

"Capricorns. It's all they care about. Security. I bet he's got three houses and a pension plan, eh?"

I could feel myself blushing. That was true, but also . . . not the point. "Astrology is a load of nonsense," I blustered crossly, feeling very protective of Jonathan. "Anyway, I think you'll find Capricorns are meant to be great lovers."

"Oh, yes," said Nicky. " 'Lie back and think of the Bank of England, darling.' Don't argue with me about astrology, you romantic, imaginative Pisces. I've made a point of knowing all about this nonsense. Girls love it."

"Well," I said, bristling at the condescension, "maybe if you spent more time brushing up on *proper* topics of conversation, you'd spend more time with intelligent *women* and . . ."

My voice trickled to a halt as Nicky lowered the newspaper and gave me the full force of his amused stare. As we passed by some trees, summer light dappled onto his tanned face, and I noticed just how smooth and flawless his golden brown skin was. My fingers twitched to touch it, to see if it was soft, like suede or peaches.

A few very charged seconds passed as he smoldered at me and I pretended to look disdainful. Inside, though, I was glad I'd remembered to put down the thick leather armrest between us. I wasn't sure whether he was having me on, with all this "Hey, ladeez" routine. Whether it wasn't just a private joke he was sharing with me, because he knew that I knew it was all an act.

Or was it?

"Pisces—very good at living double lives and *very* good at getting drunk." Nicky held out a finger toward me, as if reading my mind, then pushed a hank of blond hair behind one ear. "And, yes, there are the telltale enchanting eyes."

While my mouth was still open in protest, but before I'd thought of what to say, he winked and added, "I bet you just love having your feet rubbed, don't you? Amongst other things."

"That's enough!" I said, and grabbed the paper.

We drove through the gates of Cowdray Park, and Ray parked up next to a veritable showroom of gleaming limousines. Bentleys, Jaguars, Audis—most with uniformed drivers hovering protectively around.

"If he plays up, call me," Ray muttered as he opened my door to let me out. "I can easily take him round the block a few times."

"I'll bear that in mind," I muttered back under the cover of a smile. Ray tipped his hat to me and nodded.

Nicky and I made our way across the grass toward the large marquee, and as my heels sank into the damp grass I was glad I'd remembered to put a spare pair of shoes in my bag. We'd only gone about three steps, however, before Nicky had his phone out and was texting.

"Ah, I'll have that," I said, swiping it out of his hand.

He spun round as if I'd made a grab for his testicles. "What the hell are you doing? Give me that back!"

I dropped it into the echoing depths of my handbag and clipped it shut. "No, sorry. Can't have you getting distracted from the day's events, can we? Or taking snaps of Prince William on your camera phone."

Nicky's lovely mouth dropped into an unattractive sulk. "As if," he said. "He's very dull. And balding."

"Is he? But then he is the heir to a throne. I mean, a really big one. I'm rather looking forward to seeing him," I went on cheerfully, approaching the girl with the clipboard. "Hello there, it's—"

Nicky barged in front of me, but in a manner that made it look as if he'd been gallantly saving me from having to talk to her. "Hello. Prince Nicolas of Hollenberg." He paused. "And guest."

"Good afternoon, Your Highness," she said with the blush that I'd grown accustomed to seeing on women's faces when Nicky turned on the charm. "If you'd like to have a glass of champagne, the first chukka will start at three."

"Can't wait," he said with a sideways glance at me, but I followed him as closely as a three-legged racer toward the bar.

The main tent was decked out as splendidly as a London hotel reception room, with huge white floral decorations and arty bits of glass everywhere. Twenty or so large tables dominated the room, with heavy silver cutlery on the white tablecloths and four or more vast crystal wineglasses on each setting. The gentle tinkle of light jazz from the quartet in the corner was disturbed only by the equally gentle tinkle of champagne flutes and the flick of Cartier lighters as the other guests floated around, networking furiously.

I must admit that my eyes were skating from satin-swagged pillar to satin-swagged pillar, taking in all the faces to see who I knew. When I say "knew," I don't mean there was anyone there that I knew *personally*, but as Gabi would have put it, the place was like an *OK!* TV special. I spotted half the emergency ward of the television program *Casualty*, Kate Middleton, Sting, and Lizzy Jagger (not together). And that was just in the queue for more champagne.

"Are you going to follow me around all afternoon?" demanded Nicky, as three girls dressed in much smaller, spanglier outfits than me went into spasms of preening on the opposite side of the tent.

"Yes," I said. "Unless I can trust you not to get up to anything stupid, and I'm not entirely sure I can just yet."

"Oh, Melissa," he began with a charming sigh.

"Honey," I corrected him.

"Oh, Honey, that just turns into a challenge."

"It's not meant to," I warned. "I checked what happened last time you came to one of these. The extra-ball-on-the-pitch trick? Not going to happen this time."

"That," he said, pointing at me, "was a great laugh."

"Not," I said, pointing back at him, "for the woman who was knocked out by the extra ball when the referee man wailed it off the pitch. Don't deny it. I have researched your antics thoroughly."

Nicky made a *what can you do?* face.

"No one's looking at you," I said firmly, very aware that this time I didn't have Nelson, Gabi, and Roger for backup. This was just me and him, so I had to convince him I was beyond disobeying. "They're here to gawk at Prince William, be photographed, and drink their body weight in free champagne. You're here to listen with concern when the charity women make their speech, be photographed making small talk with the oldest guests here instead of molesting the waitresses, and to leave at a reasonable time, because you need to study for your postgraduate degree."

"My *what*?"

I flapped my hand. "It just occurred to me. It would look good if you were seen to be training in something you'll need for taking over from your grandfather. Economics, or international politics or something."

"You don't think you're taking this a bit too seriously?"

I shook my head. "Not in the least."

"Oh, God," sighed Nicky, but I dragged him off to say hello to the lady from the elephant charity. Alexander had helpfully sent me a list, and I intended to make Nicky work through it.

After thirty minutes' intensive mingling, Nicky pulled me to one side.

"Come on," he said, steering me toward the exit.

"Where are we going?"

He stopped and widened his eyes at me. "The loo. Obviously, you don't trust me to go in alone, so . . . you can get two in the cubicles at these sort of dos. Sometimes more. Don't ask me how I know that, by the way."

"I'm not coming to the loo with you!"

"No?" He tipped his head to one side, and his dark hair flopped over in a thick wave.

"No!" I knew I was blushing and wished I hadn't been—I knew he was trying to embarrass me.

Nicky rubbed his hands. "Excellent. Well, I'll see you back here then. Don't bother waiting. I'll find you."

I realized I'd fallen straight into his trap. "I could do with a walk," I said airily. "And the polo's about to start, anyway."

We made our way through the little clusters of silk-stockinged women and guffawing men, onto the wooden veranda and over to the elaborate Portaloos.

When Nicky vanished into the cabin, I rummaged in my bag for my phone.

Nicky's phone, however, came to hand first and abruptly beeped with a text message.

It was one of those phones where the first bit of the message came up on screen automatically, WHEN R WE MEETING 2NITE?

PIGXXXXXXXXXXXX, I read. Alongside a revealing snap of shimmering bony cleavage.

And, just as I was wrestling with my conscience about having read Nicky's message, that was followed by: HAV U DUMPED PORKY YET? And the cleavage again.

Furious, I typed, CAN'T MAKE TONIGHT, AM STAYING IN. Then, I added, in case that sounded too out of character, HAVE HEADACHE. Then I pressed Send just as Nicky reappeared, deep in conversation with an ash-blond woman with coltlike legs in gold sandals.

I dropped the phone into my bag as if it had been red-hot.

"Why don't we all have a fresh glass," he was saying, then hissed, "Was that my phone?" at me, as he steered us both back inside the pavilion toward the champagne table.

"No! No, it was mine. Hello," I said, extending my hand toward the lady. Now she was right next to me, I realized that she was an astonishingly well-preserved older lady. How old, I couldn't tell. "I'm Honey Blennerhesket."

"Georgina von Apfel." She took off her huge shades and gave me a very searching look. More searching than one expects at a social event. Her perfectly made-up eyes seemed to be taking all of me in and processing me accordingly. "Honey Blennerhesket?" she asked coolly, shaking my hand. "Are you related to Dilys Blennerhesket? You look just like her."

"Yes," I said. "I'm her granddaughter."

"Georgie's an old friend of my grandfather," explained Nicky. "From New York."

"More an old friend of your *grandmother*, Nicolas," she corrected him, not letting her eyes leave me. "Darling Celestine. How we all still miss her."

I sensed there was a whole sea of implication there that I wasn't getting, but suddenly a shoal of waitresses engulfed us, and suddenly I had a glass of champagne, a program, a mini macaroon, a cucumber sandwich the size of my thumbnail, and an ironic sausage on a stick to juggle. Plus my bag hanging off my forearm like a deadweight.

"I'm so sorry," I said, trying to balance it all.

"Nicolas, you're forgetting your manners," iced Georgina. "Do take Honey's bag from her while she sorts herself out."

"I'm not carrying a woman's *bag*!" began Nicky petulantly. "And have you felt how heavy that thing is?"

"Take it!" she snapped, and he took it, and set it on the ground.

"Oh, that's better," I began, but right on cue, my phone began to ring. Apologetically, I unloaded my food and drink onto a nearby table and rummaged in the murky depths of my handbag.

It was Jonathan. He'd already phoned three times and sent a terse EMERGENCY. RING ME SOONEST text. My heart sank, then started beating in double time. What had happened?

"I'm so sorry," I said again, "but I really have to return this call. It's an emergency."

"Don't let us stop you," said Nicky with a glint in his eye. "Why not step outside? No rush."

"I will," I replied, pocketing his phone too, just to be on the safe side. "Mind my handbag, won't you?"

Nicky adopted his angelic expression, which made his wicked brown eyes seem almost innocent.

Obviously, if I'd known what was going to happen next, I wouldn't have taken that phone call. Not even if it had been the pope offering to christen Emery's baby, with Gordon Ramsay on hold offering to cater Gabi's wedding.

twelve

My nerves jangled as the phone rang at the other end and a variety of awful possibilities presented themselves, escalating with every unanswered ring. When Jonathan did pick up, my heart felt as if it had bounced right up my throat.

"Jonathan?" I said as I walked urgently away from the pavilion, almost falling over myself in my haste to get somewhere private. It wasn't easy, in my heels, on the grass. "What's the matter?"

"Have you got that list of members clubs you said you'd check out for Farrah?" he demanded.

I stopped walking and nearly bumped into a pair of lissom dark-haired teenagers, who glared snootily at me. But I was too shocked to care. That was what constituted an emergency? I'd assumed Jonathan had been hurt, or that there'd been some dreadful work scene. Annoyance mingled with the relief flooding through me.

"What?" The loudspeaker commentary had begun on the match, and I had to press a finger in my ear to make out what Jonathan was saying. "Well, sort of. I'm at a polo match with Nicolas. I can't really talk about work here. Can it wait till I get home?"

Jonathan made a *tsk*ing noise. "Not really. I have a meeting scheduled with Dom in a half hour, and I know it would make a great impression if we could wow him with those details."

"Well—" Jonathan's less-than-appealing habit of texting me queries and reminders, and expecting me to jump to it as if I were one of his assistants was starting to grate. Of course I wanted to make a good impression with Dom and Farrah, but was this what working with him would be like? One snappy request after another?

"Have you got them or not, sweetie? I need to get moving," he asked, with a hint of impatience beneath his usual polite tone.

"Yes, I have," I said, fishing in my pocket for the bit of paper Nicky had given me. "But I haven't had time to get on the Internet and—"

"Can you please just tell me what they are!"

"OK! OK!" I said. "Um, La Paradise, Odille's . . ." I peered at the list, which I now saw was written on the back of a Gordon Ramsay bill. Nicky had bold, loopy writing, and he'd used a marker pen that made his scrawl look even more schoolboyish. "La Coquille?"

"Great," said Jonathan. "Great. Got that. Now, are you going to be coming to Paris on Thursday as usual?"

"Yes, I should think—"

"Good, because I need you to come earlier. Can you cancel your Thursday morning appointments and get the first train?"

No, I thought crossly, *I can't.*

"It's not as simple as that," I began, and Jonathan made a grumbling noise.

I turned round to see Nicky walking toward me, his crisp white shirt now undone another button, with a broad smile illuminating his handsome face. His teeth were as white and gleaming as his shirt. I pointed at the phone and made a *Sorry* expression. In response he pretended he was about to goose the pert behind of an unsuspecting female spectator, then laughed when I flinched forward to stop him. Then he pulled a faux-reproachful face and slapped his own wrist.

I couldn't keep myself from smiling at this performance, but I wagged my finger at him all the same.

He made a *Wind up the call* gesture and jerked his thumb toward the champagne tent. *Oh, God,* I thought. He must need me to defuse one of his awful social faux pas . . . or maybe he actually wants to talk to me? After all, there were plenty of more glamorous guests for him to occupy himself with.

I pushed a hand through my hair nervously, remembered I was wearing a wig, and stopped myself just before I shoved it off my head entirely.

"If you could get here at nine that would be ideal," Jonathan was saying. "As well as checking out those possible offices, I've managed to get a couple of key meetings scheduled, and it would be better if you could manage to . . ."

I felt a sudden pang in my chest. Since his business plans had moved into higher gear, it felt as if all Jonathan's calls seemed to be about business these days. Business, or money. Very little flirtation at all.

"Jonathan," I said, interrupting him before Nicky got within earshot. "Aren't you meant to say 'Come over earlier because I miss you'?"

There was a pause on the other end. "But you *know* I miss you."

"You never tell me you do," I said. I turned over Nicky's list in my hand. It had been a wildly expensive meal for two. They had drunk three bottles of champagne and lingered over six coffees after the tastings menu dinner. I felt unexpectedly envious of whoever had been on the other side of the candles.

"I *guess* I hoped that every time you looked at the diamond on your finger you'd realize how much I missed you," he replied with a weary sigh. "Come on, Melissa. We're not eighteen. I'm rushed off my feet here, trying to deal with the office, and get things moving on our own project. If I had thirty hours in the day, you know I'd be spending them calling you. It's only because Solange is so efficient with my schedule that I even get a chance to take lunch."

A wicked voice in my head wondered if he'd now delegated the sending of my flowers to Solange too. I pushed the idea away but heard my own voice whine, "It's just that you're starting to make me think that the reason you want me to move to Paris is because I'm a key employee of your new business, not someone you can't bear to be apart from."

"You really believe that?"

Oh, God, this was one of those moving-walkway conversations: you get on with a reasonable comment, and before you know it, you're being swept away to Recrimination City, with no means of getting off.

"Sort of," I said bravely. "Can we do something fun this weekend? As well as looking at the offices? Please?"

Nicky was now standing right next to me, so close I could smell his aftershave.

Jonathan didn't reply immediately, and when I heard him say, indistinctly, "Oh, Solange, you're a miracle worker," I realized he was multitasking even as he was trying to convince me the romance hadn't gone from our relationship. That ratcheted my irritation back up to annoyance.

"Jonathan?" I demanded.

"Melissa, please don't get whiney. You're at work, I'm at work, let's talk later, OK? OK."

My mouth dropped open at the sheer nerve of it, but before I had a chance to snap back with something appropriately tart, he'd hung up.

"Mr. Capricorn, I assume?" asked Nicky. "He does speak to you like you're a little girl, doesn't he?"

"Yes," I said, so cross I was really talking to myself. Jonathan couldn't talk to me like I was a baby while at the same time insisting I help him with these "vital" business arrangements. One or the other! "He does. Sometimes." I gathered myself. "Only when he's busy. And he's really busy right now. And anyway, you shouldn't be listening to private conversations."

Nicky looked sympathetic. "You look very stressed out, Melissa."

"Honey."

"You look very stressed out, Honey." He leaned forward and subtly straightened my wig. "If you weren't in charge of my morals, I'd offer to massage it out of you. Feet first. But can I get you a drink?"

I stopped wiping the muddy grass off my ruined heels and looked up at Nicky. There was a genuine air of concern on his face. Somehow that only made me feel more defensive.

"Are you really bothered about my stress, or have you found some cute waitress you need to get back to?" I asked.

He raised his hands. "I know you think I'm some kind of skirt-chasing lech, but I don't like to see damsels in distress. And I definitely don't like to see that horrible frown you do when you're tense."

"When have you seen my horrible frown?" I demanded, flushing.

"At the dinner, when Piglet was showing off. When I nearly got thrown out of the Blue Bar the first time we met. In Huntsman, when I asked if they could do me a Playboy print lining in my suit. Want me to go on?"

I must have looked aghast, because he added, with what I hoped was a self-deprecating wink, "I only notice because you look so edible the rest of the time. I can only assume it's something I'm doing. Which"—he winked more seductively now—"is either deeply upsetting or rather flattering."

Deep breath, I told myself. *Deep breath. Do not say the first thing that comes into your head.*

The first thing that came into my head was: *You are easily the sexiest man I have ever met, you have a previously undiscovered sense of humor, and I am developing a hideous crush on you,* but fortunately I was saved from making a total idiot of myself by the arrival of a policeman.

"Excuse me, sir, madam," the policeman said, gently steering us around, "but could you step this way? We're clearing the area temporarily."

I looked around and realized that play had stopped on the pitch and herds of thin women in fluttery dresses were being marched toward the safety of the car park, closely followed by their red-trousered companions, all making furious calls on their mobiles.

"Oh, God, what's happening?" I asked.

The policeman looked shifty and said, "We've had a security alert. Someone's spotted a suspicious package in the pavilion. Just to be on the safe side, we're calling in the bomb squad. Can't be too careful, what with Prince William here today."

"*And* me," said Nicky, pointing at himself.

The policeman stared at him.

"He's a prince too," I explained. "Prince Nicolas of Hollenberg."

"Oh, right," said the policeman, unimpressed. "Well, if you could move along . . . Should all be sorted out in no time."

"Oh my God!" said Nicky, as we hurried toward the car. "This is terrible! I should phone my grandfather. What if it's an assassination attempt by the government, to stop me from inheriting?"

"I hate to break this to you, Nicky," I said breathlessly, "but I think your inheritance is somewhere beneath parking tickets in Cowdenbeath as far as the government's concerned."

"Not your government, the government of Hollenberg!" He raked his hands through his hair. "Mama always said they were mafiosi. And I'm not saying I'm a *cad*, but some girls haven't taken it too well when I had to break it to them that—"

"Look," I said to humor him, "we'll call your grandfather." I took my phone out of my pocket and dialed the emergency number. While it was ringing, I started to get one of those vague nagging thoughts in the back of my mind, beneath the general bomb scare panic. Something wasn't right. What was it? I racked my brains.

"Nicky," I said, mentally running through any last bequests I had, should the bomb go off. Nelson would get everything, and he would distribute it with meticulous fairness between the donkey charity I supported and the Lifeboats. "I refuse to be blown up without fresh lipstick. Oh, my God, where's my bag?"

"Your bag?" said Nicky.

"Yes." Panic was rising in me now. I noticed Prince William being rushed past by a crack troupe of protection officers, still in his white polo jodhpurs, his blond hair ruffled where he'd removed his helmet. He didn't look all that bothered, to be honest. I guessed this sort of thing must happen to him a lot.

My attention was drawn back to my phone as a woman's voice answered, "Hello?" I assumed it was Alexander's secretary. "Hello, may I speak to Prince Alexander? It's Melissa Romney-Jones," I asked politely.

"Melissa, darling! It's me!"

"*Granny?*"

"How are you?"

"Fine, fine!" I said, somewhat startled to get her on what I'd assumed was Alexander's direct mobile line. "I do need to speak to Alexander quite urgently. Is he there?"

"Darling, I'll just get him." I heard her calling, "Alex! Alex!"

Where were they? And was that a seagull squawking in the background?

Nicky, meanwhile, was thinking. I could tell by the way his mouth was moving slightly as he hauled thoughts around in his head.

"Well?" I hissed. "Where's my bag? Don't tell me you checked it in at the cloakroom? I'll never get it now."

"I didn't check it," said Nicky. "I put it somewhere safe behind a flower-arrangement thing while I got some more champagne. Oh, come on!" he said. "You didn't expect me to be seen carrying a *handbag,* did you?"

I almost dropped the phone. "What? Where exactly did you leave it?"

"By the champagne table. Near where they've sealed off the tent . . . Oh."

We stared at each other as the extent of the whole truth dawned. They were going to detonate my handbag, thinking it was a suspicious package! The only suspicious thing about that poor handbag was how much I managed to cram into it.

Predictably, Nicky recovered first. "Oh, come on," he said, with a wink and a nudge, "at least it's livened things up! Life's too short to watch an *entire polo match!*"

"Your life may end up being a lot shorter than you realize if you don't get that bag back!" I hissed furiously, just as Alexander came on the line.

"Hello? Melissa?" He sounded worried. "What's happened? Are you all right?"

I glared at Nicky but tried not to let the stress show in my voice. At least Nicky hadn't done it on purpose.

Or had he?

I swallowed. "Hello. I'm frightfully sorry to disturb you, but I just thought I should let you know that we're at the polo match, and there's been a bomb scare. But there's nothing to worry about. It seems to be all in hand, but I didn't want you to hear from anywhere else."

I could hear the panic in Alexander's cultured voice, although he was clearly making an effort not to worry me. "Good Lord, are you sure? Are you safe? Get in the Bentley—it's armor-plated, you know. I had it from one of the sheiks."

Nicky was sloping off slowly, but I grabbed him by the sleeve. "Just to put your mind at rest, sir, here's Nicky." And I handed him the phone and grabbed the binoculars hanging from his pocket.

While Nicky was blathering on about hitting the deck and making the area safe, I trained my binoculars around the ground. Ponies . . . tall men in tight white trousers . . . burly royal protection officers with headsets and moustaches . . . There—the pavilion. Sure enough, the police were taping off an area around the side entrance, where we'd been downing Krug only ten minutes earlier.

I thought as fast as I could. My bag was full of stuff. And not just the usual purse, keys, and makeup—there was a spare pair of shoes, tights, knickers (Marks & Spencer size 14–16), a notebook with all kinds of potentially embarrassing facts about half of London's bachelors, Alexander's credit card, a note from my father shamelessly asking me to pretend I'd been on the Cheese Diet, all with my own name on!

Oh God. Oh God. Oh God.

I had to get it back before the police confiscated it or blew it up or, worse, looked inside.

" . . . will be fine. Yup. Cheers. OK, bye then. I will. Bye-bye. No, really, I heard you the first time. Bye now. Hang on, I think we're going into a tunnel, I might get cut—" And Nicky hung up on his grandfather.

I glared at him. "He *knows* you're not going into a tunnel."

"Whatever." Nicky shrugged. "When do you reckon the camera crews will get here? Should I change my shirt? Ray has a fresh one for me in the Bentley."

"No," I said, closing my eyes and trying to machinate as Honey-ishly as possible. What would Honey do? It was an emergency.

I opened them. "We're going to get the bag back," I said with more confidence than I felt.

"We?" Nicky raised his eyebrows with such incredulity that they almost disappeared into his hair. "But there's a bomb over there . . . Oh, right. I get you. No, I don't."

"Come with me," I said, setting off with a determined stride. "Keep up!" I added over my shoulder.

"And get in front of that wiggle? Absolutely not. It's like two puppies fighting in a sack!" said Nicky, ogling my rear end.

I covered my arse with my hands, self-consciously, though I had to admit I was a little bit flattered. "Now is *not* the time."

"Tell me when the time's going to be!" Nicky bounded after me. "And tell me what we're going to do!"

I could feel my stockings against the inside of my thighs and not for the first time marveled at how my brain suddenly seemed to whir into a higher gear as I walked.

As we got nearer the pavilion, I was pleased to see that despite the police's best efforts to clear the area there were still quite a few female guests flapping around, and more than a few ex-army chaps with red-dening faces, offering the police advice on what they should be doing. That would give us a bit of cover.

"Right," I hissed in Nicky's ear. "I hear you're good at getting out of nightclubs through toilet windows."

"Yes," said Nicky, looking proud of himself. "Not to mention the odd bedroom window, at short notice."

I gave him a disgusted look but carried on. "Right, there's a door the caterers were using round the back—sneak in there while I distract the policeman, grab my bag, and get out here as soon as you can. Throw it over the hedge if you have to. In fact, that might be a good idea. Just don't let the police get it."

"Can't I run out with it? Like a hero?"

"Don't overdo it," I said, my brain racing. "We want to make you look brave and trained in security issues, because you're a modern prince. You don't want to look like a complete cretin with foolhardy risk issues. In fact, it might just be better to get in, get the bag, and get out."

Nicky put his hand on my shoulder. His hand was warm, and his long fingers caressed my neck. Out of habit, I reckoned, rather than anything else. "Melissa," he said, gazing deep into my eyes. "Don't you think I'd look wonderful on the front of *The Times*, having saved your life?"

"Just save my handbag from being detonated," I said, preparing myself for the loss of my favorite ever bag. It was a massive Kate Spade scarlet leather number Jonathan had bought me in New York, and nothing had ever touched it for versatility, style, and sheer capacity. But it would be a small sacrifice, I told myself. And for a good cause. Nicky was right: one prince saving the life of another would make a great story. When the initial fuss died down.

"You know what this means, don't you, Melissa?" said Nicky.

"What?"

He slid an arm around my shoulders and flicked playfully at my wig. "You'll have to spend the rest of your life following me around, saving my bacon."

I fixed him with a glare. "Your bacon's still raw, Nicolas. Get a move on."

True to his word, years of vanishing from places he shouldn't have been in had given Nicky a catlike slinkiness, and I watched as he slipped unnoticed around the back of the pavilion. I didn't even need to distract anyone. Getting him out, though, would be more tricky.

I took a deep breath and strode toward the policeman nearest the door I hoped he'd emerge from. The one nearest where I hoped he'd left my handbag.

"Gosh, officer!" I said, fluttering my eyelashes shamelessly. "What's happening?"

"I'm not at liberty to tell you that, miss," he said. "Nothing for you to worry about, though. You'd be much safer standing by your car. If you wouldn't mind moving along, please?"

I peered over his shoulder. No sign of Nicolas. "Um," I said, racking my brains for something to say, "I know you're very busy, but I did hear someone in the car park mention there was some funny-looking package by the welcome tent too?"

He gave me a hard look. "I'll get someone onto that." But he made no move to investigate.

"It might even be drugs," I added hopefully.

"Let's deal with this package first, miss." Another, more impassive look.

Clearly, nothing was going to distract him. I felt a brief pride in the value for money my taxes were getting in quality policing, then dropped dramatically to the floor with a groan, clutching my chest and letting my skirt ride some way up my thighs, revealing an expanse of stocking top.

Sometimes the old tricks are the best. At once, all surrounding policemen gathered around me, and they were distracted long enough for Nicky to come bursting out of the tent, waving something in the air.

I staggered to my feet, waving away helping hands, ready to grab my handbag. But he wasn't carrying it. Cold fear gripped me. He was waving something else.

"It's OK!" he yelled. "Panic over! It's just a makeup bag!"

I stared, as every head turned his way.

"Don't worry! I've had special security training," he went on. I noticed he'd undone yet another button on his shirt and had ruffled up his hair. Trust Nicky to have made time for grooming. "Secret Service and all that. My great-great-uncle was assassinated, can't be too careful, you know, in my situation."

"As heir to Hollenberg," I added hastily. "His grandfather's the crown prince."

Policemen began to approach him with a mixture of respect and bewilderment writ large on their faces, but he motioned them aside and strode toward me.

I shook my head silently and put my hands up to stop him. The last thing I wanted was to be ceremoniously presented with the personal item that had caused all this kerfuffle.

"No, please, no fuss," Nicky was saying, still walking toward me. "Don't thank me. Let's just get this polo back on the road. Think of the elephants. Don't want them missing out on their big fund-raiser. Tell Wills the chukkas are back on, OK?"

Somehow, he managed to breeze majestically past all the policemen, all the hangers-on, everyone, then slung his arm around my shoulders.

I felt a thrill run up my spine, then forced myself to look unperturbed. I had to admit, inwardly, that I was impressed. That was more Honey than Honey. Clearly, Nicky could do commanding and competent when he wanted.

"You look peaky, darling," he said in a loud voice.

"Yes," I agreed, nodding my head for emphasis. "Take me back to the car. I could do with getting something warm inside me."

"That can be arranged," said Nicky.

And we were walking toward the car, and the police seemed to be letting us.

"Your great-great-uncle," I said, trying to sound light. "Was he really assassinated?"

"Oh, yes," Nicky nodded. "Shot by a jealous husband in a casino in Monte Carlo. Dreadful scandal. Didn't even get that evening's IOUs written off. Oh," he added, "want this?"

And he passed me my makeup bag.

"Thanks," I said, wryly wishing he'd saved the real thing. "But what did you do with my handbag? Did you leave it so they'd have something to blow up?"

Nicky winked. "It's in the trunk of the car. I got Ray to wait behind the pavilion. Didn't want to give the coppers a chance to claim it as evidence."

I paused and allowed my lips to curl into a smile. "You're quick."

He paused too and pretended to look hurt. "No one, Melissa, has ever said that to me before."

"You can be pretty resourceful too," I said, thinking of my How to Be a Prince list. Chivalry, selflessness, rational thinking: he was making some headway down it, after all. "Any reason why you . . ." I didn't want to say *chose this moment to behave properly?*

"Why I decided to go along with your plans?" His eyebrows flicked up, and underneath my jacket I felt prickly heat tingle along my arms and across my chest as he blinked slowly, letting his long, dark lashes brush his skin. "Why do you think?"

"To get this project over and done with sooner?" I suggested.

"Maybe. Or maybe I wanted to save your bag. Or our joint reputations." He widened his eyes, as if to say, *No?*

I fiddled with my makeup bag. "Or maybe you wanted to get on the front page of *The Times*? Or was it to get onto Prince William's Christmas card list?"

I didn't know why I was being so sarcastic. It was just like being back at school, and having a crush on some spotty youth from St. Peter's and only being able to converse in insulting banter. But then there was something so ludicrously dorm pin-up about this foxy, tanned, wealthy, urban *prince* that I couldn't help reverting to school-girlish behavior.

Nicky sighed, put his arm around me, and set off toward the car again. "Darling, I'm *on* Prince William's bloody Christmas card list. He's my ninth cousin, or something."

"I'm not impressed," I reminded him.

"I didn't expect you to be," he said, and I thought I detected a note of ruefulness in his voice.

We had reached the Bentley. Ray leaped out of the driver's side and went round to the back, bearing no outward signs that anything was amiss.

"Brandy, ma'am?" he said, opening the trunk to reveal a huge wicker hamper and, tucked behind that, my red bag.

"That would be lovely," I said.

As I sipped from the little silver crested tumbler, it struck me that the police had been remarkably willing to let Nicky walk away from the scene, with the evidence, too. Surely they'd have to write some report about it? There had been bomb squad cars there and everything.

In fact, that was another car full of police dogs arriving right now.

"Ray," I heard Nicky ask. "Surely now I've got the bomb out, they can let the boys in blue go home? Get the horses back out?"

"Ah, well," said Ray, "I did overhear one of the other drivers mention that the suspicious package in the loos wasn't so easy to remove."

My blood ran cold. "The *loos*?" I said. "But I thought—"

Ray coughed discreetly. "As I understand it, they had an anonymous phone tip-off, and once they started looking for suspicious packages, it seems the whole place was awash with them. I don't even think they were looking for a handbag . . ."

He didn't get a chance to explain any further, as a muffled but significant explosion from the direction of the champagne pavilion cut him off.

An explosion that sounded a lot bigger than a stray bag being exploded.

My blood ran cold. So there really had been a suspicious package in there!

I looked at Nicky and felt sick. He could have been seriously injured. Did he realize? Should I point it out? Would Alex go berserk if he knew how close Nicky had come to getting killed?

Nicky grabbed his binoculars. "Someone should tell Venetia Hammond that bomb scares are no excuse to feel up Her Majesty's policemen."

I reached up and took the binoculars off him. "I think this would be a good moment to go home," I said firmly. "Ray?"

"Yes, ma'am," he said.

By the time Ray pulled up outside my house, a pleasant warmth had spread over me, and it wasn't entirely due to the delayed relief I felt at our close call. It had more to do with the easy chat about families and their foibles that Nicky and I had fallen into, closeted behind the discreet chauffeur glass. I'd breathed in a fair amount of his intoxicating cologne too, and heard a different laugh from the look-at-me one he used in the company of other people.

It might have been the heroic recovery of my bag, or the surprisingly athletic manner in which he'd done it, but I was starting to think Nicky wasn't nearly as louche as he made out. After all, I'd hardly covered myself in glory, putting him in danger like that, but he'd glossed over it like a gentleman, spending the journey back telling me some shockingly name-dropping—but self-deprecating—gossip.

"You're not going to invite me in for a nightcap?" he asked, leaning over as I busied myself with my bag.

"No," I said. "It's only six-thirty. Nowhere near bedtime."

Nicky hoicked up one eyebrow. "Early to bed, early to rise . . ."

I blushed and ignored him. "I always wake up at seven. Anyway, Nelson texted me earlier to say he'd cooked supper."

"Fine. How about a nightcap at my place then?"

I gave him a firm look. "Nicky, you clearly have no experience of Nelson's beef Wellington. It's not something you pass up."

"Does Nelly only cook meals with historical references?" he inquired. "I expect you get a short lecture thrown in."

"You sound almost jealous," I said.

"Who wouldn't be?" he sighed. "You don't have to be so professional all the time, Melissa. You're not on duty now. In fact, what would happen if I were to slip this lovely blond wig off and . . ."

He reached for my hair, and I grabbed his wrist. "No," I said.

"Mmm!" growled Nicky. "Like that, is it? Fine with me!"

Visions of Jonathan flashed in front of my eyes. I'd let Nicky under my professional guard. I'd known it could happen, even if I was fighting against it with all my might. Honey was a seductive state of mind, for the client and for me. But it wasn't going to happen now. Besides, might this not be another of Nicky's slippery plans to get me off his case? Charm me into bed, then complain to Alexander that we could no longer work together for "personal reasons"? He wasn't the sort to keep quiet about any conquests, either.

I dropped his wrist, trying not to notice how sinewy it was beneath the soft skin.

"No," I said, more quietly. "Sorry."

Nicky leaned farther over and took my other hand. "What's the matter? Don't you trust me, Melissa?"

I swallowed. Nelson always told me I was too trusting. So did Jonathan, and Gabi. And Granny and Allegra and Mummy, come to that. No matter how charming Nicky seemed, I didn't really know him at all.

"No," I said, forcing a laugh into my voice. "I don't trust you an inch!"

He looked at me, his brown eyes suddenly unreadable. If he was trying to appear hurt and distressed in a Method Acting way, I conceded to myself that he was halfway there.

"Neither do I," he sighed.

"Oh, give it a rest," I said, grabbing my bag. "For a moment there, I thought—"

"Thought what?"

"Thought you weren't spinning me one of your Sloane fishing lines." I got out of the car, shut the door, and leaned in through the window. "I'll speak to you soon. I have a full day tomorrow and I'm off to Paris on Thursday. I need to pack."

Nicky threw himself back on his seat. "Are you? Well, have a nice time. I'm going home to watch *Coronation Street* now, as per your instructions."

"Oh, Nicky—it's not forever." I was about to wave good-bye to Ray when I suddenly remembered something. Reaching into my pocket, I handed Nicky his phone. "Yours, I believe."

"Are you sure?" he carried on, his eyes not leaving mine as he turned his phone back on. It abruptly bleeped with a hundred and one messages. All from frantic women, no doubt, worried about his well-being.

"*Coronation Street,*" I said, wagging my finger, and I left before I could be persuaded to join him.

To my surprise, Nelson wasn't in when I let myself into the flat. But then I was back a good hour or so before I'd reckoned, so I took advantage of his absence to have a really long, deep bath, completely emptying the hot water tank in the process.

At half eight he broke through my inconclusive thoughts about Jonathan and Paris by bellowing, "Hi, Honey, I'm home! How was Bonnie Prince Smarmy?"

"Fine!" I yelled. "And don't call him that. Where've you been?"

I heard him wander through the flat toward the bathroom. I knew what he'd be doing: checking through the mail I hadn't bothered to look at, picking out the overdue bills, and chucking away the catalogues.

"Oh, just having a drink after work."

"With who?"

"Whom."

"With whom then?" Was it me, or did he sound a bit furtive? I sat up with a splash.

"With Leonie."

"Leonie?"

"Yes, Leonie. Your friend, Leonie. Your friend with whom you were so keen to set me up, and *with whom* we're going on a *lugg-*sury cruise in a matter of weeks. Seriously, Mel—how many cashmere sweater catalogues does one woman need? I'm recycling all of this."

I stared at my crimson toenails through the rapidly dissipating Jo Malone bubbles. Dinner for two last night, after-work drinks tonight. I'd never really seen Nelson get serious about a girl. Was he getting serious about Leonie?

"And did you . . . did you have a good time?" I asked.

"What? Yes, s'pose so. She's very knowledgeable about tax laws, isn't she?"

"Yes," I said. "And . . . ?" I faltered. "Did you . . . you know?"

"Mmm." Nelson's attention was clearly elsewhere. I wondered if it was on my overdue Visa bill or what Leonie had been wearing. No, that was unlikely. More probably what Leonie had told him about overseas blind trusts.

"Want me to put the dinner on?" he asked. "And if your feet are clean, I'll give that foot rub I promised."

"Ooh, yes," I said. "I'll be out in five minutes."

"Don't rush," he said, moving away from the door. "You'll need a good soak to get all the secondhand charm out of your hair."

For want of anything smart enough to say, I deliberately ran some more hot water into the bath just to annoy him.

thirteen

It was back down to earth with a bump on Wednesday, but following a busy morning of paperwork, at least I got out of the office and into the sunshine in the afternoon.

Felix Harvey was an old school friend of Nelson's or else I'd never have agreed to take on a job that might involve running in public. But Nelson so rarely asked me for favors, and in any case, Felix was a nice enough chap, apart from his habit of saying nothing whatsoever for ages, then coming out with something startlingly random. It stemmed, I assumed, from an adolescence spent with monosyllabic boys who communicated by grunt alone, then compounded by getting himself hitched to a woman who never, ever shut up.

Nelson's theory was that Miriam and Felix had only married in the first place because she'd proposed and he hadn't said no quickly enough. It hadn't lasted, but they'd parted amicably enough, and now she was living in Chiswick with their young son, Hamish, to whom Nelson was a very conscientious godfather (port laid down, swimming lessons booked, etc.). Miriam, ever practical, had "moved on" and into the arms of her financial advisor, but while Felix had slipped happily back into weekend-dad bachelor life, what he couldn't bear were Miriam's constant therapist prompted inquiries about whether he too was "moving on."

He hadn't. But that didn't stop her checking every time he visited Hamish.

"There is no right answer!" Felix fulminated, in a rare burst of consecutive speech. "If I say I'm not seeing anyone, she pulls this hideous 'so you're not over me!' face, and if I say I am, she gets all fake-concerned about whether it's not all too soon, and wants to know details and then I . . . I . . . !"

He slumped into a more familiar silence, but his thwarted expression spoke volumes.

And that was why he needed someone to go to Willow House Prep School Sports Day with him—to provide solid evidence that he'd moved on. Believe me, it wasn't so I'd win the Mothers' Race.

I'd heard various scary things about supercompetitive prep school mummies, and thought I'd better make an effort before Felix picked me up at lunchtime. I didn't have time to drop three dress sizes and/or collect a new summer wardrobe, but I squeezed myself into a pretty Parisian cotton dress and cardigan, and slipped on my new cat's eye sunglasses.

Felix raced over from his legal office in the City and we drove through south London in silence. I didn't take it personally. By the time we'd reached Wimbledon Common, where the sports day was being held, I'd managed to glean that Hamish was in the sack race and that there were two credit cards for every person in the U.S.

Felix found a parking spot between the herds of Land Rovers and BMWs, and I scanned the Common, which was milling with little boys in navy shorts and parents in suits. I couldn't spot Miriam. Nelson had told me not to bother looking, but instead to listen for a woman's voice saying, "I," "me," or "honestly" a lot.

"There he is!" said Felix, suddenly, pushing his wire-framed glasses up his nose and pointing at the line-up of kids.

Thirteen identically adorable blond boys with floppy hair and Boden sports uniforms, and one dark-haired wee chap with matching glasses and a worried expression, just like his dad's, were lined up. They were all clutching sacks.

"We should head over there, before it starts," I said, shouldering my bag. "Get to the finishing line, eh?"

I looked quizzically at Felix, but his brow knitted as he stared into the middle distance. When I followed his gaze, I realized that either he was fascinated by a park bench, or trying to avoid the two women homing in on us with fixed smiles on their faces.

"Felix?" I prompted. "Who are these women? Felix? Quickly! Oh, for heaven's sake!"

Too late. They were on us before Felix could even marshal his thoughts, but I could tell by the blush spreading across his face that they were significant in some way.

I focused my attention on him, threw back my head and laughed as if he'd just said something terribly amusing.

Felix looked at me as if I were mad, but for once, I knew this client wouldn't come out with something that would blow my cover. Not for another ten minutes, anyway.

"Felix!" cooed the first woman, clasping his forearm to plant a kiss on his cheek, then, almost without moving her head, added, "Hello! I'm Miriam, Hamish's mummy! I'm not sure we've . . ."

"Honey," I said firmly, shaking her hand and deliberately not adding an explanation as I turned to smile at the younger, darker-haired woman. She was wearing sensible ballet flats which, I noted jealously, she could carry off with her muscular calves.

"This is Jessica," said Miriam. "My friend from yogalates. She's been coaching Hamish in the sack race. Lives about four streets behind me, I don't know if you know Chiswick, we're up by the park . . ."

"Ah, hello!" I said. While I was shaking hands, and murmuring something unspecific about godparents, quick glances between Felix and Jessica triggered signals in my mind. Her eyes were widening hopefully, waiting for him to strike up some conversation, and I could tell from the furrows in his brow that he was paralyzed with panic.

Meanwhile, as she yapped on about urban hayfever, Jessica's sharp eyes darted back and forth, mainly between me and Felix. It was a veritable cat's cradle of eye contact.

"We were just about to go over and get seats!" I said, to break the tension. "Don't want to miss the big race!"

Park grass and high heels aren't an easy combination at the best of times. I deliberately set off next to Miriam, so I could be sure she'd get the right idea, but I was having to juggle my bag and program, concentrate on answering Miriam's loaded questions, and keep one ear trained on Felix and Jessica's conversation.

Well, Jessica's valiant efforts at starting one. What I could hear made me itch to turn around and intervene.

"So, this weather!" she said, merrily. "I never know whether to bring my wellies or my bikini!"

There was no response from Felix, despite it clearly being an opening for some repartee. But as I opened my mouth to help out, Miriam distracted me with another question.

"Have you known Felix long?" she asked, just as Jessica went on, with a touch of desperation. "Let's hope the sunshine holds out long enough for tea! Are you staying?"

Felix managed a grunt, which I hoped was accompanied by a keen smile and nod, but I couldn't check because Miriam was quizzing me again, this time about whether I'd met Hamish before.

"I'm a good friend of Hamish's godfather," I said truthfully, willing Felix to say something, but Miriam was off again, this time about what a wonderful godfather Nelson was—as if I needed telling.

"I hear the tea is lovely!" Jessica tried finally, and I was about to turn round and clout Felix round the ear, when, to my absolute relief, I heard him clear his throat.

"Of course, the bikini is actually named after a nuclear testing range," he said.

Jessica, Miriam, and I all paused to process this.

Felix smiled shyly, revealing an unexpected dimple. "Do you want to sit anywhere in particular?"

"Mrs. Harvey? Could I have a word?"

We spun round as a chap in cricket whites appeared next to us, and Miriam made a little moue of apology.

"Headmaster. Won't be a tick," she said, then dropped her voice and squeezed Felix's shoulder. "So good to see you're *moving on*," she said in a whisper we could all hear quite plainly. "Wonderful example for Hamish."

"So, Jessica!" I said, hoping inspiration would strike if I just started speaking. "How do you coach for the sack race?"

"Sleeping bags," said Jessica. "They soften the fall." She let her eyes dance sideways toward Felix, but, inexperienced flirt that he was, he only smiled, vaguely.

"Nelson was telling me how you'd all cheat in the sack race at prep school!" I said, nodding toward Felix so he could deliver the punch-line.

Felix stared at me, and I glared back.

He rounded his pale owlish eyes, as if to say, "What?"

I wondered if he'd once been told never to interrupt ladies in con-versation or that women liked a listener, or something. You never know what strange male quirks are the result of a misinterpreted mag-azine article, read in a guest bathroom somewhere at the age of fifteen.

"Go on," I said, with a tight smile.

"Yes, do tell!" said Jessica.

"We, er, we used to cut holes in them," he said hesitantly. "And then shuffle down the course."

I laughed heartily, and while Jessica was laughing too, I muttered, toward his ear, "And the eggs?"

"Why?" He gave me a familiar "duh!" eye roll. "You know about that."

"Jessica doesn't!" I hissed, beneath the cover of a broad grin.

"Oh. Right, well, I used to use a magnet on the egg for the egg and spoon race. Nelson was furious. He gave his third prize back, said he didn't want to be part of a sporting deception. He was only seven."

"Sweet!" giggled Jessica.

I started to relax, but then realized that Felix's mouth was clamping shut again with nerves. I really felt for him. It wasn't that he lacked conversation, he just had no idea how to deliver it.

"Do tell that lovely story you were telling me in the car about Hamish going to the zoo with you and Nelson," I suggested.

Felix hadn't told me—Nelson had. That didn't matter, though. I just needed to prompt him into chat, like someone push-starting a car.

"About the giraffes?" I added.

"Ah," said Felix, grasping at a fact, "now did you know giraffes only sleep for half an hour a day, a bit like Hamish, actually. . . ."

"I can believe that!" Jessica said, and smiled.

I hovered around in the background, prompting Felix when he seemed to be going into a mute spell, and eventually, he relaxed enough to chat on his own, with only the occasional slip into silence, which Jessica filled happily enough.

Hamish's sack race gave us all something to chat about, especially when to mad cheers from us, he came in a valiant third. Miriam's barrage of yapping kept me occupied, but it also gave Felix a chance to get quite chatty with Jessica, and just to cap it all, I even surprised myself with a very creditable second in the Grown-Ups race, once I'd pulled off my high heels.

It might have had something to do with expending nervous energy.

At half past four, Jessica left with Felix's number ("You're just the random fact genius we need for our pub quiz team!"), and as he drove me back into town, alternating his usual silence with odd bursts of spontaneous conversation, like a baby bird finding its wings, I felt really warm inside.

This was what the Little Lady Agency was about, I thought, helping people be happier with themselves. It was lovely to see the difference in Felix, just from one afternoon, and I'd sensed that Miriam was more guiltily caring than interfering—something I'd tell Nelson. And if Felix was happy, then surely that would only make little Hamish happier too.

As we drove back into town, I reveled in the warm glow of a job well done. Not to mention the first rosette I'd won since my last Pony Club competition when I'd got the prize for "pony with the tidiest mane."

I was still basking in this heartening bonhomie—not to mention the lavish supper of gratitude Nelson cooked up by way of thanks—when

I rolled into the office on Thursday morning, blissfully unaware that the worst day of my life was about to kick off.

It didn't start so badly, with my bank manager calling first thing to say that my mortgage application had been approved, and I was able to call Peter, my landlord, and tell him the good news.

"I'm so glad, my dear," he told me. "I know you'll be very happy there."

"I will," I promised him, delight bubbling through my veins. "I definitely will."

I managed to hold myself back from ringing Jonathan immediately so I could keep it as a special surprise that evening. I planned to slip the spare keys on his keyring when he wasn't looking, then reveal all. It would make a lovely change—me giving *him* a set of spare keys for once.

But things started to go awry when he called me to check that I'd canceled my appointments as requested.

"It's impossible," I told him, looking at my diary.

"If you were sick, you'd have to," he argued.

"But I'm not sick. You just want me to come to some meetings, and I can't, because I have meetings here."

Jonathan said something in French that I didn't understand, and then I realized he was talking to Solange.

"I'll be there at seven," I said. If he couldn't be bothered to listen to me, that was his problem. "If you want to make them evening appointments, we can do that, but I really can't cancel these particular clients."

"Sorry, sweetheart," he said, finally returning his attention to me. "I didn't catch that."

"I'll be at the Gare du Nord as usual," I said briskly. "Call me if you arrange dinner discussions, otherwise I'll look forward to us having that romantic night that you keep promising me." And I hung up.

About five minutes later, Wesley Clayton-Phipps arrived to ask for my help in arranging a "decent burial and memorial service" for his mother's beloved black Labrador, since she was too distressed to do it herself. It was her last link with her husband, who'd died ten years ago, and a loyaler companion to boot. I could sympathize with that.

An hour later, I helped Simon Howard draft a best man's speech, as well as his own groom's speech; I advised Lionel Gill on how to phrase his Soul Mates ad for the *Guardian* so as not to offend so many readers as last time; and instead of lunch, I went out to the latest cake shop on Gabi's list, to inquire whether they could make a wedding cake featuring Aaron's favorite cars round one tier and sugar-craft shoes round another.

Gabi, of course, was disparaging about Jonathan's bossiness, thrilled about my new property-owning status, and insanely curious about my day at the polo.

"It was on *Radio London*!" she said. "I hear it was *packed* with celebs—I wish you'd learn how to use that camera on your phone, Mel. Something about a high-profile guest dismantling one bomb and the police accidentally detonating Kate Middleton's iPod? They didn't mention Nicky by name," she added. "Is that good or bad?"

"Good, I think," I said. We were eating sandwiches on a bench outside her office, and I didn't want anything to do with Nicky broadcast.

"So. Has he tried to snog you yet?" she asked.

"No!"

Gabi nudged me with a naughty gleam in her eye. "But you want him to, right?"

"No! I don't! At all! He's absolutely not my type, and anyway . . ." I stopped before I protested too much. Gabi had eagle eyes for that sort of thing.

But she wasn't concentrating. "I would," she said dreamily. "Aaron would understand. It's a one-off, snogging a prince. Even a made-up one. Mind you, Nelson would be furious. He really can't stand Nicolas, can he?"

"No," I agreed. "He drew a diagram the other night to prove how Orlando von Borsch, Hugh Grant, and Nicky are one and the same person. Honestly, he's being very *off,* if you ask me. He knows it's a job. He knows I'm really only doing it for Granny." I sighed. "I know Nelson can be a bit fussy, but it's really not like him to be so *childish.*"

Gabi gave me a funny look. "You know it's all just a big act to hide how he's really feeling."

"In what way?"

She put her sandwich down carefully on the paper bag. "Well, think about it. He's really going to miss you when you move to Paris. How long have you lived together?"

"Nearly six years," I said.

"Mel, I know three people who've got married and divorced in less time than that. Have you talked about it?"

I shook my head. "I did tell him about Jonathan's September deadline, and he said something about getting a new flatmate in, but since then we haven't really . . . you know."

It wasn't a subject either of us really wanted to bring up.

"And Roger's got Supermodel Zara to play with, and I'm getting married." Gabi readdressed her sandwich. "And you're spending your last few months in London being swept round town by a notorious playboy. No wonder he's carrying on like a bear with a sore head."

I blinked. That was a very good description of Nelson: a big brown bear, grumpy on the outside, but protective and gentle inside. With a pot of organic honey, and a warm cave he'd now have to share with a stranger. Who might not take care of him the way I had.

Unexpected tears pricked at my eyes, and I was glad I had my sunglasses on.

"So, yeah," said Gabi, not noticing, "be nice to Nelson, OK? He's really . . ." She paused and looked at me. The cheeky gleam had left her eyes and she seemed almost serious—a condition I'd only ever seen her in during sample sales. "He's a good man. You mean the world to him, you know."

"I know," I said fervently. "I love him too. He's the brother I never had."

Well, apart from that one time when something not very brotherly nearly happened between us. But that was ages ago. And we were both a bit tipsy and overemotional. And we both agreed it was a never-to-be-repeated one-off.

All that went through my head very quickly, but it must have shown on my face because Gabi opened her mouth to say something, then stopped. Then opened it again, then stopped again.

I squinted at her. Gabi didn't know. Nelson and I had solemnly sworn to keep it to ourselves.

"So you keep saying," she said, opening her can of Coke carefully so as not to break the impressive false nails she was "trialing." "Just that I don't think he sees you quite like that."

"No, you're wrong," I said. "We're very fond of each other."

"Get real," said Gabi, with a *dur* expression on her face. "Hasn't it ever crossed your mind that most men don't cook gourmet meals, administer hour-long foot massages, and straighten out the accounts of their flatmates? Or take it incredibly *personally* when the flatmate pretends to be a well-known womanizer's girlfriend?"

I stared at her, my mind whirring. "No . . . No, I'm pretty sure Nelson doesn't . . . No."

"Mel!" Gabi rolled her eyes so hard it looked like she was having some kind of seizure. "Think about it. Jonathan's fine with you dating this guy. In fact, he'd probably rifle through Nicky's address book for contacts while you had Nicky distracted. But Nelson—he spent the whole of that dinner looking as if he'd like to challenge Nicky to a *duel.* Face it! He's in love with you!"

"Gabi! Stop it!" I put my hands over my ears. "God, I wish you hadn't said that. It's the kind of thing that could really ruin my last few months here."

"I'm just saying. I just want you to consider all your options before you commit." She peered at me. "You sure you don't have some deep-down feelings for him? Hmm?"

"Yes, I am sure." I folded my arms. Gabi had never really liked Jonathan. "Fond as I am of Nelson, I'm marrying Jonathan."

Gabi balled up her sandwich bag and threw it into a nearby bin. "You've just got into the habit of seeing him like a flatmate, that's all. I'd hate for you to suddenly see Nelson for the ideal man he *really* is the minute you move out and in with Dr. No. It's my job as your best friend to say things you don't want to hear. And no," she added, "you can't sack me. Even when you're in Paris."

When she said that, it suddenly dawned on me how very different things were going to be in just a few months' time. With that, the sun went behind a cloud, and our lunch break was over.

Later that afternoon, with my clients sorted out and my work phone turned off, I boarded the Eurostar to Paris, determined to have a good weekend with Jonathan. I'd decided that instead of going out to some fabulous restaurant, as we usually did, we'd have a cozy evening in. No dressing up, no glitz, just the two of us, relaxing together. I couldn't actually think of the last time we'd stayed in with a DVD. If ever. Just sharing quiet time with someone was the biggest romantic compliment you could pay them, in my opinion.

But the first ghastly moment came practically as I set foot on the platform at the Gare du Nord.

I could tell something was up as soon as I hugged Jonathan and felt only tense muscles beneath his soft cotton shirt, instead of the yielding warmth of someone who was happy to hold me. He kissed me quite formally on the cheek and grabbed my overnight bag from me without even joking about the weight of it.

"Bonsoir, chèrie!" I said, trying to jolly him up. Maybe he'd just had a difficult meeting. Maybe Kyrle & Pope had found out about his escape plans. "*Tu sais, ce soir, je vachement voudrais rester chez nous et regarder un DVD romantique, et puis, nous coucher . . . tôt?*" I guessed. "What's to 'have an early night' in French?"

"Don't," he snapped, slinging the bag over his shoulder, taking my hand and setting off toward the exit.

"What?"

"Don't remind me how much you've got to learn about Paris."

I stopped walking, stung. "What's that supposed to mean?"

He turned to face me and glared. "I just got off the phone with Dom Scott. That list of clubs you gave me yesterday?"

"Yes?" I said, remembering Nicky's telltale Gordon Ramsay bill more than the names themselves. "What about them?"

"They're strip clubs," he hissed, with maximum disdain.

"What?"

"He says they're all *strip* clubs. Or, alternatively, clubs where I'm reliably informed ladies take their clothes off for free."

"Oh," I managed to squeak. Damn. I knew I should have checked. But I'd been so busy. "Oh. I didn't realize. I thought because Nicky lives in Paris he'd know . . ." I ground to a halt as Jonathan's face registered utter exasperation.

"You asked Nicky? Jesus. Melissa, does he strike you as a *reliable* source? I mean, thank God I managed to cover up by pretending that it was the wrong list, that you'd been doing some research into a stag night for—"

"Jonathan, stop!" I faced him angrily. "I told you I didn't know those sorts of details about Paris! I *told* you! I'm going to learn, but you have to give me some time, and you just *thrust* this on me, at a moment when there was no way I could have explained. And I did my best, but you rushed me! You called me at the polo match!"

"You had plenty of time to check it out."

"When?" My knees were trembling with shock and fury. "*When* should I have checked them, in between getting them at the polo match, dealing with a situation there, getting home knackered, then being horrendously busy at the agency all day yesterday and this morning?"

"You could have canceled your appointments."

"I told you—I could *not*!"

"You could have gone on the Internet at night. You could have got up an hour earlier this morning. That's what professionals do. They go the extra mile."

"You can be a professional and still have a life!" I retorted, although he was succeeding in making me feel appropriately guilty for the linguine con vongole and *Midsomer Murders* repeat I'd enjoyed with Nelson before turning in last night. Maybe I *should* have gotten up earlier, I thought guiltily. Jonathan made room for a jog before getting into the office at seven, after all. "Anyway," I added, as it occurred to me, "you're the one in Paris with a Parisian staff—surely it would have been easier to ask *Solange* than me."

Jonathan narrowed his eyes at me, and I swear it was like being back in my father's study, facing my report card showdown again. "I wanted *you* to have a role. I guess it depends what you consider your top priority. Use your brain, Melissa! You should have known they'd be tacky, coming from that playboy idiot, Nicolas."

"Now that's not fair," I said hotly, the glimpse of Not-Quite-as-Bad-as-I'd-Thought Nicky still fresh in my mind. "It's probably my fault for not making it clear enough. He knows what kind of business I have, advising men, and maybe he assumed I needed ideas for that sort of single man client. I'm sure he wouldn't deliberately want to make me look stupid like that."

"Wouldn't he? Why are you so sure about that? It's not like he's got any reason to embarrass the woman who's been employed by his grandfather to 'improve' him, is there?" said Jonathan sarcastically. "You're just too trusting, Melissa. You need to—"

"Jonathan, for heaven's sake!" I exploded. "Don't talk to me like I'm a baby. If I've made a fool of myself, then I'll deal with it in my own way. I'll speak to Nicky, and I'll speak to Alexander and I'll find out where the right sort of club is for Dom bloody Scott. If it makes you happy!"

We were still standing on the platform, glaring furiously at each other. Tension crackled back and forth between us, and it wasn't the good sort.

"Do you want to start again?" I asked, trying to force a smile onto my face. "Give me my bag back, go behind that pillar, and I'll pretend you're ten minutes late and I've been waiting for you."

"Let's do that," said Jonathan. He rubbed his forehead with thumb and forefinger, and his expression softened. He looked more like himself again, but the frown lines around his gray eyes were still there. "I hate yelling at you, Mel. I'm just superstressed, getting everything off the ground. I want this to work for both our sakes."

"I know, darling," I said. "I'm not taking it personally. But calm down, will you? There's no point us both getting so tense that we drive clients away, is there? They're meant to be the stressed ones, not us."

Jonathan pushed his hand through his coppery hair. "OK. I'll go out and meet you again, right?"

"Right."

I watched him spin on his heel and stride down the platform. I sank onto a metal bench, my legs as wobbly as if I'd just run a marathon. This was how whole weekends could turn bad.

I took a deep breath, pulled a smile back onto my face, tried to wipe my mind clean, and stacked up a set of conversation topics like discs on an old record player.

But although we made a great acting job of him "finding" me on the bench and apologizing for being late, it didn't quite take away the surprisingly bitter taste of those first few moments. For one thing, my brain was now set on damage limitation mode, fiddling endlessly with the Scott situation, and for another, we both knew Jonathan would never, ever have been ten minutes late for my train.

"So," I said, swaying into the sitting room in my new silk lounge pants. They were sexy *and* comfy—a bit of a find, if you ask me. "Have you got any DVDs, or shall we skip straight to the early night?"

Jonathan, I noticed, was still in his suit and was looking at his BlackBerry. "Sorry, sweetie?"

"I thought we could stay in tonight," I said, draping myself seductively along the sofa. "Watch a film, call out for a takeaway? Give each other foot rubs?"

"Foot rubs?" Jonathan pulled a funny, mock-revolted face. "I'm not letting you anywhere *near* my feet, not if I want to keep that ring on your finger. Anyway, I've got a table at L'Ambroisie for eight. I moved that meeting from this afternoon to dinner. Do you mind? You'll love L'Ambroisie," he went on, going back to his BlackBerry. "The food's to die for, apparently. The waiting list's insane—I still don't know how Solange managed to snag us a table."

I could hardly be mad at him, since I'd said on the phone that I didn't mind making a dinner appointment, but I'd been thinking about a sexy night in all the way under the Channel. . . .

"Um, OK," I said. "But we can stay in tomorrow?"

"Sure. Hey, are those things pajamas?" he asked, peering at my swishy pants.

"They're lounge pants," I replied.

"Right." His face said what he was too polite to put into words.

"I'll go and change," I said, hauling myself to my bare feet. The sofa wasn't nearly as comfortable as it looked. In fact, it wasn't a sofa for lounging on at all.

While Jonathan was at work on Friday, I put on my flat shoes and took the Metro up to Montmartre in search of a vintage boutique I'd read about in the Sunday papers. It was a breath-catching walk up the steep hills from Abbesses station, but the pretty winding streets and chocolate shops distracted me until I puffed my way to the steps of Sacré-Coeur, and Paris was laid out like a miniature city beneath me.

I spent the day browsing the boutiques (euros still felt like Monopoly money and were therefore tons easier to spend than my hard-earned pounds) and peering nosily through iron gates at the secret courtyards inside. I found a recipe book for beginner French cooks that even I could translate, so I left a message for Jonathan that I'd be cooking dinner tonight. I pictured myself flitting Frenchly from *boucherie* to *épicier* to *boulangerie*, then fastening on an apron and whisking up an intimate meal in the tiny galley kitchen. I'd decided I could put the spare set of keys to my newly purchased office in a little dish of some kind and serve them to Jonathan—it was the kind of news that deserved its own fanfare.

Before that, though, I'd arranged to meet Jonathan for a drink on the Left Bank, and—typically—he noticed my new/old vintage blouse immediately, which only increased my good mood.

"New shirt?" he said, kissing me on the cheek.

"Yes." I flicked up the collar and caught my reflection in the glass. There seemed to be mirrors all over French dining establishments—for admiring yourself and flirting, presumably. "Quite Brigitte Bardot, the lady in the shop said. I think."

"Mm." Jonathan stopped perusing the wine list. "Listen, I meant to ask you—fancy going shopping tomorrow?"

"Ooh, yes!" I said. "What for?"

"Clothes."

"For you?" My mental Rolodex whirred. "I've heard there's a marvelous American men's tailor that all the—"

"Um . . . I mean, for you. Too." he added, a fraction of a second late.

I stared at him. "But I'm fine for clothes!" I laughed. "You know me and my wardrobe."

"Well," he said, looking a little cautious, "I was thinking more of a *working* wardrobe. It isn't that I don't think what you wear is great, Melissa, but I just think, here in Paris, people are a bit more traditional than London. And we want clients to take you seriously."

I felt rather stung. Apart from the fact that my clients *did* take me seriously, thanks, Jonathan had always gone on about how gorgeous he thought I looked in my pencil skirts and nipped-in winter tweeds. Like an old-fashioned man's woman, he used to say. "What's wrong with my clothes?"

Jonathan spread his hands. "I'm not saying there's anything wrong. Just that you might want to look more . . . businesslike."

The waiter appeared and Jonathan ordered something in fluent French. He and the waiter then shared a little joke that I didn't understand, and the waiter looked at me, still chuckling, and I had to smile and pretend I had.

"Listen, you can't wear tea dresses to work, not for the type of clients we deal with," said Jonathan, getting back to the matter at hand. "It's not what they're used to. It doesn't come across well."

"Surely if I'm dealing with their cleaners and arranging nannies I should look relaxed and trustworthy," I argued.

Jonathan made a face as if he couldn't understand why I was being so difficult. "Don't take it so personally. You can save the pretty dresses for me, when you get home. You know I love them."

There was something so Daddyish in that comment that I forgot my Parisian diet and reached out crossly for the bread basket on the table.

"I'll get Solange to find you a dressmaker, if you want," he carried on. "It's the kind of thing she'd know. We really have to set up lunch with her—I'm hoping I'll be able to persuade her to jump ship and join you as an assistant." He looked over the table at me. "What do you think? You could train her."

"I'm sure she could do the job better than me already," I said pettily. I knew I was being childish, but it came out anyway. Argh.

Jonathan cocked his head. "Well, I must admit I'd been looking ahead to that—you know, so that in a year or so, you could take some time off?" He raised his ginger eyebrows.

"Sorry?" I said. Surely Jonathan wasn't bringing up the romantic topic of us starting a family in the context of his *diary*. Was he?

"Well, you know, neither of us is getting any younger. Not just you," he added, as my face registered distress, "me too! I read that men have a biological clock too—and I'm going to be forty this Christmas. And what with Brendan and Cindy having little Parker running about . . ."

Cindy was his ex-wife. Brendan was his brother. Parker was his two-year-old nephew. Doesn't take a genius to see how painful Jonathan's divorce had been.

He reached over the table to stroke my arm, but I was still tense. We'd never really talked about family plans, since Parker was such a painful topic, but it was one of my favorite romantic thoughts—you know, finding the man you'd want as your children's father. I'd always assumed it would just . . . *happen,* not be timetabled. I should have known Jonathan would want to be more specific. Since he'd been in Paris, he seemed so much more target-focused. Or maybe I was just noticing it more.

He touched my engagement ring. "Once we've got this business up and running, and the wedding over, I don't think we should wait around, do you? In case . . . you know."

The wine arrived, and Jonathan disengaged his hand to try it.

"Bon." He nodded knowledgeably to the sommelier, and he nodded again toward me to have my glass filled.

Suddenly, I really felt like I needed a drink. I took a deep slurp of red wine and braced myself to be frank. He'd suddenly brought up a whole load of stuff—not just babies but also this business of my clothes, the chalet girl nature of what I was meant to do, the fact that we hadn't actually discussed how I was going to wind things up at the agency—and now appeared to be moving on to the menu as if it had all been settled.

I felt a tightness starting in my chest and forced myself to sound relaxed.

"Actually, darling," I said, putting my wineglass down, "there were one or two things I wanted to ask you. About the business."

"Can it wait till after supper?" he asked, gazing at the specials board. "You're always telling me not to talk about work when we're off-duty."

"But I think we . . . ," I began, and he looked up, with a *no, no!* twinkle in his gray eyes.

"But—"

"Ah, ah!" he said playfully.

"OK," I said. "But shall we talk about this at home? I'm going to wow you with cooking and translation skills." It was nearly six, and if we didn't get back, the shops would be shut and my planned dinner wouldn't happen.

"I called you," I added. "About supper?"

He tore his eyes from the menu. "Oh. I didn't get that message. I thought we could eat now then maybe meet up with a couple of guys I know from New York—they're stopping over in Paris and I said we'd take them out for drinks. That OK?"

I felt my heart sink. "It's just that . . . I thought we were going to stay in this evening, spend some time together?"

Jonathan looked up. "Melissa, I only see you a few days a week. What's the point of staying in and doing nothing?"

"Because it's just nice? To relax? Be all unbuttoned together?" I tried a smile. "You know how I love my evenings in."

"Honey, I don't work this hard to spend evenings in watching television," he said. "Anyway, there's so much to catch up on—how's Emery? Tell me she's hired someone else to sort out the christening for little Egbert. There's no way you've got time to get dragged into that!"

"Cuthbert. The baby's called Cuthbert," I said automatically. Suddenly, I couldn't even be bothered to argue. A real paralyzer of a Bad Mood was starting to spread through me. "Jonathan, I'm just going to pop to the loo—if the waiter comes back before I do, I'll have the tomato salad to start, then the sole."

I pushed my chair back and weaved my way out into the fresh air.

Most people would reach into their bags and restore themselves with a cigarette. Instead, I refreshed my lipstick and checked my phone. No messages.

Nelson would be at home by now, I thought. Probably with his feet up with some homemade minestrone, watching some boring archaeological program. Unless he was out with Leonie.

Or maybe Leonie was there with him, I thought with a pang. On my side of the sofa.

My fingers started to move before I could think. WANT ANYTHING FROM PARIS? I texted and sent it to him.

Almost immediately, a reply pinged back. DUR!! YOU FORGOT TO MOVE YR CAR AGAIN! HAD TO SAVE IT FROM PARKING WARDENS—IS PARKED IN LUPUS ST.

I knew there was something I'd forgotten in my rush to catch the train yesterday: the evil hour when parking was permit only outside our house. Good old Nelson had saved me at least sixty quid there. I smiled at the image of bearlike Nelson folded up in my tiny pink Smart car, scooting away in the nick of time from the fist-waving wardens. I LOVE YOU! I texted back. YOU ARE PATRON SAINT OF FLATMATES! I breathed in the cooler air and missed London.

To my surprise, the phone beeped again with a new message. HOW'S PARIS? Nelson had texted.

Nelson didn't normally text internationally with such wanton disregard for his phone bill. This unexpected yearning for home, plus gratitude for his thoughtfulness, unlocked the building panic in me. I started to tell him about having a row with Jonathan, then stopped and deleted it. MORTGAGE IS GO! I texted instead. THANKS TO YOU!

There was a brief pause, then HOORAY! YOU'RE A BORING MORTGAGED GROWN-UP AT LAST! came back.

I smiled to myself, suddenly seeing his sardonic expression as he said that. Nelson and I could say all sorts of things to each other, knowing we didn't really mean it.

I started to text back, then reminded myself I was meant to be having dinner with Jonathan. And how mad did I get when he wouldn't turn off his BlackBerry?

I texted TALK LATER MX to Nelson, then turned off my phone and went back inside.

Jonathan compromised by rearranging his friends in favor of a romantic walk along the river, and after a little brittleness, we got through the starters and the mains in a better mood, talking about my family's various ridiculous arguments about Bertie's christening, and Jonathan's dealings with Parisians, and his plans for the apartment. Then we hit an awkward dry patch, and I found myself blurting out my news about the office, just to fill the silence.

Instead of leaping in the air with delight, Jonathan merely smiled and said, "Hey, well done."

"That's all?"

"Yeah. Good move. I kind of thought you already owned the place, actually."

I stared at him, dismayed by his lack of excitement. "But I've never owned anything in my life. This is a big deal for me."

"You own a business," he said, looking a little evasive.

"Well, yes, but . . ." I swallowed. The nearer it got, the less happy I was about closing down what I'd put so much effort into starting. "Jonathan, I need to talk to you about that. I'm not sure I can . . ."

"I thought you didn't want to talk about work," he said, signaling to the waiter.

"Well, no . . . ," I began. "But . . ."

The waiter was hovering at my shoulder.

"Go on," said Jonathan. "You can order the desserts—good practice."

I would have bet money that the waiter deliberately brought me crème brûlée instead of crème caramel, but I ate it anyway.

We left the restaurant by nine. Early, for us. When we'd first started dating, it had been a running joke that Jonathan would slip the staff cash to let us linger on, flirting over liqueurs while they'd swept up around us. And I'd argued to my wavering conscience that since it was my job to introduce him to London, I'd only been giving him value for money by staying so late. Then we'd started dating properly and there had been no need to pretend anymore. The talking and flirting had carried on just the same, but with the promise of even more to follow.

Tonight, though, we each sank into our own thoughts. I didn't understand enough French to eavesdrop on our fellow diners, and I felt uncomfortably like a tourist. Jonathan was quiet too, as if he was trying to work out how to say something awkward. When he suggested strolling to the square du Vert-Galant off the Pont Neuf "because it was famously romantic," I felt a sudden pitch in my stomach, as if that could only bode badly.

We walked hand in hand along the bridge, and I realized I was racking my brains for something to talk about. That had never happened to us before. It made me feel chilly inside.

"So come on," said Jonathan, pulling me to a sudden stop as we reached a curved sightseeing bay overlooking the Seine and the tourist boats passing beneath. "Suppose you tell me what's wrong?"

He looped his arms around my waist, and he was smiling, but his smile seemed forced. It reminded me again of our first dates, when he'd been tense and defensive, still smarting over his divorce and cracking the whip at Dean & Daniels.

"OK, I'll start," he said when I didn't reply immediately. He sat down on the stone bench and gently pulled me down next to him. "I'm sorry for shouting at you about the Scotts, and I'm sorry about that confusion with their club. I know you didn't do it on purpose. And I'm thrilled about you buying the office, OK? I just wish you'd talked to me about it first."

"I wanted it to be a surprise," I said, feeling the cold stone through my thin summer skirt. "And . . ."

He lifted up my chin with a finger and crinkled up his gray eyes to examine my face better. "What? You're still offended about the clothes thing, aren't you? Melissa, don't take it that way. Think of it as a different kind of costume. Trust me, I know this business and—"

I gathered my nerve. "That's just it. I'm just not sure about this business," I said.

Jonathan's brow furrowed. "Meaning?"

Squeezing my eyes shut, I opened my mouth and let the words that had been jostling in my head for the last month come out. "I don't think I want to do it. Not the way you want. I'm sorry."

When I opened my eyes, Paris was still there, the tourists were still strolling across the river, but for the first time ever, Jonathan was looking stunned. "What are you saying, Melissa?"

That was a very good question. It was also a much bigger one than it first appeared.

And this is where my Ghastly Day began to take on quite epic proportions of Ghastliness.

fourteen

I took a deep breath. "Jonathan," I said, "I've been trying to talk to you but there's so much we haven't discussed. When were you going to ask me what *I* saw my role in this partnership as? You didn't even check to see if I wanted to do it before you started making plans."

It was out of my mouth before I had a chance to think what I was saying. The trouble was that once that bit was out, a whole load of other stuff followed it.

"It's not that I don't think it's a good idea, but I've been running my own office for a while now, and I don't want to act as a glorified chalet maid to people too busy and self-important to pay their own parking fines!" I went on. "I mean, I'm sure they're very nice and very successful, but is that all I'm going to be doing from morning till night—filling in forms for one client after another?"

"No, there'll be far more to it than that," said Jonathan, sounding surprised at my outburst. "Some guys will be bringing their wives over, and if they're not working, they'll need someone to show them round, get them used to the way things work over here—"

"As well as fill in their forms?" I gave him a *Seriously?* look. "And their parking fines? And do their secretarial donkey work?"

He shrugged openly, with both his hands raised, as if he had no idea why I was being so unreasonable. "Seriously, what's the problem here? Is there something I'm not seeing? It's exactly what you're doing in London. It's what you're good at."

"It's totally different," I insisted.

"Is it? You're just picking up the slack for people who can't or won't sort out their own lives. Your clients *can't.* Ours, on the other hand, are professional people who don't have the time. And I know which kind I'd prefer to deal with."

Jonathan's voice suddenly got much harder. "You're happy enough to run after *Nicolas,*" he went on disparagingly. "And he's treating you like an idiot, and behaving like a child, so it can't be about that."

I bridled at his tone. This wasn't the romantic, urbane Jonathan I knew. "You know as well as I do that Nicky's a one-off, and anyway, most of my clients aren't . . ."

I stopped and stared at him. Was this really an argument about work—or was it about *my* work and *my* clients versus Jonathan again?

He lifted an eyebrow, and suddenly there was none of the tender amusement that usually accompanied the familiar gesture. His face, the face I thought I knew so well, seemed hard, and there was a cold-ness in his eyes that made me shiver inside, despite the warm evening air closing in on us.

I stopped speaking, afraid that the next words that came out of my mouth would shift everything into dangerous new ground. Here we were, about to move in together, and I just wasn't sure we were plan-ning the same things.

Jonathan, though, took my silence as some kind of agreement. "OK," he said, softening, "forget Nicky. It's not that I don't think your agency is great. You hit on a real niche, and, you know, with the divorce rate and everything, single guys everywhere, it's only going to get bigger. That's why I don't want you to sell up when you move to Paris."

"You don't?" Now I really was confused.

"No. Not in the least. In fact, I think we need to think bigger. Ex-pand. Get an office going in Edinburgh, Manchester, Birmingham. Wherever you've got single men, you're going to need a Honey."

"But I'm working four days a week in London as it is," I said, baffled. "How can I spend time in Manchester as well? And, I mean, I sort of know Edinburgh a bit, and I've got a few friends up there, but it's not like—"

Jonathan waved his hand in front of my face. "*You* don't need to be there."

"But . . ."

He clicked his finger and pointed at me. It was a brusque, glib gesture from the old days that I hated, and now it filled me with dread. "You franchise!"

"I what?"

"You franchise. Interview Honeys—I mean, come on, you wear the wig, so it's not like you're *actually* Honey Blennerhesket. She's just a persona. A work persona. Anyone could be Honey, so long as they were clever enough and practical enough." He winked. "And had good enough legs, right? I'm sure you've got plenty of contacts who could take over, or Gabi even—she's a smart cookie. She did a decent job of covering for you when you came to New York last year—why not give her a break? Just think, your very own team of Honey Bs. Isn't that a cute idea? It came to me on my run. Honey Bees—like Honey Blennerhesket?"

I stared over the stone bridge at the lamp-lit square du Vert-Galant beneath us, jutting into the Seine like the green prow of a little boat. A couple were sitting right on the point, dangling their legs over the edge, their arms wrapped around each other, heads leaning on each other's shoulders. Saying nothing.

Anyone could be Honey? Did he really think that?

Jonathan, meanwhile, was steaming on and on. "I've been looking into this for a while, to tell you the truth, and you know what? The more I've thought about it, the more perfect it gets as a solution. You keep your agency, and some financial independence, which I absolutely respect . . ." He held up his hands at this point to show me how much he respected it. "But it's not a good use of your time anymore. So you come over here with me, while the Honey Bees keep bringing in the nectar back in England. And I've even found a backer for the franchise operation."

I looked at him, unable to make sense of the tumbling emotions jostling about in my head. They were like sharp little stones, while the rest of me felt numb. What was it going to be like when we were working together, if we couldn't even see eye to eye now? Jonathan—the man who'd fallen for the woman Honey had helped me become—thought the whole agency boiled down to a wig and a Harrods discount card. And he hadn't even been there during the weeks it had taken me to undo the chaos after Gabi's well-meaning spell in charge!

But I am Honey, the voice in my head kept wailing. She's part of me. I can't sell her off!

Then I realized the voice wasn't in my head. It was coming out of my mouth.

Jonathan stroked my arm affectionately. "Don't be silly, Melissa," he said. "I thought we went through all this? I always knew the real you was underneath that Honey front—the smart, responsible, caring you. Anyway, you want to know the best bit? I think you'll like this—it's very English and ironic."

"What?" I choked.

"Where do you think I found the backer for the franchise operation? The operation that's going to create an independent income without you having to do a thing?"

A variety of awful options slid in front of my mind. Granny? Surely not. Roger? No. A client?

"I don't know," I whispered.

"Your father!" said Jonathan triumphantly. "Isn't that perfect? He's happy to sink his entire earnings from his Cheese Diet book into the start-up. We're still talking terms, but I'm being really tough. You've got to love the irony of that. You set up the agency to earn back a few thousand pounds you owed him, and now he's having to stump up the cash to make you a rich woman!"

All the blood drained from my face. I didn't care whether Daddy was doing it as a money-making or money-laundering scheme—he never invested unless he knew he could make money or wanted to lose it. Either way, I'd still be the butt of his jokes.

Worse than that—much worse than that—Jonathan thought it was a good idea.

I got up from the bench and walked over to the edge of the bridge. I looked down at the Seine flowing underneath, with the lamps glimmering through the dusk on the gray water, and felt everything slipping from under me, like a rug on a shiny floor. This wasn't how I'd imagined things working out. Not at all.

Jonathan appeared by my side. "What's the matter, Melissa? Have you got a problem with that?"

"Please tell me this is a joke," I said. My voice wobbled on the "joke."

Jonathan shrugged. "A joke? Why would I be joking? It's a great idea—you don't have to get so involved yourself, plus, you stand to make a lot of money, especially if we develop the Internet angle."

"You don't think I'd . . . I'd have a problem with my father investing in a business I started to get away from him and his meddling in my life? And I *want* to be involved! It's not up to you to decide to sell off something I've made! Something I love! Especially not to him!"

We stared at each other furiously, until finally he twisted up his face in disgust.

"Why, Melissa, does it always come back to your family? Every time? Am I being naïve here? Should I just accept now that they're always going to be there, in the background, screwing you up? I honestly thought you were over that."

"You can't *get over* your family, Jonathan," I said bitterly. "They aren't *measles*. Just because we're in Paris doesn't mean they're going to vanish from my life. And how could they, if you'd let Daddy buy into my business?"

"Because I thought it'd give you the upper hand! I honestly thought that by us both uprooting ourselves to live in Paris, we'd be able to make a fresh start. Together," he said, half to himself, as he chopped the side of his hand down onto the bridge, over and over. "No Cindy, no families, no people reminding us how we met . . ." He turned to glare at me. "No sharing you with two hundred idiots in London and the Home Counties. But you're not going to move, are you? You never really wanted to come to Paris."

"That's not true," I protested. "I do! I love you!"

"Do you? Really?"

Jonathan's cynical tone went through me like a knife. "Yes! It's just that . . ." I struggled for the right words. "You always seem to be asking me to choose between you and everything else in my life that *isn't* you!"

"I give up. I give up, Melissa. What do you want me to do?" he demanded. "It's like you're constantly putting things before me—your family, your business, London. I flew across the world to be with you! I've worked out a business we can run together!"

I blinked, feeling unbearably selfish. He *had* done all that, it was true. But something inside me still refused to stop.

"So when are you handing in *your* notice?" I demanded, and Jonathan's evasive flinch told me everything. "You haven't, have you?"

"Well . . ." He pushed his hair back with his hand. "When I told Lisa about the relocation idea she loved it. Really loved it, saw it as something we could run as a boutique service alongside our main operation." He met my stunned gaze and there was an excitement in his eyes that I knew wasn't just about working alongside me in some little office somewhere. "Lisa came up with a financial package that I'd have been insane to refuse, but think about it! This is the best of both worlds! I stay in the running for worldwide CEO, we build up our own business, which we can eventually sell back to Kyrle & Pope in a huge deal, you get your own project here, and I get to take you out for lunch whenever I want!"

I stared at him, horrified. "You were never going to leave! You want me to run this on my own, don't you?"

"With Solange. And me." He put his hand on my thigh and squeezed it as if he'd just put my mind at rest. "Melissa, I want you to have everything—security, a proper career . . ."

"I know!" I flashed back. "But not you! You won't stay in for one evening and talk to me!"

Jonathan made a *What?* face. "You're complaining that I take you out too much? Seriously?"

I looked into his baffled eyes and knew there was no point trying to explain. And that made me sad.

But at least we were talking about it, weren't we?

I put aside the business horror for a moment. This was much more important. "I'm sorry. It's not that I don't appreciate the lovely places we go. But you're so good at making quick decisions, and I'm . . . not. I need more time to think about important things."

"The business?" He bit his lips. "Or me?"

I looked down at the river. "I'm not sure," I admitted.

Jonathan fiddled with his gold cuff links. The vintage ones I'd found for his birthday. "Well, you need to learn to make some decisions, Melissa. Very soon. Or else I don't see this situation changing in the next year, two years, five years. Come and live here with me now, right now, or don't bother. But let's not waste time neither of us has."

Although I was stunned, a hot thread of anger ran through me, that he could reduce such a life-changing decision to an either/or. It might be how he got buyers to make a gut decision on a house, but I hated being backed into a corner. I'd had enough of that growing up.

"You want me to answer that now?" I asked incredulously.

"If you know what the answer is, why string me along? Or are you waiting for half the apartment?" Jonathan's voice was unnaturally cool, and I hoped it was to hide his own panic.

I gasped as if he'd hit me. That was uncalled for. I struggled with my dignity, refusing to sink to that level of bitterness. "I think you're confusing me with your ex-wife. And I thought you knew that I'm not like her at all."

Jonathan's mouth made a "no" shape and he looked ashamed. "Melissa, I'm sorry, that was very wrong, I didn't mean to—"

I lifted my chin. "I don't need half of your *anything*. And I wouldn't sell my agency to strangers for the world. It's not about the *money*. It never *was*. If you think that, then I wonder just what else you've got wrong about me. I was willing to give that up for you—and you weren't giving up anything at all. Not even your time."

My voice started cracking. This was going so wrong it felt as if it was happening to someone else.

"Listen, Melissa," Jonathan began, "I think you're being far too emotional about this. Should we talk about this tomorrow? You're tired, and—"

Something in me just snapped.

"You're right—I'm tired." I wrenched the diamond engagement ring off my finger. "Here," I said. "Take this."

"What?" Jonathan took a little step backward.

"You think money and . . . *stuff*'s important to me? It's not." I tried to push the ring into his jacket pocket. He hadn't unpicked the stitching so the jacket would hang better, so I had to shove the ring in his trouser pocket instead.

"Are you breaking off our engagement?"

We stood on the Pont Neuf, as if time had frozen for a second. Jonathan looked as shocked as I felt. Tourists were gawking at us now, but I barely registered their curious looks.

What was I doing?

It's not all about flying across the world and fancy dinners, said a calm voice in my head. It's about how you're going to live together after you stop being the girlfriend and start being the wife. When the music stops and the nights in start. If he ever lets you have a night in.

I drew a shuddering breath. "I'm saying I need some time to *think*. I don't want to let you down by not turning out to be the woman you thought you were marrying. I'm sorry. I'm sorry, Jonathan. I'll . . . I'll call you."

Then I turned on my heel. If I didn't get away now, I'd cry or apologize, and I knew I didn't want to do either. I had no idea where I was going to go, but there was absolutely no way I could stay there on that romantic old bridge, with couples walking along hand in hand, blissfully happy, when my heart was breaking. I couldn't see through the tears in my eyes.

"Where are you going?" He caught at my bare arm.

"Home!" I said, pulling away from his warm fingers.

"You can't! You don't know where anything is!" he said with a mixture of concern and exasperation. Unfortunately, I mainly heard the exasperation.

"I'm not a child, Jonathan!" I yelled, and I stormed off, walking anywhere, as fast as I could, just to get away.

I took a left turn off the bridge, following the crowds of wandering tourists, tears blinding and stinging my eyes, with no real idea where I was going, through a quiet square, then down streets—anywhere Jonathan wouldn't follow me.

Eventually, I stumbled to a halt in front of the massive facade of Notre-Dame Cathedral, its pale stonework bathed in floodlights. I sank down onto a bench and stared up at the towers, letting tears wash down my face as an unexpected stillness fell over me, and my heartbeat began to slow down. There was something very calming about the filigree windows and delicate angels, carved like lace out of the stone—it gave my racing brain something else to focus on.

I tried to take deep breaths, between my hiccups. The flower beds were planted with box, and the dark, green smell reminded me of my parents' garden. Suddenly, I felt very, very lonely and very far from home.

What had I done?

After a second's pause, I reached for my phone and dialed.

It rang and rang, and for a horrendous moment, I thought maybe he wasn't there.

"Hello?" said a familiar voice. "If you're going to sell me something, I'm terribly sorry, but I'm not interested, thanks."

The sound of Nelson's matter-of-fact tone made me want to curl up and howl, and when I opened my mouth, nothing came out but dry sobs. The anger I'd felt moments ago had evaporated, and now all I felt was a clawing sadness.

"Mel?" he said, immediately concerned. "Are you OK?"

"No," I managed. "I've had a ghastly row with Jonathan, and I . . ."

Nelson paused to let me get myself together, then said, "Whatever's happened, it's nothing that can't be put right. What was it about this time? His ties?"

"Worse than that!" I said. The words came out of my mouth in a flood. "He's franchised the agency to Daddy, has no intention of giving up his own job, and more or less told me I had to move out to Paris now, or it was all over!"

"Oh. Right. I see," said Nelson. "That's pretty off."

"Yes!" I howled. "It's very off! And I don't know if I can . . ."

I couldn't make myself say it. Not even to Nelson.

"Where are you?" he asked practically.

I couldn't hold back the tears anymore. Misery was moving up my chest in a hard lump, and I knew a great gut-wrenching sob was moments away.

"Notre-Dame," I managed. "I can't believe it's real! I just want to press rewind and go back to the start of the evening! Nelson, what am I going to do?"

Nelson made unspecific sympathy noises. I knew he'd never really liked Jonathan, but he was too gentlemanly to get into that now, unlike Gabi, who would have let rip. Instead, he said, "Listen, Melissa, do you want to come home? I can—"

He was being cut off in bleeps. I had an incoming call.

"Wait a second," I said, "this might be Jonathan."

I juggled the phone buttons. "Hello?"

"Melissa, it's me," drawled Nicky. "I decided to pop over to Paris for the weekend and just wondered if you were around for a spot of Sunday lunch." It sounded like he was calling from a club, from the loud music and the squeal of overexcited It girls. "Might end up being more of a tea fixture because I've got plans for Saturday night, but you know, if you want to bring your fiancé along . . ."

That did it. I burst into tears.

"Melissa? Are you all right?"

"I don't think I *have* a fiancé anymore!" I wailed. "We've just had a big row and it's all your fault! Partly!"

"Well, how flattering!" he replied, and I could just picture the smooth expression on his face. I longed to punch someone right now, and he was a great choice. "I did wonder how long it'd take for me to . . . Melissa?" he asked, dropping the drawl. "Are you crying?"

"Of course I'm crying!" I yelled. "I'm not like you—I have feelings!"

The background noise changed at the end of the phone, as if Nicky had walked outside. "Where are you right now?" he said, in a more worried tone.

The fight abruptly went out of me. It wasn't his fault. That business with the clubs had been more about Jonathan's attitude than anything else. I didn't have energy to waste on being angry, and I didn't know anyone else in Paris. So I told him where I was.

"Fine. Fine. I know exactly where you are. Walk over the Pont St. Louis—there's a nice little bistro two blocks down. Le Relais de l'Ile—it should still be open. Go in there, sit down, and order yourself a bottle of wine."

"And what good's that going to do?" I demanded bitterly.

"Well, you need a drink, and you can't be alone at a time like this, can you? Take deep breaths, yes? Good. Now wait there."

"Why?"

"I'm coming to get you."

Somehow, being given instructions seemed to help focus my stunned brain, and without really knowing how I managed to get there, I was in the candlelit bistro staring at a bottle of house red while three people played noisy jazz in that peculiar French way. Then the full glass in front of me was empty, then the waiter must have topped it up, and then it was empty again. My French must be improving, I thought. Then Nicky was sitting opposite me.

I knew that without looking up, because suddenly the tables around me had gone very quiet.

He slid a pair of sunglasses across the table. "Here, you'll need these," he said.

"So no one will recognize me with you?" I suggested weakly.

"No. Because you've got major mascara issues. It kind of suits you, though. Now, let's get you somewhere more private." In a few deft movements, he got me to my feet, slapped a wodge of euros on the table, nodded to the barman, said something cheeky to a waitress, and hustled me outside, where a shiny black Bentley was waiting.

I sank into the back of it and felt the wine pressing down on my head. My brain was only processing one thought at a time.

How could Jonathan have gone behind my back like that? Was that what he and Daddy had been discussing in the study? Was that the reason he'd been so happy to spend the weekend at Romney Hall—had it just been about making money?

Drinking your way out of problems went absolutely against everything I'd ever believed, but for once all I wanted was to slide into absolute oblivion and worry about it later.

"Here," said Nicky, reading my thoughts as we drove off. He shoved a silver hip flask at me, and I drained the contents, then handed it back to him.

He looked at me approvingly.

"More," I slurred. "I'm drinking to forget. And there's a lot to forget."

Nicky's eyes rounded appreciatively and glinted in the semidarkness of the backseat. "Supernanny! I knew there was some unwholesomeness in there somewhere." He opened a drawer and pulled out a bottle of champagne and two glasses. "I might even join you."

"Where are we going?" I asked—like I cared.

"Well, I *am* meant to be out with friends at the moment," he said. "Birthday party, actually."

My heart sank again at the thought of an evening with Chunder-a-likes. I didn't want to see anyone right now, much less the sort of people who made dental work seem a preferable social option. "Oh."

"But maybe you'd prefer to get wasted somewhere quieter?" Nicky sounded almost sympathetic. Some part of my brain noticed he'd been discreet enough not to ask me for details as to why I was in this state. Yet.

"Yes," I said, tipping the champagne flute unsteadily to my lips. "Somewhere quieter."

It occurred to me that it was a bit of a coincidence that Nicky just happened to be in Paris this weekend, and I was about to mention it to him when his phone rang. He had the grace to look apologetic as he answered and almost immediately had to hold it away from his ear to protect himself from the shrieky onslaught.

"No! No! Piglet . . . no, I'm not."

My brain, now tipping slightly sideways, discerned that it was Imogen Whatsit-Whatsit.

"Bloody hell! Will you . . . I'm not! No! Well, get a cab and put it on my . . . Will you calm down? No, I didn't intend to stand you up from the . . ."

I could hear her screeching from where I was sitting.

Nicky rolled his eyes at me. "No, darling, I've had to go to an emergency meeting . . . With Melissa, yes." He held the phone away from his ear again, and even I could hear the fury. "Stop it . . . No, stop it. It's not like that. No, I don't think she'll want to talk to you. I don't care if you need to talk to her. . . . Darling, if you want to leave the party with Piers, please do . . . I . . . Piglet, there is no need for . . ."

Without even thinking about it, I took the phone off Nicky, turned it off, and gave it back to him.

"Sorry," I slurred politely, as he stared at me in amused awe. "I don't have time to deal with people like that. I need to devote all my energy to feeling miserable. I've had a terrible evening."

I shut my eyes, felt dizzy, saw Jonathan's face, and opened them again, tearily.

"Let me take you home," said Nicky gently.

Nicky was not the sort of knight in shining armor I'd have hoped for, but then nothing this evening was turning out as I'd expected.

I was too tired and too stunned and too generally freaked out to do anything other than smile, and when I did, the self-mockery left his face, and I felt like he was someone I'd known for ages.

After that, time seemed to compress and blur. I don't remember going into Nicky's apartment, although I vaguely remember some kind of even-more-elaborate-than-normal elevator, and I do have a very vivid mental picture of sinking into a deep leather sofa.

As my head spun with helicopters, I closed my eyes to stop them. When I opened them again, after I don't know how long, Nicky was leaning over me, very close, and I could see the double layer of lashes that made his dark eyes seem so fascinating. They were so deep brown it was impossible to see where the pupils began and ended. His smell seemed familiar too; underneath the expensive cologne and lingering nightclub air was a pungent, exciting boy odor I remembered from school dances. Nothing special, or regal: just boy. And he was angling his head toward me in the way boys did then, when they wanted to make their intentions clear. Or was he checking to see if I was still breathing?

Whatever it was, it filled me with a horribly inappropriate longing. Partly for Nicky, whose smooth, tanned throat I could now almost reach out and touch with a fingertip if I wanted, and partly for the chance to run away from the reality of my own ruined world into this Alice in Wonderland fantasyland of princes, and polo, and Bentleys with champagne in the back and discreet drivers in the front.

But then Jonathan's face would float up in my mind's eye again, and the awful jagged pain in my chest returned too.

"You're not asleep then," Nicky whispered, and now I could almost taste the warm breath that brushed against my face.

I'm not sure what I said in response. Seriously, I wish I could remember. But the next thing I knew, I was struggling to open my eyes, and it was Saturday morning.

fifteen

When I woke up, I kept my eyes closed for as long as possible. There seemed to be a fine layer of Super Glue sealing them shut, but in any case, opening my eyes would mean acknowledging that now I had to work out what to do. Plus, I wasn't entirely sure I wanted to see what kind of unholy state I was in.

Instead, I lay there and let the invisible miners clog dancing in my head get on with their evil business and tried to think of three positive things.

Honestly, never in my life had it been so hard.

The first one I came up with, after five minutes of thinking slowly, was that at least I knew where I was.

The second was that if you were going to get embarrassingly wasted, you might as well do it in style, on vintage champagne, with a prince, however tenuous his grip on a proper princehood might be.

Unfortunately, thinking only triggered another torrent of savage clog dancing as the previous evening began to trickle back, and I would have rolled my head under a pillow if the mere thought of moving my head hadn't filled me with nausea.

After half an hour of lying very still, I tentatively ran my hands down my body and discovered, to my surprise, that I was still wearing yesterday's clothes.

That was a good thing. A very good thing.

Three, I told myself, at least I hadn't revealed the full horror of my cottage cheesy thighs to a client.

With a huge effort I opened my eyes.

I was alone on a bed the size of a small room. Disappointingly, it wasn't round or a waterbed, as far as I could see, but the décor was enough to reduce most would-be seductees to a quivering jelly even without Nicky's efforts. It was a massive bedroom, dominated by a majestic white marble fireplace and two long windows with cream curtains, through which rays of lemony sunlight streamed. Beneath my own horrible morning-after stench, I could make out the pale scent of rose water on the crisp linen sheets, and another cloud of fragrance coming from a crystal vase of lilies on a pedestal stand.

Even through my hangover, I noted it wasn't exactly the bedroom I'd imagined Nicky would have.

I levered myself up to sitting with some effort and steadied myself as my head spun in a most unpleasant manner.

Come on, Melissa, I told myself sternly. *Get a grip. Start with washing your face.*

I groped my way out of bed, clinging for balance onto various mahogany furnishings that I'd have admired had I not been so queasy, and found the en-suite bathroom. Again, it was *Vogue Homes* elegant, although the main thing I noticed was that alongside the Jo Malone oils and potions was a bottle of Johnson's Baby Bath. I'd always used it, ever since Granny had told me it was better for your skin than anything else.

While the bath was running and the comforting smell soothed my nerves a little, I studied myself in the mirror over the cool square sink.

I looked a wreck. In fact, more specifically, I looked like a Hollywood starlet gone bad, left out in the rain and put away wet. My mascara was smeared round my eyes, which were red with crying, my carefully roller-set hair had gone into mad curls, and just to add insult to injury, there was a massive white spot on the side of my nose.

For some reason, the thought of Nicky staring at the spot all night bothered me more than anything else.

Automatically, I reached for the cleansing lotion and began cleaning up my face. Then I sank into the hot bath, until the grime and misery seemed to float off my skin, then I washed my hair, over and over again, to get all the memories of last night out of it.

I always feel better for washing my hair, even with an Olympic hangover. By the time I stepped out of the bathroom, pink and glowing in a fluffy robe, I knew I at least now looked more like myself, even if I wasn't completely all there inside.

My eye fell on a pile of clothes, laid on the chair by the bed. Had they been there when I'd left? I frowned but picked up the crisp white shirt (so Parisian) and black skirt. Underneath that was a pretty cotton sundress, and a fine cashmere cardigan, all more or less my size.

I stared at them. There was no way I could put last night's clothes on. Fortunately, I had a spare pair of pants in my handbag, as usual, but beyond that, I'd have to go round to Jonathan's flat to get fresh clothes.

Jonathan's flat, I thought. *You never really thought of it as yours, did you?*

We can sort this out, I told myself. *You just need time to think it through.*

In the light of day, the apartment was about ten times bigger than I'd thought last night, with high, molded ceilings, gold light fittings, and a rather intimidating silence.

I tiptoed through to the kitchen, where there was still no sign of Nicky. Instead, someone had laid out breakfast: a silver pot of coffee, croissants, jam and English marmalade, and bone china. The china had little crests on it, and the knives were so heavy that they had to be solid silver.

As I was pouring myself a cup of black coffee with a shaky hand, a voice asked, "You have everything you need?"

I nearly jumped out of my skin. A Filipino maid was standing in the doorway. "Um, yes!" I said, spilling my coffee. "Yes, fine, thank you."

"Prince Nicolas has been called out," she said discreetly. "He leaves his apologies, and has asked me to make sure you were comfortable."

"Oh, right," I said. That didn't sound like something Nicky would say. My brain still felt coated in treacle. "Did he say when he'd be back?"

She shook her head.

"Right." I looked at her. I wasn't the sort of person to say *That will be all,* but I wasn't sure how to make her leave me to my headache. To be honest, she looked as if I wasn't the first woman she'd seen stumble out of Nicky's bedroom.

"I'm fine, thank you," I said. "Um, lovely coffee, by the way!"

She smiled in surprise. "Thank you," she said, and slid out of the kitchen again.

I sank onto a chair and massaged my temples. What was I supposed to do now? Where did I start working out what I wanted?

Handbag, I thought firmly.

My phone still had enough battery left to check my voice-mail messages, of which there were five.

The first was from Jonathan. I could hardly bear to listen to it, but I forced myself.

He sounded choked. "Melissa, it's Jonathan. Look, we've both said some hard words tonight." Pause, for him to stick his right hand into his hair. "You're right—we need some time to think about where we go from here. I don't want to rush you. So let's talk in a week. I'm so sorry. Really, I am. You're so special. I've never . . ." Then his voice cracked, and he hung up.

I had to sit very still for a moment after that.

Then I gathered myself to listen to the next one. It was Nelson. "Hi, Mel. I'm, er, I've just noticed that there's a rather good offer on some wine that we're studying at wine class at the Sainsbury's in Calais, and I thought I might, er, pop over to pick up a case or two this weekend. Roger's not around, off with Zara somewhere. . . . Anyway, I was wondering, if things aren't any better with Jonathan, you might want a lift back? I was, er, a bit worried when you didn't call me back last night, so, er, let me know."

Nelson's kind, worried voice made my eyes fill up again, but I bit my lip and dialed his mobile number. He picked up immediately, almost as if he'd been waiting for it to ring.

"Mel?"

"Hello, Nelson," I said, gulping back tears. "I think I'll take you up on that offer of a lift, if that's OK."

"Oh. Oh, splendid."

"Where are you now?" I asked.

"Um, on the outskirts of Paris?"

My heart filled up with warmth. "You're here? What if I'd said I didn't need a lift?"

"Then I'd have gone home with a trunk full of wine. Look, I'm more than happy to rescue you, but I didn't want you thinking that I assumed you'd need it. You're always saying how annoying it is when Jonathan treats you like a child, so . . ." He paused. "Only this time, you know, I thought you might need the cavalry to arrive in good time."

"Oh, Nelson," I blubbed. "I really, really want to go home!"

"Fine with me," said Nelson. "Just tell me where you are and I'll stick it in my sat nav."

"Oh," I said. "Actually, I'm not sure where I am."

"What?"

"I mean, I know where I am, I'm in Nicky's apartment," I gabbled. "But I'm just not sure whereabouts in Paris it is, let me just see if I can find someone to tell me . . ." I hurried into the big reception room in search of the maid and was immediately poleaxed by the view from the long window.

It was the Place des Vosges—the unbelievably posh square just around the corner from Jonathan's flat. The one where super-smart L'Ambroisie was. The one he told me it was harder to buy in than the most exclusive New York co-op.

Meanwhile, Nelson was going about as spare as I'd expected he would. "Bloody hell, Melissa! I thought when you didn't call me back last night that you were with Jonathan, sorting things out! What was Remington thinking, letting you go off with that cretin? If you'd told me you were with P. Nicky I wouldn't have bothered checking into the hotel last night, I'd have come straight there—"

"What do you mean you'd have come straight here?" I demanded. "Don't tell me you've been here all night?"

"Well . . . more or less," admitted Nelson. "I couldn't sit at home when you sounded so out of your mind with worry, so I just got in the car and caught the night crossing in the Channel tunnel. It's really very efficient, and much cheaper at night. Anyway," he added as an afterthought, "I was coming over for the champagne."

"Oh, yes, the champagne," I said. Anyone would think Nelson had just made that up as an excuse. "Listen, I've found the address." I read it off the top of some engraved stationery on a writing table.

"So where is the pretend prince?" he asked.

"Out. He had a bit of an argument too last night," I said wryly. "You couldn't bring some Nurofen with you?"

"No problem. I'll bring some Dettol too, if you want. I hope he didn't take advantage of your distress? Mel? You didn't let him get you drunk? Oh, no. Oh, no. He did. Oh, no."

"I'm more than capable of getting drunk on my own." I rubbed my head. "Look, I'll explain when I see you."

Nelson sighed. "Right. I'm coming to get you. Be ready."

"I'm more than ready," I said, and hung up.

Quiet descended over the apartment again. I sat down at the writing desk and gazed into the elegant square below, where a few bon-chic-bon-genre Parisiennes were walking their tiny dogs and their Barbour-jacketed children. I'd often strolled round the old arcade of shops and galleries that ran underneath the aristocratic apartments, wondering who could live above them. Now I knew.

The sun shifted and drew my attention to the cluster of silver-framed photos on the desk. I picked up the nearest for a closer look.

It seemed to have been taken by the sea in some Mediterranean resort: sitting on a rock, with an azure sea glittering in the background, was a pretty brunette woman in huge Jackie Onassis sunglasses, holding a little boy on her lap. Next to her was a rangy man with serious sideburns. I assumed this family shot was Oriane, Nicky, and the vanishing racing driver. It was impossible to see whether the man or the woman was happy or sad because of the huge shades masking their eyes and the 1970s "photograph expression" making them pout.

Nicky, on the other hand, had a smile that almost split his sun-tanned face, revealing cute gappy teeth that had obviously been corrected shortly afterward.

The other photo had been taken at the same time and was of Alexander, looking like Blake Carrington in Gucci trunks, carrying Nicky on his shoulders as they splashed through the shallow waves. They were both having a whale of a time, and laughing their heads off.

How sweet, I thought. *Nicky's got matching trunks!*

"Sweet, isn't it?" said a voice right behind me, and I jumped again.

"Didn't I tell you not to creep up on women?" I demanded. "It's very bad form. Haven't you heard of mace spray?"

Nicky put his finger on his chin and pulled his suave face, which now, with repeated exposure, I knew he was doing as a kind of self-parody, not because he thought I was taken in by it. I was beginning to suspect that much of Nicky's behavior was as put on as his too-strong cologne. "I have my own secret weapon, Miss Moneypenny."

"Well, it doesn't work on me."

"You won't let me get it out."

I put the frame down and rubbed my still-thumping head. Nicky looked perfectly fresh in his habitual red shirt, tan loafers, and jeans combo, which didn't seem as Euro-trash in Paris as it did in London.

"So, how are you feeling this morning?" he asked. "I think I can hazard a guess."

"A bit fragile, thanks." I wandered toward the black grand piano, suddenly self-conscious about exactly what I might have drunkenly confessed last night. The piano was strewn with more photo frames, some of which contained photos of people I thought I recognized. Alexander and Grace Kelly at a party. Alexander pulling a Christmas cracker with . . . Elizabeth Taylor? Either Alexander and his family rubbed shoulders with genuine Euro-celebrities or everyone had looked like minor royalty in the seventies.

That woman, though, I did recognize. Granny, about my age, with her hair whirled in a chic updo, wearing the red satin cocktail dress I'd worn to a ball at the Dorchester. With Jonathan. I turned the frame away as fear punched me square in the chest.

"This isn't quite what I imagined your flat would be like," I said, walking over to a huge sofa and sinking into it.

He sat down at the other end and leaned forward to pour the coffee from the fresh pot on the table. "What were you expecting? Black silk sheets? But no, it's *not* my apartment. It's my grandfather's place. I've got a little pied-à-terre in St. Germain. I wouldn't normally bring girls back here. But you're not normal girls."

So had that been *Alexander's* bedroom? I blinked, confused and a little uncomfortable. "Should I be flattered, or not?"

He pushed the cup toward me. "I think so." He looked up and straight into my eyes with a disarming smile, and I thought how much more boyish and less sleazy he'd have looked if the dentist had left his teeth where they'd been. "Maybe I thought you'd be impressed with the official Paris residence. Maybe I thought you *wouldn't* be impressed with my bachelor flat."

"Or maybe there was someone else sleeping in your bachelor flat?"

The eyebrows lifted slightly. "Maybe."

"Imogen?"

"Maybe." He paused. "Maybe not. In fact, that reminds me, I should go back there and check she hasn't trashed the place." He blanched. "She hadn't calmed down this morning. She's convinced you and I are on the point of eloping, which would absolutely *ruin* her plans to be a princess."

"I hope you gave it to her straight," I said.

"Melissa!" he said, with a shocked expression.

"What?"

"Oh, nothing. Do you take sugar?"

Nicky didn't seem to be displaying any signs of anything having happened between us last night. In fact, he was drinking his coffee as if it had been a perfectly normal evening. Either he was being amazingly discreet, or it had been a normal evening for him.

"So," he said, stretching out his arm along the back of the sofa.

"I'm thinking of buying some new wheels. What's the Little Lady ruling on suitable cars?"

"Ah," I said, grateful to talk instead of think, "that's quite a question. . . ."

For all his nightclub charm, Nicky had amusing daytime conversational skills too. He showed me the stained-glass windows in the apartment, and he told me some funny stories about his family, and I told him a few, heavily censored, stories about mine. Time passed and my hangover receded to a dull throb almost without me noticing.

"I don't want to pry, but what are your plans?" he asked eventually. "You're welcome to stay the weekend here. Just tell Maria and she'll sort out whatever you need. And if you want to carry on drowning your sorrows, there's a really great party I can take you to tonight . . . Oops!" He put his hand over his mouth and looked naughty. "Forgot I'm not allowed to go to parties. Are dinners in Parisian restaurants allowed? Could be good practice for me?"

I knew he was trying to cheer me up. I met his teasing eyes for a moment, and for a moment, I was seriously tempted to sidestep into Nicky's fantasy world for a few days. Be whisked from place to place, not caring about anything, or paying for anything, or thinking too hard about anything . . .

But I couldn't *not* care. It was like getting drunk: I'd only have to wake up to my own life in the morning. I owed Jonathan an answer. Anyway, it wasn't me, all that shallowness and posturing. I wasn't sure I could put it on and take it off, like my blond wig.

"Thank you, but I can't," I said. "I'm going home. I need to get back to London so I can do some thinking." My dignity wobbled. "I need to work out where the compromises are."

Nicky's teasing expression softened. "Don't worry about the fiancé," he said, in a surprisingly normal voice. "If he's got any sense, he'll be the one doing the compromising."

"I've already made him move from New York to Paris."

"Well, London to Paris might be nearer, but it's still a different country." He touched my hand—a delicate little gesture, considering he could easily have shoved up the sofa and slung his arm round me. "Home is where the heart is, and all that. At least you know where your home is. Mine are all over the place."

I did know, inside. Home was a scruffy flat in Pimlico. But surely it was time I grew up and left?

"I'm just being stupid," I said. "Sorry."

"Melissa, you're not stupid." He let his hand rest on mine, and I felt my skin tingle underneath it. Nicky's hand was soft, but quite cool. "Where's that great big diamond?"

"I gave it back to him," I said sadly.

"Ah. Now that proves you're a nice girl. You can tell how nice a girl is by how many presents she needs, and how many she sends back."

"It's not about the *present*," I said, "it's the thought that goes into it. I'd rather have tiny little gifts that someone had spent time finding, rather than ludicrously expensive ones they'd just charged to their Amex." I looked up at Nicky and blushed a little bit to see him gazing at me intently.

He raised his eyebrows good-humoredly, as if he'd never heard such a weird thing.

"It's not good form for a lady to feel she's being bought," I added, as if we were just talking theoretically about his List of Princely Attributes. "Or at least, not good form for her to establish she has a price."

"So the Rolls-Royce full of Cartier tank watches I've got waiting for you downstairs will just have to go back?"

"Maybe you should give it to Imogen," I said.

Nicky shook his head. "She's more of a Lamborghini girl."

"Expensive?"

"No, loud and thirsty. Impossible to park. Unlike you."

I wasn't sure what to make of that. Nor of the fact that he hadn't let go of my hand and showed no signs of doing so.

Actually, no—now he was threading his fingers through mine and clasping it with his other hand, while letting a shy smile play across that lusciously sexy mouth.

"Nicky," I said, "why didn't you tell me at the polo match that you were going to be in Paris this weekend? I told you I was coming over."

"Maybe because I hadn't decided I was until you told me that." He paused and looked at me again, sending hot flushes through my whole body. "Melissa," he began, "you know you—"

My phone rang on the table, making us both jump this time.

"That'll be Nelson," I said, reaching for it. "He happened to be in France this weekend too, so he's coming to pick me up."

"Nelly *happened* to be in France?" repeated Nicky, screwing up his nose incredulously. "He *happened* to be here?"

I nodded. "Why not? You were, weren't you?" I said, and answered the phone. "Hello?"

"I'm outside," barked Nelson. "Are you ready to come down? Not sure I can leave the car. God knows what sort of parking wardens there are in Paris."

"I'll, um," I said, one eye on Nicky. "I'll come down right now."

"Oh, let him pop up," drawled Nicky. "I'd love to say hello."

"No, really," I said hurriedly. That was the last thing I needed: handbags at dawn between Nicky and Nelson. "I'll see you in two seconds."

I hung up, taking a second to stare at the phone and collect myself, then I turned back to Nicky.

"I have to go," I said. "Thank you for last night."

Even I saw the double entendre in there, but he didn't rise to it.

"Glad I was there," he said quietly. "I'm sorry it was under such tricky circs."

I took his hand and squeezed it. Well, if he could do it, so could I. "Maybe I'm doing better with you than I thought."

"Meaning?"

"Meaning you rescued a damsel in distress, took her home, and didn't take advantage of her."

"Yes," he sighed. "Either I'm slipping or you're winning."

I shouldered my bag and let Nicky guide me out of the apartment, into the elaborate elevator, and down to the arcade beneath, where Nelson was standing, arms crossed, peering at the architecture.

I felt better at once, just for seeing his familiar messy blond hair and meticulously ironed blue shirt. He was a pure pocket of Englishness next to the Renault Clios and manicured French trees in the square.

"Nelson, it's so nice to see you," I said, giving him a hug.

"And you," he said, staring, I think, over my head at Nicky. "Are you OK?" he muttered into my hair. "He hasn't . . . you know?"

I pulled away. "Certainly not."

"Nicky," said Nelson, extending a hand.

"Nelly," said Nicky, shaking it. I noticed he'd gone back to his usual louche mannerisms. "It was my pleasure."

Nelson's eyes narrowed, but he made an effort to be polite. "Right. Mel, if you're ready? Don't bother waving us off. I'm sure you've got lots to be getting on with. Choosing a new flag for your castle and so on."

I wondered where he'd parked the car, and, more to the point, why he was trying to get rid of Nicky before we left. Then I looked down the arcade and realized. There was no sign of Nelson's battered Range Rover, but parked three cars away was my tiny pink Little Lady car.

I stared at it. "You drove my Smart here? All the way to France?"

I didn't add *in a pink car with a cartoon woman on the side*. That much was obvious.

Nelson coughed. "Yes, well, it was a bit cramp-inducing toward the end, but—"

"You must be buying very small bottles of wine," observed Nicky. "Babycham, perhaps?"

"I lent the Range Rover to Leonie so she could move," he explained to me, shooting a ferocious glare toward Nicky. "I forgot. And there wasn't time to go and get it back. I just thought . . . you know, time was of the essence. . . ."

I smiled. "It's the perfect car for Paris," I said, linking my arm through his. "Let's get home."

"Melissa?" called Nicky. "Shall I have your clothes laundered and sent back to the office or your home address?"

Nelson sucked in some air between his teeth.

"If I can find all the little . . . bits and pieces," Nicky added, rather unnecessarily, I thought.

"That would be really kind," I said, turning about as pink as the car.

Being with Nelson meant I could no longer ignore the reality of my argument with Jonathan, but at the same time, it wasn't quite as scary as it had felt standing alone on the bridge.

Slowly, very slowly, I was beginning to realize that I'd simply asked the questions that had needed to be asked. And Jonathan hadn't come up with answers. Or rather, the answers I wanted to hear.

Nelson listened patiently as I spilled out all the awful details, not even prompting me as I repeated conversations word for word, sucking his teeth at the worst bits and wordlessly passing me his cotton handkerchief as I confessed, to myself as well as to Nelson, that I just wasn't sure what I wanted anymore.

Eventually, he let a long pause fall, presumably to make sure I'd finished, then said, "I think you've done the right thing."

"Why?" I asked miserably.

"Look, Jonathan's not a *bad* man, and I'm sure he loves you. But there are some things that you just can't ignore, and rating a business deal above how you'd feel about being in your father's pocket again . . . He doesn't get it. And I don't care for the way he was happy to abandon that dog of his at your mother's either."

"No," I said. "I keep asking when we can bring Braveheart over, but he's not keen. I don't think Jonathan's a dog person."

"That's not the point. Well, maybe it is. And I didn't like the way he never consulted you about anything—moving to Paris, this business you were going to run together, giving up your agency which you love so much . . . And as for not giving up his own career, while assuming you'd be happy to give up yours! He just sprung things on you, so you could agree with him!"

"Mm." I didn't think I needed to tell Nelson about the way Jonathan had virtually penciled babies into my diary.

"Having said that," he conceded reluctantly, "you do need to *tell* him what you're not happy about. Have you actually spelled it out for him?"

"Yes!" I said.

"Ding!" said Nelson.

"I have," I insisted. "It's just that . . . I don't think Jonathan hears it."

Nelson took his eyes off the road to look at me directly: a sign of deep concern. "I'm not going to go on about this, Mel, but when you started that agency, it was as though you suddenly got the confidence to be yourself. I really admired the way you stood up to your dad, the way you knuckled down and made it work. It's something to be really proud of." He looked very slightly abashed. "And I don't mind admitting those tight skirts were . . . very you. But since you got engaged to Jonathan, you've started to let people boss you around again. Mainly him. One minute you were turning him down because he wanted you to move to New York, then suddenly it's all on again and you're both moving to Paris. What changed? Did you talk about it?"

"Not really," I said sadly. "It just . . . happened. But that's the thing about being with Jonathan—it's like being in a film. Lovely dinners, and dressing up, and feeling glamorous and witty . . ."

Nelson abandoned his polite driving style and pulled over onto the shoulder, causing the van on our tail to swerve and honk furiously at us. "Melissa," he said, turning toward me as much as his seat belt would allow. "You *are* glamorous. You *are* witty. Even when I see you in the kitchen with your hair in rollers, you look utterly fabulous to me. Jonathan is a *businessman,* who used to be married to a boring, ambitious, bitch of a businesswoman. No wonder he fell for you! But life—real life—can't always be dressing up and fancy dinners. Sometimes it's leaky plumbing and flu and ironing. And you need to be able to *talk* about problems, not just go along with what one person decides."

I opened my mouth to agree, but Nelson hadn't finished. "I don't want to give you a lecture." He paused. "I just want to say this. You're an incredible woman, and I know you'll make someone happy forever, and that's what you deserve in return, Mel. Someone who'll love you, and respect you, and share everything with you, whatever happens."

I met Nelson's gaze and saw the concern and affection creasing his forehead, making his blue eyes crinkle earnestly at the edges. He was a fine, decent man, I thought, through my general ache. Listening to him in full flow was like hearing "Rule Britannia!" sung by a male choir accompanied by a brass band.

"Someone who loves you for who you are," he went on, more passionately. "Who knows the real you, not just Honey." He tried a little smile. "Someone you can take your shoes off with, even when your feet reek."

And with that, he put his finger on the splinter that had been twisting into my heart: Jonathan was really in love with the Honey he'd met first, not me. That was really all Jonathan knew—me making a big effort. He'd never even seen me with leg hair.

I gasped with pain at that realization at exactly the moment Nelson put his hand on my knee, and he whisked it away as if my knee had been red-hot. It was a very small car. We were practically sitting on each other's laps as it was.

"You can put your hand back if you like," I said sadly. "I think we know each other well enough by now, Nelson."

"Quite," said Nelson awkwardly. "God, this is . . . Not a great moment, but . . . Um . . . I just hate to see you unhappy when I . . . when you mean so much to me." A flush spread across his cheekbones and down his long nose. "*Very* much to me, in fact."

I knew from my vast experience of British men that declarations of fondness that didn't involve making fun of your hair were hard to come by.

"And you mean the world to me," I replied. "Oh, Nelson!" I said, a sudden rush of affection surging through me. I flung my arms around him. "I honestly don't know what I'd do without you! Thank you so much for coming to get me! You're the only man I can really rely on."

He pulled away so he could examine my face.

"What, um, what *exactly* do you mean by that?" he asked, with an intense look that made his blue eyes seem quite dark. The boyishness had gone, and I was startled by how, well, intense he seemed.

I stared back at him, confused. Through the mists in my brain, I remembered what Gabi had said about Nelson's fondness for me, and I wondered if this was some kind of . . . of romantic overture?

Surely not. It was so the wrong time. And place. Nelson wouldn't *dream* of taking emotional advantage of an old, old friend who'd just argued with her fiancé—but not quite called things off just yet. That would be the final weirdness, and I wasn't sure I could cope with that right now.

"I mean . . . I'm so lucky to have you as a friend, and flatmate, and everything else!" I blinked, then, to break the rapidly growing strangeness in the car, I flung my arms back round him and hugged him again.

"That's what I thought you meant," sighed Nelson, which put my mind at rest.

sixteen

I spent most of Sunday in a misery coma, which Nelson helped me through in sympathetic silence. He cooked me eggy bread to tempt my dead appetite, and passed me fresh white hankies, all without saying much, for which I was grateful. Eventually, I fell asleep on his shoulder after two or three glasses of red wine too many while we watched an old Miss Marple and he hoisted me off to bed like a bag of sails, leaving a pint glass of water and some Nurofen by my bed. Just two, though. Not the whole packet. I was so moved by his gentleness that I had to pretend to be asleep when he tucked the duvet over me, or else I'd have started crying again.

However, when I woke up on Monday morning, the very thought of going into work pinned me to the pillows. The Elephant of Depression wasn't just parked on my chest, it was relaxing there with the Walrus of Gloom and the Hippo of Bleak Friday Nights in Alone. They had beers. They were settling in.

For once, I wasn't sure work was going to take my mind off things. After all, the Little Lady Agency was where Jonathan and I had met.

There were so many good memories there. And now bad ones.

I think I'd have stayed in bed and felt sorry for myself if Nelson hadn't barged in with a cup of tea and a plate of toast.

"Get up," he said, putting the toast within tempting distance. "I know you're feeling low, but there are people in this city much worse off than you."

I pulled the duvet over my head. "I'm not in the mood for your homeless-people lecture, Nelson."

"I'm not talking about them," he said, throwing open the curtains and letting in the unfeeling morning sun. "I'm talking about people like Roger."

"Roger has a *girlfriend*!" I barked from under the duvet.

"Not for much longer if you don't give him a call." I could hear Nelson rummaging in my drawers now, chucking fresh clothes on the bed for me to put on. "I spoke to him on Saturday morning—apparently Zara lost one of her earrings round at his flat last week and was all upset about it. He turned the place upside down, found it, popped it in a little box, and gave it to her over dinner."

I was sufficiently curious to pull back the duvet. "And the problem was?"

Nelson paused in his clothes selection. "If you were having dinner at the chef's table at Claridge's and your boyfriend said, 'Darling, I've got a surprise for you . . . ' then put a little pale blue box on your plate—and you opened it to discover it contained your own earring, what would you do?"

"I'll give him a call," I said, swinging my legs out of bed.

"Good," said Nelson. "That's more than Zara's done for five days. Now, red blouse or black blouse? And do you want a lift to the office?"

I hated admitting Nelson was right, but he was. As usual. Although there was a lingering dull ache in my chest, once I'd dragged myself into work I did feel better for being surrounded by my familiar things, doing stuff, and being useful.

Obviously, though, that was while my brain was safely engaged elsewhere. I had to take a break every fifteen minutes or so to be choked up at the sight of a matchbook from a romantic bar or by flicking back in my diary and remembering some special date.

I tried to make a list of pros and cons about Jonathan, but when I got stuck on whether his business sense was a pro or a con, I phoned the one person I knew who'd give me an unbiased opinion. Gabi.

"Oh my God," she gasped when I told her what had happened. "I'm coming over right now!"

"But you're at work!" When Jonathan had been in charge of Gabi's office, he'd made them sign in and out, even for cigarette breaks.

"Sod that," she replied. "Hang on . . ." I heard her cover the phone with her hand. "Paula," she went on with muffled concern, "there's been some kind of mix-up with the keys to that house in Elystan Place—I'm just going to pop out for half an hour, OK?"

Paula said something in response to which Gabi laughed uproariously. "I'll be with you any moment, Crispin," she said loudly to me, then added in a venomous whisper, "You want me to send an anonymous company email about him having alopecia? Dave from IT taught me how to fake spam. I'll have an alibi while I'm out."

"No," I said. "No, don't do anything like that. Just come over."

Gabi arrived within fifteen minutes. She had the coffee machine on and was dictating the pros/cons list to me before one arm was out of her jacket. She got up to nine cons before the coffee even started filtering.

"Drink that," she said, pressing a mug into my hand, "and ten, he had very thin lips."

"Thank you," I said automatically.

"But stuff him—how are *you*?" she asked, perching on the desk next to me. "That's all that matters. You've had a crap weekend."

"I'm . . . confused." I put the mug down. "I mean, I can't help thinking maybe I'm getting wound up about moving to *Paris*, and transferring my stress onto Jonathan and—"

"Hold it right there," said Gabi, jabbing the desk with a finger. "So far, the worst thing you've said about Paris is that the pavements are so appalling they've wrecked your high heels. That's the *worst* thing. You're two hours from Waterloo, your French isn't that bad, and you've already got the obligatory small dog." She raised her hand. "I don't accept the Paris argument. In fact . . ." Gabi peered at me. "If anything, I think you're transferring *the other way.* I think you're pushing the doubts you have about Jonathan onto Paris."

"Thank you, Dr. Freud," I said with a sarcastic frown.

"Seriously," she said. "Everything you've told me so far, you could sort out with one balls-out conversation. Your dad, the business, everything. Why are you so scared of speaking your mind? You have tougher conversations at work every day. So it must be him."

Gabi had an unerring knack of coming right out with the unsayable, then saying it again, just in case you hadn't gotten it the first time.

"I know you've never liked Jonathan . . . ," I began defensively.

"Bollocks!" she said. "He's a great catch, if you like men with red hair. But you've *got* to be able to argue, Mel. Look at your mum and dad—they've been married years."

"Gabi, I'd rather die alone with cats than have a marriage like theirs."

She arched an eyebrow. "Well, they must be doing something right. I know things have always been perfect with you and Dr. No, but you had to fall out sometime. It's what making up's all about." She paused. "If you *want* to make up, that is."

"I do!" I protested. "I just worry that . . ."

The words stuck in my throat.

"Out with it," said Gabi. "Unless it's something bedroom related, in which case, just hint, please."

I wrapped my hands around my mug and tried to put my thoughts in order. "When I'm at work, I'm bossy and organized—but I can only do that so long as I can slob out in the evenings. Jonathan's organized twenty-four hours a day, so when I'm with him, I have to be too. That's what he loves about me. It's exhausting being the girl he thinks I am." I raised my eyes pleadingly to Gabi. "But you can't break up with someone just because they think you're perfect, can you?"

"You can if you're too scared to let them see you be less than perfect." She looked at me. "You've seriously never slobbed out in front of him before? I feel like I know your corns better than your chiropodist."

I'd had no idea my feet were such a center of attention for my friends.

"It's like we're always on our tenth date," I said. "Still sexy, still romantic, still thrilling . . . but I just don't know how much I can ever relax."

Gabi put her coffee down and hugged me. "It's OK to admit things aren't perfect," she said more softly. "But it's very stupid to let yourself be swept down the aisle without ever actually working out if you can fix them. Not being upfront about whether he was giving up his job is a big deal."

I blinked back tears. "I know. Can we talk about something more cheery?"

"Sure!" she said, and creased her brow in concentration. "You've still got your cruise to look forward to!"

"Which cruise?"

"The charity cruise on Prince Nicolas's yacht. The one Aaron and I should have won. The one that that horse-faced accountant Leonie won. With her *one* ticket."

"Oh, that." I opened my desk diary and disconsolately flicked through the pages. "It's not for weeks yet. I wish you *were* coming. I don't fancy spending a weekend listening to Leonie Hargreaves tell me how I should have gone for an offset mortgage instead of a tracker. Still," I sighed, "Nelson seems to like her. He's been out for drinks with her and everything. It sounds as if they might actually be . . . you know."

"Mmm, no," said Gabi. "I think he might just be humoring you and your blind date fixation."

"No, I think he's quite keen." I picked up my coffee mug and took a sip. Gabi had added my pre-Paris-diet milk and two sugars. "He lent her his Range Rover so she could move this weekend," I went on. "You don't do that out of the goodness of your heart."

"Unless you're *Nelson.* Dur!" said Gabi, popping her eyes at me. "He lent her his *big,* comfortable car, then drove five hundred miles in a mobile shoebox to rescue you! I bet she was *sick* when he dropped off the keys and left her to it. Talk about dropping hints!"

"I know Leonie. She's not one for clutter. At boarding school, she used to fit all her stuff into one small box at the end of term when everyone else practically needed a trailer. I doubt she'd need Nelson's help to hump anything," I replied.

Gabi sniggered. "I doubt that very much too."

"What?"

"Nothing."

I slipped off my shoes and tucked my feet up under me. "He was so sweet this weekend, looking after me. He'll make someone a lovely husband."

At that moment both our gazes fell on the stack of wedding magazines Gabi had left by my desk for future reference.

"Mel," said Gabi, suddenly looking guilt-stricken, "you really don't have to help me with my wedding anymore."

"I don't mind," I said bravely.

My rising "coffee and best mate" spirits slumped again, but Gabi knew me too well to miss the signs of impending gloom.

"You know what? Why don't you redecorate?" she suggested, waving her hand toward the walls. "Freshen things up. If we pop out now, get some color cards and samples—Nelson and Aaron could sort it out in a weekend. New paint, new start."

If only everything else was that simple.

Still, I let myself be dragged down the stairs and out to the Kings Road.

Gabi was swooning over some purple and gold flock wallpaper in Osborne & Little when my phone rang.

Thinking it might be Jonathan, I dug it out of my bag with trembling hands. I wasn't sure I was ready to talk to him, but I still couldn't help wanting to hear his voice.

"Hey, at last!" said a smooth yet sympathetic voice. "Your phone's been off all weekend. How are you getting on?"

It was Nicky, calling from the parallel universe he lived in. Having him ring me for no good reason while I was very much in my own universe—and with Gabi—was a bit unsettling, to be honest.

"Um, fine, thanks," I said, failing to sound cool. "I mean, not great, but coping OK. Sort of."

"Good, good." Nicky had a very bedroomy phone manner, now with added concern for my well-being. It didn't help.

"How are you?" I squeaked, to get off the sticky topic of myself.

"Not so bad. Spent Sunday calming Piglet down by taking her shopping. It was *her* birthday party on Friday, actually—the party I bailed out of? Didn't want to tell you at the time in case you forced me to go back to it out of manners. I tried to buy her a little present, but after what you said about women and their prices . . ." I heard a faint laugh.

"And what's Imogen's?"

"An Hermès overnight bag. Which came in handy, as it turned out."

"Why?" I could see Gabi moving nearer, and from the look on her face, she'd worked out who I was talking to. I waved her away, unsuccessfully.

"Because she packed nearly all her stuff in it when she stormed out. We've split up. So it was a going-away present as well as a birthday one."

"Nicky, I'm sorry! Was that my fault?" I gasped, not actually feeling that sorry at all. Imogen was ghastly, with her ratty extensions and her snotty, grabby attitude. At least if he wasn't with her, he stood a chance of attracting someone nicer.

"It was your fault," he confirmed, and I wished I could see his face to tell if he was joking. I stared hard at some wallpaper and tried to concentrate even harder on his voice. "You inspired me to break it off after you were so honest with your fiancé," he went on. "I thought about what you said, and she's not the sort of girl I'd want to spend the rest of my life with, even if she is determined to get her hands on my crown jewels at every opportunity."

"She did seem a bit of a social climber," I agreed.

"What?" said Nicky.

"Your crown jewels."

"Oh, right, yes. Is that all you're going to say? Not 'Well done, Nicky'? 'You're on your way to becoming Prince Idol'?"

"Well, yes, well done," I stammered. Gabi was standing so close that she was practically on the phone herself now. I was surprised Nicky couldn't hear her breathing.

"So, what's next for me?" he asked. "I'd understand if you wanted to give it a rest for a little while, but on the other hand, I have heard the best thing for one's troubles is keeping busy."

"I suppose so," I said, kicking myself for not coming out with something smarter.

"Grandfather's still banging on about this Act being ratified or what have you in a month or so, and you know how quickly I slip into bad ways," said Nicky. "How about dinner this week? I'm sure you had something on your list about dinner. What was it?"

"Having dinner with a lady without trying to get her into bed," I said. "It's an important gentlemanly skill."

Gabi made a *What?!* face, which I ignored.

"I quite agree! I definitely think that's one lesson worth practicing," said Nicky. "I mean, it's win-win, isn't it? Give me a date. I'll cancel anything."

His voice was so flirty that I could feel my entire body blushing, including my feet.

"I'm not at my desk right now," I said, trying not to sound too keen, "so I don't have my diary in front of me . . ."

Gabi rolled her eyes and offered me hers.

I glared at her. "But I'll ring you this afternoon and let you know when's a good time."

"How about tonight?"

"Erm . . ."

"Don't pretend Nelly's cooking you lamb chops or something. Come on, let me take you out."

"Tomorrow," I said firmly.

"Excellent. I'll look forward to that," said Nicky with an audible smile, and hung up.

"That sounded a lot like flirting to me," observed Gabi, when I managed to get my phone back in the bag.

I shook my head weakly. "Yes. But no, I think he's like that with everyone."

Gabi did her double eye roll. "Ding!"

"Don't you start with that," I said, picking up a wallpaper sample book. "Nelson's bad enough." But to be honest, Nicky's charm was like sinking my weary body into a warm, scented bath. It didn't solve anything, but it felt nice. I just hoped I could get out again.

When I got back to the office with my new lamp and a pep talk from Gabi, I'd regrouped enough to deal with Ranald Harris, who'd spun himself into an appalling web of lies by fibbing on his speed-dating form, then inadvertently speed-dating four different women, to whom he'd each told increasingly elaborate porkies, without making notes. Slowly, Ranald and I unraveled them between us, to the point where he could at least contact two of them with reasonable explanations. The other two, I told him sadly, he'd have to write off. You've pretty much boxed yourself into a conversational corner once you've insisted you're an international fast bowler and/or a keen tuba player.

Flushed with success, I called Roger about Zara and how he could make it up to her after the jewelry clanger.

"It's not about *what* you give her," I told him for what felt like the millionth time this weekend. "It's the thought you've put into it."

"I don't have any thoughts," he said wildly. "I'm a bloke!"

"Well, take her on a minibreak or something—surprise her. What does she like doing? Which bits of England hasn't she seen? Why don't you take her back to Hereford and show her your apple orchards?" I improvised.

"Riiight," said Roger, in a far-from-encouraging manner. "I did hear they've got the new tractor now, might be quite interesting for her. By the way, sorry to hear about your bad news."

"Oh, thank you," I said automatically, then wondered what Nelson had told him.

"How are you coping? Are you eating?" Roger's voice had taken on the ghastly solicitous tone he used when dealing with women in distress. I only had myself to blame; I'd taught him to use it instead of his old blunt *Why are you crying? Are you up the duff?* approach. "You don't want to eat too much," he went on. "Or drink too much. I expect Nelson's looking after you."

"For your information, Roger," I said crossly, "I don't need looking after. I haven't broken things off with Jonathan at all. We're just . . . thinking."

"You'll go through various stages," he reassured me. "Including denial. Anger is perfectly normal."

"Let me know how you get on with Zara, won't you?" I said as sweetly as I could. "And for future reference, any jewelry gift that is not an engagement ring should be presented in nothing smaller than a shoebox. Got that?"

"Yurp!" said Roger, and he hung up, presumably to get the tractor polished and ready for Zara.

I made my way through a fair amount of paperwork and was drafting a tactful email to a client who seemed to think I'd actually go to his godchild's birthday party *for* him, as well as sort out the gift, when my mobile rang again.

I saw from the caller ID that it was my mother.

I stretched out my hand to take the call, then I chickened out. She loved Jonathan.

Later, I told myself guiltily. I'd call her back later, when I wasn't at work, and had no distractions.

I went back to my emails, and ten minutes later, Daddy rang. I had a special ring tone to alert me to his calls. It was the *Blackadder* theme tune.

I definitely wasn't talking to *him.*

When I didn't take his call, he added a voice-mail message to Mummy's, and when Emery rang at four o'clock, I thought I'd better not answer that either. So she left a message too.

At four-thirty, just as I was about to nip out to Baker & Spice for a cake reward for getting through the day, the phone rang again, and this time there was no Romney-Jones caller ID, so I picked up.

Mistake.

"Hello, darling!" cooed Granny. "I just wanted to pass on a little compliment! I was talking to Georgie von Apfel at a party I went to with Alex over the weekend—she's a snobby old boot, to be honest—and she said she'd bumped into a granddaughter of mine. Called Honey!"

"Oh," I said. "Yes. At the polo. She seemed . . . quite nice."

Obviously, Granny had brushed off the small matter of Nicky and the bomb scare, because she babbled on, "Yes! Anyway, I didn't disclose details, even though she was obviously *desperate* for information. I was vague, you know. And I must say Alex was very good too—he didn't even crack a smile." She paused to sigh happily. "He's so discreet. Anyway, what she *did* say was that Nicky was looking positively smitten, and when you went off to make a phone call, he told her you were the most charming woman he'd ever met!"

"Really?"

"Yes! I think Georgie was a bit miffed, because she's been lining up her granddaughter, Bitsy, for years. . . . Anyway, she made a few barbed comments about the family charm, which I'm afraid were aimed at me, but in the end, she couldn't help but be rather complimentary about you too. Said you made a very handsome couple and that you had the sort of forehead that could carry off a tiara. Which I think was her ham-fisted attempt at fishing for gossip about whether the two of you were romantically linked, as they say!"

"We aren't," I said. "But he has dumped his horrible girlfriend. Imogen Leys."

"Has he? Alex *will* be pleased. He only met her once, but she asked him if there were any family tiaras she could wear for their wedding, or should she get her dad to buy one? Honestly, from what I hear the girl practically had a list . . ."

"Oh," I said, reassessing just how horrendous *that* dumping conversation must have been for Nicky.

"So how was Paris this weekend?" she asked airily. "Jonathan all right?"

I flinched. I hated lying to Granny. "Oh, you know . . ."

There was a long silence on the line. "Anything you're not telling me, darling?"

I bit my lip. There was no point. She'd find out; Nicky would tell Alexander, and he would tell Granny.

"We had a big row," I confessed. "I've asked for some time to think about moving to Paris. And everything else."

"Oh no!" cried Granny. "You poor angel! Are you all right?"

"Yes, I'm fine," I said. "Well, not fine. But I'm managing. Jonathan . . ." I pressed my lips together to keep the ache in my heart from spreading to my throat. "Jonathan wanted to sell off the agency to Daddy. And I just knew things weren't right. I was *trying* to be happy, not *being* happy. I know that doesn't sound—"

"No, no!" I could almost see Granny holding up a long finger. "You don't have to give me any reason, darling! If you don't think it was going to work out, for whatever reason, that's all you have to say. I must admit," she went on a little naughtily, "I did *wonder*—"

"Why?"

"Oh, a little bird told me that you might have stayed the night in a certain person's apartment over the weekend . . ."

I turned bright red. "How did you know that?"

"The little bird might have needed a forwarding address for some laundry. Don't worry," she added, still in that same naughty voice, "I won't tell a soul!"

"It's not what it looks like!" I insisted hotly. "Nicky offered me somewhere to stay—I was in a total state. He was very gallant, if you must know."

"So I should think. In any case, I'm saying nothing."

That would be a first, I thought, seeing the baroque fantasies already spinning their way around Granny's brain. "There's nothing going on between me and Nicky," I protested. "Honestly. Please don't start thinking that. It isn't why Jonathan and I split up."

"Of course not," said Granny.

"I haven't spoken to Mummy about it yet," I said, "so please don't say anything until I know what I'm doing."

Granny paused and sounded more like herself. "I understand, darling," she said. "My lips are sealed."

And I knew she meant that, at least.

At the end of the day, when I'd done all the chores I could find, I steeled myself to listen to the messages from home.

Mummy's was first.

"Hello, darling. I want to have a little chat with you about a drinks thing I'm trying to arrange? I thought it might be a good time for Jonathan to meet the vicar and some of Daddy's constituency people. I know they're a bit hard work, but that's the beauty of Jonathan—he always has something to say. And your father's very keen to talk to him too. Says he needs his opinion on something . . ." There was a bark of deranged laughter. "So there's a first time for everything! Do call me back, darling."

Then Daddy.

"Melissa, it's your father. I'm trying to get hold of Jonathan—I need to . . . discuss something with him, but he's not answering his phone. Been trying all weekend." I could hear weird sucking noises in the background. Was that a fault on the line? Then Daddy said, "By God, you finished that quickly, you greedy little bugger. A second bottle? Is it? Is it? Is it a second bottle for Bertie? Good chap! Anyway, don't know what Jonathan's playing at, but it's imperative I speak to him in the next twenty-four hours. Get onto it, will you?"

Then Emery.

"Hi, Mel, it's Em. Listen, I need to talk to you about the naming ceremony. Daddy's getting on my case about dates, because he wants to get some magazine to pay for the food in return for photo access or something, so I need you to come and help me. And I was wondering if Jonathan would like to be godfather? I haven't discussed it with anyone yet, but thought it might be an idea for Bertie to have at least one sensible man in his life. Daddy's turning him into a little clone—he's changed the Baby Mozart CD in the cot for his Winston Churchill speeches one. Actually, Nanny Ag's driving me a bit mad too." She sounded like she was calling from under the stairs or in the shed or something—her voice was nearly a whisper, but it had a purposeful note to it, which I took to be the New Emery breaking through. "I'm supposed to be expressing milk. But I'm hiding in the stables. Oh, shit!" The phone dropped to the floor and a muffled exchange took place. I recognized the fearsome tone of Nanny Ag above Emery's whining.

I deleted the messages, put the phone down on the desk, and listened to the sounds of London going home for the day until the light started to fade.

seventeen

I will say this for Nicky: he certainly did his best to take my mind off my constant, miserable, round-and-round agonizing about Jonathan. I don't know whether it was because his ladykiller pride refused to let another man be foremost in my thoughts, or whether he was genuinely keen to cheer me up. No need to say which option Gabi preferred, obviously. Whichever it was, not only did he call me every day that week "just for a quick chat," but he also insisted on taking me out for dinner, despite my pleas that I'd be rotten company.

"You'll feel better once you've got yourself dressed up," he insisted, with worldly experience. "Girls always do."

Annoyingly, he was right.

From the moment I hauled the strings tight on my black satin Honey corset—why not?—I felt a defiant sexiness return, along with my wasp waist. As I got dressed, I saw a gratifyingly glamorous woman start to emerge in the mirror, and by the time I slipped into a wrap dress and pinned on my long blond wig, it was as if I'd put armor around my heart and I could tackle anything. Honey was a winner, even if I wasn't.

And, I told myself as I fastened my diamanté earrings, it was all part of Nicky's old-fashioned gentleman boot camp, so it was my duty to go—both as Honey, to pass on my hard-earned knowledge, and as Melissa, to keep up my promise to Granny.

I finished off my going-out face with a glossy slick of crimson lipstick and smacked my lips together.

Honey smiled at me from the mirror.

Nicky texted me to say he'd booked a table at The Wolseley on Piccadilly, and he was already there when I arrived, gazing around the high-ceilinged room, presumably using the mirrors to see if he recognized any of the swishy-haired clientele or, more to the point, their husbands. I noticed he'd gotten one of the best tables in the central bullring area—something I'd never managed to do, even using my best wheedling skills.

When he saw me, a broad smile broke across his face.

"Hello," I said as he rose to kiss my cheek. "You get five points to start with, for being early."

"Excellent," he said. "Is it like a driving test, where you have a list you can check off when I get things right?"

"No," I said, meeting his teasing dark eyes with a cool gaze. "I've got a list I check off when you get things wrong."

"Oh, dear," he said seriously. "And you know how much I like getting things wrong. I must try harder. You look ravishing, by the way. Blue is a marvelous color on you. Any reason why you're here as a blonde tonight?"

My cool gaze wavered as I touched my hair self-consciously. "No, I—"

"I hope you're not hiding behind it?" he went on, lifting an eyebrow.

"Not at all," I said quickly. "I just thought that since The Wolseley is a people-spotting kind of place, you might be spotted by someone you knew, and since I've already been to a couple of events with you as a blonde, it just seemed . . . logical. And it is a business meeting, to discuss your dining skills, isn't it?"

"Is it?" asked Nicky. "It can't be me taking a friend out to dinner to cheer her up after her undeserved weekend from hell?"

I looked at him, and a little tingly frisson passed between us across the table. "I think it would be more straightforward to chalk it up to business," I said. "That way you can write me off against tax."

Even though it was a totally Leonie-ish comment, it had come out more flirtatiously than I'd meant. Or maybe I had meant it. Nicky seemed to tap into something very Honey in me. Still, it took my mind off Melissa and her troubles for a welcome hour or two.

"OK, OK," said Nicky. "Fine with me. I like the fact that we have a little secret already. And only I know what lies beneath." He winked.

I winked back, then made my face cross. "No, no, no," I said sternly. "Do not make references to anything lying beneath anything at all. In fact, steer clear of the whole lying image altogether."

"Right," said Nicky. He reached into his manbag and pulled out a notebook and pen.

"And lose the manbag," I added. "It's so awfully Euro-trash."

"How am I meant to carry anything?" he asked, uncapping his Montblanc by biting the top off.

"Jacket pockets. Or a briefcase."

He lifted a warning finger. "Now, there are limits, Melissa. What are you meant to do with a briefcase in a nightclub? I'd look highly suspicious." He jotted down *Do not refer to lying down.* "I mean, I don't mind looking slightly suspicious, that's quite hot."

"No, it isn't," I said. "You think Rex Harrison ever looked slightly suspicious? The whole point of not being overtly sexy over dinner is that if there is some . . . attraction between you and your dinner companion, she'll be all the more fascinated by your apparent restraint. If you're *really* well behaved, you might even find *she* starts with the flirty comments, in the hope of penetrating your gentlemanly manner and stripping away the politeness to get to the passionate man beneath."

"I see," said Nicky. "So *you're* allowed to talk about penetrating and stripping but I'm not?"

I blushed. "Um, that's just an illustration."

"Good," he said. "Now what am I allowed to talk about? Tell me while you're ordering."

I studied the menu and tried to find something I could eat that wouldn't lead to me licking my fingers or slurping or doing anything that might end up looking like Nigella Lawson. "You can talk about books you've read, or places you've been, or people you know. But no salacious gossip," I added. "Just in case it turns out your date is related to them. I'm terrible at that. And you know *loads* more people than me so . . . Just don't."

"Anything else?"

"Don't so much as breathe a word about religion, politics, Big Brother, your exes, her exes, or what kind of diet she's on. Write that down."

"Oh, Melissa, you're so strict," he sighed. "And so wise. It's what every man dreams of—a woman who'll tell him what to do, but wear corsets while she does it. Do all your clients end up falling in love with you?"

"No," I pinged back saucily. "Just my fia—" A sudden pang hit me, so hard I felt tears spring to my eyes. *No,* I told myself, *you* have *to get over this.*

"Just Jonathan," I said bravely. "And I'm not sure he really knows where Honey stops and Mel starts. That's why I'm wearing the wig— partly. It's complicated."

Nicky looked stricken and grabbed my hand. The bantering disappeared from his manner. "God, I'm sorry, that was so stupid of me. I didn't mean to be so crass. I'm such a cretin."

"That's why I'm here!" I said, trying to be light. "To teach you stuff!"

"I was having such a good time I forgot I was learning," he said simply. "You're very easy to relax with."

"Am I?"

"Yes." He nodded. "I don't think I've ever met a girl who was so easy to talk to."

"That's because most of the girls you meet aren't exactly conversationalists," I replied, studying the menu. "But then I suppose you're not dating them for their views on current affairs, are you?"

He held my gaze in an unsettlingly direct way. "Is that where I'm going wrong?"

Then the waiter appeared and saved me from having to come up with a smart answer.

We talked and ate and drank and talked, and though the flirtatious Nicky rose to the surface once or twice, he seemed to open up throughout the evening, letting more of the serious, thoughtful side he'd shown me in Paris slip out. I was surprised—in a nice way—by how frank he was about his childhood in various schools, like me, and the traveling and the nannies and the feeling of never having quite enough attention.

Although the restaurant was big and filled with chatter and the clatter of a fashionable dinner, it felt as if it was just him and me, in a very small room. Miles and miles away from that first dinner we'd had, in Petrus.

"So," he said, stirring two sugars into his espresso. "I suppose my grandfather's given you instructions about finding me a more appropriate girlfriend? I know he had a special loathing for Piglet. And pretty much everyone else I've been out with."

"Not specifically," I said. "Although he seems quite adamant one should be with someone one loves and respects. I assume he would include you in that."

"The implication being what? That I don't respect girls like Imogen?"

"Guess so," I said. "Call me a hairy-armpit feminist, but men who don't respect women—they're pretty unattractive. And women who date men who don't respect women are pretty stupid. That's just asking to be taken advantage of. You need to stand up for yourself."

Nicky nodded thoughtfully.

"Personally," I went on, with feeling. "I don't go in for *pretending* to be ditzy. It's just a waste of time. I miss enough as it is—I don't need to make people think I'm *more* dense. And grown women pretending to be schoolgirls is just . . . ugh."

"Well, I don't know, it has its charms . . . ," he began. Then, to my surprise, he dropped the insouciance altogether. "But you're right. It's good to be able to sit here, talking to someone properly. About . . . real things. Piglet would have played with a salad, drunk two bottles of the most expensive white wine on the list on principle, then dragged me out to a club by now." He checked his watch. "We'd have been leaving for the second club about now."

"And I haven't even got on to my second coffee," I said.

Nicky sighed and pushed his cup away. "I wish I met more girls like you, Melissa. Girls who aren't all about the money, or about being in magazines." He looked up at me from under his dark lashes and smiled. He had eyes like a baby calf. A very sexy baby calf. "I just don't seem to meet them unless my grandfather sets me up with them. And how wrong is that?"

I struggled to maintain my grown-up composure.

"That's why I'm trying to keep you out of nightclubs," I reminded him. "You meet a nicer type of girl at charity sailing dinners."

He tipped his glass toward me in a little salute of recognition. "And what do you think?" he asked. "What do you think is important?"

"I'm not sure I'm the right person to be asking," I said wryly.

"Ah, but I think you are. I think you know perfectly well what's important in a relationship. You've just told me, for a start. I hope you're going to tell Jonathan what you've just told me."

I blinked, taken aback by his insight.

"Well?" he repeated, tilting his head so his thick hair flopped to one side. The tealights on the table made deep chestnut highlights gleam in his hair. "What's important in a relationship?"

More frissons crackled across the table. This time, though, I knew it was because we were being really honest, not because we were playing games.

"Well," I began, sidestepping the whole Jonathan thing. "I think you need respect for the other person as an adult—you need to see them as an individual, with strengths and weaknesses, and quirks and flaws. That's what attraction's about, really, not how blue their eyes are, or how cute their figure is. That's what lasts fifty years. It's that something you can't quite put your finger on. You need to feel comfortable enough to be yourself, but not so comfortable that you stop bothering."

"Should I write this down?"

"Try remembering it. Doesn't look good, taking a checklist on a date."

"So," said Nicky, holding my gaze and counting on his fingers. "You think I should be looking out for a sensible English girl, with her feet on the ground, and plenty to talk about. Someone who has her own money and isn't interested in mine, who eats her meal instead of playing with it, who has enough self-confidence to dress like a real woman, can make me laugh, and who has hidden talents."

"Did I mention hidden talents?" I asked. My tummy was quivering with the combined effort of holding it in and noting that I hadn't mentioned anything about an English girl, or polishing off meals, or dressing like a real woman.

"I'd want any girlfriend of mine to have hidden talents," explained Nicky, so intensely that he made me forget to breathe. "Especially if she was going to be my wife."

I'm sorry to say I couldn't stop myself. "And I suppose *you* have hidden talents to offer?" I asked.

He nodded.

"Which are?"

"Oh, they're hidden." Without missing a beat, he signaled to the waiter for the bill, then returned his eyes to mine. "You'd have to find that out. Or, rather, whoever I dated . . . would."

Somehow, mindful of the lesson I was supposed to be giving him in not trying to get a lady into bed over dinner, I stopped myself from swooning on the spot. Instead, I pushed myself away from the table.

"Thank you for a fabulous dinner," I said. "It's been enchanting and instructive. And," I added in more normal tones, "you have cheered me up. Really."

"Have I? Mission accomplished," he said, punching his PIN into the machine. "And you've given me a lot to think about too." He let me get out from the table. "I'll be thinking about it all night."

Ray was waiting outside with the Bentley, and when he saw me, he smiled and tipped his hat. "Good evening, miss," he said, opening the door for Nicky, who slid across the backseat to make room for me.

"Lovely evening, thanks," I said, slipping into the car, keeping my knees neatly together in top finishing-school fashion, mainly for the benefit of the passing tourists, who stopped and stared at us, wondering if we were famous.

I had to admit, it was something one could get quite used to.

Nicky was quiet as we set off toward Victoria, but I didn't mind savoring the unreality of the moment: the handsome prince next to me, the purring luxury car, the fashionable dinner. It was like being Cinderella—the moment I stepped into my flat and took off my wig, I'd be back to normal.

Or would I? How much of what Nicky had said tonight had been genuine? How much of what *I'd* said had been me and how much had been Honey's mannerly instruction? We'd gone over an invisible line this evening, and I wasn't sure where it was. More to the point, I wasn't sure if Nicky thought it was in the same place that I did. That was the trouble about his life. It didn't seem to have the same reference points as mine.

Far too soon, Ray pulled up outside home, where he let the engine idle discreetly while we said our good-byes.

I was suddenly gripped by the fear that maybe I'd been swept away more than Nicky, and that I too looked like one of the starstruck climbers who fawned over him in Boujis. OK, I might have been enjoying a little escapism in my head, but the last thing I wanted was for him to think I was developing a crush on him.

"Well, this is me," I said, probably a bit too cheerily. "Thanks for a lovely evening."

"No, thank you," said Nicky, sliding across the backseat so I could feel his breath on my bare neck. "Can I cheer you up again soon? I think you need it."

"Absolutely," I said, with one hand on the door. "Next week, we can tackle being safe in taxis."

"Next week? I hope not," he said, lowering his voice to an intimate murmur. "I was thinking . . . in the next *day* or two?"

Nicky's eyes were almost black in the half-light, and full of suggestiveness. I gazed into them like a rabbit frozen in the headlights of an oncoming tractor.

"Good night!" I squeaked, just about managing to keep my voice normal.

"Good night," echoed Nicky, and leaned forward. He paused, his lips a tantalizing breath away from my own, then, after a heart-stopping moment, he changed course and touched my cheek, brushing my cheek with his lips, but not gently—with a sort of reined-in, very grown-up passion. I felt his eyelashes flutter against my cheekbone, and his skin, slightly rough but smooth at the same time, pressed close to mine. I could smell him: lemony cologne and champagne, and something musky and sexy and miles more dangerous than any man I'd ever kissed before.

He could have kissed me. He knew I knew he could have kissed me. But he didn't, and yet we were both left imagining what that unkissed kiss would have felt like.

He pulled away to see what my reaction was, and in that second, I managed to grab control of myself.

You can't let him do this, barked a stern voice inside my head. *You're in no emotional state to do anything, and besides which, you've spent all night telling him how he needs to respect women. DUR!*

"Don't kiss me!" I heard my own voice gabble.

Nicky's eyebrow hooked up in amused query. My heart melted again at the shadows falling onto his handsome face from the streetlights around us, reminding me of the vulnerability he'd shown me earlier.

"Don't want you turning back into a frog!" I explained goofily.

"That's not all princes," he reminded me.

"Well, I know, but, um, I mean," I gabbled, clutching at straws, "from a *behavior* point of view it's much better to . . ."

Nicky sighed. "Please don't. I wouldn't presume to kiss you anyway. Respect, and all that. I've learned quite a lot about nice girls tonight."

"Good," I said, opening the door and getting myself out before I said anything that might undo my previous hard work. "I'll call you."

He leaned out from the backseat. "I'll be watching my phone."

I let myself in with trembling hands that scraped the key around the lock a few times before I could get it in. But when I climbed the stairs to find that Nelson had gone out to see a film with Roger, leaving half a chicken pie in the oven and a gas bill on the table for me, it really did feel as if it had been me who'd turned back into a frog, and not Nicky.

Even with Nicky doing his best to distract me, I couldn't stop tormenting myself about Jonathan and what I should do. I couldn't concentrate on anything, even the most mundane paperwork, and in the end, I realized I was doing exactly what I'd yelled at Jonathan for— working, instead of concentrating on our relationship. So I abandoned Freddie Curran's wardrobe invoice, grabbed my big bag, and headed for Green Park to think.

It was a typically clammy English summer afternoon, and the streets were busy with tourists heading for Buckingham Palace and office workers hurrying back with Pret a Manger bags and coffee. I gave myself one lap of the paths to work things out, and set off with a determined stride.

I'd had so much advice by now that it was hard to separate what I truly felt from what everyone else thought I should feel, but two things kept coming back to me: Gabi had been right when she'd said I could have had one tough conversation to make my feelings clear about the business, so why hadn't I? What was I afraid of?

And Nelson had been right when he'd said I needed someone I could relax with, and I knew I couldn't with Jonathan. In the beginning, I'd thought he'd be less hyper once his personal life was happy, but now I realized stress was as much a part of Jonathan's life as good manners were of mine.

But we'd met so perfectly! I argued. Surely a relationship that had started in such a romantic way deserved to be given every chance?

I stared at the trees and the overflowing litter bins. What was more important here? The idea of the relationship—or the real me and Jonathan?

The truth was, I realized sorrowfully, Jonathan and I were more in love with the idea of each other than the reality, romantic though the ideas of each other were. I couldn't ignore the fact that he was a cool businessman, ten years older than me, who'd never understand the mesh of my family loyalties. And he couldn't keep trying to make me into a soignée, driven businesswoman. It was fine for dating, but neither of us could keep that up over an entire marriage. Not unless we had two houses and permanently clashing diaries, and that wasn't what I wanted.

But hadn't my parents managed to stay together, despite being so different and so argumentative?

Desperate for one last shot of advice from someone who actually liked Jonathan, I did the unthinkable: I rang my mother.

From the background noise, she seemed to be in the middle of some industrial process. "Hello? Melissa? You'll have to shout, I'm having my hair done!"

It wasn't ideal, but I really needed to talk to her now.

"Mummy, I know this sounds weird, but"—I bit my lip—"are you and Daddy happy? I mean, together?"

"Darling, I've been telling you for the last twenty years," she bellowed over the dryer, "your father and I are not getting divorced. It would cost a *fortune*!"

"But—"

"Is this about Jonathan?" yelled Mummy. Like Granny, she could be very shrewd when she wanted.

"Yes," I said, hugging my bag.

"Trouble?"

I paused, cringing at what the woman in the next chair must be thinking. "Yes."

"Darling, could you turn that off?" I jumped, thinking she was talking to me, but the loud whirring stopped. "Thank you. Tell Mario I'll just be a moment. Now, Melissa," she went on, only slightly less loudly, "I'll say to you what I said to Emery and Allegra when they got engaged. I know your father and I don't have the most conventional marriage. But it works because we know the absolute worst and best about each other. Sometimes he's utterly vile. Sometimes, though, he's charm personified. But he's always himself. And so am I. That's the secret of happy marriages, in my opinion. It's like waxing your moustache—once you've pretended to be something you're not, you'll be doing it for the rest of your life. It means something's not quite right."

I was still blenching at the thought of Daddy being charm personified.

"Oh," she added, as an afterthought, "and always check the laundry basket for rogue underwear."

"Thank you," I said weakly.

"I hope everything's OK, darling?" Mummy went on. "You know how much we like Jonathan."

"I know." That was part of the problem: he was the first boyfriend I'd had that they hadn't actively repelled.

I reminded myself that my father had liked him so much he'd bought my agency. Or tried to.

"Are you coming to see us soon?" Mummy asked hopefully. "I know Emery would love to see you. She's having trouble with Nanny Ag, I'm afraid. Bit of a personality clash, I think, and then there's the christening—"

"I don't know," I said, slinging my bag over my shoulder. My mind was about two hundred miles elsewhere. "Soon. Mummy, I have to go. I have to book a Eurostar ticket."

I hurried back past the white houses of Belgravia to the office, stiffening my resolve with every click of my heels on the pavement. But when I shoved open the door to the office, I took an involuntary step backward. My desk was surrounded by dozens and dozens and dozens of velvety red roses, and standing in the middle of them all was Jonathan.

eighteen

"Hello," he said, pushing a hand into his red hair. "I'm afraid I couldn't wait until the whole week was up. Do you mind?"

I struggled to breathe normally, and not just because I'd run up two flights of stairs.

This huge romantic gesture was so typical of Jonathan—the roses, the surprise appearance, the flying-to-win-me-back—but suddenly I felt annoyed rather than overwhelmed, as if he'd wrong-footed me here in my own office. I didn't want grandstanding gestures. I wanted a proper talk. The proper talk we should have had ages ago.

"No. Of course not. Can I get you a drink?" I said automatically. Jonathan looked surprised. "What? Oh, OK. Coffee would be nice."

I turned on the coffee machine and tried to steady my thoughts. I couldn't help aching at how gorgeous Jonathan looked, leaning against my desk with his suit hanging perfectly and his hair freshly cut. I wished I'd washed my hair that morning.

"If I'd known you were coming I'd have tidied up," I said lightly. "The office, and myself."

"Both look just as cute as ever," he said, running his gaze around the room. "Makes me feel quite nostalgic, coming in here, catching you on the run." He directed his gray eyes toward me. "Although it's all changed since then, of course."

"Well, yes and no." I squirmed. "Look, sit down."

Jonathan raised an eyebrow and shifted a pile of paperwork off the chair. It included Gabi's paint charts and wallpaper samples. "You're planning on redecorating?" he asked, holding one aloft.

I nodded.

"Call me Sherlock Holmes, but that doesn't sound like something you'd do if you were about to move to Paris," he observed.

"It's what I'd do as a business owner," I replied, putting out a cup and saucer for him. "It's nice to freshen up the place."

"Shall we cut to the chase, Melissa?" he said, and pulled my hand so I was suddenly sitting on his knee, close enough to feel his warm skin through the fine cotton of his shirt. "I've missed you. I'm sorry. I don't know what I have to say to you to get things back on track, but just tell me, and I'll say it."

As his arms tightened around me, my heart lurched in my chest, as if he'd pulled it toward him on a string. How churlish was I being, for God's sake? Here was a man who was more romantic and independent and . . . *more ideal* than anyone else I'd ever met—and he loved me! What was I waiting for?

And yet, deep down, I knew something was missing, and it just wasn't fair to keep ignoring it.

"Say you'll come back with me," said Jonathan softly, raising my hand to his lips as he looked up into my eyes. "Please? I got you a ticket. First class. Let's start again, from the beginning."

I looked back at him, and though I felt my heart breaking, I realized that was the problem in a nutshell: did he think two hundred roses and a first-class one-way ticket were enough to brush all the unspoken problems out of the way? Was I that easy to manage?

"Jonathan, it's really hard for me to say this—" I began, but he interrupted me.

"If it's about the business, then I'm prepared to work something—"

"It's not about the business," I said firmly, and he stopped. "It's us."

"Ah," he said instead, visibly bracing himself. "OK, out with it."

I cupped Jonathan's strong jaw in my hand, feeling the first prickles of ginger stubble against my palm. A lump was making its way into my throat and I knew it wouldn't be long before tears followed. It was like being right at the top of a roller coaster, knowing the plunge was ahead, and inescapable.

"I've been thinking about nothing else but you since the weekend. And about me, and about our future."

"Me too," said Jonathan.

"But . . ." I summoned up all my inner courage. "I just can't see what that future *is*. I mean, I can picture us going out to dinner, and holding posh drinks parties, and strolling round the Place des Vosges, but I just can't see the dull everyday stuff."

"And that's important to you? Dull stuff?" His voice wasn't cross, just confused.

"Yes!" I stroked the arm that was holding me on his knee.

"Dull stuff. . . . Can you be more specific?"

I racked my brains for examples. "Like reading the Sunday papers with a hangover, or getting messy painting the nursery. Relaxing. Not talking. Not having to try so hard to be what each other wants." I paused, trying to find the right words, words that would let him see it wasn't his fault, or mine. "It's been like starring in a film, being with you, Jonathan. A film where London is gorgeous and everything sparkles, and I feel like a million dollars. But the thing is, my life's more like a sitcom. Low budget. Ad breaks. I need that vegging-out-in-front-of-the-television time that you hate. You're in love with a *part* of me, but I can't be like that *all the time*. I'd end up a nervous wreck, and you'd end up disappointed, I know. I can't bear the thought of that, when it's been so wonderful up to now—I'd rather end things now, while those memories are still perfect. I'm so sorry, Jonathan."

"No. God, Melissa. Please don't give me all that Honey crap again," he groaned.

"That's not what I'm saying," I insisted. He really wasn't getting this. "I'm *always* Melissa, but that efficient side of me you think is so great and effortless? That's work. I love it, but it's my *job*. You want someone who'll power through your social calendar as hard as she'll drive your business—that's not me. Just like I can't force you to enjoy country walks and drooly dogs." I tried a sad smile. "It wouldn't be fair. It's selfish, I know, but I love you too much to let you be disappointed again."

"How long have you been thinking this?" he asked, hurt. "Without telling me?"

"I've tried not to think about it," I admitted. "I don't really want to do it now, but I can't *not.*"

"Is there . . . someone else?" he asked, and his face was so tight with pain that he might as well have said *as there was with Cindy?*

I shook my head. "No, Jonathan, there's no one else, I promise you."

"And it's not just to do with that franchising business?"

I hesitated, knowing I owed it to him to be truthful. "That . . . that wasn't something I was happy about. But it was more of a sign that things weren't going to work out."

He took my hand and kissed it again, resting his lips tenderly on each knuckle. There was a painful silence as we both digested what I'd said. I felt sick, but strangely calm.

"I appreciate you being honest with me," he said at last. "I've always loved that about you—you're so . . . honorable. I know I'm not so great at big emotional moments. Maybe that's the problem. But you know I love you, right? Like I've never loved anyone else."

He looked up at me, and his eyes, normally so cool and amused, were filled with a pleading expression I didn't recognize. And tears. It tore at my heart to hurt him like this. "There's really nothing I can say?"

I shook my head again, not trusting myself to speak as tears filled my eyes too.

"I hope we won't . . ." He cleared his throat. "You're right—we owe it to each other to part in as elegant a way as we met. Melissa, I hope I can still be a special friend to you?"

I flung my arms around him. "Jonathan, I never want us to be less than special friends!" I sobbed. "That's not even in question!"

"Then that's something," he said, and I think he was crying too.

Jonathan left half an hour later, and I spent the rest of the afternoon just sitting there in my chair, staring at the wall, ignoring the phone, unable to move or stop the tears rolling silently down my face until the light began to fade and shadows started to fall in the office.

At seven, there was a tentative knock on the door, and when I didn't answer, it pushed slowly open and Nelson peered round, wearing his cricket whites.

I'd forgotten he had nets that evening. I'd promised to go along and videotape his bowling for later dissection.

When he saw my tear-ravaged face, and the roses, and the piles of Kleenex covering the desk, his expression changed into one of infinite kindness as he put two and two together and made about ninety. Without speaking, he crossed the room in a few steps and engulfed me in a huge bear hug, pressing my nose into his cricket sweater. There was such tender concern in that simple, spontaneous gesture that a new reservoir of blubbing burst open and I howled for the romantic cocktail nights and sexy mornings in Jonathan's New York town house, for the surprise birthday plans I'd made for him, for the well-mannered red-haired children we'd never have, and for the fact that you could love someone who loved you but still not be able to make things work.

Nelson, meanwhile, just stroked my hair until I hiccuped to a blotchy-faced halt.

"Come on, Mel," he murmured soothingly, helping me to my feet. "Let's go home."

If I was heartbroken at calling off my engagement, I knew it would be nothing compared to the disappointment my parents would feel—something akin to that of a small child who's been told that Santa's been dropped from the Christmas gig. My father had only started treating me like an adult since Jonathan had come on the scene, and my mother was besotted with him.

But I had to tell them, and, more to the point, I had something to get off my chest with Daddy.

True to form, Mummy spotted that I wasn't wearing my engagement ring the moment I walked through the drawing-room door.

"Are you having your diamond cleaned, darling?" she asked delicately.

"No," I said. "I've given it back. I'm afraid I've broken off my engagement."

"Oh dear!" Mummy sank into the nearest chair, nearly spiking herself on the knitting needles sticking up out of it. Attached to them was what looked like a life-size knitted barn owl, but with fins. "Why?"

"Because of what you said. Jonathan and I . . . we just weren't being ourselves." I sank into a chair myself, but not before checking it for knitted wildlife. "I don't think I could have made him happy, but it would have broken my heart to make him *un*happy."

"I'm so sorry, darling. Would you like a quick stiffener?" she asked, concerned. "I could do with one." Before I could reply, she reached into an ornamental flower stand, withdrew the crystal whisky decanter and a couple of glasses, and poured us both a generous drink. "Don't ask," she said as she dropped in some ice, concealed in a tissue box. "Nanny's got us all on rations, your father included."

"Good God," I said and sipped the Scotch. I needed something to buck me up to challenge Daddy, especially if he was in a foul mood. If there was one thing I was determined to do, it was to give him a piece of my mind before I left. Make him feel guilty. Make him realize that he couldn't treat me like that. If I didn't say anything now, I'd never be able to face myself again.

"Where is everyone?" I asked. "It's very quiet."

Your father's in his study, reading P. G. Wodehouse to poor Bertie. Emery's hiding from Nanny, I think, and your grandmother left for Nice this morning in a helicopter." She pulled a face. "Apparently that helipad out back your father's always showing off about is for decorative purposes only. Still, Alexander was terribly sweet about it."

"Did it damage his chopper?" I asked, wondering what Nicky would have to say about that.

Mummy coughed on her Scotch. "In a manner of speaking. Anyway, are you sure about Jonathan? It's not just pre-wedding jitters?" she asked hopefully.

I shook my head. "No. Sorry."

She leaned over and patted my knee. "Well, it's a brave thing to do.

I had to do it once or twice myself, and it's frightful. I'm sure you've got good reasons."

"Yes, I have," I said, assuming Daddy had told her about the franchise investment. "I was furious. I felt like I'd been horse-traded!"

Mummy's brow creased as far as her Botox would let it, which was an imperceptible wrinkle. "Steady on, darling, Granny didn't mean to—"

"What's Granny got to do with it?"

"You split up with Jonathan because you're seeing Nicolas now, aren't you?"

"What?" I stared at her. "No! Of *course* not! Didn't you know? Jonathan and Daddy were planning to sell my agency across the country like—"

"Like Office Angels but with stockings and a bit of sauce. It's the best idea I've had in years!"

I spun round, and there was Daddy in the doorway, Bertie strapped to his chest. Both were pink around the nose and a bit drooly.

I ground my teeth. I'd hoped for a bit of run-up before tackling Daddy, but here he was, like a terrifying three-fence and water-jump combination, all from a standing start.

What made it even more disconcerting was that he was wearing an ingratiating smile. He obviously hadn't heard the first bit of our conversation.

"I was wondering when you might pitch up. Let me guess," he went on jovially, "you've popped over to play hardball about your marital stake in the company, eh? I don't blame Jonathan for letting you do the negotiating—after all, it is my little lady who owns The Little Lady Agency, isn't it? And what a businesslike Little Lady she's become! But I must warn you, it's better to leave the numbers to the chaps. You stick to those clever wardrobe tips, popsy."

"Martin . . . ," hissed Mummy, making *No, no!* gestures.

I stared at him as fury coursed through my veins. It was precisely this blend of condescension and bullying that had led me to set up the agency in the first place. "If you must know, Jonathan and I have called off our engagement. And this deal he and you were cooking up—without bothering to consult me—was a major factor. I can absolutely believe it of you, but for him to go behind my back like that was the final straw."

I didn't think now was the time to add that there were other equally valid contributory factors. All the fury and unhappiness that had been swilling around me for the past few days erupted like molten lava, and I wasn't about to let details get in the way.

"All my life you've put me down, and belittled me, and now I've built up something to be proud of, you think you can just buy your way into it!" I raged. "Well, you can't! And if you think I'd marry someone who'd connive with you to . . . to . . . disempower me, then you don't even know your own daughter!"

"But I did it *for you,* you stupid woman!" yelled Daddy. "I wanted to make sure you weren't on your own, up to your neck in it with some silver-tongued estate agent!" He actually managed to look hurt. "I wanted to support you!"

I boggled. "Don't give me that! Since when have you ever done anything for anyone but yourself? Marriage isn't something normal people need to be protected from, in any case! And for your information, Jonathan was well aware of what you were up to. He was out to use you about as much as you were trying to use me!"

Daddy looked positively stunned, and he covered Bertie's ears. I supposed I was shouting now.

Not that I'd finished, either. "Most girls have fathers who care about them, and love them unconditionally, but you've just treated us like idiots from the day we—"

He held up his hand, and, thinking he wanted to apologize, I stopped short.

Instead, he narrowed his eyes. "What did you just say?"

That threw me. "Which bit? You letting me down? Or going behind my back?"

"No, no, the bit about Jonathan exploiting my investment."

"Martin, you pig!" snapped my mother. "Apologize to Melissa right now!"

I held my shuddering breath while Daddy rearranged his features into something approximating remorse. To be fair, he did look fairly rueful. But that might have been the vision of having to redo his tax accounts.

"Melissa, darling, of course I'm very sorry that you're so upset, and it's terribly sad about the engagement. . . ." He pulled a sympathetic face, but then his real nature broke back through. "But in what way was that sneaky bastard ripping me off?"

My voice was shaking. So were my hands. And my knees, come to that. "How can that matter to you more than my feelings, you . . . you monster?"

Daddy heaved a patronizing sigh. "Melissa, my darling girl, it's business. You really shouldn't mix the two if you're going to get so emotionally involved like this."

I bored my most hate-filled glare through his forehead. "I am thirty years old. I am not your little girl anymore. And if you didn't have Emery's baby strapped to your chest," I snarled, "I swear to God I would throw my drink over you."

I stormed across the room, nearly in tears, and Daddy stepped aside to let me out, widening his eyes at my mother. As I passed, without stopping to think, I grabbed hold of his newly candy-flossed hair and yanked.

As I thought, a large section of it came away in my hands, like a clump of mangy urban fox.

To my great delight, Bertie unleashed the most almighty wail, right under Daddy's nose, and showed no signs of stopping.

In an ideal world, I would have leaped straight into my car and driven away in a cloud of triumphant dust. Actually, if I'd been living Nicky's film-star life, I'd have gotten back into the Bentley and told Ray to take me back to London, but since I'd had a large scotch, I was trapped at home until my blood alcohol went down and forced to take refuge in the rambling upper stories.

As I wandered around upstairs, blinking back tears in front of previous generations of Romney-Joneses and some other portraits of

unknowns (bought at auction to replace the ones Daddy's grandfather had sold to mend the roof), my blood pressure started to
come down.

You told him, at least. I thought. *You're not carrying it around inside
you. And that's a step forward.*

Out of long-forgotten habit, I headed toward the attic, where
Emery and I had spent much of our childhood playing darts and hiding from people. It came as no great shock when I found her up there,
reading *Heat* magazine and eating a chocolate orange.

"Don't worry, it's just me," I said, as she scrabbled to hide evidence
of all three.

"You look ghastly," she observed now, with a directness I'd come to
expect from Allegra, not her. Childbirth's surprising effect on Emery's
personality had meant it wasn't so much like gaining a nephew as
gaining a whole new sister, as well. The filmy veil of ethereality had
been drawn away to reveal quite an acid drop.

"Budge up and give me some chocolate," I sniffed.

"Crisis?" she asked.

"You could say that," I replied, and filled her in.

"You know, in an odd way, I do think Daddy *was* doing it for you,"
she mused. "He doesn't ever show it, *obviously,* but he's always banging
on to me and Allegra about how you're the only one who's ever managed to make any money, standing on your own two feet." She looked
thoughtful. "As opposed to us lying on our backs and thinking of al-
imony, I guess."

If that was meant to be witty, it went over my head. "What?"

Emery swung her long hair at me. "Forget it. Look, he was probably just trying to sneak in an extra prenup for you. Safeguard your
business by getting his own foot in the door. I know it's warped, but
he's like that, isn't he?"

"Safeguard it? From Jonathan?" I felt like crying again.

"Oh, what do I know," said Emery, falling back onto more familiar
tactics of vaguery. "Why don't I take your mind off it by telling you
how bloody awful my life is?"

I helped myself to some chocolate and sank against an old Chester-field sofa as Em began a long, long whine about ex-wives, Daddy's hogging of Bertie, Allegra's continued attempts to stress Mummy into freaky knitting, and winding up with motherhood in general.

"Nanny Ag is driving me utterly bonkers, Mel. And Daddy refuses to get rid of her, because he enjoys tormenting her more than any other human being he's worked with, according to him."

"Where is she now?" I asked.

"It's her half day. Probably in town getting her broomstick re-strung." Emery stuffed the spine of the chocolate orange in her mouth before I could nab it myself. "You know she confiscated my iPod this morning? Said the radio waves would upset the baby. I need it," she added, more to herself than me. "I *need* those dolphin songs."

"Well, let's go and get it." I heaved myself to my feet and brushed the dust off my skirt. "Come on," I said, looking back at the depress-ingly large fresh area I'd cleaned on the sofa. "No time like the present."

"What's got into you?" demanded Emery.

I set my jaw. "The worm is turning."

We hadn't been allowed in Nanny Ag's room as children. Even though it had been a spare guest room for the subsequent fifteen years, our shoulders automatically went timorous and we both started to tiptoe as we approached.

"Do you think . . . ?" she whispered, turning to me.

The adrenaline was still in my system from earlier, however. Nanny Ag didn't scare me, especially when she wasn't there. "For God's sake," I snapped, and swung the door open.

The pink and white room was supernaturally neat, with brushes lined up at meticulous intervals on the dressing table and only one book by the bed: *Potty Training in One Week* by Gina Ford. Even her slippers were lined up next to the fireplace, next to her sensible shoes (shoe trees included). It was the sort of neat you see in the photos of serial killers' homes.

"Where do you think it is?" Emery whispered.

"Probably hidden somewhere," I said, and began opening the dressing table drawers. "Where's the last place anyone would look? In her knicker drawer."

"Mel," Emery began. "Are you sure you should be—"

"Yes," I snapped. "She has no right to confiscate your iPod. You're a married mother of one! And this is your house!"

I couldn't see it among the neatly folded Sloggi armpit-high pants and industrial girdlage. But as I rummaged through Nanny Ag's identical Marks & Spencer blouses, my hand closed on something boxlike. Triumphantly, I drew it out.

It was a box file. "Here you go," I said, passing it to her, "have a look in here—you'll probably find Allegra's underwater Walkman and your old Smash Hits sticker album."

Emery opened it and her jaw dropped. "Mel!" she said.

I was busy folding everything back in the right place. "What?"

"It's not my iPod."

I looked over to the bed, where Emery was flipping through a notebook with undisguised horror.

"Well, what is it?"

"It's . . . us!" She thrust the book at me. "Everything we've done! How much Daddy drinks in an evening! Where Mummy's hidden her Vicodin! The real reasons Allegra was expelled!" She put the book down and picked up another. "It's . . . oh my God! Kitty Blake! I went to school with her! I had no idea she . . . Blimey! So *that's* why she only ever talked to her pony."

"What?" I scrambled across the bed to look.

The box file was packed full of old photographs of Happy Meal birthday parties at McDonald's and unflattering fancy dress outfits, printed-out emails, computer discs, tapes marked "baby monitor—Gingold/Patterson Affairs 3-7"—stacks of what could only be described as *evidence.*

"The sneaky cow must have been collecting this stuff for years!" I gasped. "And I know some of these people too!"

Emery raised her eyes in horror. "We probably recommended her to them."

I scrabbled through the assembled notebooks. "But I don't see how she could have had time to work for all these people. . . ." Blimey— that was Godric Ponsonby and his sister, Aelthred! And that, if I wasn't mistaken, was Bobsy Parkin, complete with a faceful of braces that made her look like a human pencil sharpener.

Bobsy had never mentioned Nanny Ag to me, and most of the girls I'd been at school with kept in touch with their nannies for years. I frowned. How was that possible?

I searched through the box and soon found out why: letter after letter revealed that Nanny Ag had been operating a network of nanny informers, from one end of the country to another.

Gracious. I'd had no idea Bobsy's father had a lovechild in South Africa. She certainly kept that quiet.

"Mel, look at this," breathed Emery, thrusting a sheaf of notes at me. "She's been taking notes on us! 'Emery has passive-aggressive issues,' indeed. I'll give her passive . . ."

She broke off as we heard the front door close and Daddy yell, "It was only a small one! And the bloody sun's well over the yardarm, you fascist old boot!"

We froze, surrounded by the evidence.

"She's back!" gasped Emery, "What do we do?"

I thought quickly. "Put everything back. She's not going anywhere. We need to think about this."

Hastily, we repacked and stowed the letters and photos with trembling fingers.

"Mummy? Where is Mummy?" bellowed Nanny Ag, clumping up the stairs toward us. "You are late for bed and stories!"

"Bertie likes staying up, you mad old biddy," muttered Emery, as we slid out of the room as silently as we could.

Unfortunately, we'd misjudged Nanny Ag's SAS-like ability to get up stairs faster than you'd expect from someone of her size and age, and we bumped into her just outside her room.

"What are you two doing?" she thundered.

"I wanted to put some flowers in your room," I said quickly. "Emery was checking you didn't have any already."

Emery made a low hissing noise as Nanny Ag thought, then simpered. Not a pretty sight.

"How thoughtful, Melissa. Maybe we can wipe that nasty London attitude away, after all."

"Mmm!" I said, and shoved Emery down the passage.

"What was that about?" she demanded. "You creep! After what she said about you . . ."

"Emery," I said, relishing the sound of Bertie howling downstairs and Daddy attempting to soothe him by singing "Three Little Maids from School." "If there's one thing I've learned from living in this house, it's that revenge is a dish best served cold." I pursed my lips and thought of the unkind comments I'd read about my puppy fat. I was very disappointed in Nanny Ag. "There's usually enough left for seconds, then."

Emery gave me a sideways glance. "Sometimes, Mel, you really do sound like Daddy, you know."

"Don't," I said.

nineteen

Word got round that I was back to five full days in the office, and work flooded in. It was nice to feel needed, I suppose, and it helped to keep busy. But every time I came across some old matchbook that brought back a particularly romantic evening, or when I found a date in my diary that I now had to cross out, I was felled anew by gloom. Nelson, Gabi, and Roger did their best to drag me out to the cinema and cricket and whatever they could think of that didn't involve weddings, but surprisingly, it was Nicky who did the best job of taking my mind off things.

My corsets started straining even more than normal as a culinary war broke out, with Nelson cooking up a storm at home on the nights Nicky wasn't squiring me out for dinner—which was at least two or three times a week. Though I spent some of the evening lecturing him about the minefields of proper behavior, mostly we talked about other things, like families or old flames (ninety percent his, to ten percent mine, naturally). His flippant mask slipped more and more often, and I started to see that Nicky's wilder behavior was actually pretty sad—his only way of competing with his grandfather's celebrated charm, and his father's racing success. It was hard just to be himself. I knew that feeling well. By August, I felt as though I was dining with the real Nicky, and the showing-off was down to a bare minimum. Well, until he spotted the paparazzi outside, and even then I think he acted up so I could tell him off.

Most of all, I was touched by his genuine desire to make me laugh when I never wanted to laugh again. And that was more attractive than any of his ludicrous chat-up lines. When I told him that, he just smiled.

Granny tried to cheer me up too, by sending me a stream of invitations: "Alex would love you to take Nicky to"—the Henley Regatta, the Goodwood Festival of Speed, tennis parties, and dinners. She took to popping into my office, hauling me round the shops for a "second opinion" on clothes for her, which inevitably turned into "a teeny treat" for me too. She made the occasional gentle inquiry into how things were with Jonathan, but I could tell her honestly that, out of mutual hope that we might still be friends, we'd decided not to be in touch until we'd both moved a little further on.

That, naturally, was much easier for me to say than to do, but Nelson and Gabi were both on eagle-eyed drunk-text alert.

Even though I was sure I'd started to wreak a positive effect on Nicky, relations between him and Nelson hadn't improved. If anything, they'd got worse, and the cruise was now only a few weeks away.

"Nelson," I said at home one night in late July. "I need you to do me a favor."

"If it's anything to do with more office decorating, then no," he said, without raising his eyes from the *Guardian* crossword. "I've got a grumbling coccyx from all that sandpapering."

"It's to do with Nicolas, actually," I said.

Nelson responded with a gagging noise, as did Roger, who'd come round to "pick my brains about lingerie"—a ghastly prospect I'd been putting off for two hours now.

"Oh, come on," I wheedled. "I just need you to coach him a little bit. For an interview."

"About what? How to do up all the buttons on his shirt and then apply a tie?" Nelson looked up. "Or are they interviewing him about his much-loved homeland and he needs a refresher course about where it is?"

I ignored all this. "You remember when we were at that charity dinner and Leonie won the weekend away on Nicky's yacht?"

"I can hardly forget."

"Well, do you remember someone from a magazine offering to send their paparazzi?"

"Melissa," said Nelson patiently. "I assumed that was a joke. No one *expects* the British paparazzi."

Roger giggled in a high-pitched voice. "Their chief weapon is surprise! And fear! And ruthless efficiency! Monty Python," he added, looking at me patronizingly.

I sighed. That was the biggest common factor among my public school clients: a near photographic recall of all British comedies of the past forty years, and a primeval urge to reenact them with other men. It was like religion, right up to the point where they paused to let everyone laugh in unison at the appropriate moments.

"Well, apparently they give notice these days. Someone's going to ring us up in advance, so we can glam ourselves up and look relaxed. And the magazine wants to have a chat with Nicky beforehand so they can run a little interview alongside the pictures, about his sailing and so on, so I was wondering if you could come along to the office for a spot of lunch and sort of . . . brief him?"

Nelson looked at me with his Grade Two Head Prefect expression. "Like he briefed *you* about Parisian clubs? And dropped you right in it with Jonathan?"

I went pink. "I don't think he meant to drop me in it, and anyway, I should have checked it out myself. And it wasn't . . . Look, let's not talk about that. Anyway, it won't take long—I just want him to sound as knowledgeable and seaworthy as you do. It's really very attractive in a man," I added, with shameless flattery.

Nelson upped the Prefect expression to a Grade One. "Mel, you do realize that there'll come a point when your spin machine steps aside and he'll be revealed as the moronic freeloader he really is?"

"Honestly, you just have to get to know him!" I insisted. "When he's not in shallow social situations, he's actually quite sensitive. I mean, when Jonathan and I—"

I stopped mid-defense, recalling with a little surprise how sensitive Nicky *had* been about Jonathan. Almost as if he genuinely cared about my happiness. Almost as if . . .

"Are you trying to remember when you last saw him in a non-shallow social situation?" suggested Nelson helpfully. "Or just assessing how badly he'll go off the rails when you're not spoon-feeding him?"

"You are his social water wings," intoned Roger. "Or, as might be appropriate to this interview, his self-inflating life jacket of re-spectability."

I glared at Nelson and Roger. "I intend to teach him to swim without my support. In the . . . in the blue waters of . . . of . . . his own inheritance."

"Whatever that means," added Roger.

"Don't forget the poor journalist has to talk to the little creep in person," Nelson reminded me. "Unless you've added ventriloquism to your impressive list of skills?"

"Why don't you just do it over the phone—get Nelson to pretend to be Nicky?" offered Roger.

"I could not be that slimy," huffed Nelson. "I'd give myself away by not asking enough questions about the color of the poor woman's underwear."

Roger went puce. "He didn't ask about the color of Zara's. He asked if she was *wearing any.*"

Nelson made a *grrr*ing noise and shook his head as if trying to dislodge a bee from his ear.

"Come round to the office for lunch tomorrow." I stroked Nelson's arm. "You can do your bit to put him on the straight and narrow."

"Make no mistake, Mel," said Nelson. "I'm doing this for you, and you alone."

The following morning, Nicky surprised me by answering his phone on the second attempt, then frankly astonished me by claiming he was at Tate Britain.

"I'm soaking in the culture so I've got plenty to talk about over dinner," he informed me. "'Develop an interest in art,' it says here. Well, I am."

"That's good to hear," I said, not believing him for an instant. "Now, get out of bed and come over to the office for your sailing briefing."

"Melissa, I am out of bed! I'm in . . ." I could hear him consulting a passerby. "I'm in Millbank!"

"Of course you are. Do you want to put Foo-Foo or whoever it is on the phone so she can tell me about Turner's revolutionary depiction of speed?"

That was a phrase I'd learned for my History of Art A-level. I'd known it would come in handy one day.

"Don't you mean the brilliant depiction of light which paved the way for the later Modernists?"

I stared at the telephone. "Um . . ."

"I did do a year of a History of Art degree," said Nicky offhandedly. "I'm not a complete philistine."

"I'm sure that's where you developed your appreciation of the female form," I whizzed back.

"There's a lot you don't know about me, Melissa," said Nicky archly. "What did you say you wanted me to do?"

"Come over here and be briefed for your interview this afternoon." I pushed my tortoiseshell glasses up my nose in an attempt to regain my serious composure. "Remember? The one I wrote in your diary."

"How could I miss your handwriting? Do you want to have lunch with me first?"

"No," I said. "I've got clients all morning, and Nelson's only squeezing you in by having sandwiches in this office."

"Nelly? Jesus. I don't want to be squeezed anywhere by that tedious do-gooder, thanks."

"You'll be here by twelve forty-five or else. He's going to share his immense sailing wisdom with you."

"Of course! I'm a passionate sailor," said Nicky. "I keep forgetting there are a lot of things you know about me that *I* don't. Well, OK. I'll be there. I'm doing this for you," he reminded me.

"And your inheritance," I said, trying to sound businesslike. It was the only way to deal with that sort of flirtation. Then I hung up quickly.

Nelson arrived on the dot of twelve thirty-five, ten minutes early. Nicky arrived at twelve-forty, so if Nelson hadn't been making such a big point, Nicky would have won the timekeeping standoff.

If he was annoyed to see Nelson rise from the comfy leather chair to greet him, he hid it well.

As they shook hands, I noted Nicky was a few inches shorter than Nelson, who looked terribly sober in his gray suit (which, I might add, he never, *ever* wore to work unless they had tax inspectors in). Nicky, on the other hand, was dressed as if he'd been about to set off on the cruise already, in linen trousers and deck shoes, with a pair of Gucci shades tucked into the open neck of his deep red shirt, dragging it down enough to expose a flash of chest hair.

I knew I should tell him off about the playboy shirt, but I just . . . couldn't. I could already see Nelson eyeing the deck shoes with contempt.

"Right," I said, perching on the edge of my desk and pushing the plate of sandwiches toward them. "Let's get going. I had a bit of a chat with the journalist when I was setting up the interview . . ." I glanced at Nicky. "I was being your press secretary, by the way—called Flora, just so you know . . ."

"Am I sleeping with you?" asked Nicky, raising his eyebrow.

"No, Flora is not like that," I said.

"Or so she says."

Nelson coughed.

"And I managed to get a rough idea from the journalist the sort of things she'll want to hear about—what your grandfather's yacht is like, how old you were when you started sailing, any funny stories you have, why you think it's a great sport for young people to get involved in . . ." I turned to Nelson. "Nelson's sailed round the Adriatic with young offenders, haven't you?"

"Yes," said Nelson, "but that was proper sailing, with *sails*. Not just steering a drinks cabinet from one port to another."

"Two very different kinds of sailing," I said hastily. "Well, perhaps you could make that point, Nicky? That you're more experienced with . . ."

Nicky shrugged.

"Motor yachts," supplied Nelson.

"I don't see why I have to pretend anything." Nicky pouted. "Do you know how much our yacht is chartered out for? For a week?"

"Heaps, I imagine," I said quickly, as Nelson inquired, "Is that a tax dodge?" "But I think it would work well if you had a few stories about skippering something smaller. With sails? It'll make you look more traditional. Besides, girls *love* men who can do knots and cope with bad weather," I added, more for Nelson.

"My ancestors were known for their seafaring prowess," Nicky pointed out, with a side glance at Nelson.

"And also for stealing their castle in the fifteenth century from a bunch of nuns, or so I read," replied Nelson casually. "Gambling debt, wasn't it? With the abbess?"

"Don't believe everything you read," snapped Nicky. "At least I *know* what my family was doing in the fifteenth century."

I groaned inwardly. He'd picked the wrong topic there. Nelson, with his characteristic thoroughness, had traced his ancestry back to one farm near Harrogate and had turned up no fewer than ten judges, magistrates, and lord lieutenants in previous generations of Barbers.

"Mine were raising sheep in Yorkshire," said Nelson. "And chopping the hands off miscreants."

"Nelson," I said firmly, taking control of the bickering, "tell Nicky about how you started sailing. Nicky, listen to him, and remember some key phrases."

They both looked at me, with *I'm so doing this under sufferance* expressions.

"Go on," I said encouragingly.

"I learned to sail my father's dinghy up in Yorkshire when I was about five," started Nelson crossly. "I nearly drowned because my brother Woolfe undid my life jacket as a joke."

"Don't bother remembering the Yorkshire bits," I muttered.

"I wasn't going to," said Nicky.

Once Nelson got onto the joys of sailing, it was quite hard to stop him. So I didn't try. I just kept topping up everyone's coffee and jotting things down on my pad.

". . . and that's why you should always have a manual bilge pump as backup." Without warning, Nelson stopped, and Nicky and I jerked back to wakefulness.

"Thanks, Nelson!" I said brightly. "That was really helpful! Just so Nicky knows, what sort of sailing yacht should he pretend to have had?"

"Yah. Tell me what kind and I'll pop out and buy one," drawled Nicky. "Might as well."

I glared at him. If he was trying to impress me, that was absolutely the wrong way to go about it. To be honest, I didn't like it when Nicky went back into his awful princy persona, not now that I'd seen a sweeter side of him. I could only assume he was doing it for Nelson's benefit.

Nelson's blue eyes narrowed, then he reached into his pocket and brought out his phone. "Something like Roger's yacht would do. It's a Pickleton," he said, passing it over so we could see a little picture of it.

"Right," I said. "And what . . . sort?"

Nelson looked hard at Nicky. "It's a bark-rigged scoop."

"Bark-rigged scoop," I repeated. "Got that, Nicky?"

He nodded, bored. "Yeah, yeah."

"I have to go now," said Nelson, checking his watch. "I've got a meeting at two."

"Thanks so much for coming over," I said, kissing his cheek. "I really appreciate this help."

"Yeah, thanks," said Nicky. "I really feel as if I've sailed round the world myself. In real time."

Nelson glowered at him, as if he was about to deliver one of his Home Truths, then evidently decided against it. "I'll see you later," he said to me. "Bouillabaisse all right for dinner? There's a new fishmonger's open down the road, and they're saving some fish heads for stock."

"Oh," I said, "I was going to pop home this evening. Emery's called me three times today about the christening—did I tell you Daddy's postponed it this time? Something to do with the Cheese Diet book going into paperback and it making better coverage if Bertie's christened in November."

"Why don't you invite that girl over?" drawled Nicky unexpectedly. "Leonie, wasn't it? I'm sure she'll be looking forward to the cruise next weekend? Maybe you can brief her too. Or debrief her," he added with a wink.

"Brief her," I said. "Debrief would be her telling him what had happened."

"Yes," said Nelson, shrugging on his jacket. "We'll run through the whole gin-and-tonic-making process. Call me if you need anything, won't you? Afternoon, Nicolas."

"Have fun boiling your heads," called Nicky as he left.

We listened to Nelson clumping down the carpeted steps, and the front door banging.

Suddenly, a buzzy tension filled the little room, along with the warm afternoon sunshine, as Nicky and I were left alone. I couldn't put my finger on quite why I felt so hot and bothered, but it had something to do, I think, with the clashing of antlers that had just taken place. And I wasn't sure how much I liked the idea of Leonie getting my rightful bouillabaisse.

"I like what you've done with the place," observed Nicky, lounging comfortably on the sofa. "Less like a sick bay, more like . . . a lady's boudoir."

"But without the bed," I said, and felt myself blush. I opened the huge, color-coded appointments book and fiddled with a pen to hide my abrupt rise in temperature.

"Hot in here, isn't it?" said Nicky. "Or is that just you?"

I pushed my chair back and got to my feet. Though I was glad I'd dressed up for work today, the lacey tops of my stockings squeezing my thighs were making me feel quite body-conscious, and Nicky's flirtatious manner wasn't helping. "Much as I'd love to sit and chat with you all afternoon, I have to boss someone into getting their hair cut. Might I chuck you out?"

"Can't I stay and watch you be bossy?" he pleaded, lounging on the leather sofa, one long leg swung over the arm. "It's so sexy."

"No," I said, "and no. Out."

"Fine." He got to his feet, and I pretended to be checking some files on the shelf.

"Enjoy the afternoon," I said absently. "Buy a copy of *Yachting World* or something."

"I'd rather do the something." Seeing I wasn't going to be drawn further, he sloped toward the door, but then suddenly turned back. "Present for you."

And he chucked a paper bag on the desk, with the Tate Britain logo on the front.

"All right," I said. "So you *were* at an art museum this morning. I believe you! I'm glad you're listening to some of what I say!"

He paused at the door. "I listen to everything you say, Melissa," he said, blinking slowly at me so I got the full benefit of his long, dark lashes. "Everything. Little things, right?"

And he left.

When I was sure he'd gone, I tipped the postcards out onto my desk, and my heart beat faster in my chest. Every single one featured beautiful women—by Rossetti, Singer Sargent, Millais—but all with long brown hair, and brown eyes, and hips like cellos. Like mine.

I sank into my chair and fanned myself with them.

Honestly, I'd never had a more flattering five pounds spent on me before.

twenty

I was usually pretty confident about what suited me and when to wear it, but packing for a weekend on a motor yacht with two princes, my flatmate, my grandmother, and some paparazzi—in an Indian summer heat wave? I was gripped with indecision.

"Nelson, what am I supposed to wear?" I wailed, staring at the explosion of clothes on my bed. "None of this looks right."

"You're asking the wrong person," he said, trying to find somewhere to put down the cup of tea he'd brought me. "You're probably better off watching UKTV Gold until an old Agatha Christie film comes on. They usually have questionable princes wafting around in patent leather shoes too, come to think of it."

I ignored that.

"What about this?" I held up my least restrictive cocktail dress.

"It's a cocktail dress." Nelson scratched his ear. "Is that a good idea?"

"I'm not going to be scrubbing the decks," I replied crossly.

"Well, presumably you're not going to be manning the roulette wheel either. OK, OK," he added hastily. "What have you packed so far?"

I pointed to my wig, in its little traveling box, and a large sun hat.

He raised his eyebrow at the wig. "Why are you taking that? Won't it get wet? No! Don't tell me—are you and the part-time prince planning to steal everyone's jewels and make a break for the Swiss border?"

I gave him a patient look. "It won't get wet, because *I* won't get wet. I have to take it, because I'll be photographed with Nicky, as Honey, his refined and suitable new companion. Along with you and the charitable Leonie, we'll be sipping martinis in a decorous fashion, rather than cavorting grotesquely, and it'll end up in the magazine, next to his lovely interview about how sailing makes him feel spiritually closer to his seaside principality. Everyone's happy."

"Apart from that Imogen woman," said Nelson.

"Don't talk about her." I pulled a face. "She's been *plaguing* Nicky with phone calls—she rang while we were having lunch the other day, and I could hear her calling me a . . . tart, among other things."

"Sure it was you she was talking about, and not him?"

"Nelson!"

"OK, OK." He chewed his nail—a dead giveaway that he was nervous—and began rearranging the many hair products on my dressing table. "And, um, any dress code for chaps on the SS *Gin Palace* or whatever it's called?"

"I wouldn't presume to tell you what to wear on a yacht," I said.

"But . . . if I asked you?" he pressed a little shyly, then added, "I wouldn't want to give P. Nicky the chance to have a laugh at the expense of the English abroad."

I felt a rush of warmth toward him. Nelson *never* asked my advice on sartorial matters. "Well . . . what you'd wear to a garden party, I expect—blazer, linen trousers, light shirt? Deck shoes?" I wagged my finger jokingly. "They're the only place it's really OK to wear them, you know, so you might as well."

"Fine," he said. "Will do."

In the end, I decided to let someone else choose for me and took myself off to Harvey Nichols. Four hours later, I left, floating on an intoxicating cloud of retail therapy, clutching, in three bags, the ingredients for looking like a film star:

One pair white silk wide-legged pants
One pair industrial pants for wearing beneath the white trousers
One navy and white striped top—très chic!
One pair elegant gold sandals
One "uncreaseable" little black dress
One brown polka-dot bikini with cute tie sides and structurally miraculous underwiring
One mad Pucci print halter dress for sitting around drinking martinis in and generally attracting the attention of paparazzi
One large kaftan
One pair huge Sophia Loren–size shades
One delicious new silk scarf for tying around my head in jaunty nautical fashion
Plus, obviously, a new bag to stuff it all in

Nelson's travel plans always involved setting off "in good time," a flexible formula that roughly equaled estimated journey time plus one major accident en route plus me forgetting one vital item and/or him insisting on going home to check the oven had been turned off. Since I'd been rushed off my feet all week, I'd left the travel arrangements to him and Leonie, who had been in touch with Alexander's secretary.

Nicky, apparently, would "see us at the gate." I made him promise he wouldn't be late.

Needless to say, Nelson called round at my office a good half hour before he'd said he would, and he proceeded to conduct a verbal cross-examination of my travel bag.

"Passport?"

"Yes! Nelson, I'm trying to finish this email before we go, so—"

"Euros?"

"I doubt we'll need any, but yes—"

"Travel insurance?"

I gave up on my email. "Nelson, if anything goes wrong I fully expect Alexander to fly me back to London. Blimey, you look nice."

Nelson did look rather dashing, in a biscuit-colored linen suit and an open-necked blue shirt that brought out the bright color of his eyes.

"Have I seen that suit before?" I added curiously.

"Um, maybe, maybe not. Bought it for the cricket club dinner and, er, haven't got round to wearing it yet," he replied casually. "You don't look so bad yourself. If a bit *nautique*."

"What on earth do you mean?" I demanded. I was wearing very smart navy sailor pants, with a sleeveless print blouse and flat pumps with adorable little gold buttons. It was hardly as if I was kitted out in a captain's hat and eye patch. *"Nautique?"*

"Oh, you know, what people who don't sail think people who do sail wear," he said obliquely, then distracted me by fussing furiously about the time.

We called round by Leonie's office in Hammersmith to pick her up, but with Nelson creating a drama about stopping on a yellow line, she leaped into the back of the Range Rover before I could get a decent look at her. As usual, she was traveling light, with just a very small bag.

"Hi, Melons! Hi, Nelson!" she yelled. "You don't mind if I make a few calls, do you? I've had to take a half day off. I just hope it's going to be worth it!"

"You know no one calls me Melons anymore?"

The thought of the mileage Nicky would get from that was too much to bear.

"Really? Sorry!" But she was already on the phone, yapping away.

Nelson gave me a little smile, and I put my shades on.

The traffic out of London was thick and the weather was hot. I could feel my outfit becoming less and less chic with every mile we crawled.

"Are we flying from Farnborough?" I asked Nelson. At least there'd be no hanging about if Alexander had sent his plane. Granny had been positively lyrical about the delights of private air travel.

"No, Luton."

"Luton?"

"Yes, Leonie booked it. There's an easyJet flight straight to Nice."

"EasyJet?" I swiveled in my seat.

Leonie gave me a thumbs-up. "I booked online! Bargain!" she mouthed, in between ripping into some wretched business contact.

I was startled to see that the sensible city hairdo had gone, replaced with a funkier bob, complete with a generous scattering of creamy blond highlights. She'd evidently been to a personal shopper too, judging by her complicatedly casual navy outfit. I didn't remember her looking so . . . put together before.

I wondered oddly if that was why Nelson had gotten a new suit— to make an impression on Leonie.

"Nelson," I hissed, swiveling back. "Didn't Alexander offer to take us in his jet? I know that's how Granny's getting there. She's all 'I don't do British Airways these days.'"

"Oh, well, Leonie and I talked about it, and she was keen on easy-Jet, and I tend to think you should minimize the carbon footprint where you can, so . . ."

It's very hard to get cross with someone that saintly.

"He's sending a car to collect us at the other end," he offered. "That should be a nice posh one, if it cheers you up."

My phone was ringing in my handbag. "I haven't finished with this!" I warned him, and answered it.

"Hi, can I speak to Honey Blennerhesket, please?" said an unfamiliar voice.

"This is Honey," I said, ignoring Nelson's snort.

"Yeah, hi, my name's Tyra—I'm calling from the subs desk about the interview we did with Prince Nicolas? About his sailing?"

"Oh, yes! Great! How can I help?"

"Well, I just had a few queries. . . ." I could hear the rattle of a keyboard. "Like, he says at one point that his favorite yacht is a . . . where is it? A Pickleton? Was that a mistake?"

"Ummm . . ." I flicked my eyes sideways toward Nelson, who was suddenly concentrating very hard on driving.

"Because the chief sub questioned it—she says there's no such thing. And, yeah, he also said it was a 'bark-rigged scoop'? No such thing either."

"Really? No such thing? How strange!" I said. "I wonder if the tape wasn't clear. Hang on a moment, Tyra, I'm with him at the moment—let me check. Nicky," I said through gritted teeth. "You didn't describe your boat as a *Pickleton,* did you?"

Nelson glared at me.

I glared at him.

"*Did* you?" I repeated.

"Yah! I need to talk to Eddie Rothery in Legal, right now!" brayed Leonie in the back.

"Who's that?" inquired Tyra.

"Um, his other press secretary," I said quickly. "Nicky?"

Nelson made a *why should I?* face.

"*Nicky!*" I hissed, and Nelson caved in.

"It's a Nicholson, darling," drawled Nelson, in a dreadful impression of Nicky. "With a *ch.* And it's a sloop."

"Oh, yes, of course!" I gushed down the phone while glaring fiercely at Nelson. "Gosh, you're not always too clear. You really ought to speak up."

"Hangover," said Nelson. "Darling."

There was a pause on the other end of the line, and I hoped it wasn't a pause of disbelief. "Is that . . ."

I quickly spelled out both words.

"Oh, right . . . ," said the sub. "Glad we got that cleared up."

"Absolutely!" I agreed.

"Things like that have a nasty way of getting into *Private Eye,*" she went on ominously.

Blanching, I made some polite chitchat about us just being on our way to the yacht now and quickly hung up.

"Nelson!" I hissed, once the phone was safely in my bag. "What in the name of God was that about!"

"Oh, come on," he scoffed. "It was just desserts. I didn't see Nicky writhing with guilt when he dropped you in it with Jonathan. How much trouble did that cause between you?"

"That wasn't on purpose!"

"Wasn't it?" he said. "Didn't hear him apologize. Anyway, if he's too bone idle to do his own research . . ."

I took deep yoga breaths. What if it did appear in *Private Eye*? I didn't know anyone who worked on that: I couldn't stop it. My blood ran cold.

"It wasn't me being bitchy," Nelson added. "I don't care about him—it was to settle the scores for you."

"Nelson," I said in a strained voice. "I appreciate that you were trying to help me get my own back for . . . for all that, but don't you see that if Nicky looks stupid because of some PR thing I set up, *I'm* the one who looks stupid, not him?"

Nelson's sarcastic expression shifted.

"And it won't just be Nicky who's furious with me, but Alexander as well?" I went on, dropping my voice to an undertone, in case Leonie was eavesdropping. "And probably Granny, for good measure? I'm meant to be stopping him making a fool of himself—it just makes me look *incompetent*."

"God, I'm sorry, Mel," muttered Nelson. "Really sorry. I didn't think of it like that."

"Anything else I need to know about before they go to press?"

He shook his head and looked ashamed of himself.

"Fine," I said. Then, because Nelson had turned uncharacteristically schoolboyish, I added, "I do appreciate your help with the whole thing, though. It was good of you." I nudged him. "You'll have to think of a favor you can pull in from him sometime."

Nelson looked as if he was about to say something, then restrained himself. "Hmm," he said ambiguously.

As soon as we got to the airport, Leonie insisted on hustling us to check-in, so we'd get the first seat allocations. That done, she made a beeline for Duty Free and stocked up on a new pair of half-price

Nicole Richie sunnies and two pots of Clarins moisturizer (for someone from her office—she was charging a very reasonable 10 percent handling fee). I bought the usual girder-sized bar of Toblerone, which we were about to tear into when a familiar figure sauntered across the concourse, a Louis Vuitton overnight bag slung over one shoulder.

Instantly, Leonie and I put down the chocolate, and Nelson's back stiffened.

"Hi there," said Nicky, pulling down his Gucci shades and pretending he hadn't noticed the stares following his progress. He was wearing a ludicrous pair of red deck trousers, with a crumpled white shirt that made his golden skin glow, finished off with a pair of tan shoes. It was hard not to stare at him.

Leonie did a sort of automatic bob, then looked flustered.

"Hello, Nicky," I said, kissing his cheek. "You remember Leonie, don't you? Nelson's *date* this weekend."

"Leonie?" he said, taking his shades off fully. "From that dinner? Good God."

To be fair to Leonie, she did warrant a Good God. Fabulous outfit and glossy new hairdo aside, she'd also slathered on a fair amount of lip gloss in Duty Free and might have had her teeth bleached. The overall effect was very Foxy Chelsea Primary School Teacher, a look I knew Nicky would find irresistible.

"You get what you pay for," she said by way of explanation. "And we saved a fair amount on the tickets, so—"

"Yes," I said, "thanks for arranging the flights, Leonie. But I didn't know you'd booked for Nicky too?"

"She didn't," said Nicky. "I thought it might be a good idea to be *seen* traveling on a *budget* airline—see? I do listen to what you tell me." He then spoiled it by adding, "Anyway, I must admit, I probably did get a bit of a deal on the tickets . . ." He winked. "Go on, guess. Guess how much I paid."

"Fifty quid?"

"No!" he crowed smugly.

"Forty quid?"

"Thirty-five pounds!" He looked round, waiting for us to be impressed.

"That's a shame," said Leonie. "You should have told me—I got ours for fifteen quid return." She pulled a sympathetic face. "Never mind."

Nicky's smugness vanished. "How did you do that?"

"Oh, the prices change all the time, if you get on the right search engine. Just a matter of setting your alarm. Four-fifteen's a good time. In the morning, of course."

Nelson and I exchanged brief, shocked glances, although I must admit I wasn't that shocked—I'd never seen anyone haggle in Duty Free before, either.

"I think that's our gate being called," Nelson pointed out. "Shall we go?"

Leonie grabbed her bag. "Absolutely. We need to be right at the front of the queue or else we won't get seats together. I'll go first."

And with a ferocity that would have put England's rugby team to shame, she barged and elbowed her way through the crawling trolleys.

We followed her, at a little distance.

I soon realized, looking at everyone else's bags, that I'd packed far, far too much, even taking into account my dual personality for the weekend. But the driver who met us at Nice airport didn't comment about the weight of my bag as he lifted it into the trunk of the vintage Rolls-Royce, and soon we were wafting along in air-conditioned luxury toward Monaco, through the mountain tunnels and toward the quieter, twisting coastal road, with the crystal blue sea on one side and the rocky hillsides on the other.

Nelson volunteered to sit in front, since his father had an old Roller too, and he couldn't resist fiddling with the various buttons and dials and asking questions about coach builders.

If you ask me, I don't think Nelson was that keen to sit in the back watching Nicky be charming to two women at the same time, one on each side of him in the luxurious leather bucket seats.

Not that Nicky's charm was getting him very far with Leonie, but the more she resisted, the more he laid it on.

"I think you'll like the *Kitty Cat*," he smarmed. "She's been in the family for years. We've had all kinds of famous people stay on her. I know it seems quite extravagant, keeping a yacht, but she really is a floating work of art, and it's so important to maintain pieces of one's history, don't you think?"

He shot an approval-seeking glance at me from the corner of his brown eyes and casually extended his arm along the back of the seat.

"One's really a curator, as much as an owner," he added.

"Really?" said Leonie. "I understand you charter it out now. That's quite an efficient way of maintaining it, I suppose, getting other people to fund the upkeep."

"Well, yes, but she's still ours—"

"Mm," said Leonie. "I Googled it."

"Her," said Nicky. "Boats are always ladies. Nelly told me that, so it must be right." He relaxed so that his left knee made contact with mine. Leonie was sitting with her knees clamped together, well out of reach. "I like to think of yachts as being very like women."

"Really?" said Leonie.

"Really?" I said, desperately trying to think of a way to keep him from saying whatever he was going to come out with.

"Oh, yes. Tricky to steer, expensive to maintain, beautiful to look at . . ."

I started to relax, at which point he added, " . . . fairly easy to tie up—"

"We must be getting near Monaco!" I exclaimed loudly, as a crop of white apartment blocks and palm trees rose up from the craggy waterfront ahead of us. "Look, Leonie! Isn't it beautiful?"

She peered out the window at the spectacular view, and I took the opportunity to point my finger warningly at Nicky.

"Best behavior!" I mouthed.

He responded by taking my finger and biting the end of it gently, which utterly undermined my attempts at sternness.

I slapped his knee.

Nelson's voice crackled through the old intercom connecting the driver to the back. "This was all reclaimed from the sea, and Monaco itself is actually smaller than Hyde Park. And," he added, as Nicky's hand trapped mine on his knee, "I can see you, by the way."

The three of us sat very upright in our seats for the remaining three minutes of the journey down the twisting road to the marina.

The *Kitty Cat* was moored alongside a gigantic white motor cruiser and an even bigger fast-looking monster straight out of *Miami Vice*. Nelson, who had been making gentle scoffing noises as we'd followed Alexander's driver along the quayside of gold-encrusted, million-dollar extravagances, abruptly went silent and appeared to have slipped into some kind of love trance.

"Is that it?" asked Leonie.

Nicky nodded. "Not bad, eh?"

"She's absolutely beautiful," barked Nelson, as if Nicky had just insulted his mother.

I had to agree with him, even though I knew nothing about motor yachts. She wasn't as big or as flashy as most of her show-off neighbors, but the *Kitty Cat* was pure old-fashioned glamour, with sleek Art Deco lines and polished wooden decks. Every inch of brass gleamed with years of polishing, the ropes were brilliant white, and the portholes sparkled clean in the sunshine. Well, I say portholes. They were more like windows. It was that big. Although it seemed quite small compared to the other boats, the *Kitty Cat* must have been nearly as long as a hockey field.

"Welcome aboard!" Alexander appeared at the top of the stairs leading up to the deck. I was pleased to see he wasn't wearing a jolly captain's hat like a few of the other owners I'd noticed on the way over. Unlike Nicky, who was clambering aboard as if the whole thing might just take off at any moment, Alexander seemed perfectly relaxed in his shirt and chinos.

The first awful *Am I overdressed?* worries began to steal over me. Was this hat a bit much? It *was* very hot in the sun, and I didn't know when the paparazzi were scheduled for—I didn't want them to snap me unwigged.

"Darling!" said Granny, appearing from behind him.

I needn't have worried. Granny was wearing silky white palazzo pants and a floppy blouse, having apparently stepped straight out of Katharine Hepburn wardrobe services. A white scarf protected her head from the sun, and gold chains glinted round her neck. To keep her from looking entirely like a stray sail, her bare feet were accented with the brightest red nail varnish I'd ever seen. The effect was unfairly glamorous.

"How lovely to see you again," said Alexander, kissing me on each cheek. He greeted Nicky the same way, muttering something terse in Greek, albeit with a smile on his face, then he shook Nelson's hand and kissed Leonie's.

"Ah, the Lady Luck! You have brought us beautiful weather," he said to Leonie, who blushed. "I hope we'll have a splendid weekend! Now, what will you have to drink? You must need refreshing after your flight. . . ."

We found ourselves being moved toward the sun deck of the yacht, where a sunken pit was filled with blue and white cushions, next to an oval relaxation pool, tiled in turquoise and silver. An ice bucket of champagne was waiting for us, and as we approached, a crew member in a red crested polo shirt began pouring into the chilled flutes. The whole effect was so like being on a J. Lo video set that I itched to wander around the deck, touching all the smooth surfaces and peering into the windows, but instead we sat and chatted politely about Marinas We Have Known and Nicky's new interest in art galleries.

"You really must come along to Belinda's private show," said Granny, more to Alexander than Nicky. "It turns out she's the most tremendous knitter! Makes all these little knitted creatures with too many arms and legs. She has all those blasé critics gobbling her up."

"They don't know whether to take her seriously or not," I added. "They think she might be a real artist pretending to be a posh blond socialite. So they err on the side of caution and say she's a genius of artistic subversion."

"I can't think where she gets it from," sighed Granny.

"Who knows where any of our children get things from," said

Alexander, glaring at Nicky, who had already drained his glass and was fiddling with his mobile phone.

Another steward glided up to Alexander and muttered something in his ear, which made him nod and smile.

"Thank you. John has just told me that your bags are unpacked in your cabins, so if you'd like to freshen up, or have a dip in the pool . . ." He lifted his hands and beamed at us. "Dilys and I had planned to have an early dinner on board and then perhaps visit the casino later, but you must do exactly what you want."

"Ooh," said Nicky. "Really?"

I kicked him discreetly, but he sighed at me so loudly that Nelson stopped admiring the yacht and glared so hard the varnish nearly bubbled on the deck.

The crew began milling about efficiently as we went below, and soon we were heading out of the marina into the open water "for a short cruise before dinner." If I hadn't seen the seascape changing out of the windows, I'd barely have known we were moving, it was all so smooth and quiet.

Frankly, I could have spent a whole hour just in my cabin, opening and closing the hidden fittings and admiring its pine green and cream elegance. The double bed, made up with proper linen sheets, was surrounded by little cupboards, with round-edged mirrors everywhere to make it seem twice as big. The tiny bathroom was just as smart, with one of those huge rainstorm showerheads and big old-fashioned brass taps on the sink. It smelled of polish, and beeswax, with only a very faint tang of ozone to remind you that you weren't in fact in a Mayfair hotel. Inside the wardrobes were matching cream and green satin padded hangers, on which some invisible maid had hung my clothes, lining up my shoes underneath. The latest magazines were stacked by my bed, along with CDs for the stereo and a pink silk sleep mask.

I sank onto the bed and marveled at the luxury of it all. Then I had a shower, just because I could, and washed my hair, because the bathroom was filled with Aveda products, and when I'd finished drying myself with at least three towels, I put on my new magic bikini, with the palazzo pants over it, and wrapped a long scarf around my hair. I was admiring the raffish effect of my big hoop earrings when there was a knock on the door.

"Enter!" I said, getting into the spirit of things.

It was Nelson. "Are you coming up for a go in the . . . Wow." He stepped back a little. "You look very glamorous."

"Thank you," I said, twisting round to look in the mirror. "Sure you can't see my love handles over the top?"

"No one will be looking at your love handles with that top going on," Nelson assured me, then added, in more familiar tones, "Have you got plenty of sun cream?"

"Yes," I said. "Oh, apart from my back." I didn't usually expose that much of myself. "Would you mind?"

"Um, no," he said, after a moment's hesitation.

"Cheers," I said, and handed him the tube of sunscreen, adding, "Oooh!" as the cold cream touched my warm back. Nelson's hands moved with quick, firm strokes across my skin, over my shoulders, under the straps of my bikini, down to the small of my back where my palazzo pants started.

"Mmm, that feels nice," I started to say, then stopped, realizing just *how* nice it did feel. Nelson had very strong hands. He'd done my feet for years, but he'd never massaged any part of me above the ankle before. Clearly, I'd been missing out.

"Better do it now than let Nicky lech all over you," he said as he stroked the rounds of my shoulders with his palms. "I'd hate to think where the cream might end up. By accident."

"Oh . . . Um, yes." I hadn't thought of that. The idea of Nicky massaging sun cream into my back, or indeed, anywhere, was rather a cheek-pinkening one.

Nelson's hands carried on moving across my skin, squeezing my arms, pushing my neck forward to cover the sides of my throat, and a warm glow spread through me. I wondered if he'd be offering to rub Leonie's sun cream in too.

"Funny," I said. "When I did my arms and legs it absorbed much more quickly than this."

"Right, there you go, all done," said Nelson, finishing abruptly, and I was quite sorry when he did.

We cruised along the coast for a few hours, relaxing in the Jacuzzi and playing deck quoits, until the hot afternoon began to soften into a balmy evening and the chief steward informed Alexander that dinner would be served in half an hour. Naturally, having brought about nine changes of clothes for three days, I was more than happy to pop back to my cabin and dress for dinner.

Dinner was served in the dining room, a wood-paneled affair with a full-size dining table that could have seated twelve people easily. Tomato and fresh buffalo mozzarella salad was followed by gigantic prawns and sea bass, with wineglasses that seemed to fill themselves by magic.

"So, tonight," said Nicky, rubbing his hands as the final plate was whisked away by the steward, "you'll be pleased to know, Leonie, that we're on the VIP list at Jimmy'z, which is a very well known club here in Monaco, and it's always packed with racing drivers and hot models—"

"Ah," said Alexander, patting his lips with a linen napkin.

"What?" Nicky demanded.

"I've been talking to John . . ." John was the captain; he'd given me and Nelson a lovely tour of the boat. "And he says there have been a few set-tos between the paparazzi and some actor who's here on honeymoon. The place is seething with photographers. So, with that in mind, perhaps it might be a good idea to go out on Saturday night instead?"

"Yes," I said quickly, seeing what Alexander was hinting at. "If we give the paparazzi lots of pictures of you on the boat tomorrow, they'll go away happy and leave you alone, whereas if you go out tonight and they're spoiling for a scrap, they'll be trying to provoke you."

"Well . . . ," said Nicky reluctantly.

"And you don't want a repeat of the Cuckoo Club incident!" I reminded him, more pointedly.

A few months before I met Nicky, he'd steamed out the back door of the Cuckoo Club and decked a couple of photographers whom he'd assumed had been there to get an exclusive shot of him drunk. They hadn't been. They'd been waiting for Prince Harry. One of them hadn't even known who Nicky was. It had all been most embarrassing.

He glared at me. "I think you'll find we're under far more scrutiny here than we ever are in England."

I knew Nelson would be biting back some retort about no one knowing who the hell they were outside Hollenberg, but he was far too polite to do anything more than shoot a quizzical glance at me.

I had to bite back my smile.

I must admit it was quite disconcerting, seeing Nelson in his new suit, making witty dinner table chitchat with Leonie and Granny. Obviously, I'd seen him entertain Roger and his school friends with his dry anecdotes, but tonight he was positively charming, whether out of competition with Nicky or not, I didn't know. It was really rather attractive. Granny, especially, had been giggling all evening at his observations about London restaurants. I didn't even know he'd *been* to The Ivy. Certainly not with me, anyway.

"Why don't you leave it till tomorrow when you can really let your hair down?" Granny suggested now. "There's plenty to entertain you on board—films and PlayStations and what have you."

"It's all right for you to say that when you're heading off to the casino," grumbled Nicky, but he knew it was a losing battle and gave up before Alexander had to glare at him.

After dinner, it was still very warm, and we took our coffee up to the aft deck and watched the red sunset melt into the sea as we sailed back into the marina. The lights had come on in every window in the flat-roofed houses rising all the way up the Monte Carlo hillside, and the shoreline glittered as if someone had strung diamonds along the streets and between the yachts in their moorings.

"Doesn't that look fabulous!" I sighed, helping myself to another chocolate and relaxing back into the cushions. "Just think of all those clubs and little bars . . ."

"Have you been to the Blackpool Illuminations?" inquired Leonie. "That's quite similar. And much less pretentious."

"Do you know, I haven't?" said Nicky. "You must take me some-time."

I checked to see if he was being sarcastic, but he didn't seem to be. In fact, he was making more than his usual effort with Leonie. I'd muttered as much to him as we'd been making our way up to the deck, and he'd pulled a very descriptive face and murmured something about "the quiet ones" and how much he "enjoyed rising to a challenge."

"Not on a par with you, of course," he added, with a knee-wobbling dip of his eyelashes. "But then you're more than a challenge. You're completely out of bounds."

"Yes," I'd said, "I am."

OK, I smoldered Honey-ishly when I said it. I couldn't help myself. I was on a yacht, in an evening gown and gold sandals, for heaven's sake. When Nicky was around, I didn't need the blond wig to be Honey. He sort of brought her out, like a snake charmer teasing the snake out of the basket.

In a manner of speaking. He even had me thinking in faintly saucy metaphors.

In addition to this, Nelson also seemed to be making an effort to bring Leonie out of her shell, although this led to quite a long discussion of inheritance law, which wasn't so interesting, although Nelson did an admirable job of nodding and *mm*ing in the right places.

All in all, I thought, as we motored elegantly into the harbor, given the selection of people there, it seemed to be going astonishingly well.

"Anyone fancy a drink?" asked Nicky, pushing himself away from the prow we were all leaning on, watching the pretty lights of the harbor sharpen and sparkle in the first evening dusk. "Or I can have them make you a pot of tea if you prefer, Nelly?"

"I'm fine," replied Nelson through tight lips, as Leonie said, "Ooh, yes, I'd like one of those Irish coffees, I think."

"Something hot and intoxicating, eh? I think we can manage that—come below with me . . . ," he said to Leonie as he winked saucily in my direction.

I pretended to ignore it, but I shivered a little when he was out of view.

"Cold?" asked Nelson at once, and before I could answer, he'd slipped off his sweater and draped it round my bare shoulders.

"Thanks," I said, tucking it around me. I wasn't cold, but it was nice of him all the same. "Isn't it a gorgeous view!"

"Yes," said Nelson, looking at me rather oddly. "It is." Then he coughed awkwardly.

I put that down to his inability to like anything connected with Nicky and slipped my arm into his. "Thanks for making such an effort this weekend. I really appreciate it. You're an angel."

"I'm doing this for you," he reminded me.

"I know." I leaned against his reassuringly solid side, rested my head against his shoulder, and sighed. "I don't think there's anywhere else I'd rather be just now."

Nelson put his arm around me. "Me neither."

We stayed leaning shoulder to shoulder against the ropes as the crew expertly docked the ship in a berth that must have cost more than my parents' house. And I'd have happily stayed there, watching the Gucci espadrilles and gold jewelry parade up and down the marina, if Nicky hadn't summoned us both to the Jacuzzi.

I wasn't hurrying for myself, you understand, but for Leonie's sake.

twenty-one

I don't know what time Granny and Alexander returned to their stateroom, but it must have been well after half one, since that was when we turned in for the night and there was no sign of them then.

They didn't appear for breakfast either, which was laid out by the sun loungers—hot coffee in silver pots, warm croissants with fat pats of unsalted butter, sliced fruit, juice, and homemade muesli—but when Granny did emerge, shortly after we'd put to sea for the day, she was wearing large sunglasses, so I couldn't tell how worse for wear she was. Alexander followed her, positively bursting with cheerfulness, and after he greeted us, he excused himself to dive off the back of the boat for his morning constitutional.

"I think he's made a pact with the devil," observed Nicky, helping himself to another croissant. "There must be a painting somewhere of a very, very old man. With arthritis and lumbago."

I cast a look at Granny, who was sipping a black coffee. "We have one of those too," I said. "An old lady with embroidery and sensible shoes."

"Are those the paparazzi then?" asked Leonie, shading her eyes with her hand.

We looked out to sea, and sure enough, there were a few little motorboats following in our wake. Little flashes of light glinted off what I guessed were camera lenses.

I squeaked and rushed off to get changed. When I returned, in a Pucci sundress and the gold sandals, with my blond wig cascading over my bare shoulders, Nelson and Nicky both stared at me as if they'd never seen me before.

"It's only a *wig*," I said, very conscious of their attention, especially Nelson, who was staring at me as intently as Nicky was.

"Take it off," ordered Nicky coolly.

"What?" I squeaked.

"The wig. Take it off."

"I can't! You're meant to be seen with an amazing *blond* girl!"

"So?" His gaze was steady and knee-wobblingly sexy. "It's far too hot, and besides, I can just as well be seen with an amazing brunette, surely?"

I stared back. What exactly was he saying? There was more than just *the wig* here. Was he saying . . . he'd happily let them photograph *me* as his mystery girlfriend?

Or me as a not-mystery-at-all girlfriend?

We held each other's gaze, and despite my sternest warnings, my stomach flipped and fluttered.

"*Mel!*" warned Nelson tersely, but I ignored him.

"I suppose . . . I could say I'd had a dye job," I murmured.

"May I?" said Nicky, moving slowly toward me with his hand out-stretched.

It was such an intimate, sexy gesture that I nearly let him, until I re-membered that underneath the flowing locks were a nylon skull cap, twenty hairpins, and my own flattened hair.

"I'll just be a moment!" I squeaked, and ducked down into the cabin to make the necessary adjustments. I refreshed my lipstick at the same time, and when I emerged, the little boats were much nearer.

It wasn't just the one photographer either. There must have been at least ten proper Euro-snappers as well, with their shirts off, riding toward us on the clear blue water on aggressive little speedboats.

"Right," I said, looking around the deck. "Let's get that empty bottle moved and some bottles of mineral water brought on. Have you got any books?"

"Books?" demanded Nicky, as though I'd asked for rhinoceroses.

"Those are very long lenses," I reminded him. "They'll pick up anything on deck. Every wrinkle and crisp packet. Have you got a chessboard?"

"I think Twister's more Nicky's style," said Nelson.

"Bring the chessboard," Alexander instructed a steward. "And the backgammon set."

In a few moments, I'd staged a charming tableau—Leonie and Nelson lying on cushions, playing backgammon, while Nicky and I were engaged in a game of chess, as Granny and Alexander sunbathed. They weren't to know Nicky and I were playing chess according to checkers rules.

What they could see, I hoped, was that we were all having a great time, because—actually—we were.

"Melissa, am I looking serious enough?" Nicky asked, stroking his chin. "Is this the chess play of a future ruler?"

"Nelson, you're letting me win!" protested Leonie before I could reply, and when I turned to see what was going on, I saw her bat Nelson playfully with a cushion. His grin was wide, and relaxed, and I realized with a shock that not only was he (a) in possession of a decent pair of legs beneath those deck shorts, he was (b) flirting with Leonie, who was giggling like a girl who'd never even heard of personal tax allowances.

"Melissa?" said Nicky. "Am I meeting your expectations here?"

"Oh, er, yes, you're looking very serious," I said, flashing him a smile. "How long can you keep it up for, though?"

"All night," he said.

"I think another twenty minutes should be ample," I said, leapfrogging two of his pawns.

Nelson snorted behind me, but I serenely ignored him.

We gave them lots of shots of us playing deck quoits, and then most of them waved and vanished, at exactly the same time as lunch arrived in big silver domes.

*   *   *

After lunch, we lay dozing in the gentle sea breeze while the *Kitty Cat* slid through the limpid waters of the Mediterranean.

"They're back," said Nicky suddenly.

"Who?" I said, without opening my eyes.

"The photographers."

I opened one eye, and with a sinking heart, I could see him twitching with the unmistakable urge to show off.

"Mel," he said, "have you ever been on a rib?"

"A what?"

"The little inflatables we keep on the back of the boat. They've got outboard motors—top fun!" Nicky winked. "Fancy a ride?"

"Not so soon after lunch," I said firmly.

"On the rib, I mean."

"I *know* that's what you meant. I'll stay here, thanks."

"I'm a very good ribsman," he cajoled. "Go on."

"No," I insisted. Nelson had gone below to chat with the crew, which was maybe why Nicky was eager to show off. "I'm not brilliant in the water, to be honest. I only got my one-width swimming badge."

"You're missing out," he wheedled, obviously desperate to get his photo taken in action. "Leonie?"

Leonie shook her head. "No, thank you. My travel insurance doesn't cover dangerous water sports."

Nicky thought for a second, then called over to the sun loungers, where Granny and Alexander were reclining in the sun, giggling to one another.

"Melissa's just come up with a marvelous idea—wouldn't it be good if those photographers got some shots of me and Melissa on the rib?" He turned back to me and added, in a loud voice, "I did do that interview all about how experienced I am on the water—"

"Splendid idea, Melissa!" Alexander called back. "Off you go!"

"Yes, well done, darling," murmured Granny. "Don't fall in."

I glared at Nicky. There was obviously no arguing. "Well, come on then. But if I fall in, or you muck around, I will kill you."

"You're in safe hands," he said, rubbing them together gleefully.

The crew helped us into the little inflated rib, and Nicky took off at a manic pace, riding the waves and letting us crash up and down, as we wove around the photographers' speedboats in huge circles.

I must admit, it was fun. I could feel my hair streaming out behind me, the warm sunshine on my face was divine, and the life jacket hid my stomach nicely. Nicky was grinning with a boyish pleasure that was quite charming to share, and he clearly loved hearing me squeal with delight as we zoomed around.

"They're getting some great pics!" he shouted in my ear. "You look gorgeous!"

"And so do you!" I yelled back. "Very princelike, in charge of your vessel!"

Nicky held my gaze, even though we were sitting shoulder to shoulder, so close I could feel his breath, as well as the salt spray on my face. "And you look just like a princess."

I couldn't tear my eyes away from him when he said that. My heart was doing loops quite unrelated to the action of the boat.

But I had to look away before I said something stupid, so I turned back to the yacht, where Leonie and Nelson were standing watching us from the sundeck. Nelson seemed to be waving.

I waved back.

Then Alexander and Granny joined them. And Alexander started waving too.

"Shit," muttered Nicky.

We seemed to be going in much smaller circles all of a sudden.

Much smaller circles, and much, much faster ones. Then, mad figures-of-eight.

"Nicky, is there something wrong?" I asked, watching him yanking the rudder back and forth.

"No," he snapped, "I just thought I'd see how quickly I could make you seasick. Of course there's something wrong! The rudder's stuck!"

The photographers could see something was afoot, but rather than doing anything useful, they seemed to be taking more photographs.

A nauseous feeling swamped me, and I clutched the sides with both hands. The sea, which had seemed blue and inviting a moment ago, now seemed rough, sinister, and very deep.

"We've got two options," announced Nicky, as the rib jerked and rocked beneath us.

"Which are?"

"We can swim for it, or wait until it runs out of petrol."

I looked at him in horror. "I *can't* swim for it, you moron. Apart from anything, I've got more makeup on than I normally wear to go out, and this is a sunbathing-only bikini! We'll just have to wait it out!"

Nicky shrugged. "I hate to tell you this, Mel, but the fuel economy on this is superb."

"How's your lifesaving?"

"How's yours?"

"Oh, for God's sake," I said, glaring at him fiercely. This was the trouble with Nicky—he was perfectly charming until you actually needed him to *do* something. That was the downside of being boyish. Sometimes *manly* was what was needed. "Do something!" I yelled at him.

Nicky responded by getting up to gain greater purchase on the stuck tiller, but he only succeeded in unbalancing the boat even more. As it started to roll, he let go of the tiller entirely and started screaming, windmilling his arms round and round in panic, as we lurched sickeningly from one side to another, tipping me nearer and nearer the water.

"I'm going to be sick!" I gasped.

"Well, lean over the side. Oh, *Christ.* I forgot there'd be *that* option."

I managed to lift my head away from the surging water. "And what option's that?"

"Being rescued by bloody Admirable Nelson."

Bouncing toward us on the waves was another rib, and I could see the sun glinting off the driver's mop of blond hair.

Through my rising nausea, I felt a sharp clutch of relief. "Oh, thank goodness for that."

Nicky raised his eyebrows at me. "Any chance of pretending I did this on purpose?"

"No!" I snapped.

The next moment, Nicky stood up just as a stealth wave lifted the rib, and it rocked us right up, tipping me toward the water. I screamed as the wave washed over me, much colder than I expected, soaking through my bikini and sarong, plastering my hair to my face. My feet and hands slipped and slid as I scrabbled to keep my grip on the unstable boat.

"Nelson!" I howled above the roar of the engines. Salty water rushed into my mouth, and suddenly someone yanked me backward by the life jacket, and I was lying on my back in the rib, looking up at the china blue sky. My heart felt like it had stopped and started again.

Above me was Nelson's familiar face, now drawn with intense concern. "Mel!" he said urgently, forehead creasing as he leaned over to check my breathing. "Are you all right? Say something to me. Are you OK?" He cradled my face in his big hands and stroked the wet hair off my forehead as I stared, stunned, back up into his worried eyes.

And that's when I realized that Nelson wasn't a lovable Labrador, or a grumpy teddy bear, but a bloke. Nelson was a real, fanciable bloke with muscles and courage and sensitive hands, who could do dinner-table chat without being smarmy, who wore the right thing but never in an attention-seeking way, who could talk to my Granny or the crew equally easily. And he really cared about me. I was scared, but I'd only had a bit of a splash. What would he have done if I'd actually gone in?

"I'm fine," I croaked.

"There's no need to be brave about it," he began, leaning nearer. "I know you're rubbish at swimming. Why on earth did you let that idiot—"

"You might want to wipe her mascara," said Nicky. "You don't want to look like Chi-Chi the panda for all those photographers."

I'd forgotten he was there. Nelson seemed to have forgotten too. We stared at each other, rocking gently as the waves lifted the rib.

"Hello?" said Nicky, pointing toward the stalling motor. "Hello? We have an escaping boat here?"

"Oh, for God's sake," said Nelson, and he sprang into efficient sea-goer mode. My eyes followed him, since I was too limp with shock to do much more.

I realized now that Nelson had thrown me into his own boat, and Nicky had evidently gotten aboard too, because our runaway rib was now some distance away. Nelson headed after it, and when he caught up, he did a sort of cowboy maneuver, placing one foot in his rib, his hand still gripping the tiller, and the other foot in ours, dragging it alongside.

His thighs looked great in his shorts, I observed from my prone position. Strong and blond and hairy.

"One of the crew lost a testicle doing that," remarked Nicky.

Nelson glared at him, and so did I.

"Shut up," Nelson snapped. "Unless you want to lose one too."

Then, timing it perfectly, with one athletic, seafaring vault, he was in the out-of-control rib, yanking at the emergency lines on the rudder. The engine gave a last grunt, then came to a spluttering halt. He jumped back to us, lassoed the other rib with a mooring rope, and pulled it in, securing it with quick, deft knots.

In the distance, there was a round of applause from the snappers, and from the yacht, where Granny, Leonie, Alexander, and all the crew were lined up against the railings.

"Nelson!" I said. "That was the most amazing thing I've ever seen."

But Nelson was glowering at Nicky. "You could have capsized, you cretin!"

"Don't be such a girl!" snorted Nicky, restored to full confidence now that everything was back under control.

Nelson shot back, "I don't give a toss about your safety, but if anything had happened to Melissa, I promise you I'd have—"

I raised myself to a nauseous sitting position. "Nelson," I said. "Don't let's give them a row to photograph."

"Fine," he said with a final glare, and set us off in the direction of the yacht.

"Are you all right?" he said, holding my shoulders as the crew helped Nicky aboard.

"I . . ."

What was I meant to say? My emotions were as shaken up as my stomach. I wasn't sure *what* I thought.

Nelson raised his eyebrows in query. His blond hair was spiked with seawater and his wet T-shirt was sticking to his chest, outlining his broad shoulders. Something about his hands on my shoulders made me feel absolutely safe and yet tingly at the same time.

The chances of saying the wrong thing were so high, as usual, that my throat seized up.

"Really, I'm fine," I managed. "Just a bit . . . seasick. What?"

A smile tugged at the corner of his mouth, and he rubbed his thumbs underneath my eyes, gently smearing away my bedraggled makeup. "You do look a bit panda-y."

"I think you've seen me looking a lot worse," I replied.

"I have," he agreed. "But never worse than when I thought you were going in the water." He leaned forward and kissed my forehead with a tenderness that sent shivers across my scalp and down through my whole body.

And then hands were reaching down to help us up. I staggered a few steps, then my knees gave way with delayed shock and I pretended to sink onto a lounger.

"Marvelous!" cried Alexander, shaking Nelson's hand furiously. "What a marvelous rescue! Well done!"

"Oh, Nelson!" exclaimed Granny, kissing him enthusiastically. "It could have been Daniel Craig out there!"

"That rib was dangerously *faulty*!" announced Nicky, as loudly as he could. "*Faulty*! The rudder was broken! Melissa and I could have been in grave danger!"

"But we're safe and sound now," I managed, ever on duty. "I think I'll just go and . . . freshen up."

What I actually did was go to my berth and throw up.

I stood under the shower and tried to keep my mind from racing in different directions. The adrenaline was still pumping furiously round my system, but more than that, I couldn't stop thinking about

Nelson. It wasn't just gratitude for being rescued, it was the look on his face when he'd thought I was going to fall in the water—and the feeling in my heart when I'd seen him coming to get me.

And, now I thought about it, it was the twinge of jealousy when I'd seen him laughing at Leonie's jokes, and the burst of pride when he'd emerged in his just-right suit. The happiness I'd felt at pushing open our front door after a weekend in Paris, and the utter bliss of a foot rub and his roast chicken. I'd seen all that. I just hadn't seen that my flatmate was also a very attractive man.

I stumbled out of the shower, dressed myself, then flopped on the bed.

Honestly. How could I have missed all that?

Granny's head popped round the cabin door, her eyes agleam with nosiness. "Hello, darling," she said. "Just came to see if you were all right after your ordeal."

"I am, thanks," I replied, hastily rising to my feet.

"Alex is worried about you, and absolutely furious with Nicky. But I think he's going to make Nelson honorary head of the Hollenberg navy or something—wouldn't that be fun? Nelson would look *marvelous* in one of those three-cornered hats!"

"Yes," I said. Nelson in uniform. Of course.

"Now," Granny went on, "do you have any sun cream? I've run out."

"I do, but I gave it to Nicky, because he didn't bring any. I think it's in his cabin." I got up, wobbled slightly, and went to the door. "I'll get it for you."

"Are you sure you're all right?" she asked, putting out a hand to steady me. "I'll come with you."

She followed me through to Nicky's stateroom, which was yet another splendid Art Deco hotel room in miniature. Or rather, I could see splendid aspects of it—the curving brass reading lamps, the crystal glasses—beneath the jumble of clothes, magazines, and discarded towels strewn about the place.

Granny and I frowned. "As if the crew don't have enough to do but tidy up after him. He needs a good talking-to."

"It's here somewhere," I said, going over to the mahogany writing desk, shifting papers and iPod paraphernalia. "I gave it to him this morning. It's . . ." My voice trailed away. Under the sports section of *The Times* was a red morocco ring box.

"What's that?" asked Granny at once. "Is that a ring box?"

"Yes, I think it is," I said, picking it up. It was an old one, with gold lettering. "Shouldn't this be in a safe or something?" I flicked the little gold hook and opened it. On a bed of very old velvet the color of crushed raspberries was the most enormous diamond I'd ever seen, surrounded by round petals of brilliant-cut sapphires. It was an antique setting, on a delicate band of platinum, and it flashed and sparkled in the sunlight coming through the porthole above the desk. It was so exquisitely perfect that it almost didn't look real.

"Crikey," I said. "Is that real?"

"Let me see." Granny deftly removed the ring and scratched it against a glass. "Yes, that's a real one, all right. Oh, a girl learns to check," she added, in response to my shocked expression.

"Why on earth has Nicky got that?" I wondered. "Do you think Imogen gave it back to him when he dumped her?"

"I very much doubt it," snorted Granny. "Anyway, I think that's a family piece. Alexander's mother used to wear it." She turned to me with a curious look on her face.

"What?"

"Oh, I was just wondering . . ."

"What?"

"Well," she said. "There are only three women on this yacht. I doubt Nicky's planning to give it to me, and it would be awfully precipitous for him to give it to Leonie after one day, even for Nicky, so . . ." She raised her eyebrow. "Maybe it's a thank-you gift for doing such a good job on his prospects?"

"But this is an engagement ring!" I blurted out.

Granny and I stared at each other.

"Is it?" I demanded. "Do you know anything about this?"

She shook her head. "Darling, I know he admires you more than he lets on, and I know Alexander thinks you're the bee's knees, but no one's said anything to me. At least . . ." She looked thoughtful.

Various flashes of conversation at home now came back to me. Had Granny been planning this all along? To throw me and Nicky together, so *I'd* be the suitable girl to marry him and bring decency and balanced accounting to the New Hollenberg? And instead of me training Nicky up to be an old-fashioned prince, had this been their way of introducing *me* to *his* lifestyle? The clothes, the dinners, the credit card—had it all been some kind of test?

That might explain why she looked both ecstatic and very shifty at the same time.

"But we haven't even . . ." I faltered, embarrassed. It was utterly incomprehensible to me that Nicky the Playboy would even consider proposing to someone he hadn't managed to get into bed, but maybe Nicky the Heir to the Throne had different criteria. I wasn't all that up on royal marriageability, and suddenly I was out of my depth.

"Kissed?" asked Granny, lifting her elegant eyebrow in a conspiratorial manner.

"Well, no, not exactly," I confessed. That moment in the car after dinner crackled in my mind. I could have kissed him on any number of occasions now, I realized, and he would definitely have kissed me back. In fact, some of the openhearted moments we'd shared had been more romantic than a grope in a taxi would have been. "Sort of, but not like that, and we definitely haven't . . . You know." I opened my eyes wide.

"I see," said Granny solemnly. "Whatever you told him about respecting a woman must have sunk in, in that case. I'm most impressed, darling!"

I squirmed, despite the thudding of my heart. You try discussing your sex life with your grandmother, and coming to the grim conclusion that it'll never match up to hers.

"Well, what are you going to say?" she asked, clasping my arms.

I hung my head, unable to think straight. What *was* I going to say? I couldn't possibly marry Nicky, but I felt we'd become friends, if nothing else. What with our dysfunctional families and odd backgrounds, we understood each other, and I'd been more honest with him than I had with anyone, Jonathan included. Maybe he *was* in love with me. Weirder things had happened, and God knew I'd been cringe-makingly wrong about these things before.

"I absolutely adore Nicky . . . ," I began, then ran out of words.

Granny peered at me, mistaking my inner turmoil for massive emotion overload. "Melissa, darling! I know it's very soon after Jonathan, but I'm sure Nicky would be happy to wait, if you needed more time to think, but I must tell you, this is the most sensible thing he's ever done. Just tell me . . ." She tipped my chin up so she could see into my face with her cool blue eyes. "But you must tell me honestly, darling, because this is terribly important. Do you *love* Nicky?"

Oh, dear. I blinked hard, searching for the best words. It obviously meant a lot to Granny, me, and Nicky. Maybe she saw it as the chance she and Alexander had never had. But at the same time I was deeply annoyed that Granny of all people should have been planning my future behind my back—just like Daddy and Jonathan!

"Granny, of course I have feelings for Nicky, but if you must know, I'm rather cross that you could be planning something like this without telling me!"

"What?" said Granny. "I don't follow, darling. I really had no idea . . ."

We stared at each other, then we stared at the ring. Then back at each other.

"Oh, *dear,*" I said. "I know he's a prince and everything . . ."

Granny tipped her head to one side, resting one feline cheekbone on her knuckles, and looked up at me, her mouth curving ruefully. "Darling," she said. "It's not done me the slightest good, but let me at least give you the benefit of my hard-won experience. Let me tell you about me and Alexander. . . ."

twenty-two

"There are no such things as princes, not really," she began wryly. "And I have been courted by at least three in my time. They're just men, and men with better excuses than usual. Real princes are normal chaps who treat you like a queen."

"But Alexander!" I protested. "He's a prince *and* he's totally charming!"

Granny sighed. "I met Alexander when I was nineteen, when I was singing at the Cavalier Club off Regent Street after the war. I just got up on stage one night as a dare, when I was there on a date. I sang 'Hard Hearted Hannah.' The manager asked me to come back—and I said why not? You would have loved the Cavalier Club, darling—it was all velvet drapes and huge crystal chandeliers, and you never knew who would be sitting at the next table. There'd be dukes, gangsters, actresses, all throwing back the cocktails and carrying on until breakfast the next morning. Quite scandalous, but terribly chic."

"Didn't your parents mind?" I asked.

"Oh, I'm afraid to say I ran rather wild in those days. Daddy and Mummy were in the middle of their divorce by then, and it was all getting pretty unpleasant—put me off marriage for years. I bought a little flat in Kensington and let them get on with it. Besides, I had stacks of admirers. Champagne every night, and hothouse peonies from country estates sent to the back door, and men proposing . . ." She smiled. "I was only nineteen, but I pretended to be twenty-two."

I'd seen photographs of Granny singing in her figure-skimming lamé evening gowns and long gloves, lit up in a smoky spotlight, surrounded by dinner jackets and ladies in tricky little veiled cocktail hats. She might have been nineteen, but she'd had the heavy-lidded expression of a thirty-two-year-old thrice divorcée.

"Alex came in one night with a group of friends, and they had the special VIP front-row table. As soon as I saw him looking up at me, I felt I'd known his face for years. It was divine, just like electric shocks. We couldn't tear our eyes away from one another, and I was almost too nervous to sing, but he waited until the club closed at five and took me out for breakfast. We went to a café he knew that opened for the flower traders at Covent Garden—he bought me coffee and every single orchid on sale that morning."

"How romantic," I breathed.

Granny nodded. "It was terribly romantic. Anyway," she went on, "I moved into the flat he kept in Mayfair and I became what you'd call his mistress. But," she said quickly, "it was a lot *more* than that, Melissa. We spent all the time he had in London together, going to the theater, and to parties, and concerts. Alex talked about marriage, and where we'd live, and what our children would look like, and I absolutely longed to be swept away by him. We were desperately in love. But business came first. Hollenberg. His father was negotiating with practically everyone to get the family reinstated in some form, and he had some far more suitable specimens lined up than me."

"But, Granny, you were perfectly suitable!" I protested. "Your father was a High Court judge!"

She pulled a face. "Well, lots of people were in those days, darling. And they were divorced, and Mummy was quite notorious, and I'd had . . . a few admirers, shall we say? But what you must understand is that despite all this, Alex and I were *very serious* about each other." She gripped my hand tightly, and I got the impression that we were now approaching the tricky part.

"Alex started to spend a lot of time abroad, dealing with his family.

They were all over the place—Paris, New York, the south of France—and I started to get a bit, well, cheesed off. Just like you were cross about Jonathan. I was about your age by now, darling, and in those days, a girl was on the shelf by the time she was twenty-two. I wanted to know where I stood. I didn't care for the idea of being his mistress forever, twiddling my thumbs until he flew in. And I didn't like the idea that being his *mistress* meant there was a full-time *official* post for someone else. I was quite the society girl by then—I'd given up singing, you see—"

"After the hit record," I added.

"Yeeees," said Granny. "And quite frankly, it wasn't as though I was short of potential husbands. *Everyone* used to come to my bashes in Mayfair—I had chinless wonders hanging off the fire escape. Percy, your grandfather, was sending me some special peony he'd crossbred in my honor three times a week, constantly taking me for tea at the Ritz, *begging* me to marry him. Not to mention a certain rather charming actor who shall remain nameless. Oh, yes, and *him*. I'd almost forgotten *him*," she added, more to herself, then stopped.

I held my breath.

"Alex flew me to Paris on Valentine's Day, in 1958. He said he had something to tell me. I thought he was going to propose, more fool me. He didn't. He told me he was going to marry some countess called Celestine—a second cousin, or something—because it would more or less guarantee them getting their castle back." Granny's lips tightened, but I couldn't tell who she was angry with: herself, I suspected. "He was upset, and I was *devastated,* but I think he expected we could carry on as normal, once I'd calmed down. Of course we couldn't. That is *not* what I call princely behavior." She twisted her mouth ruefully. "It didn't get him his castle back in the end, either."

"So what did you do?" I asked, though I think I already knew.

"I flew home and married your grandfather. He knew all about Alexander, but he waited for me, and when he asked me again, I said yes."

"Did you *love* Granddad?" I asked. I couldn't bear to imagine Granny heartlessly marrying herself off to someone she hadn't loved, just to have gotten her own back. It just didn't fit with the Granny I'd adored all my life.

Her eyes met mine, and for the first time, we were seeing each other as women, with the same vulnerable hearts, and romantic but pragmatic blood in our veins. I knew whatever she said would be honest, and I braced myself for my opinion of her to be changed forever.

"Yes, I did," she said, after a pause. "Not the same way that I loved Alex, but I did love your grandfather. He was a sweet man, much older than me, you know, with grown-up children from his first marriage. But he was kindhearted, and quite dry once you got to know him. He had his peonies, and his table tennis, and someone to run his houses and his cellar, and I had the security and the company, and someone to beat at the crossword. And the title, of course." She tutted ruefully. "Quite nice to be an official Lady. It might not have been a whirlwind romance, but we had the sort of love that lasted thirty years, whether life was stormy or dull, and that counts for a lot, you know, Melissa. Respect."

"And what about Alexander? Did you stay in touch?"

Granny sighed and didn't answer at once. "It's very hard, isn't it, when people you love turn out to be not the way you hoped?" She touched my hand and I nodded, sadly, knowing she meant Jonathan.

"Alex tried to get in touch with me many times, but I knew that if we met, we'd just be tempted to start an affair, and I promised myself I'd never, ever get involved with a married man. And I was cross for a long time about the way . . . things ended." Granny looked quite fierce. "After Percy died, Alex called me and asked if he could take me out to dinner. I wasn't sure, but he's so charming, he persuaded me. I realized we were old enough to let things go and be friends. I'm glad he did." She looked down at her own diamond rings. "Then when Celestine died last year . . . Well, that changed things again. I'd always like to think there's room for forgiveness. But what I wanted to say to *you*, darling, is . . . If I'd waited for Alexander to give me a fairy-tale life, I'd be a bitter, lonely old woman by now. And instead, I've been very happy."

She touched my cheek tenderly. "If I hadn't married Percy, I wouldn't have had your mother, and there wouldn't have been any you! Darling, I know you're feeling down about Jonathan, but please don't expect Nicky to provide some kind of happy ever after for you. Because it's not up to him, it's up to you."

"I don't expect him to!" I protested. "I mean, he's gorgeous and much less of a moron than he seems, but really, Granny—do you *honestly* think he's my type?"

"We all like to *think* we know what Our Type is," she pointed out. "But hormones have a habit of bypassing that."

"It's not that, there's . . . there's someone else."

"Really?" asked Granny. "Who?"

I blushed.

"Please God don't say Jonathan," she groaned.

"No!"

"Thank heaven for small mercies. Who, then? Nelson?"

I nodded, and a little smile broke through the tension on Granny's face. "Oh. Well, now, he really is a prince, Melissa. Nelson Barber is everything I'd wish for you, and he absolutely adores you, that's quite clear."

"Do you think so?" I asked hopefully.

"Oh, yes." She took my hand and squeezed it. "Hardworking and honest might not be as glamorous as a yacht and helicopters, but believe me, darling, it's a lot more precious. Does Nelson know how you feel?"

I shook my head. "No. Well, I've been engaged to Jonathan, haven't I? God, I've been so *stupid,* trying to fix him up on blind dates—and now here he is with Leonie and they're getting on like a house on fire! She's had a makeover, and now even Nicky's been listening to her lectures about international tax havens. It's amazing what a half head of highlights and a push-up bra can do."

Granny went silent, then said, "Well, what if *Nicky* suddenly took an interest in Leonie?"

"What?"

"Well, if Nelson thought Leonie was interested in Nicky, he

wouldn't touch her with a barge pole. And if Leonie thought Nicky fancied her—she's an accountant, isn't she? Which fund would you rather invest in?"

"I see what you mean," I said. "Isn't that a bit sneaky though?"

"*Ingenious,* darling."

I looked at the red ring box on the desk, and the inner joy I'd started to feel curdled in my stomach. It didn't change the fact that Nicky had an engagement ring in his cabin. Not only was this going to lead to a terrible, embarrassing situation, but we were stuck on a yacht. With no taxis to spirit us to safety.

"What am I going to say if Nicky does propose?" I wailed. "I've only ever been proposed to once, and that didn't go very well!"

"You say, 'I'm terribly honored that you'd consider spending the rest of your life with me,'" Granny began, with a suspiciously practiced air, but before she could carry on, I heard footsteps pass the porthole on the deck above and Nicky's voice say, "I don't know—I'll just go and find her, shall I?"

I nearly jumped out of my palazzo pants. "Quick!" I said. "Out!"

Fortunately, the boat's palatial dimensions meant that we had just enough time to slip out and pretend to be emerging from Granny's stateroom when Nicky sauntered down the steps.

Granny and I both stared at him, as if seeing him for the very first time.

"What?" he drawled, running a hand through his thick dark hair. He raised an eyebrow in my direction. "Hey, I know I'm a good-looking guy, Melissa, but you're making me feel quite shy, staring at me like that!"

"I'm fine!" I squeaked, not knowing what to say.

He peered more closely at me. "Melissa?"

"She's still a little shaken after your cavortings," Granny said, intervening smoothly, putting a hand on the small of my back and shoving me toward the stairs. My eyes stayed on Nicky, despite myself. "I prescribe a stiff gin and tonic, darling. Nicky, can you arrange that for us? We're just going for a spot of sun."

"Yeah," he said, creasing his brow. "Leonie's wondering where you

are, by the way. Nelly's boring her senseless with his reef knot anecdotes."

"Hahahahahahaha!" tinkled Granny, and led me upstairs.

I'd barely settled myself into the soft mass of cushions in the sun pit
when a generous G&T arrived in a huge tumbler, and I drank deeply
from it, my hands shaking so much the ice rattled.

Granny arranged herself and her gauzy layers of designer linen on a
sun lounger next to Alexander, who was already tanned to the deep
bronze of Daddy's dinner gong. Nelson had gone off to inspect some
new GPS system, according to Leonie, for which I was quite grateful,
but she seemed eager to chat, for which I wasn't.

I lay back on the cushions, in the shade of a broad green umbrella,
and tried to think what Honey would do. It was all so bizarre. What
was the etiquette on being proposed to by a prince? How could I let
Nelson know how I felt?

"Nelson's a nice man, isn't he?" Leonie observed, breaking into my
thoughts. "Bit like a Labrador."

"Sort of," I said. A twinge of jealousy bit me. *I* was the only one allowed to see him as a Labrador, thank you. "He's a bit grumpy in the
mornings, though. And he won't drink nonorganic milk because of
dairy mastitis."

I wondered, guiltily, just how far I could put her off, in the name of
telling the truth. Not that I had any right to interfere in Nelson's life,
when it was me who had set him up with Leonie in the first place. Especially if he liked her.

"Hmm," said Leonie. "I don't go in for organic food personally.
Just ten percent extra for a bit of mud, isn't it? Paranoia tax. But I'm
really impressed with his ethical investments," she went on. "He's obviously very clued up on tax breaks."

"Yes," I agreed. "Very much so."

"And he's quite handsome, I suppose."

"He's *very* handsome," I insisted. "He has gorgeous eyes, and his
hair isn't even *starting* to recede, unlike that of most of his friends."

"Like a teddy bear," agreed Leonie.

"No," I said stoutly. That was what I'd been getting wrong all these years. "*Not* like a teddy bear. Like a . . . very handsome man."

One of the crew came past and offered to refresh Leonie's glass, at which she giggled. "No, shouldn't," she said. "This is my fourth! And I've had nothing to eat since . . . Oh, go on, then!"

She rolled over on her side and looked at me over her Duty Free sunglasses. Her bosom made a bid for freedom from her bikini, but she didn't seem to notice. "Nelson's very nice, but you must be looking forward to all this," she confided.

"Sorry?"

"This life . . ." Leonie waved a vague hand around at the yacht. Four might have been a polite scaling down of her drinks tally. "I'd *love* to have a lifestyle like this! Yachts, and castles, and tans, and staff, and"—she stared lustfully at her drink—"huge crystal tumblers . . ."

I frowned. Tipsy or not, this wasn't the disapproving Leoneezer I knew. Those blond highlights must have gone to her head.

"And as for Nicky!" She giggled again, and then sighed lustfully. "He's so scrummy. So . . . naughty."

"Leonie," I said, propping myself up on one elbow. Ingenious plan or not, I had to be honest with her, as a fellow St. Cathalian. "I don't really think he's your type. You know he once undid my wrap dress in front of everyone at Petrus? For a laugh? Without even thinking how mortified I might be?"

Her eyes widened even further. "Oh, you lucky, lucky cow!"

I sank back into the cushions. Clearly, Leonie had a hidden side I knew nothing about.

"And to think all this is going to be yours," she went on.

"It certainly isn't," I corrected her, then it dawned on me that Nicky could do a lot worse than a Very Sensible Girl with a suppressed naughty streak. "Nicky and I are just old family friends. You know," I added, "I rather think it's *you* he fancies."

"Oh, no, don't be silly!" she simpered.

"I think he does, though," I insisted. "Didn't he tell you how much he loved your new look? And he told *me* he's bored of brainless heiresses and gold diggers. He wants someone with their feet on the ground, someone normal who won't be impressed by material things, and love him for who he is, instead of what he can pay for."

"That's so sweet!" she near sobbed.

"He's rather keen on strict girls, you know," I pressed on. "And now they're all moving back to Hollenberg, someone's going to have to step in and modernize the castle, and that sort of thing. I doubt Alexander will want to have to deal with it."

"The castle," breathed Leonie. "Prince Alexander's been telling me all about it. It sounds . . . magical! But probably quite dilapidated in some respects," she went on, in more recognizably Leoneezer tones. "Have they negotiated any conservation grants to help with the restoration?"

I sank back and closed my eyes, adjusting my huge sun hat so that my face was shaded. "I don't know," I said. "Perhaps that's something you could ask Nicky over dinner?"

"Yes, I will," she gasped. "Oh, God, what should I wear?"

"The smallest outfit you've got," I said, and pretended to go to sleep.

Obviously, I didn't go to sleep. I lay there fretting. Fretting about Nelson, about whether Granddad Wasdalemere had been a knight in shining armor or just an old man with a red nose, about whether Alexander was going to break Granny's heart again. And also about Nicky and that enormous diamond ring.

A shadow fell over my face, and I felt someone squat down next to me. Whoever it was smelled of cologne, and the knees didn't click, so I knew it wasn't Nelson or Alexander.

"Melissa," whispered Nicky.

Oh, bollocks.

I kept my eyes shut beneath my shades.

"Melissa, I need to talk to you." His voice sounded unusually serious, and quite urgent. "In private."

This was it. My heart hammered. *Right,* I told myself, *be dignified. Respect the fact that he really seems to have grown up recently.*

An ice cube dropped on my cleavage and I sat up, scrabbling for it as it vanished into the dark caverns of my kaftan.

"So you weren't asleep," Nicky remarked, then added, as if he just couldn't stop himself, "Want some help fishing it out?"

Out of the corner of my eye, I saw Leonie struggle between desire and disapproval.

"Don't do that," I snapped. "Unless you want one down your trousers?"

Nicky pretended to swoon, but I could see tension lines around his mouth. "I love it when you get cross with me. Come on, I need to talk to you." And he grabbed my hand and dragged me off the cushions.

Giving Leonie a significant look, I followed Nicky down into the salon, mentally preparing myself to be kind yet firm.

He dropped the lighthearted banter as soon as we were out of sight, and when we were safely in his cabin, he shut the door and went over to his desk.

Oh, God, I couldn't let him do this.

"Nicky," I said hastily, "you know I absolutely adore you, and I really do feel we have a special friendship . . ."

And the rest, I blanched but drove on.

"Which I hope we'll never lose, but I've had a very upsetting time of it lately, and I just need some space and time on my own to . . . What?"

He was staring at me impatiently. Then, to my horror, he dropped to one knee.

"Nicky, I can't marry you! I love someone else!" I roared, at the same time as loud music started blasting out of the carefully concealed speakers all round the cabin.

"What?" he said, getting up.

I realized he'd gone down on one knee to turn on the stereo, not to propose at all. The first pricklings of humiliation stabbed at my chest, but fortunately, he didn't seem to have caught what I'd said.

"I don't want to be overheard," said Nicky, nodding toward the music. "Something bloody awful's happened."

He flipped open the lid of his laptop and clicked on an email. Curiously, I drew nearer and saw the email was from Imogen. It was composed in capital letters. She was clearly very angry or else wasn't familiar with the caps lock.

Nicky sank into his chair, pulled open the drawer of the desk, and withdrew a hip flask, from which he took a mighty swig. "Read it," he urged.

I skimmed Imogen's shouty email, flinching at the foul language. The gist of it was that she was very annoyed at being dumped for some "fat chav," as she charmingly described me, and to repay Nicky for making her look like a fool—something I felt she was doing perfectly adequately without his help—she was going to the magazines with some "interesting" photos she had of him. Which, she felt, might well provide an obstacle to his getting the keys to Castle Hollenberg. In fact, Imogen was fairly confident they might even lead to a visit from Her Majesty's Constabulary.

I scrolled down. Imogen had attached one of the photographs to the email as an illustration. It started innocuously enough: a dark nightclub, the tops of people's heads . . .

I reeled back from the desk at the sight of two flushed, seminaked girls grappling with Nicky and his awful shouty friend Chunder. Both of them were just about wearing unraveling togas, and there were empty bottles and bits of discarded clothing everywhere. Imogen had typed IT GETS MUCH WORSE—REMEMBER THE TWINS?!?!?!?!!?! beneath.

"Nicky, what on earth was going on there?" I peered closer at the arrangement of bare arms and legs. "Were you having a wheelbarrow race?"

He looked shifty. "Um, not exactly."

I winced just looking at his tattoo, which seemed to be some kind of heraldic thing. "Is that a snake rampant? Gosh, it must have really hurt getting it down there . . ."

"Fine, OK!" said Nicky, and slammed the lid down, swigging again from his hip flask.

I sank back onto the chair in dismay. Just when I thought a nicer Nicky was emerging from the Euro-trash shell. It really was my day for being let down by people.

"Melissa, I'm really sorry you had to see that," he said, biting his nails.

"Why?" I said bitterly. "Did you think you had me completely taken in with your sensitive act?"

"No, because I've moved on since that was taken! Jesus, don't look at me like that!" he protested, taking a step backward. "Don't you think I feel bad enough without having you give me the full disappointment treatment?"

"It's not you I'm disappointed with," I said, "it's me. I feel *sorry* for you. What the hell were you thinking?"

"It's camera phones," he whined. "They've ruined everything—"

"*You're* going to ruin everything!" I yelled at him. "On your own! For everyone! Can you imagine how embarrassing this'll be for Alexander? Quite apart from anything else?"

Without warning, the defiance turned to contrition, and Nicky crumpled onto the bed, his head in his hands.

I turned off the stereo so we didn't have to yell. Although I really, really wanted to yell at him right then.

"Look, I know I've been stupid in the past," he said. "OK? I've been stupid. But I swear to God, Melissa, this is an oooold photograph. It happened sometime last year. Before I met you."

That made me feel quite awkward. "I didn't know my opinion mattered so much," I said.

"It docs. I do care what you think. Very much. And you're right—I don't want Grandfather dragged into it. He'd be . . . he'd be gutted." Nicky's face went pale beneath his tan, and he started chewing his nails again. "Fine, maybe I've left it a bit late to grow up, but I *have*, OK, and I don't want things to be screwed because of something I've done. And God knows what else Piglet's got. I've been to some . . . pretty wild parties." He looked up at me appealingly. "But you have to believe me when I tell you I haven't been to a single one since you started doing whatever it is you're doing with me."

I returned his gaze, but with a more cynical lift of the eyebrows. "I might be naïve, Nicolas, but I'm not stupid."

His innocent face slipped a little. "OK, but I haven't done anything prisonworthy, and I definitely haven't done anything Piglet could have happy-snapped."

"And there's the small matter of your inheritance," I went on mercilessly, determined to wring full contrition out of him. "I suppose that hadn't crossed your mind?"

Nicky flinched. "Of course not! Are you trying to make me cry?"

"No," I said. "I'm trying to make you feel guilty."

"Well, I bloody am, OK? This is entirely my fault! I can see that! I have been an idiot! But please help me sort it out! You're the only person I really trust!"

"OK." I took pity on him: poor Nicky looked positively bewildered at the new emotions he was feeling.

We sat and stared at each other.

"Right," I said at last, when it was clear that he wasn't going to propose as an afterthought. "Did she give you a deadline? What exactly does she want?"

"Nothing. She just wants to punish me," he said bitterly. "Piglet's like that—it's all about publicity for *her*. She's going on some celebrity pirate ship thing next month, you know, as the random posh totty, so you can bet there'll be some big picture of her with her tits out, alongside any of me."

"You'll have to stall her until we can think of something," I said. "Tell her where you are—"

"She knows exactly where I am," he interrupted. "That's half the problem." He nodded meaningfully toward me.

"Well, that's ridiculous," I said briskly. "She ought to know we're old family friends. Tell her you want to talk about it face-to-face. Tell her whatever she wants to hear, but make sure she doesn't *do* anything."

"Then what?" Nicky asked, with new hope in his eyes.

"I don't know! I'll have to think of something."

"By when?"

"Oh, I don't know! Soon!" I threw my hands in the air. "I've never

been in a blackmail situation before! Ask Granny—she's more likely to
have experience of this than me."

Nicky looked horrified. "Melissa, this is *our secret.*"

Yeah. I thought, *until it's just between me, you, and the readership of*
Hello! But I didn't say anything.

"Fine. But this week is looking mad already—I won't be in the office from Thursday, and I'm going home to help my sister sort out the
plans for my nephew's christening—"

"Yeah," said Nicky. "Your father rang me this week—asked me to
be a godfather."

"Really?" It didn't surprise me. "I thought that was up to the parents."

"Grandparents usually have their own agendas," said Nicky.

"Tell me about it," I said.

There was a knock at the cabin door, and Alison, the stewardess,
put her head round. "Excuse me, but Prince Alexander asks if you'd
both come up on deck for a moment?"

Nicky rolled his eyes. "Can you tell him we're quite—"

"Fine!" I interrupted him. "Quite fine! We'll be right along."

"Thanks so much," she said, and vanished.

"Come on," I said. Nicky looked utterly deflated, and almost boyish, with his rolled-up deck trousers revealing his skinny ankles and
long, tanned feet. The sexiness had evaporated, but he looked much
more human. I felt a sudden, protective urge toward him and grabbed
his wrists. "Let's get up there. It'll seem better in the sunlight."

He let himself be hauled to his feet, then hesitated, still holding my
hand.

For one ghastly moment, I thought he was going to propose while
I was off-guard, but instead he gave me a hug. "Thanks, Mel," he
mumbled into my shoulder. "I wish I'd had a friend like you before
now. Might not be in such a bloody mess."

I hugged him back. "Well, quite. And I'd have had miles better
holidays. Come on," I said, breaking apart. "I think I heard a champagne cork pop."

*   *   *

It was a champagne cork. When we arrived on the sun deck, Nelson and Leonie were standing by the loungers, awkwardly holding onto massive flutes, while two of the crew bustled about with silver ice buckets and stands. Leonie was swaying tipsily in the breeze, and Nelson glared at Nicky as we emerged.

"Ah, here they are at last!" cried Alexander, in a voice that could have carried back to Nice airport. He was wearing a fresh linen jacket over his white shirt and looked as if he was about to burst with delight. "Come on, you two! Take a glass!"

I signaled frantically with my eyes to Granny in case she thought Nicky had popped the question and held up my bare left hand in what I hoped was a casual gesture.

"Something the matter with your hand, darling?" she asked, tearing her gaze away from Alexander for a second and shading her eyes to see me better.

It was then that I was nearly blinded by a ray of sunshine hitting the enormous diamond ring she was wearing. The same ring that had been in Nicky's cabin hours before.

"What?" hissed Nicky.

"That ring . . . ," I began.

"Oh, that. Yeah, he had me look after it for him. Apparently, no drawer is safe from your grandmother."

I opened my mouth to defend her honor just as Alexander cleared his throat and addressed the assembled gathering.

"I want you to be the very first to know that Dilys has made me the happiest old man in the world and agreed to marry me," he said. He took her hands as if the rest of us hadn't been there and went on, "I should have realized long ago that castles and lands mean nothing unless the woman you love is there to share it with you."

"Although obviously now you can have both," Granny pointed out. "Which is simply marvelous."

Alexander inclined his silvery head. "It is marvelous. I can't believe my luck. Eh, Nicky? I think this will be a gala year for our family!"

Poor Nicky looked so sick that I rushed in and proposed the toast for him. And when Leonie sat herself between him and Alexander at dinner and proceeded to regale them with endless clever advice about financial planning, he didn't even have the energy to tell her the buttons on her dress had popped open.

Nelson was strangely subdued; I was thinking how I could help Nicky; Granny was clearly planning her wedding in her head—needless to say, for our own various reasons, we all got roaring drunk and, VIP list or not, no one went to Jimmy'z that night.

twenty-three

I realize it sounds insane to be on a luxurious superyacht with ten staff, two speedboats, a full bar, and a Jacuzzi at your disposal and yet be whiling away the endless hours until you can fly back to London and your office job, but that's how Sunday went for me, Nelson, Leonie, and Nicky.

At least Leonie had the delights of flirting with Nicky, who managed a halfhearted sort of response, out of habit more than anything else. As for me, I was suddenly awkward with Nelson for the first time in my whole life.

"Has Nicky said something?" he asked, when he caught me disconsolately grazing on the finger buffet.

"No!" I said quickly. "He's . . . fine."

Nelson gave me a funny look. "And you're OK?"

I hazarded a guess. "Yes?"

"He seems to be getting on with Leonie."

"Mmm," I said, not sure if he was annoyed because he fancied her or annoyed on my behalf because he thought I fancied Nicky.

"Good," said Nelson, equally cryptically, and went back on deck.

Clearly, romantic complications weren't an issue for Granny and Alexander. They were in their own private world of champagne and in-jokes, which they intended to extend on the yacht for a few more days. And technically Nicky didn't have a job to get back to, but the hungover hours passed very slowly until at last the cars arrived at the marina to take us to the airport.

"Aren't you going on to some faaabulous party or other?" Nelson inquired of a downcast Nicky as the driver loaded our bags into the trunk. "No one opening an envelope in Biarritz? Don't tell me you're reduced to flying back with us."

"Give it a rest, Nelly," said Nicky, not even bothering to rise to it. "I've got things to do in London. This is the quickest way to get back. And if I take the private jet, I'll have to sit within one seat of you for the entire flight, whereas on easyJet there's no chance of us getting seats anywhere near each other."

Nelson looked surprised, but he had the decency not to prod him further.

My heart swelled with admiration for his maturity, then contracted shrewishly as he gallantly opened the car door for Leonie.

And I thought life had been complicated before.

At Luton, Nicky kissed us all good-bye and vanished off with Ray, who had come to collect him. He raised his eyebrows at me, as if to say, *You can tell me all the gossip later!* but I shook my head, and Ray looked surprised at the resigned way Nicky slid into the backseat.

Nelson, Leonie, and I trudged out to the long-stay car park, where a bird had pooed on the hood of Nelson's Range Rover. London was muggy, the sky above the airport was a very Sunday-afternoon gray, and there was a massive queue on the M25 that not even my half-melted Toblerone could make up for.

It was not good to be back.

We dropped Leonie off at a Tube station ("I like to get maximum value out of my Oyster card, otherwise Ken Livingstone has won!") then set off back to our flat.

It was the first time since my inner revelation about Nelson that we'd been properly alone together, and I was as nervous as if we'd been on some dreadful blind date.

I racked my brains for some witty observation, but I couldn't think of *anything to say.* To Nelson!

Argh, I moaned inwardly. This was terrible. *Unnatural.*

At the same time, I couldn't help sneaking a sideways glance at his tanned hands tapping along to the radio on the steering wheel, and his elbow leaning on the open window. His checked shirt was rolled up, showing golden strands of hair that shimmered, and one or two deep brown moles. I really wanted those arms around me. How had I missed all this before?

He caught me looking at him.

"You're very quiet," he said with a smile. "Missing P. Nicky already?"

"No!" I said, too emphatically. "No, no, he's got himself into . . ." Actually, this wasn't the time to tell Nelson about the photos. I didn't want to talk about Nicky. "He's . . ."

"He's not that bad, I suppose," said Nelson, with more mellowness than the enraging Sunday driver traffic warranted. "Leonie seems to have taken to him. And you know how hard she is to please."

"Mmm!" I wanted to ask, *How much have you been pleasing her then?* But I couldn't.

If this was going to happen all the time from now on, it was going to make daily life very complicated.

We drove through west London listening to taxi drivers arguing on LBC 97.3 FM, in the kind of companionable silence I'd normally have enjoyed after such a frenetic weekend but which now made me squirm as I realized how important it was to me.

Nelson, of course, didn't seem bothered at all, tutting at the news, stopping for old ladies at crossings, cursing saltily at the Congestion Charge cameras.

"Do you think Roger will have sorted things out with Zara?" he asked easily, when we were nearly home. "You told him what to do to put it right with her, didn't you?"

"I did what I could," I said.

"He's an idiot, but I'm really chuffed for him," he went on, signaling to overtake a cyclist. "Just goes to show, doesn't it?"

"Yes," I said, seizing the chance. "Yes, you can find love where you least expect it!"

"Oh, he told you, did he?"

"Told me what?" I asked nervously.

"Where he met Zara."

"No?" I said, trying to sound as if that's what I thought he meant.

"Online. In some Internet war game. She was playing the role of a biological warfare specialist in his invasion force, and Roger was being an embedded journalist with unexpected hand-to-hand martial arts skills."

"And romance blossomed over the grenade fire?" I said, trying to picture it.

"Apparently so. Got to the point where Zara wouldn't go into battle without Roger—or, Troy Absolom, as I suppose we should call him—at her side."

"Right . . ."

"Anyway, they got chatting while that night's raid was held up after the troop commander was stuck in detention in Idaho Falls, and it turned out she lived in Kensington. So they met up one evening, and the rest, as they say, is history."

"That's amazing," I said, turning in my seat. Nelson was parking the Range Rover now outside the house, with heartbreaking precision. He scorned parking sensors. I opened and shut my mouth like a goldfish.

"Means there's hope for me yet, eh?" he joked.

Like an idiot, I leaped into the opening. "You're a wonderful, eligible man," I gushed. "You're bound to find someone, someone who'll really make you happy. That's what you *deserve*. A friend, and a lover and a—"

He gave me a funny look. "Steady on, Mel. Anyone would think you were applying for the position yourself."

I braced myself. "I am."

The engine ticked as it cooled down. Nelson's brow furrowed. "Sorry?"

"I want to make you happy. I've been so stupid, not realizing until now how I really felt about you, but now I *know*. I want to be more than just your friend, Nelson . . . I want to—"

"Don't," he said, holding up a hand. "Don't say anything else."

I thought he meant *There's no need for words*, as in *Let me sweep you soundlessly into my arms for a Hollywood kiss*, and closed my eyes, ready.

But apparently he didn't mean that.

At all.

"I know it's been a bit of a fantasy weekend, Mel, but we're back in London now," he said awkwardly, and then laughed even more awkwardly.

My eyes snapped open. "What? Quite the opposite," I stammered. "It's as if everything's suddenly really clear. I saw you on the boat and I realized that I've been completely blind—you and I . . . we're meant to be together. You're the perfect man for me!"

Nelson said nothing, but he pressed his lips together, which was the first sign of polite annoyance.

"What?" I demanded. "You might say something."

"What do you want me to say? What *can* I say—you *suddenly realized*, after splitting up with your fiancé, who you still haven't properly got over, while on the *yacht of the playboy*, who's been flirting outrageously with you for the past few months, that actually, scrub those two, it was *me* you really wanted?"

"There's no need to make it sound so—"

Nelson undid his seat belt. "I'm not some kind of comfy crash mat you can rebound onto, you know."

"It's not rebound!" I insisted. "It's just . . . delayed realization!"

"Come on, Mel," he sighed. "We've been here before, remember? When you thought Jonathan didn't fancy you unless you were dressed up as Honey? You can't just use me as someone to take your mind off feelings you should be dealing with!"

"I'm not!"

"How do you think that makes me feel?" he went on. "I've got feelings too, you know."

"I know! That's just it!" I struggled to find the words. "I always saw you as a teddy bear, not as a man with real feelings, and now I do it's—"

"Teddy bear," said Nelson flatly. "Cheers."

I stared at him in horror. This was going so badly awry that I had no idea how to get it back on track. Whatever I said now was going to sound wrong, even though it was absolutely right in my head. Hot tears of shock and embarrassment and mortification sprang into my eyes.

Nelson saw them, and—*because he was such a nice man*—he softened and patted me on the knee. Like you would your sister. "Look, Melissa, you know you mean the world to me. And, actually . . . it's very flattering. You're a charming, beautiful woman, and I'd walk over hot coals for you. But what sort of bastard would I be if I took advantage of you when you're obviously still getting over Jonathan?"

"I'm *over* Jonathan!" I wailed. "The reason I could never have made things work with him is because I wanted him to be you! Because you are *every single thing* that he's not!"

He grimaced and stared out of the windshield. The hot summer had frazzled the leaves on the tree next to the flat. Everything looked very worn-out and dirty after the ice-cream-colored extravagance of Monaco.

"Melissa, you've spent the past six months trying to fix me up with your friends. If that's reverse psychology or something, it's a lot of game playing I just don't want to get into. I've lived with you and your awful magazines in the loo long enough to know that you have to give yourself time to get over little hitches like broken engagements. Come on," he said, opening his door. "Let's get in and have a cup of tea. It's been quite a weekend, what with one thing and another."

I stared after him, my stomach feeling as if I'd swallowed a lead weight.

Nelson leaned back into the car. He looked like the familiar, cheerful Nelson I'd grown up with, and yet not. I wasn't sure if he could ever be that Nelson again to me now.

"Come on," he said gently. "We're old enough friends to have the occasional brain fade. I won't hold it against you. Fancy a curry for supper?"

I forced a smile onto my face. "I think I'll pop round to Gabi's, actually," I said. "I'll see you later."

Gabi's advice was straighforward.

"You'll just have to make him see you as a woman, not his flatmate," she said.

My expression must have looked suitably aghast, because she topped up my glass without even asking.

"You were shocked when you suddenly saw him as a potential date—Nelson'll just have to be shocked too," she elaborated. "I don't see why it should be such a big deal—everyone else seems to fall in love with you easily enough when you put that tight skirt on and start bossing them around."

"It's not as easy as that," I moaned. "He *has* seen me all dolled up—Nelson's seen me at work often enough." I downed half the wine in my glass and glared at her balefully. "*You* said he was in love with me all along. *You* said . . . More wine, please."

Gabi removed the glass from my hands. "Mel, hon, don't you think he might have a point about you giving yourself some time to get over Jonathan? It's only been a few months."

"Oh . . . I suppose so. But to be honest, Gabi, I'm not half as miserable about Jonathan as I thought I would be." I looked up at her. "I do miss him, but it's more 'I wonder what he's up to?' or 'Wouldn't it be great to try that restaurant?' Not 'My life is now completely rubbish and it's because he's not here with me.' Like I'd miss a really good friend. I did *mean* it when I said I hoped we'd be friends."

"Have you heard from him since you . . . since you and Nelson went over to collect your things?" she asked carefully.

"Not really. We've decided to give each other some space, you know, to move on a bit." Not that I'd managed to move very far. "I rang him last week, actually, to ask if he'd found some jewelry I left, but I got Solange. He must have been out with a client. She was pretty frosty with me," I added. "She's probably taken against me, like a good PA. But then I suppose I have been pretty mean to Jonathan. I've been pretty stupid all around. . . ."

Gabi grabbed my hands, but I couldn't stop the tears pouring out, even when she wrapped her arms round me and pressed my head into her chest.

I couldn't distract myself anymore, as the events of the past few months replayed themselves in my head, crashing into each other like runaway train carriages. Jonathan, Paris, arguing with Daddy, messing things up with Nelson . . . It was as if everything I'd managed to build up in the last few years had never happened and I was right back to where I'd started: single, stressed out, being made a fool of by everyone, but, most of all, by myself.

All I had was Nelson, but he didn't see me the way I saw him, and probably never would now. How on earth had I messed up something so perfect?

"Poor Mel," soothed Gabi as my tears dripped onto her new velvet sofa (engagement present from Aaron). "You've had a rotten few months. Can't you just cancel your appointments this week and go off somewhere? I'll come with you if you want. You need some time away from everyone else, concentrating on you and what you want."

It wasn't such a bad idea, and for a moment, I did briefly toy with the idea of me and Gabi jetting off to Vegas, or Disneyworld, somewhere I'd only have to eat, not think. But wasn't there a reason I couldn't just pull a sickie? What was it?

Bertie's christening—and nanny-related issues arising.

I really *was* back where I started.

"I bloody can't!" I wailed. "I've got to help Emery organize this christening, if she doesn't decide to cancel it again. *And* help her get rid of Nanny Adolf. *And* help Nicky sort out his stupid blackmail problems."

"Blackmail problems?" Gabi's eyes widened.

Sniffing, I gestured toward my handbag, out of reach by Gabi's foot. She passed it to me and I reached into its depths and pulled out a huge white hanky. It was one of Nelson's, and it smelled of him:

Pears soap, and shirt collar starch, and a hint of old Range Rover. That set off my crying again.

Gabi hugged me. "Sometimes, Mel, I think you need a PA of your own, you know. Someone who'll say no for you. If you don't start saying no, I'm going to." She lifted my head. "Give me your Rolodex and I'll cancel all your clients *and* your family."

There was something in her fierce expression that warmed my heart. OK, so at least I had a friend like Gabi. That was one positive thing, out of three. I'd find another two.

I don't know how I got through the next few days, really. Nelson was making a determined effort to act as if nothing had happened, but it was impossible. Now that my eyes had been opened, I realized I'd never wanted anyone more. And the fact that he was behaving so decently about it only rubbed that in further.

Even working didn't help. Emery called, after I spent three days sourcing "the right kind of fruitcake," to tell me Bertie's christening had moved dates again because William's mother had found out that Princes Alexander and Nicolas of Hollenberg would be attending and had booked herself some emergency lipo.

Good job, really, since Emery hadn't gotten round to doing much more than writing out half the invitations I'd sent her and she wanted to recall ten of those.

"Emery," I said, "are you sure you haven't changed your invite list? Uncle Gilbert didn't even know you'd *had* a baby."

"Yes," she said. "Pretty sure. Unless Daddy's been nicking the invitations to invite extra people. I did think the pile had got a bit low, you know. Has he told you he's asked his publishers to come? They think it's going to be a Cheese Diet reception!"

"How many?" I asked, looking aghast at the catering quote. It was for fifty people, tops, and didn't feature cheese that heavily. If Daddy wanted cheese and pineapple hedgehogs he'd have to make them himself.

"I don't know . . . ten? And there's the Women's Institute ladies too."

"What?"

"Mummy's asked the WI. To say thank you for helping her knit her animals for that last big exhibition. I think they're going to bring some cakes, if that helps—"

"You know she'll be in trouble if the press find out she's tendering out her artworks," I said, jabbing at my calculator to see how far fifteen plates of sandwiches could go. Not far enough, unless Jesus was in the Little Swillbridge WI. "I'm going to have to ring the caterers, Em. So you'd better tell me right now if it looks like eighty people will be coming."

She paused.

"Come on," I said testily. "Remember what happened at your wedding, when you forgot to count in Uncle Tybalt's wife and kids and they had to sit on the stage with the band?"

"It's not that, I just thought I heard that bloody woman," she hissed. "She keeps that breast pump in her apron. I never know when she's going to barge in and stick me with it! When are you going to deal with her, Mel? Because if you don't do something soon, I swear I really am going to take matters into my own hands."

In all the fuss, I'd almost forgotten about Nanny Ag.

"Soon," I sighed. "Just let's get the christening out of the way first. So it's definitely on for October fifteenth?"

"Definitely," Emery confirmed.

I wasn't so sure. At this rate, Bertie would be christened shortly before he went off to university.

twenty-four

The atmosphere in Nelson's flat was now so strained that I knew something had to be done. We were both acting self-consciously, and I only had myself to blame. It was as though there had been a gas leak, slowly poisoning us both and making us behave weirdly.

Besides, as Gabi had counseled me, the best way for him to stop seeing me as his flatmate was to stop *being* his flatmate.

And so, with a heavy heart, I cleared out all the junk from my spare room at the office and prepared to camp out there until I could find a place of my own to rent. That was another good thing, I reminded myself: I was now officially a property owner, since the deeds had arrived, plus for once I had some cash in the bank. A massive check had arrived from Alexander's office, accompanied by an even more humongous bouquet of flowers, thanking me for my efforts with Nicky, which had apparently greatly pleased the Hollenberg powers-that-be, with the Act due to be passed any day now.

I just prayed it would happen before I could think of a way to get Piglet to come around about those photos of Nicky.

I chose an evening when I was heading home for christening negotiations to break the news of my move to Nelson.

"I'll be back on Sunday evening," I said, dumping my bag in the hall. Normally, I'd have gone over to give him a hug good-bye. Not now.

"Drive carefully," he said, not looking up from the chopping board, where he was reducing a pepper to a zillion tiny pieces. "And give my love to Her Royal Highness-to-be."

I took a deep breath and forced myself to say the words I'd been dreading. At least now I could say them and make a sharp exit. "Nelson, I've been thinking. It's time I moved out and got a place of my own."

The heavy knife clunked on the chopping board. "Ow! Shit!" He sucked his injured finger and swung around to face me. "Why do you want to move out?"

"Well . . . you know." I shrugged. "I think I need a little time on my own. Maybe we both do."

Argh. *Agony.*

"Oh. Oh, right." Nelson looked hurt. "Um, well, if that's what you want."

Of course it's not what I want, I longed to yell. *I want to live here with you! Forever!*

But I didn't. I just hauled on my Brave Little Soldier face. "Well, you know, the London house market isn't going down, and I need to get on the housing ladder at some point, or else you'll have a lodger for the rest of your life!"

"Is this because you're in the money now?" Nelson asked, trying to look cheerful. He was a rotten actor though, and his unhappiness showed through. "My lowly flat's no longer good enough for you, now you're used to staff and helicopters?"

"Absolutely not!" I exclaimed. "You know I'd happily stay here forever with you! But if you . . ." I couldn't. It was just too demeaning.

Nelson gazed at me expectantly, still sucking his bleeding finger.

God, how I wished he felt the same as I did, all tingling at the rightness of him. But he didn't.

"It's time I got a place of my own," I finished.

"And you're sure?" Nelson's gaze was searching. "You really don't have to, you know."

I paused, digesting all the things we suddenly didn't feel able to say. "I think I do."

"I see. Well, good for you." He picked up his knife and an onion and began chopping again. "You should get a move on, if you're going home. You know there are roadworks on the M4? We can talk about . . . moving out and stuff after." The words seemed to stick in his throat.

I nodded, suddenly overcome with emotion.

Nelson put down his knife, turned round, and held his arms open. I ran into them.

He didn't kiss me passionately or admit he was *terribly, terribly fond of me* in a clipped *Brief Encounter* confession but instead wrapped his arms tightly around me, tangling his fingers into my hair so my nose pressed into his shoulder. I wondered if he could feel my hot breath through his blue shirt, or the tears leaking from my eyes.

We hugged each other for about five minutes, not speaking, and when I finally pulled away, Nelson wiped his eyes with the back of his hand.

"Onions," he explained. "They're a real bugger."

"I know," I said, and waited a second in case he said anything else. But he didn't, so I shouldered my bag and left.

Over the next few weeks, as the Indian summer tipped over into a crisp London autumn, I found three good, honest things about moving out.

1. I rescued Braveheart from my parents and brought him home to live with me in the office/flat. It was good to have his smelly white self around, even if he did remind me of Jonathan. His warm snoring kept me company on the long evenings when I'd normally have been squabbling happily with Nelson about who was the better Dr. Who, and his constant need for walks counteracted the comfort eating. As a bonus, he was a splendid icebreaker for nervous clients, who couldn't discuss their love lives straight out but could chat happily about dogs.

2. Nelson now had to ring me up and ask me if I wanted to come over for dinner, which I always did. And Gabi had been right: now I wasn't living there, seeing each other was something we actively looked forward to, and he always looked as if he'd just changed into a fresh shirt.

3. I found, to my surprise, that though my spare room was tiny, though I had to go round to Gabi's for a bath, though the novelty of being able to get to work in under ten seconds wore off, I actually liked living on my own. I'd been in such a whirl of romance over the past few years that I'd forgotten how good I was at being on my own. It made me realize I *could* change fuses and cope with middle-of-the-night panics—not just for my clients but for myself as well. Most of all, those long walks around Green Park with Braveheart, watching the leaves turn gold, then brown, then finally fall into rustling piles, gave me time to think. And the more I thought, the more I knew who my real prince was.

Speaking of princes, I saw Nicky for dinner soon after, although my work there was officially done. I felt bad that I hadn't dealt with his blackmail problems—I just hadn't had the emotional energy to spare on someone else for once.

"We've got a few weeks," he said, nervously ordering a second bottle of champagne. "Imogen's still in Bali doing that reality television show. But she's such a cow that she's bound to be voted off almost before it's started, and I just know she'll go to the papers as soon as she's back."

I patted his hand, something I felt I could do now, with no fear of misinterpretation. "Don't worry, Nicky. I'll think of something."

Then he got a text message, and it was Leonie, which answered my next question before I even asked it.

It was during one of our regular treks around Green Park that I finally found the courage to ring Jonathan. Braveheart had shot off in pursuit of a squirrel, managing to wrap his leash round a tree *and* a litter bin in the process—and I found myself thinking, *I must tell Jonathan how native Braveheart's gone.*

Then, before the thought could slink away, I pulled out my phone and called him. It was what a friend would do, after all.

As it rang at his end, I stood silent for a minute, the cold October air nipping through my gloves and hat. When he answered, I felt a pang of nostalgia at that familiar, gorgeous New York accent, but I thought of hot chocolate in a china cup so my voice would sound as cheery as possible.

"Hello, Jonathan!" I said. "I'm ringing to tell you Braveheart's manners are no better in London than they were in New York! And," I added, more normally, "to see how you are."

"Melissa! Great to hear from you!"

There was a moment's uncertain pause, then we both said, "So! How *are* you?" followed by a pause, then, "No, how are *you*?"

I told him about the cruise, and about Alexander's upcoming reinstatement ceremony or whatever it was called. He told me some places we could have gone to eat in Monte Carlo had we ever gotten off the yacht.

He told me Lisa had promoted him again as a reward for staying with Kyrle & Pope and that he was setting up the relocation business too with the redoubtable Solange at the helm. I told him it would be a massive success, and I'd point everyone I knew in his direction.

"You'll be fine with Solange's contact book!" I said, more jokily than I felt. "She puts my office managing to shame!"

"She's efficient, but she doesn't have your . . . people skills," said Jonathan, rather wistfully. Then he brightened up. I couldn't see his face to tell if the brightness reached his gray eyes. "You must let me know next time you're in Paris—I've found some really great little neighborhood bistros you'd love. I totally get what you mean about hunting down backstreet gems. Hey, why not come over for a day's Christmas shopping? Bring Gabi, if you want," he added over-casually.

"That's a wonderful idea," I said. "But I can't keep up with her shopping. I might just come on my own, if that's OK? It'd give us a chance to get more than two words in over lunch, if nothing else."

There was a pause, in which we both thought things but didn't say them. It wasn't a bad pause, though.

"I'll look forward to that," said Jonathan.

"So will I." We chatted a little more, about nothing much, but by the time I hung up, I'd begun to think that maybe that road to Special Friendship wasn't as littered with potholes and speed bumps as I'd thought.

Emery called to say that she and William had delayed the christening once more, over a name standoff this time. Then, finally, under serious pressure from Mummy, who realized she could tie the whole thing in with their village Christmas party and just have one major tidy-up of the house, Emery caved in and confirmed the date for the beginning of December.

It goes without saying that they kept me pretty busy in the weeks that followed.

Since Bertie's christening/naming ceremony was planned for Sunday lunchtime, I decided to wait until Friday afternoon before I headed home. Any earlier and my family would have had me doing everything from fixing the leaky roof to worming the dogs; any later and I'd only have had to deal with the chaos created by letting them deal with the final arrangements on their own.

I packed Braveheart into the Smart with my own overnight bag and set off in good time. The weather was cold but very crisp and quite Christmassy.

When I rapped at the door, William, Emery's husband, opened it.

"Hi, Melinda," he said, kissing my cheek and aiming kicks at the pack of dogs who surrounded Braveheart in a sea of friendly barking.

I forgave him for getting my name wrong. He looked totally jet-lagged—although that might just have been the effects of stumbling into a Romney-Jones family event he'd been doing his best to avoid for months now.

"How are things going?" I asked as we walked down the hall, the dogs' claws skittering on the tiles.

"Er, to be honest? I have no idea," said William. "They shout even when they're not arguing about stuff."

As we approached the drawing room, the gentle roar of muted debate seemed to bear out what he'd said. But just as William's hand touched the doorknob, a black-clad blur swooped down on him.

"Daddy! It's your turn for feed and nap! Chop, chop! Mustn't keep Baby waiting!" barked Nanny Ag, tapping her enormous watch.

William looked stunned and allowed himself to be propelled up the stairs. When they were halfway up she turned back to me and said, "You're looking very puffy, Melissa! Are you regular?"

I spluttered.

"Roughage, that's what you need. I'll be back to deal with you later," she warned, wagging her finger, then resumed shoving William upstairs. "Now, what have you done with Mummy? I can't find her anywhere," I heard her say to him as they went.

God Almighty, Emery was right. I had to do something about that woman.

I pushed open the drawing-room door and found Mummy, Daddy, Granny, and Allegra sitting round a tray of coffee and biscuits, arguing fiercely about which of us had weighed the most when we were born. Daddy was smoking a large cigar to annoy my mother, who was knitting furiously. There was no sign of Emery.

"Ah, it's the woman with the Teflon ring finger!" bellowed Daddy when he saw me. "I hear you're not engaged to that prince either now."

"Martin!" snapped Mummy. "Shut up. It's so good of you to come over, darling," she said, kissing my cheek. "You're so terribly busy at the moment, what with one thing or another. I know Emery's awfully grateful for your help so far."

"How can you tell?" demanded Allegra. "We haven't seen her for days. Anyone would think she was trying to avoid poor Nanny."

I boggled. If Allegra knew what sort of embarrassing pictures Nanny Ag had of her on her pony, Buttons, she'd soon change her tune. "Is everything else ready?" I asked. "I spoke to the caterers yesterday and they seem ready to go. No . . . extra guests?"

Mummy sighed theatrically. "Nothing's ready. Nothing! The dogs got into the linen press and ruined all the sheets, so we've had to wash everything before your uncles arrive tomorrow, and your father had a ton of cheddar delivered about an hour ago, and poor Mrs. Lloyd is having to cut it all up for the reception. Emery's gone AWOL and now your grandmother tells me her *fiancé* will be arriving tomorrow and I have no idea what the protocol is about introducing a soon-to-be but not-quite head of state." She glared at Granny. "It makes him sound like he's auditioning for something."

"Which he is, really," added Daddy. "Surely they're only having him back as king on approval? Until he's learned his ceremonial dances?"

Granny waved her hand airily, all the better to sparkle her diamond ring at him.

I decided to go to the kitchen and help Mrs. Lloyd with her cheese hedgehogs.

For the rest of the evening, I whirled around sorting stuff out: getting bedrooms ready for various family members, checking exactly who was coming, calling in favors from various ex-cleaners in the village to get the house looking halfway decent, and tracking down Emery. There were still things I didn't know about this christening—like exactly what was going to happen at it.

I eventually ran her to ground in the pantry, evidently raiding it for supplies. William had gone off in disgrace with the dogs, having casually demolished the entire pie Mrs. Lloyd had made for supper, and Emery was looking as if she'd have happily broken her usual vow of inactivity and gone with him.

"Right," I said, concerning her. "Have you spoken to the vicar about fees and such like?"

"We're not having a vicar," she said. "Daddy and I had a fearful row. He wanted it to be in the chapel, for the snob value, but the vicar said it hadn't been consecrated ground since before the Civil War and he refused to do it."

"Good for him," I said. The so-called chapel was practically falling down, and it had had chickens in it for the last ten years. "So who *is* doing the ceremony?"

Emery's eyes skated back and forth between jars of jam. "Well, that's it. Daddy still wanted to have it in the chapel, because he'd told the magazine people it would be, and they're paying a huge amount to cover it, what with Granny marrying Alexander and Nicky being a godfather, so we had to improvise. I wanted it in the woods," she complained. "But Daddy wasn't having that either. Something to do with man traps he'd set to catch poachers?"

"So what *is* happening?" I demanded impatiently.

"It's going to be in the chapel, with a registrar. Who may or may not *seem* to be a vicar. Don't look at me!" she protested. "I did my best! Daddy's had some set-building people Allegra knows in there, turning it into some kind of mini St. Paul's! Didn't you see the vans round by the stables?"

"No," I said. "I can't say I did."

"Looks rather good, actually," Emery added, helping herself to a Tunnock's tea cake. "Daddy's ordered a shedload of booze, and virtually everyone we know is coming. Will and I snuck off down to the pub with Allegra the other night and invited some locals so, you know, if there's anyone else you want to invite . . . Actually, shouldn't we have a few extra sandwiches laid on, in case they stop for tea?"

I covered my face with my hands and tried to sound calm. "Shouldn't *you* have told me this before now?"

Emery turned her most sympathetic gaze on me. "But you've been so busy! I didn't think you needed more stress."

"Emery!" I began, but then another voice barked, "Emery! Mummy!"

We froze, stared at each other, and Emery made a bolt for the door. I hesitated for a moment, then followed her.

I went back to my room, shut the door firmly, and calmed myself down by making a list.

1. Arrange extra sandwiches
2. Deal with Nanny Ag
3. Deal with Nicky's blackmail issue

I bit my pen and felt guilty. I'd been saved so far by Imogen's unexpectedly long run in that celebrity pirate show, but I still hadn't thought about what I could do, aside from talking reasonably to her—which was sheer wishful thinking. Nicky would be arriving tomorrow, expecting me to have come up with some magic solution, just as I had done with everything else.

I threw myself back on the pillows, utterly weary of being deal-with-everyone-else's-problems Mel.

As I stared at the same crack in the ceiling that had been spreading ominously toward the window since I was a child, the organizational part of my brain pointed out that I could maybe soothe my conscience a little bit by making sure Leonie would be there for Nicky. If it was a free-for-all, who'd notice an extra body?

I rolled over and rang her.

"Hi, Melons!" she said. "I was just doing my accounts."

"Please don't call me Melons," I said automatically. "You're not really doing accounts on Friday night, are you?"

"Yes," said Leonie. "Isn't that when you do yours?"

"Um, not usually. Are you doing much this weekend, apart from that?"

"Just my pole-dancing aerobics class on Sunday morning."

I choked a little. "I beg your pardon?"

"Oh, you know, it's a class I go to. Just thought it made sense to acquire a new skill as well as keep fit, and it's always something I could turn to if needs be. Very lucrative, in time/recompense terms."

The mental image of a spangly Leonie pole dancing while briskly negotiating her fee with drunken businessmen somehow made total sense.

"How sensible!" I managed. "Um, well, it's very short notice, but we're having some people over for my nephew's christening on Sunday—Nicky's going to be a godfather—and you'd—"

"Love to," she interrupted. "What time?"

After a few minutes' chitchat, I put down the phone and crossed Nicky off my to-do list. Business acumen and pole dancing in the comfort and privacy of your own home: Leonie got more perfect for Nicky by the minute.

Various Romney-Jones relations started arriving on Saturday morning, so as to lay first dibs on the rooms with twenty-first-century mattresses. That was the trouble with having the ancestral pile, however falling down and leaky it was: the rest of the family assumed you had hotel-grade accommodations. Mummy's immense jam stock, coupled with Daddy's freebie cheese mountain, meant that poor Mrs. Lloyd, who'd been making mini scones since daybreak, wasn't short of supplies as the crowd of ravenous Romney-Joneses built up in the drawing room.

Since these reunions had a habit of getting testy, I made the round of greetings, acknowledged that yes, I had grown, and no, I wasn't thinking of getting married yet, then sloped off to help Mrs. Lloyd set up for the caterers.

Emery was collared by Nanny Ag as we were called into supper and dragged upstairs for "Baby's bath and bed," leaving William to fend off the terrifying directness of my cousin Polly's questions about why he and Emery spent so much time in different countries. Emery returned at eight with a face like thunder, apologized for not joining us, and went straight to the kitchen to eat her supper there.

I slipped away when the trifle appeared. ("Isn't that Auntie Enid's trifle bowl? She left that to me in her will." "No, she didn't, it's definitely mine!" etc., etc.)

Emery was sitting cross-legged in the vast dog basket by the stove, scarfing rice pudding out of a can while Mrs. Lloyd made sympathetic noises. When they heard me come in, the pair of them flinched defensively, then relaxed.

"She's got to go," said Emery fiercely. "Mrs. Lloyd was telling me Nanny's been snooping around the kitchen, counting the empty bottles in the recycling bag."

"And telling me what to do," said Mrs. Lloyd. She shut the dishwasher with a bang. "Not that I mind having a list of instructions."

I knew this to be a fib, but even so.

Emery pointed her spoon at me. "Since Bertie's asleep half the time under her evil regime, she's got nothing to do, so the old witch has taken to bossing everyone else around! Even Bruce who comes to do the garden. Can you believe it?"

"Telling me what to cook for dinner, running her fingers round the grill pan," muttered Mrs. Lloyd grimly. "I could go on, but I shan't . . . And then the bins, and where I keep the bleach—"

"Right," I said. "The time has come. Where is she?"

"In her room. Preparing her spells for tomorrow."

"Great. Emery, go up there right now, get her down here, and ask her about soft foods or something."

"What?" Emery looked blank.

"I don't know! I'm not the one with the baby! Ask her about how you can turn tonight's leftovers into baby food or something. Anything that's going to keep her occupied and down here for as long as it takes me to get that file. . . ."

Emery put her hand to her mouth. She looked thrilled. "Gosh!" she said. "Just like Nancy Drew!"

The baby monitor in her pocket crackled as Bertie let out a preliminary squawk. Even I recognized it as a warm-up to something more ear-shredding. Emery's face puckered with concern and she looked up at me. "I'm not allowed to go to him. Not until he's been doing it for about fifteen minutes."

I felt sorry for her. Clearly, Em's initial lack of interest in Bertie had turned into something much more maternal, possibly as a direct result of feeling he and she were on the same side against Nanny Ag.

"I'll take my mobile," I said. "Text me the second she starts heading upstairs. . . ."

I hid in the cloakroom under the stairs while Emery returned with Nanny Ag in full flow.

"You can never get yourself and your staff prepared too soon," she was saying. Above my head, her feet clumped emphatically. "That was always the problem with your mother—always had lemons for her G & Ts, never Milupa . . ."

"Still . . . ," said Emery. I could practically hear her biting her tongue.

Once they were safely out of earshot, I ran up the stairs, two at a time, and let myself into Nanny Ag's room, avoiding all the creaking steps.

I barely had time to register her worrying "tell-all" bedtime reading—*Fashion Babylon, Hotel Babylon, Air Babylon*—before pulling open the bottom knicker drawer and starting to rifle methodically through it for the file Em and I had found.

But my hands weren't finding anything solid. Well, not more solid than a couple of reinforced corselettes.

My blood ran cold. The file wasn't there. It was gone.

Damn! I thought, rocking back on my heels. *She must have noticed we'd found it!*

I probed frantically with my fingers, but there was nothing in there except pants and the odd lavender bag. Shaking, I shut the drawer and tried the others.

Socks. Blouses. Millions of underskirts. Nothing I wanted.

My legs nearly buckled as I stood up and looked around the room. I knew I didn't have very long, but my brain suddenly went blank as to where else she might have hidden it. I looked around. The wardrobe?

As I was moving pair after pair of stout walking shoes around to no avail, a furious Welsh voice suddenly bellowed in my ear.

"What the hell do you think you're doing?"

I promise you, I nearly wet my pants. Bloody Emery! I'd told her to text me as soon as Nanny Ag was on the move.

I spun round, gabbling. "Oh, God, I'm so, *so* sorry, Nanny, it's not what it looks like, I was just . . ."

Allegra was standing there, a huge smile splitting her pale face, her arms folded across her chest. She was wearing her usual long black dress, with trumpet sleeves that hung down halfway to her knees. What with the smug grin and the red lipstick, the effect was very Elvira Munster.

"What are you up to, eh?" she demanded. "Not like you to be getting into trouble."

I clapped a hand to my exploding chest. "Allegra! You nearly killed me. Where did you spring from?"

"Just got here. Saw the light on my way up to the loo—then I saw your fat arse sticking up investigating Nanny's drawers so I thought I'd pop in. I see her taste in quasi-nun's outfits hasn't changed since 1985," she observed, flicking through the hangers. "Think she's got a Madonna and whore complex?"

"Allegra," I said, taking advantage of her experience in stashing contraband in a hurry. "If you were trying to hide something in here, where would you put it? Quickly!"

She raised her plucked eyebrows at me and stalked immediately over to the paneled fireplace. With one practiced shove of the nearest carved rosette, a hidden panel opened, to reveal not one but three box files and a bottle of Baileys.

"This what you were looking for?" she asked, as I grabbed the lot.

"How did you know that was there?" I demanded, stacking them in my arms.

"Oh, I've known for ages," she said. "One of the cleaners told me about it. How do you think I got rid of that sniveling au pair Francine?"

"You didn't get rid of her," I said, momentarily distracted from my rescue mission. "She left because the room was haunted."

"She left because there was a recording hidden in the fireplace of you and Emery playing your recorders," Allegra corrected me.

"You conniving cow!" I breathed. Then a sudden chiming sound came from my pocket making us both jump.

THE EAGLE IS LANDING, Emery had texted.

"Quick," I said, shoving the remaining files into Allegra's arms. "You know how fast she gets up stairs. Leave the Baileys," I added. "She'll need it when she realizes this is gone . . ."

"What are you talking about?" asked Allegra as I hustled her out the room as fast as I could, turning off the lights as I passed. "You could at least tell me what you're up to. . . ."

Nanny Ag's flat shoes hit the squeaky step I knew was three down from the landing, and in desperation, I opened the nearest door and pushed Allegra in.

It was the green guest bathroom. Hastily I locked the door, put a finger over my lips to silence her, and opened the first box.

Quite by chance the first photograph was of Allegra in her school netball match, clearly fouling the goalkeeper by holding her back by the pigtails while kicking the goal defense. It was during her "heavy thighs" phase. On the back, Nanny Ag had written: "Allegra Romney-Jones—might one day be arrested—father MP, mother possible sex scandal."

"Bloody hell!" she roared in outrage. "Bloody, bloody hell!"

There was a sharp knock on the door. "Are you all right in there?" barked Nanny Ag. "Is that you, Allegra? Are you constipated again?"

I made *No, no!* faces.

"Of course not," she yelled back. "I'm just . . . waxing my legs."

"I expect you're not doing it right," Nanny Ag bossed through the keyhole.

"Oh, I am," growled Allegra, ripping up the photograph into angry shreds. "I'm just having trouble . . . getting rid of the annoying little ingrowers!"

Nanny Ag coughed.

"Bye!" shouted Allegra. "I'll see you downstairs!"

Meanwhile I was sorting through the photographs, cringing on behalf of the many friends and acquaintances I now recognized. I say recognized—some of them were nearly unrecognizable.

But this one was familiar. I stopped dealing out the photos and stared more carefully at one in particular, clipped to a printed sheet of notes.

The dumpy little brown-haired girl, enjoying a McDonald's Happy Meal—didn't I know her? There was something about the way she was snarling at the camera, with three boxes lined up in front of her, while everyone else just had one. . . .

I checked the form underneath—a printout checklist with tickboxes of popular problems that Nanny Ag had obviously compiled for ease of gossip.

Oh my God.

The notes, as compiled by Nanny Barnes (heretofore known as Nanny B, Nanny Ag had noted in her plain handwriting), revealed that it was one Chanel Imogen Leys, of Mon Repose, Esher, Surrey; brat rating 10; born 12th April 1980 (so not twenty-three, as Nicky thought); worst habit(s): fibbing, stealing, biting; school: home schooled since expulsion from third school for blackmail. Under other details, Nanny B had noted, "Insists that she is not Malcolm and Denise's daughter but is adopted love child of a princess. Wants to be a princess or an international showjumper. See file 2 for more pics, incl. shoplifting folder."

A sudden feeling of glee and relief began to rise in me.

"Someone you know?" asked Allegra, showing me a photograph of myself as the world's fattest angel in my prep school nativity play. "Was there ever a cloud big enough to hold that angel? What's all this for, anyway?"

I opened an accounts book and boggled at the figures listed. "That give you a clue?" I asked Allegra, showing her.

"Good Lord." Allegra grabbed it off me. "If I'd known people would pay that much to keep things quiet, I'd have hung on to my school diaries."

I folded Piglet's details in half and stuffed them in my pocket. "Right," I said. "I want you to hide these files somewhere so secure and cunning Nanny Ag won't even begin to know where to look for them."

Allegra wriggled her fingers. "My pleasure," she said evilly.

twenty-five

The day of Cuthbert Rock Hunter McDonald's christening dawned bright and crisp, although this was in no way guaranteed to last the day, given the assortment of storm clouds heading into view, from one direction or another.

I got up early to check that the chairs were set up in the chapel, and for once, I had to admit that my father's delusions of grandeur hit the spot. The set designers had managed to turn the semiderelict building into a fairy-tale chapel, with ivy creeping around the empty arches and stained glass filling the large windows at the end, so that the clear morning sun filtered across the gold chairs in pools of red, green, and blue light. It didn't matter that half the roof was missing, since forget-me-not blue sky filled the gaps beautifully, leaving it open to birdsong and the fresh smell of pine trees.

That might have been a tape of birdsong and a pine tree candle, since we didn't actually have any in the garden, but I didn't want to look too closely.

The crumbly old font that Emery and I used to wash our My Little Ponies in had been cleaned and treated with something so it looked like an Arthurian relic, and they'd gone round the worn plaques on the walls, restoring what they could of the long-gone

Romneys, Romney-Joneses, and the smattering of Barclays who'd temporarily had the place in the 1750s (in lieu of a gambling debt).

I sighed and felt a tiny pang of envy. Lucky Emery—with her baby, and her husband, she was making her own family dynasty. So was Allegra. Even Granny was getting another go at winding herself into a family tree.

All I had was myself and my business.

I looked up at the fluffy white clouds moving across the broken roof beams. And a flat to find, and a fresh start to make. On my own.

I shook myself. "And that's plenty to be happy about," I said sternly.

I walked back into the kitchen to find a makeup artist and two hairdressers working busily on Mummy, Granny, and Emery, while Daddy, with Bertie strapped to his chest as usual, was lecturing the caterers about the order in which the cheeses were to be served according to various "private sponsorship arrangements."

"Ah, Melissa!" he barked as I walked in. "See if you can raise Nanny, will you? Haven't seen hide nor hair of her since last night."

"No," said Emery. "She didn't come to wake me up for my six o'clock milking." She put a finger on her chin and pretended to look concerned. "Poor Nanny. I wonder what's happened to her?"

I winked. "Can't think. Shall I go and find her?"

"Do, darling," said Mummy, as well as she could with someone applying lip gloss and someone else tonging her hair. "She's got the family christening gown."

Emery's eyes shifted from side to side. "Actually, William was wondering if we could maybe dress him in—"

"Get the gown," said Daddy. "Every Romney-Jones baby since 1870 has been christened in that. Well, the legitimate ones, anyway."

"Any sign of Nelson yet?" I asked before he could elaborate.

Everyone shook their heads.

"He'll be here soon," said Granny, giving me a reassuring glance. "He wouldn't miss this."

Better get any yelling out of the way before Nelson arrived. "I'll go and find Nanny," I said, and steeled myself for some straight talking.

Nanny Ag was waiting for me in her room and cut straight to the chase when I asked if anything was wrong.

"Something has gone missing from my room, Melissa," she hissed, probing my face for clues with the searchlight gaze that had had me singing like a canary as a child. Not anymore. "Something personal. I'm very disappointed in Allegra. I thought we'd dealt with those klep-tomaniac tendencies after—"

"It wasn't Allegra, it was me," I said.

"No one's at home to Interrupting Ingrid," she began, then stared at me in shock. "*You* stole it?"

"I stole your horrible files? Yes!" I snapped. "I can't believe it of you. I am absolutely aghast to think you could have let us—and your-self—down so very badly. Not to mention breaking the law. People go to prison for blackmail, you know."

Nanny Ag glared at me, but I glared back, I was used to training my disappointed gaze on recalcitrant bankers, not small children, and the extra power showed.

"What would your charges think if they knew you'd been spying on them?" I went on remorselessly. "After the trust they put in you. I'm dismayed, Nanny Ag. Dismayed. If this is found out, you might never work with children again! Think of that!"

"I hate children!" she snarled. "Do you think it's fun being a status symbol for social-climbing snobs who think a nanny can turn their grabby brats into little angels because they can't stand the sight of them themselves? Getting a clapped-out Fiat Panda to drive while the parents swan around in a BMW? It's just about the most miserable ex-istence known to man. And as soon as they hit adolescence, you have to start all over again! Usually with their in-bred relatives!"

I stared at her, shocked, and not a little hurt. But I quickly rallied. "They're children! It's not their fault! It's beyond mean to upset and embarrass people like this. I'm asking you to stop it, right here."

"Or what?"

"Or I'll get William to start court proceedings against you. I've got all of your files, you know. And I've copied all your correspondence, so the various families can be informed and they can sue you too."

Nanny Ag looked stunned, then devious. "This isn't like you, Melissa," she said in a wheedling voice. "You don't think I was including you in all this? Of course not. You were always my favorite."

I narrowed my eyes. "And that was why you kept the picture of me as Boy George at a fancy dress party, with 'unlikely to do much' written on the back?"

Nanny Ag narrowed her eyes back at me. "Give me everything, or I accidentally put the iron through the christening gown." She nodded toward the back of her wardrobe, where the precious lace gown hung, then she flicked a switch on the steam iron set up by the bed.

I took one look at it, then turned back to her. "Burn what you like. I have some burning of my own to be getting on with."

And I left her to it.

Things started happening pretty quickly after that. The entire WI arrived in a minibus and nine cars, followed by seven cars' worth of Cheese Diet publishers, two cars and a motorbike of photographers, three cars of journalists, reams of Emery's vague friends, a gaggle from the local pub, The Lamb and Flag, Nelson, Leonie, and the caterer's van. As soon as Nelson arrived he was dispatched to patrol the makeshift car park in the paddock, a job he threw himself into with gusto.

Granny, Alexander, and Nicky arrived in the Bentley, which I heard Daddy insist be parked as far away from his own car as possible on account of unflattering comparisons. This didn't bother Granny in the slightest, as it gave her even farther to walk, very slowly, turning heads in her enormous feather hat and matching royal fiancé.

After posing for a few photographs with Emery and the baby, Nicky slid over to where Leonie and I were making somewhat stiff conversation about the impossibility of finding a flat anywhere within the M25. When Leonie and Nicky spotted each other, they went through a very elaborate greeting ritual, in which, rather oddly, he claimed not to have seen her for weeks, at the same time as she claimed not to have seen him for days.

But Imogen's imminent revelations were obviously bothering him.

"I can't put her off any longer," he said, his eyes flicking nervously to where Granny and Alexander were laughing uproariously at Mummy's story about knitting a nude WI calendar for Charles Saatchi. "She's out of the jungle or wherever she's been and she wants to see me tonight. She's talking about the *News of the World,* Mel!" His face was pale beneath his tan. "Grandfather warned me there's a year's probation on the reinstation! I'm seriously bricking it."

"Aha!" I said, reaching into my handbag. "Brick no longer! I think I have your answer." And I handed him the Nanny File on Imogen. "She's not quite the cut-glass socialite she's been making herself out to be. In fact, I'm sure the *News of the World* would like to get their hands on some of *these* pictures."

Nicky and Leonie gasped as the pre-nose-job, post-shoplifting-charge Imogen emerged. I know I should have felt more guilty than I did, but she was a repellent adult, and she didn't seem like a very nice child, to be perfectly honest. Allegra's sense of humor might be warped, but at least she had one.

"My friend Gabi says you can date the photos she's got of you, by the way," I added. "She says digital photos have dates on them, so you can even pretend they've been doctored or something. Ring her now!"

Nicky reached into his jacket pocket and withdrew his phone. I was pleased to see he was wearing one of the new English suits I'd taken him to buy, and with his hair less carefully messed up than usual and no sunglasses, he looked very godfatherly—in the lowercase sense of the word.

"Hello, Imogen?" he said. "Yes, I need to talk to you . . ." Then he held the phone away from his ear and winced at the torrent of screeching.

"Give it to me," said Leonie, snatching it off him. "Ms. Leys? This is Leonie Hargreaves. I'm a libel specialist representing Prince Nicolas of Hollenberg."

Nicky looked at Leonie, then looked at me with approval. She wasn't dressed to impress particularly much—just a tweed suit and a furry bcrct—but I could see from her toned calves that she'd put in a fair amount of time on her pole.

"She's a pole dancer in her spare time," I whispered to him.

Nicky's eyes nearly popped out of his head.

Leonie didn't notice. She was too busy giving Piglet the mother of all headaches, in fearsomely efficient tones. "I see . . . I see . . . While that is your legal right, I should also let you know that we have certain images within our possession which do throw new light on proceedings . . ." She gave us the thumbs-up.

"She's very . . . stern, isn't she?" Nicky murmured approvingly. "It's always the quiet ones that surprise you."

"Is it? I wouldn't know."

He cut me a familiar flirty look. "Oh, I bet you would."

"I *wouldn't*. Anyway," I said, changing the subject, "your grandfather seemed to like her."

"Oh, yes. She had him at 'international tax break.'" Nicky turned to me, squinting in the sun. "He *really* likes you, though."

"Does he?"

"He says you remind him of your granny. Which is about the highest compliment he pays women."

Over by the table of drinks, Mummy, Granny, and Alexander were laughing on their own. She put a hand on his arm affectionately, and he lifted it to kiss in a deliberate, gallant gesture.

"He's very keen to get to know you all better," Nicky went on, watching them. "He says it's all down to you that he's so happy now. Getting you to sort me out brought him and Dilys back together."

"Well, I think Granny's the one to thank for that," I said. Granny was happy, Mummy looked happy, Alexander looked delighted.

"And," he went on, "you'll be pleased to hear that I have gainful employment at last! We're opening a special tourism and investment embassy in Mayfair, and I'm in charge of events."

"Parties, you mean," I said.

"Networking," he corrected me. "Very important for rebuilding international relationships. Guess who my boss is?"

"Whoever it is," I said, "I feel intensely sorry for them."

"Your granny! Or, should I say, my stepgranny!"

Granny and Nicky. London's champion socializers. "Any job vacancies going?" I asked, only half joking.

"Sorted!" said Leonie, snapping the phone shut and handing it back to Nicky. "We might need to have a chat later so I can bring you up to date on our position. I think I've made things quite firm."

He winked at her, more like the old Nicky. "That sounds like my sort of date."

Leonie giggled, in a most un-Leonie way. Fortunately for everyone, at that moment Emery shimmered up in a confection of silvery lace that made her look like a beached mermaid and dragged me and Nicky off to brief us on our roles in the ceremony.

For a ceremony organized by Daddy and Emery in conjunction, the whole thing went off extremely well. So well that I found myself wiping away tears as Emery and William promised always to laugh *with* Bertie, not *at* him, to keep their promises about Christmas presents, and never to dress him in clothes that would come back to haunt him later.

I thought they might have considered that last one more carefully, since Bertie had been dressed for his naming ceremony in some sort of hippie dungaree ensemble, chosen by Emery, topped off with a tiny pair of Nike running shoes, chosen by William.

Allegra leaned forward and whispered, "I locked the old trout in her room. Didn't think the christening robe was that important, right?"

"Right!" I whispered back.

Then Nicky and I got up and stood in front of the registrar-dressed-as-a-vicar, and promised to do our best to help Bertie be himself, whatever that turned out to be, and to surround him with love, support, and lifts home from school.

It was a sweet service, and it was over too quickly, even with Emery's school friend Margot singing some god-awful Whitney

Houston song while the photographers got all their shots. Bertie didn't cry once, except for when Daddy insisted on promising to look out for his little mini-me, and even then, I think it was a howl of solidarity.

I hung back while everyone piled out of the chapel and headed for the enormous spread set out on tables in the dining hall. I didn't think I could face another lump of cheddar, after helping Mrs. Lloyd spear foil-covered oranges with a ton of the stuff. Instead, I hugged my coat to me and tried to put my finger on just why I felt so . . . brooding.

I didn't even think I could pin it down to one specific problem. It was one of those end-of-term depressions, a knowledge that everything had shifted, and I couldn't go back. I had to go on, but I wasn't sure where that was going to be.

"Where've you been hiding?" asked a familiar voice. A familiar arm slung itself round my shoulders as a familiar body sat down on the chair next to me.

My stomach lifted at the comfort Nelson always brought.

"What's up?" he asked, seeing my downcast face.

"I don't know. Nothing."

"Come on," said Nelson kindly. "Don't give me that. You've been acting weird for months now. I don't like it when we don't talk to each other. Come on, it can't be dafter than anything I've heard before."

I twisted round. He gave me an encouraging smile and raised his blond eyebrows. "There's nothing you can't tell me, Melissa."

I twisted back and clung to the back of the chair.

"I'm not that keen on myself anymore," I admitted. "I just seem to hop from what one person wants me to be to another. And the person who makes me feel most like myself . . ." I screwed up my courage. "I miss you. I've stopped rebounding, and I still think I love you. But you think of me as a sister."

"No, I don't," said Nelson.

I looked at him. "You do."

"Only because you've always treated me as a brother. Telling Roger you wished you'd had a brother like me growing up to explain how men think. Telling Gabi living with me was like having a girl-friend who knew about rugby. If I'd told you I had un-brotherly feelings toward you, you'd have freaked out—it would have been an epic disaster."

"No, it wouldn't," I objected. "Well, it might have done before. But now—"

"The important thing," said Nelson, taking my hands, "is that *you* feel happy about who you are. I *like* who you are, but it's not up to me, is it?"

"But how can I know who I am when my whole livelihood is based on pretending to be someone else?" I wailed.

Nelson rolled his eyes. "When you finally accept that you're not pretending? That you're a bossy, sexy, confident, imperious woman in real life? You just have to learn to be as amazed by yourself as the rest of us are." He squeezed my hands. "And I am at the top of that list. I've always been your biggest fan."

"Really?" My heart lifted dangerously.

"Really. Now, can I say anything that might persuade you to move back into my flat?"

"Like?"

Nelson's expression changed, and the teasing went out of his voice. "Like, Melissa, I . . . ?"

Nelson leaned forward, his eyes beginning to close in a prekiss movement, and I forgot to breathe with excitement as I felt myself lean closer too.

I swear we were about to have the most amazing moment, when my parents burst into the chapel, Daddy first, with Bertie in his front-loading sling, but with Mummy in hot pursuit. Both of them were carrying champagne flutes, and Mummy had a note in her hand that she was waving about.

"Martin!" she shrieked. "Walk away from me and I'll make sure you're not walking anywhere for a year!"

"I'm just trying to get somewhere quiet, woman!" he snarled. "Place is crawling with journalists and bloody *family*. Right. Now. Tell me what it is that's got your knickers in a twist. Oh, hello,

Melissa, Nelson," he said, as if noticing us for the first time. "Not interrupting, are we?"

"No, no," said Nelson, lifting his hand politely. "Do go ahead."

I could quite happily have stabbed them both with the Anne Boleyn sword.

"This could ruin us, Martin, she wants thousands," Mummy began, just as the door opened again and William and Emery came rushing in.

"Daddy, William was about to tell you something!" she wailed. "You can't just walk away from him like that!"

"Emery, we are in the middle of a terrible family crisis," said Daddy. "Aren't we, Belinda?"

"We are." Mummy nodded.

"Again?" said Emery. "What is it now?"

"Yes," I said testily. "What is it?"

We all turned to Mummy.

"Well?" demanded Daddy.

"It's that bloody awful nanny you insisted on hiring—she's going to sue for unfair dismissal! All of us!" wailed Mummy. "And if we don't do what she wants, she says she's got photographs of me while I was recovering from my nose job!"

"Which one? Anyway, she wouldn't do anything about it," scoffed Daddy. "Let's call her bluff. Silly old woman."

"My *first nose job,* Martin!" Mummy glared at him. "Don't you remember—we went into that clinic at the same time? And if she's got photos of my nose job, she's bound to have photos of you after—"

"The wicked old harpy!" snarled Daddy, turning puce and thrusting Bertie into the nearest pair of arms.

To his surprise they were Nelson's. Manfully, though, Nelson held on tight, and Bertie didn't seem to mind.

"Photographs of what?" I inquired.

"Oh, your father had some . . . minor cosmetic surgery on his . . . Um, I'll tell you about it later," murmured Mummy, and hastened out of the chapel after him. I sincerely hoped she *wouldn't* tell me about it later.

"Don't worry—William's a lawyer!" Emery called after them, just as he kicked her to shut up.

"I wouldn't worry," I said. "Leonie's still here. She has a very persuasive phone manner with blackmailers."

"I. So. Don't. Want. To. Get. Involved," said William, holding his hands up like a crash barrier.

The four of us stared after my parents as they hurried across the lawn, waving their arms around.

"I sometimes wonder if it's the constant threat of legal action that keeps them together," said Emery. "You live and learn. Still . . . ," she finished, gazing into space.

"Emery?" Nelson looked at her and nodded toward the baby. "You want this little chap back?"

"Not specially. Why don't you let his godmother get to know him?" Emery put her arm through William's. "So, darling," she said to her husband, "now we've got the christening out of the way and Bertie and I are all right to fly—when are we heading back?" She squeezed his bicep. "It'll be nice to get back to Chicago, do some proper shopping, see our friends . . ."

"Ah," said William. "Now, that's what I wanted to tell your parents about. Might as well tell you now. Good news!"

Emery beamed absently. I could practically see her returning to her old vague self, supplemented by more amenable nannies and American plumbing.

"I've been transferred to the London offices again," he went on cheerfully. "So you and Bertie can stay here, while the company sorts out a London place for us. Isn't that great? I'll be over just as soon as they've found a house. You know how bad I felt about dragging you away from your family in the first place, and now . . ."

The color drained from Emery's face. "Darling, is this a joke?" she demanded.

"Not in the least," said William, beaming.

"We need to have a little chat. In private," she hissed, and grabbed him by the sleeve to haul him out into the gardens.

That left me and Nelson once again, this time plus Bertie.

To say my family had ruined the moment would be a predictable understatement.

"So," said Nelson.

"So," I said, tongue-tied.

I wanted to tell Nelson how utterly adorable he looked with tiny Bertie in his arms. As Nelson smiled and growled, Bertie gazed up at him with round, trusting eyes, as if Nelson had been a horse whisperer. A baby whisperer.

I really, really wanted to tell him how much I loved him.

Nelson tickled Bertie's tummy and smiled as Bertie giggled and kicked his feet up in the air.

"You know, Mel, when we have kids they're not going to have these ludicrous baby sneakers," he said without thinking. "Proper baby clothes only, and nothing with writing on."

"Absolutely not," I agreed, then stopped, like in a cartoon when someone clouts you with a frying pan.

Nelson seemed to realize what he'd said, because he looked up at me, shocked.

I was shocked too, but somehow I managed to recover first. "Do you mean . . . when I have kids . . . And when you have kids," I stammered. "Or when . . . *we* have kids?"

Nelson hesitated for the most agonizing few seconds of my life. They felt like hours. I could hear music from the reception and the distant sound of champagne corks. Even Bertie seemed to know it was a moment of great tension and kept his trap shut. Then a shy, crooked smile started on Nelson's lovely, kind mouth, and he said, tentatively, "When . . . *we* have kids?"

"You want to have children with me?" I asked, just to clarify.

"Eventually," he said. "Not right this minute. But I can't think of any other woman I'd want to spend the rest of my life with, apart from you."

"Are you sure?"

Nelson put out his spare arm and tried to embrace me, but Bertie was in the way.

Gently, but firmly, I plucked him out of Nelson's arms, put a cushion and a shawl in the font, and laid him on top, with a warning finger not to live up to his genes and ruin my moment.

Nelson put his arms round me and pulled me close to him. I marveled at how neatly our bodies fit together, my curves against his strong chest, my cold nose level with the crook of his neck, as if we'd been made as a pair. But I could also smell his familiar clean smell, now excitingly unfamiliar, and masculine, and it made me so hot and bothered that I was sure he'd be able to feel my heart racing through his shirt.

"Melissa," he said, holding me away a little so I could see the sincerity in his blue eyes, "I've sat through your many attempts to change who you are, and I feel I know you better than anyone else. So when I say you are the kindest, funniest, most beautiful girl I've ever met, wig or no wig, you *have* to believe me. I love you, Melissa."

He paused, smiled a little, then said it again, in case I hadn't believed it the first time. "I love you, Melissa."

"I love you, Nelson," I said, and the words were barely out of my mouth before he was kissing me, and suddenly he was a man I'd never met before. His lips were warm, and the sureness of his kiss turned my legs to jelly, while his hand stroked the small of my back and I melted into his broad chest. And then the kiss hardened and deepened into something so sexy the sensible Nelson vanished forever from my mind.

Too soon, he broke it off and said, as if he didn't want me to be thinking the wrong thing, "Don't get me wrong, I don't want children straightaway. It's not like I'm lining you up for imminent breeding."

"I should hope not," I said, tracing my finger along the freckles on his jaw.

"We'd need to get the nursery planned out and everything, and that's not a ten-minute job."

"Quite," I said, letting my finger trace up to his mouth and around his lips.

"Good," he whispered back, pulling my face closer to his. "And I'm not sure I'm quite ready to share you with anyone just yet." And he kissed me again, this time letting his hands wander in a way I'd never even imagined he knew about, given his boys' school background.

We were rudely interrupted, however, by Bertie deciding the spotlight had been off him for quite long enough, and letting rip with his unholy screeching. This time, even Nelson couldn't shut him up.

"Give Bertie to me," I said, and I held him at arm's length and fixed him with my disappointed glare.

Bertie hiccuped, and stopped in shock.

"Still got it," I said happily.

"You never lost it," Nelson said, and led me off to the champagne.

Reading Group Guide

The Little Lady Agency and the Prince

HESTER BROWNE

Description

In *The Little Lady Agency and the Prince,* the intrepid Melissa Romney-Jones, London's ultimate freelance girlfriend, takes on her biggest challenge yet: taming a playboy prince. Her task is to transform the notorious Nicolas von Helsing-Alexandros into a proper gentleman for the sake of preserving a family inheritance.

As Melissa applies her talents to the wayward royal, her personal life is also proving hard to handle. Her American fiancé, Jonathan Riley, is pressuring her to give up The Little Lady Agency and move to Paris. She's planning a christening for the newest member of the Romney-Jones family and dealing with a rogue nanny, and her flatmate, Nelson, needs her to find him someone new to split the rent with since she'll be moving out soon. But when Melissa leaves the chaos behind and joins the exasperating yet charming Prince Nicky on a Mediterranean cruise, she realizes her fairy-tale ending might not be the one she envisioned.

Discussion Questions

1. "I can't be bossy when I'm everyday Melissa, yet somehow when I'm walking in Honey's stilettos I turn into a whirlwind of retro-

glamour and female dynamism" (p. 2). Compare and contrast Melissa's personality with that of her alter ego, Honey Blenner-hesket. Why does Melissa feel compelled to transform herself into Honey for The Little Lady Agency? What does it suggest about her self-esteem?

2. How would you describe Melissa and Jonathan's relationship? Are they, as Melissa comes to believe, "more in love with the idea of each other than the reality" (p. 279)? Why or why not?

3. Is Melissa's reluctance to move to Paris indicative of larger issues in her relationship with Jonathan? How so? Discuss Jonathan's plan for the business he envisions running with Melissa. How do they each view her role in the company?

4. Melissa is convinced that Jonathan will never agree to her taking on the assignment with Nicky. Why, in fact, does her fiancé readily support the idea? And why is Melissa so surprised by his compliance?

5. Why does Melissa initially have misgivings about working with Nicky? Which of her methods of transforming him into a gentleman are effective, and why? Does Nicky truly change, or is it only an act?

6. Which aspects of Nicky's glamorous world intrigue Melissa?

7. Discuss Melissa's relationship with her family, whom she describes as "a bunch of melodramatic, self-centered schemers" (p. 12). If, as she says, "pretty much everything that went wrong chez Romney-Jones was my fault" (p. 27), why does she continually go to their aid and help them sort out their problems?

8. How do Nelson and Jonathan each view The Little Lady Agency and what it means to Melissa?

9. Melissa confides in Nicky that she is not sure Jonathan "really knows where Honey stops and Mel starts" (p. 272). Is Jonathan actually in love with Honey? Why or why not? How much of Melissa and Jonathan's relationship issues stem from the fact that he first met her as Honey?

10. When Melissa experiences some intense emotional turbulence, she says, "It was Nicky who did the best job of taking my mind off things" (p. 295). Why is Nicky the person with whom Melissa finds the most comfort? How do they progress from a contentious working relationship to something warmer? What do they have in common?

11. Melissa and Nelson have been flatmates and friends for years. How and why do Melissa's feelings about him change? On the way home from the yachting trip, why does Nelson push her away? Do his feelings about Melissa change?

12. What does Melissa learn about relationships from witnessing Granny's revived romance with Alexander? Of the three men in her life—Jonathan, Nelson, and Nicky—which do you think is the right match for Melissa?

13. Have you read the previous two novels featuring Melissa Romney-Jones, *The Little Lady Agency* and *Little Lady, Big Apple*? If so, how do they compare with *The Little Lady Agency and the Prince*? In what ways does Melissa change throughout the stories?

A Conversation with Hester Browne

Q: In your previous novel, *Little Lady, Big Apple,* the story was set in New York. This time part of the action takes place in Paris. What appealed to you about using Paris as a backdrop? Did you spend time in the city doing research?

A: Paris is such a blissfully romantic city for lovers, and it seemed like a good compromise for Jonathan and Melissa to make their fresh start in a place new to both of them. Melissa tends to walk around in her own little black-and-white movie anyway, and Paris is the perfect backdrop for her imagination; there are so many intriguing alleys and gorgeous, red-geranium-lined balconies that even popping out for a breakfast croissant feels like the height of continental chic. But, that said, as Melissa discovers, it isn't always April in Paris and relationships aren't always sunny. . . . I was more than happy to spend a few weekends "researching" in the bars and boutiques of the Marais and the surrounding areas, as well as taking a summer visit or two to glamorous Nice and Monaco on the Côte d'Azur, which really is the ice-cream-colored seaside paradise that the iconic 1950s travel posters depict.

Q: What made you decide on a wayward prince as the latest challenge for Melissa and The Little Lady Agency?

A: You'd think that a prince would be the very pinnacle of good manners, and in no need of Honey's help—and yet Nicky's one of the rudest clients Melissa's ever had to deal with, thanks to his arrogant assumption that his money and title are some kind of "get out of jail free" card. It's a sign of her growing confidence that the sort of shenanigans that make his harem of airheads swoon not at all fazes her; in her eyes, he's not a real prince until he learns to behave like one. I wanted to emphasize Melissa's belief that good manners are free. Courtesy isn't just about which knife to use or when to wear a dinner jacket, it's about making other people feel at ease, being generous and thoughtful, and acting with responsibility and good humor. Of course, when she's finished with Nicky, he's positively Prince Charming, but it's something of a learning curve for him, as well as for Melissa—who realizes that her own prince is a lot nearer than she thought.

Q: **How did you research the royals' lifestyle? Have you been to a polo match or on a Mediterranean cruise? Have you ever met members of the royal family?**

A: Thanks to the sterling efforts of our tabloid press, the British public is pretty au fait with the lifestyles of our aristos without having to do much more than glance at a newspaper in the mornings. I've been to a few polo matches, at which Prince William was playing, thankfully without any dramatic security alerts! However, as far as cruising goes, my very English complexion means I can't holiday anywhere hotter than Calais, so my yachting experience is firmly restricted to local waters, where it's more seagulls and fish-and-chips than champagne and onboard Jacuzzis. Nelson's kind of vacation, come to think of it!

Q: **When writing your novels, what challenges are there in bridging the gaps between British and American cultures? Which things stay the same no matter what side of the Atlantic a reader is on?**

A: On a small scale, it's always fascinating to see which brand names and cultural references change in editing to convey the same sort of familiar daily shorthand on the other side of the Atlantic. And on a bigger scale, I've found that the English sense of humor is somewhat different—we're much ruder and more sarcastic in the name of both comedy and affectionate teasing, and sometimes that needs to be toned down a little.

What stays the same, however—I hope!—is the romance, and Melissa's belief that her heart is a better judge than her head. The delicious dizziness of falling in love is universal, as well as is the ache of losing that perfection and the twists and turns of a relationship taking a natural course. Everyone wants to fall in love. And have the luxurious corsets and Honey's vintage wardrobe, which run a close second for me, anyway.

Q: You once said in an interview that "American readers took parts of Melissa's story quite seriously, especially her struggles with her family, who they felt should be in therapy or, possibly, in court." How does Melissa's relationship with her family change in *The Little Lady Agency and the Prince*?

A: The battling, yelling family of hard-drinking, hard-living eccentrics who can only show their love for each other through sloppy adoration of their Labradors is something of a tradition in British comedy, and the casual insults of the Romney-Joneses are definitely meant to be tongue-in-cheek. Melissa's problem has always been that although she knows in theory that they don't mean to sound so cruel, she can't help taking it personally, thanks to her own low self-esteem. But after her Parisian experiences, I'd like to think that, finally, she gains the confidence to stand up to her father more—or at least to understand him well enough to play him at his own manipulative games. Martin does love Melissa, honestly!

Melissa also grows to understand her own grandmother much better in this novel. She's always idealized her as the chic, irresistible woman she'd like to grow into, but as Melissa learns more about the tangled relationships in Dilys's past, it makes her realize that her grandmother's life hasn't always been so charmed. Love sometimes requires sacrifice or compromise, and doesn't always follow the path you'd like it to. That really helps Melissa's perspective on her own dilemmas, as well as gives her a bit more patience with Allegra, Emery, and her own mother.

Q: Is the romantic revelation in this novel something you had planned since the beginning of the series, or is it a turn of events that happened while writing this book?

A: I don't want to spoil the ending for anyone who's flicked through to the back of the book before reading it, so all I'll say is that I knew where the story was going, but I didn't always know how it was going to get there. And like all relationships, there were twists and surprises for me, as well as for Melissa, in the writing of it!

Q: What is it about Melissa (and Honey) that you think most appeals to readers? Are there any traits you have in common with Melissa and Honey?

A: Melissa is such a cheerful, hopeful soul, who always wants to believe the best in everyone, apart from herself. I think that combination of optimism and vulnerability makes her lovable. If she were my friend, I'd do anything for her, because I'd know she'd happily offer cups of tea and sympathy at three in the morning whatever the crisis. She's also the only person you'd know who could tack up your hem.

Honey, on the other hand, is the woman we'd all like to unleash on ill-tempered customer service reps or in cocktail bars that we're not totally sure we're chic enough to be in. She's a fabulous excuse to behave out of character, and for that alone I'd recommend that everyone go out and buy her own long blond wig! (Or a tumbling Titian red mane, if you're a blonde already.)

Q: What can readers expect from you next? Will there be any further adventures for Melissa?

A: Melissa, Nelson, Gabi, and the Romney-Joneses are so real to me in my mind that they still rattle around between books, arguing and carrying on, so who knows? I'm currently writing a novel about an old-fashioned English finishing school in the posh Mayfair section of London, which has to be brought up-to-date by a very modern, independent young woman when it's in danger of being closed down. It's a lot of fun exploring what women were expected to know thirty years ago, and what my friends now wish they'd been taught at eighteen before facing the adult world: parallel parking, the right way to apply concealer, and how to turn down a date seem to feature highly!

Enhance Your Book Club

1. Follow Nelson's culinary lead and serve a traditional English dish such as Shepherd's Pie, paired with a bottle of Bordeaux. Or toast your discussion with champagne and indulge in French chocolates, a box of which Melissa keeps in her desk drawer "to be doled out as daily rewards."

2. Channel your inner Honey Blennerhesket and dress like Melissa when she transforms herself, donning apparel and accessories like stilettos, a corset, red lipstick, and maybe even a wig. Or, dress like the alter ego you'd most like to be.

3. Have a "Little Lady Agency" marathon and read all three novels featuring Melissa Romney-Jones, either for one discussion or as three months' worth of selections.

Lady Frances Phillimore's rule for knocking on doors was that one should always knock at the exact moment that one stops walking, before one can get nervous about what one is going to say when it's opened and then be caught dithering unattractively when the door swings open. But when I reached the front door of the Phillimore Academy for Ladies, an invisible hand seemed to grab my wrist before I could lift the heavy lion's head knocker. I stared at the London grime on the brass plaque, feeling my stomach churn.

I hadn't felt my stomach churn in years, and this time I knew it wasn't the fifth cup of tea I'd had with my hearty breakfast. It was a weird sense of déjà vu, laced with all sorts of other stuff I couldn't quite explain.

Why are you coming round to the front? murmured a voice in my head. You live round the back, with the staff.

Then another voice said, more robustly, that plaque needs a good splash of lemon juice and some elbow grease. Hardly the first impression to convince new pupils of the Academy's polishing prowess—literal or metaphorical.

Before either voice could get into any sort of conversation, I lifted the brass ring and rapped it hard against the door, then stepped back, unclipped my bag and got out my notebook and silver pencil.

"Polish plaque" I wrote, trying not to let my ears listen for footsteps, and then, hearing nothing, found I had time to add, "polish lion, sweep steps."

I understood that the Academy aimed to be discreet, but frankly things had gone too far the other way. The neighboring houses on the narrow street were more than presentable, with white-painted sash window frames punctuating their five stories, and a few historic blue plaques dotted around. Smart, in other words. Whereas the air of neglect hanging around the Academy's murky windows made it stand out like the one embarrassed guest at the elegant party who didn't spot the black tie dress code and came straight from work, in her third-best suit with the grease stain.

I couldn't help feeling a pang of shame for the place. This wasn't the elegant town house of my memories. It was her tipsy-at-three, care-worn sister.

I gazed up at the high windows, remembering how, as a little girl, I used to love peeking up at the higher floors on winter afternoons after my constitutional through Green Park with Nanny Nancy. In the winter, the house had seemed like an advent calendar, with different surprises hidden behind each window. The crystal chandeliers in the second-floor ballroom sparkled out into the dusk. Sometimes I'd see a whole class of girls practicing their curtseys in there, bobbing out of sight, then reappearing all at the same time.

Well, more or less at the same time. There was usually one who bobbed back up at the wrong time, or just fell over.

Above those windows were the classrooms, where I might catch sight of a cross-eyed blond girl balancing *The Guinness Book of Records* on her head for deportment, or more likely a bored blond girl (they were always blond) staring out of the window watching the taxis go past while Mrs. Quinn droned on about planning meals for a sick person on a tray—"Always remember a rose, and remove mirrors from the room so as not to distress the invalid with the reality of her own complexion."

Even though bright winter morning light flooded the rest of the street, those windows were dark now. Lace curtains, I noticed, still decorously protected the ground floor windows, as they always had, but the curtains were graying, and the climbing ivy now had a distinctly ratty look to it.

I dropped my gaze to the worn top step where I'd been left in the marmalade box as a week-old baby, with a note asking Lady Phillimore to turn me into a lady. I'd never come in through the front door again, since I grew up behind the Academy with Lady

Phillimore's nanny and cook. Given all that, I'd grown into a fairly normal child, if one extraordinarily well versed in thank-you notes and napkin folding—the finishing touches of a proper lady.

The step also needed a good brush.

Who was in charge of cleaning this place? I wondered, and wrote down "cleaner!" on my notepad. My hand wobbled, and I realized I was both sad and strangely excited at the same time.

Still no sign of life behind the door. Honestly! What ever happened to "Punctuality is the politeness of princes"?

A few window boxes would brighten the facade up too, and more quickly than a paint job. I frowned, jotted down "gardener" underneath my notes, and then finally the door was yanked open.

"I'm so terribly sorry. I'm just about to move the car!" gabbled a dark-haired woman. Her mouth was smiling in a more or less welcoming way, but her eyes nervously darted back and forth.

How stupid of me to imagine the same teachers would still be here after fifteen years, I thought, taking in the crisp white shirt, half-covered by a cardigan, and a knee-length skirt—the unofficial staff uniform. She had no pearls, so she had to be quite junior; like admirals, the teachers at the Academy seemed to acquire extra strings according to rank.

"I know you've spoken to her about it before, but I don't think they have parking restrictions where she lives, and I do know she's been awfully naughty about . . ." She trailed off, seeing my blank face. "You're not here about that nasty business with Anastasia's car and the traffic warden? And the white paint? And the . . . Oh."

I shook my head, and the woman's face relaxed for a second, before springing back into damage-control mode. "Oh, silly me! So sorry! You've come about that little mix-up with *Venetia* and that chap at the Dorchester. . . ."

"I'm here to see the principal," I said, although it was tempting to say nothing and let her reveal all the school's current crises. "Miss Thorne's expecting me. My name's—"

"You're here to see Miss Thorne? Oh God, I mean . . . oh . . . hello!" she said, recovering quickly, and stepping back so she could usher me in. "I'm so sorry, such a busy start to the week, you know, after the weekend, and, er . . . um, come in, come in . . ."

I stepped into the grand entrance hall, and tried not to let the shock of familiarity undo the cool, collected image I was working hard to present. But it was tricky, seeing it all again: the staircase sweeping up to the teaching rooms, the black-and-white tiled floor, the majestic oil portraits on the wall, the huge bowls of dried rose petals.

"Would you like a cup of . . . No, hang on, I should let Miss Thorne know you're . . ." Her forehead creased.

I gave her my best calming smile. "Start from the beginning. You're . . . ?"

"I'm Paulette."

"Good morning, Paulette," I said, shaking her hand. "I'm—"

"Cup of coffee?" she interrupted.

"Yes, I'd love a cup of coffee, but why don't you show me through to the reception room, then let Miss Thorne know I'm here?"

"Good idea," she agreed, and without realizing it, she let me direct her through the hall toward the principal's office, a large room toward the back of the house.

I tried to let her get ahead of me as we clicked our way across the tiles, so my professional eye could flit back and forth like a spy's, taking in the cobwebs trailing from the higher chandeliers, the faded framed photographs of lacrosse teams, and an explosive, chest-height display of white calla lilies, which I supposed was meant to be modern but instead resembled the work of an inappropriately jaunty funeral parlor.

I should have been taking proper notes, but it was too hard to be rational when my heart was hammering in my chest, as tiny details I'd forgotten came flooding back to me. Everything looked just as it had fifteen years ago, give or take quite a lot of dust. As it probably had done for fifteen years before that, there was a strange sense of time standing still behind the Georgian door, while the modern world went on outside, over the threshold into Piccadilly.

Paulette stopped a few feet away from the office door and dropped her voice conspiratorially.

"Now, just to give you a bit of background, the previous principal, Miss Vanderbilt, retired a few weeks ago, and Miss Thorne is currently the acting principal."

I nodded—not because I didn't know that already, but because I had an instinct that Paulette would tell me more about the state of the

Academy in the space of three sentences than Lord Phillimore had in an hour.

"I just thought I should mention . . . Miss Thorne's quite sensitive about . . . people expecting Miss Vanderbilt. . . ." Paulette did some heavy hinting with her owlish brown eyes. "I just don't want you to get off on the wrong foot," she finished. "As a prospective student, you know."

I put my hand on her arm to stop her. "Paulette, I think we've got our wires crossed somewhere," I said gently. "I'm not a new student. I'm here to have a meeting with Miss Thorne about the Academy. I'm Betsy Cooper, Lord Phillimore's . . ."

I sort of hesitated, as I always did. It made me sound like a refugee from the eighteenth century, but I said it anyway, for the sake of making myself clear: "I'm the Phillimores's ward."

Paulette looked as if she was about to faint backward with mortification. "Oh God, no. Are you the abandoned orphan who the Phillimores took in and who . . . ?"

She managed to stop herself in time, and, sweet as Paulette appeared, I had to wonder what on earth had happened to the standards of the school if the secretary was about as diplomatic as a Soho hairdresser on truth serum.

"Yes," I said, firmly. "I'm the abandoned baby who grew up to take a First in Mathematics at St. Andrews, and who is now running her own marketing consulting firm in Edinburgh. Technically, I'm not an orphan!" I smiled, so she wouldn't think I was being pointed. "I just don't know who my biological parents are."

"God, I'm so sorry. You must think . . ." Paulette ground to a halt and gazed up at me contritely. "I'm still learning! I didn't mean to apply for the secretary's job," she confessed in a rush. "I thought this was a foreign language school."

If I did one favor for Lord Phillimore, I thought, it would be to give his school secretary the rudiments of office management.

"Paulette," I said, "would you let Miss Thorne know I'm here?"

"Yes," she whispered. "But please don't tell her about the business with the traffic wardens, I'm not meant to be covering up for Anastasia, but she can be really persuasive and her dad's something quite scary in the Russian mafia. She says."

"I won't," I promised. "Now. Would you like to take my coat?"

"Oh, er, yes, of course," said Paulette.

I pulled myself up to full height, took a deep breath, and knocked on the white painted door of the principal's office.

After a count of five, a voice trilled "Enter!" from within, and I entered.

The principal's office was elegantly decorated in Wedgwood blue, with one wall taken up with a full-length bookshelf and another by a pair of French windows that led into the small, enclosed garden where students were supposed to cultivate herbs, and not sunbathe.

The room was dominated by a huge antique desk, behind which sat a petite woman, her white hair set like swirls of whipped cream around her placid, doll-like face, with a quadruple string of pearls beneath, balanced on a shelf-like bosom. The desk would have dwarfed her were it not for the forceful personality radiating out from behind it. There was no computer in sight, just a silver desk set, three Rolodexes, and a Limoges bowl full of mint imperials.

Miss Thorne looked up as I stepped into the room, and her expression of welcome had just the right amount of pleasure and surprise, with just a dash of affection. She didn't rise as I approached the desk, my hand at the ready for shaking, but instead added a flourishing signature to some document and pressed an old-fashioned blotter over it.

"Elizabeth!" she said. "Do have a seat! You've caught me finishing some letters—would you excuse me a moment?"

"Of course," I said, mentally retracting my hand and taking a seat in the chair opposite her. "Am I early?"

"Ohh, no, no. Well. Maybe by just a moment or two."

A tiny breath escaped me at that. I knew I was dead on time because I always was. As much as I wanted to give nice Miss Thorne the benefit of the doubt, my business mind games radar told me that despite the smiles and warmth, she'd embarked on one of those "unsettle the newcomer" tactics. It was an old chestnut, and I didn't think it was terribly polite, especially for the headmistress of a finishing school who'd known me since I was a baby.

She knows you're not here for a nostalgic reunion, though, I reminded myself. You're here as Lord Phillimore's agent of change—and that's totally different. Her job's on the line—after waiting twenty-five years to get her hands on it. Of course she's not going to roll over and let you take charge.

Instead of letting my discomfort show, I smoothed down my skirt and arranged my bag on my knee, knowing that Miss Thorne would be assessing my outfit. I was wearing Combination four of my carefully constructed capsule wardrobe: a slate-gray Joseph skirt suit with a deep purple sweater. All my clothes matched, to allow me to get dressed in the four minutes that remained in the morning after I'd wrestled my mad red curls into sleek professional submission, using my salon-strength hairdryer and a serum so powerful I had to bribe my stylist to get it for me under the counter. If my hair was under control, so was I.

"So sorry! Now! Welcome back to the Phillimore Academy, Elizabeth," said Miss Thorne, a delicate smile bulging her pink cheeks.

"Thank you," I said, thinking that this was more like the cozy Miss Thorne I remembered. "It's wonderful to be back, and to see everything just as I . . ."

"Although you were never actually a pupil here, were you? Strictly speaking."

"Well, no," I said, faltering a little. "Not strictly speaking. But I think I must have absorbed everything the teachers had to impart with all the time I spent sitting in the classes!"

"Yes." Miss Thorne's smile became more rigid. "You always were sitting in the classes, weren't you? And running up and down the corridors."

I returned the smile, and opened my mouth to agree that, yes, the teachers and the girls had been terribly sweet to treat me like the school pet, but Miss Thorne wasn't finished.

"And playing in the beauty studio."

"Yes, well . . ."

"And letting the girls practice their hair styling on you."

"I was only seven . . ."

"And eating cake. When there wasn't meant to be any cake for tea." She wagged her finger at me. "The places we used to find you! When you should have been safely tucked up in Matron's house, not gallivanting around with the real ladies!"

The *real* ladies? I'd rehearsed several "conversations with the principal" in my head on the flight down from Edinburgh, but I wasn't at all prepared for this genteel attack, right from the moment I sat down. It was like being assaulted with acupuncture needles: tiny, deadly, effective pricks, right on my most sensitive spots. What on earth had Lord Phillimore told Miss Thorne about my visit to put her back up so much?

But rather than making me want to turn on my heel and go, something about Miss Thorne's attitude made me determined to stand my ground. The Academy was as much my home as it was her domain. And more to the point, the business was in dire need of my help, or else this time next year it would be sold off and subdivided into fifteen luxury apartments all boasting views of Green Park.

I tried to keep my voice level, and said, with a charming twinkle, "Well, as Lady Frances used to say, those steps are the nearest things I have to a birthplace."

"Indeed," said Miss Thorne, with a nod that managed to convey the minimum of agreement. "And now you're back."

"Yes." I put my handbag on the floor and removed my leather-bound notebook and pen, ready to take notes. "Lord Phillimore asked me to come, so here I am."

"I must say, you are looking very chic these days," said Miss Thorne, suddenly switching tack to affection. "I don't think I'd have recognized you, looking so grown-up—where did those adorable corkscrew curls go? And those dear little hands that were always covered in something . . . sticky?"

I reminded myself that this was just a genteel variation on any other first interview with a nervous manager. I'd met plenty of them in the past few years, and not one failing enterprise had carried on failing after I'd waded in to save it. "Oh, you don't grow up in such a famous finishing school without absorbing a little finishing," I replied. "Even if you're not, strictly speaking, a pupil."

We looked at each other across the desk, warm smiles matched in ruthless intensity.

"But it is lovely to be back! I just wish it were for a happier reason." I tried to look business-like as I opened my notebook. "I'm sure Lord

Phillimore's discussed the purpose of my visit with you. I understand the Academy is going through something of a rough patch? He mentioned that this year's enrollment is only five girls, which seems terribly low. He asked me to come in and have a look around, and perhaps think of ways to increase applications. That's my field these days, you see—revitalizing businesses, helping them make the best of what they have."

I made one final attempt at levity in the face of Miss Thorne's unnerving silence. "Not unlike what the Academy does for its students, you might say! A bit of polishing."

Miss Thorne's pursed lips curved into a tight smile, but she didn't seem very amused. "Oh, dear Lord Phillimore," she trilled. "He is an old mother hen!"

He's a mother hen who's about to lose his henhouse, his collection of vintage hens, and possibly even the whole egg production business, I thought, but I kept quiet out of discretion.

"We're just going through one of our sporadic dips in enrollment," Miss Thorne went on. "Often happens when the foreign money markets go a bit wobbly, but there's nothing to worry about, and certainly nothing that our wonderful staff can't sort out between us. Good manners will never go out of fashion, now, will they, Elizabeth?"

I wished she wouldn't call me Elizabeth. No one did.

"Absolutely not." I turned my head to one side, so my hair swung like a shiny copper bell around my face—a miracle of grooming which I hoped would melt Miss Thorne's defenses. "Would you call me Betsy, Miss Thorne? Everyone does now."

"Do they indeed?"

"Yes." I nodded.

"I think I prefer Elizabeth," she mused.

I picked up my bag and placed it on my knee like an Hermès barrier. If that was the way Miss Thorne wanted it, then that was the way she could have it. "Do you think I could have a guided tour first? Just to refresh my memory, before we get down to a proper chat about where the Academy is, and where you see it heading?"

Miss Thorne looked a tiny bit surprised, as if she hadn't expected the conversation to turn so brisk. "Do we really need to? I was under the impression from Lord Phillimore that it was more a formality, your little . . . inspection . . ." She trailed off, and increased the wattage of her smile to compensate for what she wasn't saying.

"But I'd love to have a look around." I checked my watch. "Isn't it about time for the first lesson? Perhaps we could drop in and see what the girls are learning these days."

"Oh, but my dear, we shouldn't interrupt them! You have the prospectus, don't you? Surely that should give you an idea. Why don't I have Paulette bring us some tea and biscuits, and we can have a nice catch-up?" Miss Thorne's deep-set green eyes took on a confiding twinkle. "You haven't told me whether wedding bells are in the offing yet!"

I ignored the mean dig at my bare left hand, focusing instead on the shameless delaying tactic, and gave Miss Thorne a hard look. I knew obstruction when I ran into it, even if it was wearing cashmere and pearls. "Miss Thorne, I'm very much on your team," I said earnestly. "I, more than anyone, want the Academy to carry on doing the same wonderful job it's been doing all these years. And I know you must too—now that you're in charge of steering it through tricky times."

Miss Thorne blinked innocently and smoothed her pearls. "I wouldn't say tricky, dear, when you have as much experience as I do. . . . Now, how about that cup of tea? I'll call Paulette." And she pressed a little bell on the side of the desk.

Two could play at that game.

I put my notebook back in my handbag and looked her squarely in the eye. "Miss Thorne, you don't understand. I'm here as Lord Phillimore's consultant. He's asked me to make an assessment of the Academy and advise him on what changes need to be made, or—" I paused, significantly.

"Or?" Miss Thorne prompted.

I let her have the full force of my hardest stare. "Or whether it's too late for changes."

The ormolu clock ticked on the mantelpiece. After ten or so ticks, she pushed back her chair, and said, tightly, "I believe Miss McGregor is teaching the Fine Dining class upstairs."